BLACKSOULS

Also by NICOLE CASTROMAN

BLACKHEARTS

BLACKSOULS

NICOLE CASTROMAN

SIMON PULSE

New York London Toronto Sydney New Delhi

SIMON PULSE

An imprint of Simon & Schuster Children's Publishing Division
1230 Avenue of the Americas, New York, New York 10020
First Simon Pulse paperback edition April 2018
Text copyright © 2017 by Nicole Castroman
Cover photograph copyright © 2017 by Winter Media/Corbis
Also available in a Simon Pulse hardcover edition.

For information about special discounts for bulk purchases, please contact
Simon & Schuster Special Sales at 1-866-506-1949 or business@simonandschuster.com.
The Simon & Schuster Speakers Bureau can bring authors to your live event. For more
information or to book an event contact the Simon & Schuster Speakers Bureau
at 1-866-248-3049 or visit our website at www.simonspeakers.com.
Cover designed by Karina Granda
Interior designed by Greg Stadnyk
The text of this book was set in Adobe Garamond Pro.
Manufactured in the United States of America
2 4 6 8 10 9 7 5 3 1
The Library of Congress has cataloged the hardcover edition as follows:
Names: Castroman, Nicole, author.
Title: Blacksouls / by Nicole Castroman.
Description: First Simon Pulse hardcover edition. | New York : Simon Pulse, 2017. |
Sequel to: Blackhearts | Summary: In the late 1690s, Edward "Teach" Drummond, the
soon-to-be Blackbeard, and his beloved Anne, the daughter of a wealthy merchant and his
West India slave, are both on separate journeys to Nassau, but their paths cross when they
become entangled with the treacherous Governor Webb, forcing Teach and Anne to take
on a dangerous mission to save both their friends and his men.
Identifiers: LCCN 2016050242 | ISBN 9781481491051 (hardcover) |
ISBN 9781481491075 (eBook)
Subjects: LCSH: Blackbeard, -1718—Juvenile fiction. | CYAC: Blackbeard, -1718—Fiction. |
Pirates—Fiction. | Love—Fiction. | Racially mixed people—Fiction. |
Caribbean Area—History—17th century—Fiction.
Classification: LCC PZ7.1.C46 Bls 2017 | DDC [Fic]—dc23
LC record available at https://lccn.loc.gov/2016050242
ISBN 9781481491068 (pbk)

To Sophia and Anthony. I'm so proud of who you are and who you will become. I can't wait to see you two captain your own ships.

CHAPTER 1

Anne

Anne's father had often told her that a smooth sea never made a skilled sailor, but this morning she was grateful for the tranquility as the *Providence* cut the surface like a finger trailing in the water. The blue sky overhead stretched to the horizon with lazy white clouds floating on the breeze.

She tried to convince herself that her calm surroundings made her present task somewhat less repellant, but the expressions of her fellow passengers told her otherwise, which was why the duty had fallen to her. No one else had stepped forward to help.

Kneeling on the deck, the skin on Anne's arms and face was tight from prolonged exposure to the sun and seawater. The dull needle in her hand pierced the bloody canvas with a gentle *pop* as she pulled the edges of the hammock closer together to create a makeshift shroud.

She avoided looking at the dead man's eyes as they stared sightlessly up at the heavens. Holding her breath against the rancid smell of his rotting teeth and gums, she said a silent prayer, hoping he had not felt the rats gnawing on the soles of his feet as he lay dying.

The sailor standing beside her shifted, momentarily blocking the sun. "That's only twelve stitches. He'll come back if you don't have thirteen."

"Perhaps you'd like to do the last one," Anne snapped up at him, unable to hold her tongue any longer.

The sailor took a hasty step back, shaking his head, his eyes wide with fear. *These men and their silly superstitions,* she thought.

Bracing herself, Anne pushed the needle through one side of the canvas before passing it through the dead man's nose. She winced as she tugged at the thread to complete the last and final stitch to close the hammock. The sailors claimed that the law of the sea demanded it, a way to make sure that the person wasn't simply sleeping.

Anne knew for a fact that the man before her was dead, for she was the one who had found him. Hidden behind a large crate on the quarterdeck of the *Providence*, he had crawled away to suffer the scurvy alone and in silence. He'd had no family on board, no one to claim him.

Her task complete, Anne sat back on her haunches, waiting as a few sailors lifted the body. Gaunt and exhausted themselves, they rested it briefly on the railing before rolling it over the edge into the serene sea below.

Anne closed her eyes when she heard the splash, knowing the cannonball they'd placed in the hammock would drag the emaciated form down to the murky depths of the ocean. A small part of her couldn't help thinking that perhaps he was the lucky one. His suffering was over. For the rest left on board, their hardships would continue.

In the five weeks since they'd left the shores of England behind, he was the sixth person to succumb to the disease, and unless they reached their destination soon, he would not be the last.

From the beginning, the vessel had been plagued by exceptionally bad luck.

A lack of foresight or funds had left them with an inadequate supply of provisions. Their salted pork and dried fish had long run out, with only hardtack remaining. The biscuits themselves were barely edible, teeming with beetles and weevils. After her mother's death, Anne had thought she'd known hunger. That was nothing compared to the famine she endured now.

The weary people surrounding Anne wore threadbare clothes and haunted expressions, resembling the ship on which they sailed. It was a miracle the *Providence* had made it this far, with its tattered sails and slowly leaking hull.

While the other onlookers drifted to different parts of the deck, Cara helped Anne to her feet. "How do you do it?" Cara asked, her freckled face pale underneath her sunburn. Her once plump features had significantly thinned in the weeks since their departure.

Anne had told Cara and her brother, Coyle, how she'd been taken from the Drummond estate and put on the *Providence* against Richard Drummond's instructions. In turn, Anne had learned that Coyle and Cara's uncle had sent them enough funds to sail on a grand ship, but someone had robbed them, and the two were left to sail on the *Providence* as well. Anne was grateful for their friendship.

Looking up from the needle in her hand, Anne gave Cara a sad smile. "It's not much different than mending the sails." Cara had a fine hand for stitching and had been invaluable to the crew of the *Providence* for patching and repairing the old canvas sails ripped during the storms they'd encountered. Cara hoped to earn a living as a seamstress one day, and put her talent to use.

"I don't believe you. Some of these lads have been sailing for years and none of them offered to help the poor man."

"It was the least I could do. I like to think that if anything happened to me, someone would take the time to give me a proper burial at sea."

Cara crossed herself before shaking her head at Anne. "Don't be talking like that. Nothing's going to happen to you. Coyle won't allow it. And neither will I."

"Aye, she's right," Coyle said, coming toward them. His blond hair, so similar to his sister's, had lightened considerably in the sun, while his fair skin had darkened. He'd lost at least two stones since they'd set sail. "We're glad you're here, even if we were all supposed to be on the *Deliverance*."

Cara linked her arm with Anne's. "And when we get to Nassau, you can stay with us. I'm sure our uncle would welcome an extra hand in his tavern. From what we've heard, he seems to be doing well, with plenty of thirsty folk on the island."

"It will only be until I can earn enough to continue my journey. I don't wish to be a burden," Anne said, hating the fact that she was once again penniless, with no way to send word back to Teach. Every time she thought of him, the pain of his absence was like a cruel fist squeezing her heart.

It would take weeks for any letter to reach Bristol, but she had to try something to get in touch with him. Perhaps he'd left word with her father's solicitor. It was quite possible Teach had quit the country, in an attempt to find her.

If she closed her eyes, she could almost picture him aloft in the rigging of a ship, adjusting the sails and making repairs. The work of a sailor was physically demanding, yet Teach would never shrink from his responsibilities. He wouldn't have hesitated to sew the dead man up in the hammock. Not because he was unfeeling, but because Teach knew there was enough filth and disease on a ship without a decaying body adding to the misery.

A part of Anne couldn't help being grateful that she would soon reach land and have to stay there for some time. The trip across the Atlantic had been more challenging and difficult than anything she'd imagined. They'd endured unending hours of monotony, only to be surprised by storms so violent and fierce that Anne had been convinced the ship would send her to a watery grave.

Cara gave Anne a comforting squeeze. "You could never be a burden. If you hadn't allowed me to share your cabin, I would still be forced to sleep with the passengers below and Coyle would never get any rest."

"I still don't get any rest. But at least I don't worry as much," Coyle said, striking the small biscuit in his hand on the railing. Several weevils fell out and he brushed the tiny black insects overboard, before dipping the hardtack into a mug of diluted brandy. "Care for some?" he asked, offering it to Anne.

She shook her head. They'd all learned the hard way that the simple wafers were unbreakable and had to first be immersed in liquid in order to make them edible. Hardtack might be inexpensive to make and long-lasting for a voyage, but flavorful it was not.

Coyle shrugged and took a bite. Cara wrinkled her nose at him. "Aren't you going to offer *me* anything?" Cara asked.

"No. George ate your portion."

"Which George?" Cara had taken it upon herself to try to name every rat on the *Providence*. An impossible task considering how many there were, but it was a simple game that helped fight the monotony of the voyage.

"How should I know?"

"Was he missing a hind foot? If so, it was George III. If part of his tail was gone, then that's George I."

"I'm too bloody tired for this, Cara," Coyle muttered, rubbing his weary eyes.

Anne shook her head at him. "You don't need to sleep outside our cabin, Coyle. You've heard Captain Oxley. He's said no harm will come to us." After weeks observing the coarse crew, Anne had come to realize that the sailors mostly kept to themselves, leaving the passengers alone. Cara's outgoing nature bordered on flirtatious, but the men were too busy trying to keep the ship afloat to pay much attention to her. Especially with Coyle remaining nearby.

"I want to be close by in case anything does happen," Coyle said, looking off the port side.

Anne followed his gaze, a thread of unease winding its way through her chest. In the distance, two ships cruised the open waters, their dark outlines visible against the stark blue of the sky. For weeks, the *Providence* had sailed along, separated from familiar landmarks without a glimpse of another vessel on the horizon.

But two days ago as they neared their destination, the call had gone out that a ship had been spotted. And shortly after, a second ship had appeared. Like two shadows, they followed the *Providence*, but made no move to get any closer.

Anne drew a deep breath. "Have they shown their flags?"

"No. We're too far for them to raise an ensign," Coyle said.

"What do you think they want?" Cara asked, her eyes narrowed. "We don't have anything worth taking." The *Providence* was a pitiable merchant vessel. With rotting timbers and old rigging, the ship transported more people than cargo. Whatever goods she *did* carry, it couldn't have amounted to more than a few hundred schillings at best.

"I don't know," Coyle said, downing the rest of his brandy. "But it's not normal."

"It seems to me that they're waiting for something," Anne said.

"Like what?" Cara asked, her voice sharp.

Coyle wiped his mouth with the back of his hand. "Don't know, but I think Anne's right. See how they keep their distance?"

Cara looked between her brother and Anne. "But we're only a few days away from Nassau. It's to be expected that we see other ships."

"Yes, but they should move on, shouldn't they? If they're merchants, they would be heading to their next port," Anne said. "Do you think the tales are true?"

A few of the crew members had claimed that life was difficult for many settlers in Nassau. The Spanish had burned and destroyed the town in 1684. English settlers had arrived two years later and more continued to arrive each year, but stability was difficult to maintain, even with a governor in residence. In order to survive, many in the population had turned to piracy to earn their living. Nassau was rumored to be a lawless nest of adventurers and thieves.

"Surely they wouldn't attack a ship flying under the English flag," Cara said.

Anne remained silent, the *Providence* rising and falling gently beneath her feet. Was it possible that the life she'd left behind in Bristol was better than the one she now faced, living amongst thieves in Nassau?

The first part of their journey was nearly complete. In a few days' time, they would make port. But what kind of future awaited her?

"Sail ho!"

Looking up, Anne raised a hand to shield her eyes, squinting against the brightness of the sun. In the distance, the unmistakable outline of another vessel dotted the horizon.

A murmur spread across the deck like a wave approaching shore as other passengers and crew crowded along the railing. If they hadn't been so spooked by the two ships already following them, Anne doubted the appearance of a third would have caused such a stir.

But cause a stir it did.

The downy hair on Anne's nape prickled. Glancing back up at the cloudless blue sky, she saw that there was no sign of an approaching storm, but she sensed danger on the horizon nonetheless.

CHAPTER 2

Teach

The coppery scent of blood tainted the briny air. A thin trail of red trickled across the slick deck of the *Deliverance*. The cat-'o-nine-tails whistled once more, striking the young boy's back with parallel stripes and lacerating the skin. He let out an anguished cry as tears ran down his grimy cheeks.

"Captain Murrell, surely that's enough," Teach ground out, his shoulders tensing at the agony on the boy's face.

The thin man at Teach's side shot him a stern look, his cold gray eyes unforgiving. "If I don't maintain discipline on this ship, then someone else might try to steal from you."

"I realize that, sir. But perhaps the punishment does not fit the crime. After all, Matthew didn't get away with it."

"Because I saw him when he exited your cabin. Would you have reported the theft if I hadn't caught him in the act?"

If Teach had caught young Matthew stealing the small

chest of coins, he would have dealt with it in a different manner. Scarcely twelve years old, Matthew did not belong at sea.

"If you don't have the stomach for disciplining the crew, perhaps I should have Peter replace you as first mate?" Murrell said. His thin lips curled in a sneer.

Peter weighed the whip in his hands and gave Teach an impassive stare. Teach suspected he enjoyed the whippings as much as Murrell did. In truth, Teach was not supposed to be second in command, but back in Bristol it had been a simple task to forge his father's signature and falsify Teach's papers. A significant bribe had helped the real first mate decide to stay behind, and Teach had assumed his responsibilities on board the *Deliverance*.

At times, Teach had regretted his decision. He detested Murrell, but Teach had been desperate to be on the first ship leaving Bristol to go in search of Anne. His father's vessel had been his only option, with Nassau as its first port in the West Indies. Since the *Providence* was also scheduled to stop in Nassau, Teach had had no other choice.

Peter raised his arm once more, ready to deliver another blow to the small figure bound to the mainmast. He was one of the few men loyal to the captain. With his pale blue eyes and equally pale skin, Peter reminded Teach of a fish.

Teach stepped forward, his pulse pounding in his ears, but Captain Murrell caught Teach by the arm, halting him.

Teach glared down at the offending appendage before

meeting the captain's eyes. "Do not touch me again," he said, his quiet voice filled with malice.

Murrell slowly removed his hand, his nostrils flaring. "Do not interfere with my orders again."

The man grasping the whip looked askance between the two, and the crew seemed to be holding a collective breath, waiting to see who would win the confrontation. It had been like this for weeks, the will of the captain at odds with the will of the first mate. The few passengers who'd booked passage on the great ship had learned to retreat to their cabins when Murrell decided to discipline his men.

A soft whimper escaped from Matthew, and Teach clenched his fists at his sides. Murrell caught the slight movement, and a wicked gleam entered his eyes.

"Do you have something you'd like to say?" Murrell asked.

"No, sir," Teach said, fearing more punishment for the young boy.

After an interminable pause, the captain gave a negligent flick of his wrist. "Cut him loose. I have no wish to have his death on my hands."

Teach muttered an oath, sliding his knife from the scabbard in his boot, before moving forward to free the boy.

Matthew's breathing was ragged, his eyes narrowed from pain and fear, as Teach knelt at his side, slicing through his bonds.

"Take him to my cabin," Teach murmured to the two sailors

who also came forward to help. "I'll be there shortly to see how he fares."

"Aye, sir."

Grabbing a bucket, Teach filled it with seawater from a nearby barrel and splashed the deck where Matthew had knelt. The crew, including Murrell himself, watched silently as Teach filled bucket after bucket, dousing the spot until the blood was gone. Teach wished he could make Matthew's pain disappear just as easily, but he knew from experience that it would take several days for the welts on the boy's back to heal.

There was a much larger stain still visible on the deck, one Teach hadn't been able to wash away. Beneath the baking sun, it had darkened to black, but it, too, had started out a bright crimson.

"Would you rather I had him keelhauled?" the captain asked.

Teach replaced the bucket before turning. "I don't think dragging Matthew beneath the ship is necessary. Since he stole from me, I'd rather you let me determine the punishment, sir," he said, wiping the sweat from his brow. Although it was November, the weather was warm, indicating their proximity to the West Indies. Teach could not wait to get off the ship and be rid of Murrell once and for all.

"Yes, well, I've taken control of the chest and had it locked in my cabin."

Teach froze. "That's not necessary, Captain."

"The name on the inside of the chest reads Anne Barrett. How did you come by it?"

Hearing Anne's name spoken by Captain Murrell caused Teach's stomach to clench and his heart to contract painfully. Robert Murrell was one of the most repulsive men he had ever had the misfortune to meet, and he sincerely hoped Anne's passage to the West Indies had been easier than his.

"The chest belongs to my betrothed," Teach said tightly.

Murrell's eyes widened. "Waiting for you back in England, is she?"

Unwilling to let the captain know the truth, Teach gave a short nod. Teach would never forget the last time he'd seen Anne in Bristol. He'd asked her to go into town with him, but she'd refused. He'd kissed her, a kiss that still haunted his dreams. By the time he'd returned to his father's house, she was gone.

Every time Teach thought about her, it drove him mad not knowing how Anne fared. Was she frightened? Did she suffer from seasickness? Did her fellow passengers leave her in peace? It was the uncertainty of her situation that caused Teach the most pain. He would withstand a hundred lashes if only he could be sure that she was safe.

Murrell opened his mouth once more, but a cry from overhead arrested everyone's attention.

"Sails ho!"

A murmur went up around the deck as sailors lined along

the rails. They'd been too preoccupied with Matthew's whipping to keep a proper lookout.

"I spy three ships, Captain. Two sailing portside, the other to starboard."

Captain Murrell held out his hand for the spyglass at Teach's waist. Now that young Matthew was out of harm's way, Teach slapped it into Murrell's outstretched palm, wishing he could break it over the captain's head.

"They're most likely English or French," Murrell said, studying the distant ships. "It's to be expected. This is one of the busiest shipping lanes in the Atlantic."

"Aye, but we're still a good distance from Nassau. They could be Spanish," Teach said. It was no secret that Spain struggled to maintain their stronghold in the Caribbean. The battle for dominance was fierce.

Murrell's head whipped around. "We're too far from the Spanish main. They wouldn't attack us here. They could be Dutch."

In the end, it didn't truly matter what flags the two ships flew. Their appearance meant trouble.

For the hundredth time, Teach wondered how Murrell had ever secured his post as captain of the *Deliverance*. He was a skilled navigator, with an uncanny ability to sail close to the wind on a course that led him directly to his destination. But his conceit often got in the way of his logic. Instead of inspiring his crew's respect, Murrell resorted to violence and fear to maintain control. "Sir, the *Deliverance* is one of the largest merchant ships ever built, and this is its maiden voyage. We've been a target since we left port," Teach said, unable to control the disdain in his voice. Teach was surprised they hadn't been attacked before now.

Frowning, Murrell seemed to consider Teach's words before glancing around at his crew. When they'd left Bristol, the men had stood straight and eager, most of them former soldiers and proud to be chosen for such a grand vessel. But after four weeks under Murrell's leadership, they were now skittish and tense, never sure when they would be on the receiving end of the captain's brutal tirades.

"Ready the ship," Murrell said.

"For what, exactly, sir?" Teach asked, studying the captain. If the vessels were friendly, there was no need to ready the *Deliverance* for anything. Did the captain wish them to fight? If so, then it was *Murrell's* job to rally the men. He needed to give the final order. Teach had learned that to assume anything under Murrell's command was a grave mistake. Although it had been three weeks, the wounds on Teach's back had not fully healed. He'd carry the scars for the rest of his life.

"We'll try to outrun them," Murrell said dismissively.

"That won't work. The *Deliverance* is too large and sits too low in the water," Teach said.

Captain Murrell flushed a dull shade of red. "Then we'll throw some of the cargo overboard. And some of the cannons if we need to."

"We can't outrun them, Captain. They're most likely in sloops that are swifter and more maneuverable than we are." Teach's gut told him a fight was coming. Although they were still some distance away, the other ships were clearly smaller. They had most likely spotted the *Deliverance* some time ago and were now giving chase.

Murrell pursed his lips. His eyes traveled once more over the crew, as if gauging their loyalty, before coming to rest on Teach. The anger in his eyes was palpable. "Ready the ship for battle."

Teach nodded. "We'll need all hands on deck, sir. That includes the men locked in the hold."

Murrell glared at Teach. There was a strained silence as the two men regarded each other. "Fine. Let them out." Turning, the captain stalked away, leaving Teach and the rest of the men to stare after his departing back.

The gun crew on the *Deliverance* rushed to roll the cannons into position in their lower deck ports, stacking twelve-pounders by their sides. Above, others raced to secure ropes and check the masts and mainsails.

The two men Captain Murrell had locked in the hold joined in the activity, but the four days they'd spent below in the cramped quarters had taken their toll, especially on Teach's friend, John. Built with a broad back and stout legs, John winced every time he moved.

Teach had met John the previous year on board one of

Andrew Barrett's merchant ships. The two had been fast friends ever since. It was John who had help secure Teach's position on board the *Deliverance* by bribing the original first mate to abandon the voyage, and Teach was grateful for John's presence.

"Murrell's addled," John muttered to Teach as he readied his flintlock pistol. "Punishing us for a game of dice. How else does the fool expect us to spend our time? Perfecting our rope work?"

Cleaning his own firearm, Teach shook his head. "He didn't lock you away because of the game. It's because you and Thurston came to blows."

John scowled. "We meant no harm."

"That's not how it looked to the rest of us," Teach said. Jack Thurston was built much like John. Thurston had accused John of cheating at the game. Naturally, John hadn't taken kindly to the insult, and the pair had seemed like two bulls charging at each other.

"I s'pose I should be glad he didn't have me whipped. How's young Matthew?" John asked.

"He'll live. But it will take several days for him to heal," Teach said, his voice grim.

"How are you faring?"

The tightness across Teach's back was lessening as his own wounds healed. "I'm fine."

"You should be in control of this ship. Not that fool captain."

"Careful what you say, John. That smacks of mutiny," Teach

warned in an undertone, glancing over his shoulder. After years of living under his father's control, Teach was less than heartened to find himself under the command of a tyrant even worse than his father.

John followed Teach's gaze.

At the moment, Murrell was berating the helmsman for the direction he had chosen. "I don't care if they are leeward. I want you to stay on course."

John rolled his eyes. "The man's daft. He doesn't know the first thing about fighting."

"We have no choice. Those ships are going to attack."

"Aye, and when they do, he won't have any idea how to respond."

"Then it will be up to us to make sure they don't board us." During his year at sea, Teach had developed some skills with the saber, but he wouldn't stand a chance in a close fight with more experienced swordsmen. He simply relied on his size to intimidate any opponents.

"Don't know if we can stop them. We'll be exposed to their shot between wind and water, and with Murrell leading us, we won't stand a chance."

"Yes, we will."

John looked at Teach. "How do you know?"

"Because I know this ship. And I have a plan."

CHAPTER 3

Anne

As the day progressed, the sun arched across the sky, and the *Providence*'s shadow grew on the sea. In the distance, the two smaller vessels veered toward the larger one. Now that the *Providence* was no longer a target, the crew went about their usual tasks. The able seamen tended to worn or split riggings. The ordinary seamen were charged with coiling rope or touching up tar to prevent further leaking, while the green hands were left to swab the deck.

Only Anne stood immobile, riveted to the spot, as she witnessed a hunt on the open water, the sight before her giving proof to her fears

"I've never been on a ship that grand before," Cara muttered, coming up to her side.

Anne had. Even from this distance, the familiar outline of the *Deliverance* was unmistakable. When she'd first recognized it, her heart had fluttered with hope. It was like looking at an old friend, a tie to her past. And there was a very real possibility that Teach could be on it.

But when the two ships had changed their course and sailed toward it, that hope had turned to dread.

"We have to do something," Anne said, gripping the railing until her knuckles turned white. "We can't just sit by and let them attack."

"We don't know for sure that's what they're going to do," Cara said.

Anne couldn't help the scornful look she threw at her friend. "Don't be ridiculous. It's one of the largest vessels in the world. Do you think those ships are planning on escorting it into port?"

Cara flushed, and Anne immediately felt guilty. If it hadn't been for Cara's friendship and Coyle's protection, Anne could have suffered a much harsher voyage than the one she'd endured.

"I'm sorry, Cara. I didn't mean to be cruel. It's just . . . there are people from Bristol on the *Deliverance*. It's strange to think I might know one of them." Just mentioning the name of her hometown caused Anne's throat to tighten, and she swallowed with difficulty. Although she hadn't left under the best of circumstances, she had grown up in the English port. It was all she'd known for the past sixteen years, and until her father's death, she'd been content there, secure in her mother's love. "I can't stand the thought of people suffering, or worse, dying, if we don't come to their aid."

21

"What can we do?"

"Speak with the captain."

Cara shook her head. "My father always said it's not wise to quarrel with the boatman when you're crossing the river."

"Wise words, I'm sure, but this is no river. And if our roles were reversed, wouldn't you want the people on that other ship to come to our aid?" Anne could tell from the look in Cara's eyes that she'd struck a nerve.

"All right. But let me go get Coyle."

"I can't wait. It might be too late already."

"But—"

Anne placed a hand on Cara's arm. "Let your brother sleep, Cara. He needs the rest. I know what to say to the captain. Trust me." Turning, Anne lifted her skirts, but Cara stopped her.

"Then I'm coming with you. It wouldn't be right for you to face him alone."

Nodding, Anne allowed her friend to follow her down the dank stairway and along the dark hall to the captain's cabin. She preferred to spend as much time as possible on deck, for the cramped and damp quarters below felt like a tomb.

Knocking on the door, Anne waited until Captain Oxley called out for them to enter. His eyes widened when he saw the two girls. Anne could understand his surprise. Aside from a few exchanges in the last five weeks, neither the captain nor Anne had gone out of their way to speak to each other.

An older, severe man, Oxley was balding on top with the

rest of his hair pulled back in a queue. He was slender of frame and by the look of his tanned face, a seasoned sailor.

"Yes?" he asked, leaning back in his chair.

"I'm sorry to interrupt you, Captain, but I was wondering what you intended to do about those two ships," Anne said, fighting the urge to squirm beneath his direct gaze. His small cabin was cluttered, the papers on his desk untidily stacked, and books littered the floor.

"I hadn't planned to do anything."

"But, sir, they're going to attack that other ship."

"Better them than us," was his deliberate response.

Anne went hot and cold at the same time, gasping at his words. "How can you say that? There are passengers on board, possibly women and children."

"We have women and children on board our ship as well. Do you think that just because those people paid more money for their passage on the *Deliverance*, their lives are worth more than the poor souls on this ship, yourself included?" It was clear Oxley had heard of the large merchantman. He'd recognized it from this distance as well.

"No, but if we don't do something, they'll—"

Captain Oxley snorted. "Look around you. You've been on the *Providence* long enough to know its condition. Do you think it could handle a hit from a cannonball?"

Although a single cannonball would not likely sink the *Providence*, Anne knew it wouldn't take much more to send the ship to the bottom of the ocean. "It might not come to that. If they see us coming to the aid of the *Deliverance*, perhaps they'll change course."

"It's not my job to come to anyone's aid. I'm paid to deliver my passengers and cargo."

Anne refused to give up. "But the owner of the *Deliverance* is one of the wealthiest men in Bristol. I'm sure Richard Drummond would pay you handsomely for any support you could extend."

"He can't pay me if I'm not alive to collect. I'm sorry, but my answer is no."

"How can you say that? People will die!"

Captain Oxley stood up and leaned forward on the desk. "Do you think they would come to our aid if our roles were reversed?"

"They just might," Cara said.

"You're wrong, Miss Flynn. I know the captain of that ship. Murrell's a heartless bastard who cares more for his own skin than anyone else's."

Shaking with frustration and anger, Anne glared at Captain Oxley. "The same might be said of you," she said, ignoring Cara's sharply indrawn breath.

"You're wrong, Miss Barrett. I care a great deal for my men, which is why I won't drag them into a fight we have no hope of winning. I have no desire to send them to their deaths."

"A brave man dies only once. A coward dies a hundred times," Anne said, lifting her chin.

"Anne!" Cara interjected, but Oxley raised his hand, his face a dull red.

"You may call me what you like, but my main concern is to see that we make it safely to port." He strode toward the door and pulled it open. "And I will not discuss the running of my ship with a *woman*. If you don't wish to be confined to your cabin, I suggest you leave now."

Feeling heat rise to her own cheeks, Anne refused to move.

Cara touched her arm. "Anne, please."

Struggling to control her fury, Anne gave the captain one last withering look before stalking out of the cabin.

CHAPTER 4

Teach

Captain Murrell's expression grew progressively more alarmed as the day wore on, and his skin took on an ashen hue beneath his tan. He combed his hands through his receding hairline repeatedly. Teach was convinced Murrell would be bald by the end of the day.

Murrell was a coward. Teach could easily picture him meeting Richard Drummond and regaling him with stories of grandeur about his life at sea. If only Teach's father could see the man he'd chosen for the *Deliverance*'s maiden voyage. Drummond had gone to the trouble of hiring soldiers to sail his precious ship, but somehow he'd failed to provide a fit leader.

Teach wished the captain would retire to his cabin like the rest of the wealthy passengers, but Murrell roved the deck like a squawking rooster, his arms flailing while he shouted commands. Peter trailed after him, like a silent shadow following a storm. At first Teach had done his best to ignore what the captain was saying, but the more directions he gave, the more Teach feared they would lose their lives before they ever reached land. The thought of leaving Anne alone in the world was incentive enough for Teach to take action.

Most of the crew now looked to Teach once Murrell and Peter stalked away. Teach gave them a slight nod if they were to indeed follow the captain's orders or he would give them brief instructions once the older man was out of earshot. Murrell was too agitated to make sure if his directions were carried out or not.

Teach's behavior was a criminal act, but there was no other option. He'd tried to reason with the captain, but Murrell wouldn't heed anyone's advice. Murrell had made enemies of almost everyone on board the *Deliverance*, and very few would think to speak against Teach. They seemed to understand that now was not the time to switch direction or lower half of the sails. Teach intended to meet the other ships head-on and not show any signs of weakness or vulnerability.

"What do you make of the ships?" John asked, standing at Teach's side as Teach viewed the approaching vessels through a spyglass.

"The smaller one has eight cannons, all of them six pounders. I count twelve cannons on the larger one."

John whistled beneath his breath. "They've come looking for a fight."

Teach lowered the spyglass and attached it to his belt. From a distance he could see men scurrying back and forth across the decks of the two approaching ships. Unconsciously, he reached for the thin leather cords hanging around his neck. They were attached to a small leather pouch containing the ring he'd intended to give to Anne. Teach kept it with him at all times, often toying with the twine. "We can't outmaneuver them; they're too small. But they won't try to sink us. They want our cargo."

"They might not want to sink us, but I'll wager they'd be only too happy to take out some of our crew."

"We'll have to do our best to stop them, then, won't we?"

Jack Thurston approached, his expression harried. "Teach, we need you belowdecks."

Teach frowned. Jack never called him Teach. He'd given Teach the nickname Blackbeard when he first boarded the *Deliverance*. "What's wrong?"

"Murrell is trying to send our cannons to the bottom of the sea."

Turning, Teach rushed to the stairs that led below. He found the captain along with Peter and another of his loyal sailors crouched on the gun deck. Murrell gestured wildly to the cannons. "I want them gone! All of them! Everything that isn't strapped down needs to go!"

The two men moved to follow the captain's instructions, but Teach snapped his fingers and sent Jack Thurston and another sailor to bar their way. "Captain! It's too late to get rid of our guns and supplies. We can't outrun them!" Teach insisted for what seemed like the hundredth time, the blood pounding in his head. From his vantage point on the stairs between the top and the gun deck, he took in the worried looks of the crew. It was clear to most of them that Murrell was close to collapsing beneath the stress of the impending battle. The two ships were practically upon them, their decks swarming with men.

"We're a merchantman! We have no need for so many cannons!" Murrell shrieked, looking worriedly out the port side.

"We'll need them to fight!"

"I'll raise the white flag! I can negotiate with them."

"If you surrender, we're dead. There's no guarantee any of us will live."

Murrell whirled, pointing an accusing finger at Teach. "You tricked me into this! This is your fault!"

It took all of Teach's self-control not to slam the man into the wall. "*You* said to ready the ship for battle!"

"Because you told me we couldn't outrun them!" Murrell shouted back.

"We can't! Throwing the cannons and cargo overboard would only have delayed the inevitable and left us defenseless!"

"Mutiny! This is mutiny! I'll have your head for this! See if I don't!"

The telltale shot of a cannon in the distance prevented any response. It was accompanied a few seconds later by a resounding splash next to the hull of the *Deliverance*.

It was only a warning shot. The next one would not miss.

"Captain! Captain Murrell, what are your orders, sir?" Peter asked.

All eyes turned to the captain.

Teach clenched the railing, convinced it would splinter beneath his grip.

"Raise the flag. We're going to surrender," Murrell said.

"No!" Teach bounded down the rest of the stairs and shoved his way past the captain.

Peter grabbed Teach by the arms to restrain him, but Jack Thurston threw a punch, catching Peter squarely in the jaw. In the cramped space, Peter fell into Murrell and the two tumbled to the floor.

Nobody moved to help them as they struggled to their feet.

Murrell pulled his pistol and pointed it at Teach, his hand shaking like a leaf in the wind. He motioned to the nearest gunners. "Take him. Lock him in the hold."

The air was thick, the low beams of the upper deck pressing down on them. The two men hesitated. Peter was the only one to attempt to restrain Teach, but Teach easily shook him off, while Jack drew his own pistol, pointing it at Peter.

The hammer of Teach's pulse caused his head to hurt. He knew what disobeying Murrell would cost them. They would be tried and executed for mutiny.

"Captain, please. Trust me. I know what to do. We can come out of this alive."

Murrell stood there with his mouth gaping. He looked out through the gun ports, at the two ships, close enough now that they could see the men preparing their muskets. His eyes drifted over the gun crews before him, the cannons secured with thick ropes as the men of the *Deliverance* waited for their orders. Finally, he met Teach's piercing gaze with a vacant look of his own, and shook his head. "We're all doomed," he whispered, his voice hoarse. He stumbled toward the stairs, with Peter close on his heels.

Not waiting to see where he went, Teach turned to the gunners, crouching low in the dimly lit space. Adrenaline coursed through his veins. "As soon as they come broadside, fire on the upward roll. They don't expect us to fight. The only chance we have is to take out their rigging and canvas and make our escape."

The men nodded, their bodies tensed as they waited for the first true shot to be fired. It didn't take long. The *Deliverance* shuddered as two cannonballs crashed into her hull. Teach's heart leaped in his chest, but he knew that his father had prepared for this and had purposefully reinforced the ship's structure. Teach didn't wait for the others to take another shot.

"Fire!" he yelled as the *Deliverance* rode up on the swell. The gunners jumped, touching their sizzling torches to the fuses.

Boom! Boom! Boom!

Teach's teeth shook with the impact as cannons went off in quick succession. He nearly choked on the thick smoke encircling his head. The deafening sound left his ears ringing as smoldering scraps of soft cloth drifted upward.

He did not see the flight of the balls, but in a matter of seconds, a hole appeared in the middle of the topsail of the closest ship. Another ball hit the bower anchor with an echoing clang.

From behind the safety of the cannon, Teach waited while the sponger cleaned out any powder char or burning cloth left behind before he loaded more powder into it. Working together, the gun crews prepared their cannons, ramming the wad in before rolling the balls home.

"Fire!" Teach yelled once more. The cannons responded with another round of resounding booms. This time Teach heard the shouts and screams of men as the balls ripped through the other ships. He hoped they'd disabled more of their sails.

Musket fire exploded from the other vessels as their big guns ceased. If the *Deliverance* didn't get away soon, their attackers would send them all to the ocean floor.

"I want you to continue firing. Don't stop! As soon as you have the cannons loaded, send them off!" Teach cried out.

Grabbing a musket from a nearby barrel, Teach raced up the stairs to check on the men stationed on the top deck of the *Deliverance*. With a practiced eye he saw that thus far, none of the riggings had been damaged.

Something soared passed Teach's ear, and splinters of wood flew through the air. Diving behind a crate, he took a second to secure a target and fired. One of the men from the other ships fell over the railing into the ocean below. Another sailor quickly took his place as someone handed him a loaded musket.

Teach heard an agonized cry. He turned in time to see Murrell drop, clutching his neck as blood gushed over his hands and arms. Peter was at his side in an instant, his usually emotionless face contorted with shock.

Scrambling toward the captain, Teach did his best to try to stanch the flow, but it was no use. Murrell was losing too much blood.

Peter grabbed the nearest musket and reloaded it. Taking aim, he downed one of the nearest assailants.

After a few more seconds, the *Deliverance* sailed clear of one of the ships. The smoke lay heavy, but Teach could see where the stern and quarter had suffered on the other vessel. A quick glance off the starboard side showed that the smaller ship still sailed on a parallel course with the *Deliverance*, so Teach called for the cannons once more. John raced past him and down the stairs to do his bidding.

The entire time, Murrell clutched Teach's wrist, gurgling noises emitting from his throat, his eyes pleading with Teach to do something. But Teach could do nothing more than stay with him and watch the life slowly ebb from the older man's face. Peter was like a man possessed, loading and firing without hesitation, and shooting at anything that moved on the other ship.

The battle raged on around them and each vessel hammered the other with a continuous din. Murrell's grip loosened until his hand finally fell to the deck. As much as Teach had disliked the man, he had not wished for him to meet such a grisly end.

The sound of men shouting and the incessant cracking of muskets propelled Teach forward. He picked up another musket, reloading it with an expert hand. Sweat poured down his back and his blood hammered in his ears as he watched the small ship reel beneath the impact of three cannonballs. One went through her mizzen topsail, the other two crashed through the deck. *Surely she could no longer give chase,* Teach thought.

The men surrounding him gave a cheerful shout as the *Deliverance* hauled her wind. In a matter of minutes, she was free, benefiting from the favor of the breeze and sailing once more toward her intended destination.

Taking a deep breath, Teach sat back. The acrid smell of smoke choked the air. That had been close. Too close. Once again, Teach hoped that Anne's crossing had been easier than his. The thought of her experiencing a battle left him cold, despite the heat of the day.

"Teach," John called as he ran up the stairs, stopping when he saw Murrell's body.

Peter stared down at the captain's lifeless form, the telltale glint of tears in his eyes.

John crossed himself and muttered a prayer, before meeting Teach's gaze. "The gunners are all accounted for. We cut up the ships' rigging and ruined their looks. That's the last we'll see of them."

Wiping his brow with the back of his hand, Teach nodded at John. "See to the wounded. And tell the men to start patching the sails and repairing the hull."

"Aye, Captain."

Teach turned to Peter. "Help me take care of him."

"Aye, *Captain*," Peter said, his voice bitter.

Ignoring Peter's resentment, Teach sent him off to fetch a hammock. Once he returned, the two of them wrapped Murrell's body in it with a cannonball, and Peter quickly sewed it shut. He didn't bother with the stitch through Murrell's nose. The dead man's skin had already taken on a chalky hue. Several members of the crew stopped what they were doing to watch as Teach and Peter hoisted the body in the air before tossing it into the waves. As Murrell sank below the surface of the turquoise waters, there was almost a collective sigh of relief. The tyrant was gone.

About to turn away, Teach hesitated when Peter spoke.

"He wasn't always like that," Peter said, his voice soft. He continued to stare at the water, his eyes unblinking. "When I first saw him, he was a gunner on a naval ship. A press-gang caught me unawares in an alley of London. I was only eleven at the time and they turned me into a bloody powder monkey."

Teach knew about the navy's practice of using small youth, chosen for their speed and height, to ferry gunpowder from the ship's hold to the artillery. It was a dangerous job. In inexperienced hands, the powder could often start fires or cause explosions, especially during a battle at sea.

"I tried to run away, but they caught me. And beat me. My fingers were broken and bruised. Murrell taught me how to carry the powder from the hold to the cannons without dropping it. He told me I had to be strong. Not to let them see any weakness."

An image of young Matthew tied to the mast flashed before Teach's eyes. "There are other ways to show strength. Kindness is not a flaw. Neither is mercy."

Peter's lips twisted as he finally met Teach's gaze. "Where will those emotions get you? People take advantage of you. They don't respect you, neither. Remember who was captain of this ship."

Teach knew he should keep his mouth shut, but he couldn't stand to see Peter looking so superior. "Where is your captain now?" Teach asked before striding away, silently cursing his own reckless words. It was possible that once they reached shore, Peter would accuse Teach of mutiny. It would be Peter's word against that of the crew, but the danger was still there.

Knowing how the others felt about Murrell and Peter, Teach doubted anyone would corroborate Peter's claim. But would the authorities believe him?

Once again, Teach reached for the cords around his neck, working the thin leather between his fingers.

Even in death, Murrell still posed a threat. What had made the older man become so cold and brutal? What kind of a legacy was fear to leave behind? Not one that Teach wanted for himself. He never wanted people to dread him or the sound of his name so much that the only emotion they felt at his death was relief.

What Teach wanted most in life was to find Anne and build a quiet life together somewhere, away from the rest of the world. Only then would he truly be happy.

Only then would he truly be free.

CHAPTER 5

Anne

The port of Nassau assaulted the senses. The azure sky overhead was a darker mirror of the aquamarine waters below. It was like viewing the world through a green glass, with everything more alive and vibrant than the gray-washed landscape of Bristol. Fish of various sizes swam with the current of the *Providence*, breaking the crystalline surface as it reached the port.

Anne walked with unsteady legs as she took her first steps on land in more than a month, the dock seeming to roll beneath her feet. The briny scent in the air was familiar and yet somehow different, richer. The breeze bathed the waterfront with a mixture of fragrances from spices and oils, combating the putrid smells of wet canvas and rotting fish.

Countless boats dotted the harbor—longboats and barges from Europe's northern coasts anchored beside cutters, frigates, and men-of-war from Asia and Africa. Vessels from every corner of the earth swayed with the calming waves. Shouts and cries in different languages rang through the air as figures scrambled across the rigging and decks, loading and unloading merchandise as well as passengers. Warehouses lining the wharves opened their arms to receive cargo.

Anne had never seen so much activity, not even in Bristol. And the heat was stifling. Sweat dripped from every brow, including Anne's. Her skin was sticky and her dress clung to her as the roasting sun smothered her neck and back like a wool blanket. She could feel the warmth all the way to her feet.

Nassau burst with color. Not only did the inhabitants' skin tones vary, from deep mahogany to angry red, thanks to the ever present sun, but their clothing boasted bright hues as well. There were men in striped trousers, some in plain sailcloth. Others wore fine red waistcoats and tarpaulin hats, though Anne wondered how they could stand the heat. Women marched across the docks in petticoat skirts and blouses, in brown, yellow, and even russet tones.

Here, at last, were people like her. How often had she longed for this day back in Bristol? Anne wanted to marvel at the sights and sounds, but her fear and anxiety prevented too much admiration. The image of those two ships bearing down on the *Deliverance* still plagued her mind.

Frustrated that Coyle wasn't moving any faster, Anne wished she could force the crowds to part. She was determined to find someone who could help the *Deliverance*, but Coyle insisted on leading them along the crowded docks.

"Do you truly believe your uncle will know someone who can help us?" Anne asked, raising her voice over the commotion. It appeared the people of Nassau only knew how to shout, their voices rising to meet the sun's rays.

Coyle nodded, perspiration beading on his ruddy complexion. "I do. Uncle Alastair has been here for eleven years. From what he's told our da, he's a powerful man, even if he does only run a tavern," he yelled. "Alastair was one of the first wave of colonists to come back to Nassau after the Spanish destroyed it."

Anne hoped he was right, as she followed his broad back, pushing through the heaving throng until something crashed into her. Startled, Anne threw out her arms, pushing Cara to the side. Anne landed painfully on her left wrist, her knees slamming into the hard earth below. People crowded quickly around her, threatening to trample her to death with every heavy step. She felt helpless, a mouse trying to survive in a world of hungry lions, and her fear made her angry. Anne shoved back with all her strength, struggling to get to her feet. She hadn't survived the Drummond household and that awful boat ride to be trampled alive on the dock.

Finally, the weight on her body lessened as a stout man hauled a small figure off her legs. Cara pushed others aside and helped Anne to stand. Rushing toward them, Coyle stepped between the girls and the fighting pair, a circle forming as the crowd watched in anticipation. Some cheered, others hollered, throwing curses into the thick, humid air.

Both men were dirty, their shirts and breeches soiled from weeks' worth of filth, and their beards were messy and unkempt. The smaller one spoke in a foreign tongue, spitting words that Anne didn't understand. The larger man circled him, slowly. Teasingly.

Anne had no idea what they were fighting about, but the bigger one was drunk, his movements strained and his speech slurred. His meaty fists hit air instead of the shorter man's face.

"Let's go," Coyle urged, trying to push his way through the multitudes, but it was no use. An unwilling captive to the bloody spectacle, Anne watched in a mixture of horror and fascination as the small man suddenly brandished a blade.

No one intervened. Instead, the crowd chanted and the drunken man roared before charging the smaller man like a bull seeing red. Suddenly, he dropped to his knees, a look of shock lining his face. Anne closed her eyes, but not before she saw the knife sticking out of the man's chest.

Coyle tried once again to shove his way through the assembly and this time he succeeded. Lightheaded and sick to her stomach, Anne held her arms out, hoping to escape the crush. She knew the people wouldn't think twice about mercilessly trampling her beneath their feet.

Back in England, she had been aware of pickpockets and other petty criminals. The only victim she'd seen of a brutal crime was her mother, who'd scorned the advances of an earl's son. He'd beaten her for her refusal and she'd later died from her injuries.

But as they made their way along the crowded docks, Anne couldn't fully shake the image of the man stabbed with the knife.

Coyle and Cara appeared to be equally stunned. "What are we doing here?" Cara asked, her features pinched.

"It'll be all right, Cara. You and Anne just stay close."

"We can't be close to you all the time, Coyle Flynn," Cara said, her voice sharp. "We shouldn't have come."

"We had no choice," Coyle snapped.

"Let's just find your uncle," Anne said, hoping to avoid another fight. Deep down, she agreed with Cara. She didn't want to be another body lying in the street.

Although their situations were different, Cara and Coyle were victims of their own circumstances as well. Work was scarce in rural Ireland, and their family had lived on the margins of survival. When their uncle Alastair had offered them both a place to work, they had readily accepted.

The three of them were silent as they left the bustling docks behind. Coyle halted briefly to ask someone the way to The Laughing Fox tavern. A few streets away, they stopped at a clapboard building with a sign sporting a fox hanging in front. The structure appeared to be much newer than the other buildings lining the street. It smelled of fresh pine and pitch.

Inside, it took a moment for Anne's eyes to adjust to the dim interior after the brilliance of the afternoon sun outside. Sawdust covered the floor and a long wooden bar dominated one side of the room, its surface scratched and worn. Only a handful of patrons occupied the tables in The Laughing Fox. A single serving girl strolled through their ranks with large tankards of ale.

Coyle approached the barkeep while Anne and Cara remained by the front door. Anne did her best to ignore the looks of the curious patrons by keeping her eyes leveled on an area just above their heads. The men were rough, their clothing worn, and their hair grimy. They were mostly likely sailors and dockworkers.

"I'm looking for Alastair Flynn. Is he here?" Coyle asked.

The barkeep wiped a glass with a rag, but paused at Coyle's question, his thick eyebrows drawing together in a frown. "Who's asking?"

"My name's Coyle Flynn. Alastair Flynn is my uncle."

Nodding to the back of the room, the man continued with his task. "You'll be wantin' to speak with Beth. If she's here, she'll be in the back," he said.

Anne took Cara's hand as they followed Coyle toward the back. One man reached out and grabbed Cara around the waist. Yanking out of his grip, Cara turned on him, her face filled with disgust at the lecherous grin he gave her. The man laughed and reached for Cara again, but Anne grasped the man's fingers and bent them back toward his arm.

"Unless you want to lose that hand, I suggest you keep it for sipping ale."

The man's eyes watered and he glared at Anne. "You stupid who—"

Coyle's fist slammed into the man's jaw, and he sank to the floor at Anne's feet. His companion jumped up, clearly ready to come to his friend's defense. Coyle turned on him, his shoulders squared and his fists clenched.

Anne watched each man closely, in case anyone pulled a blade. She'd spotted a tankard nearby and wouldn't hesitate to use it.

A loud voice boomed above them. "Get out of here, Amos, before I tear you apart myself."

The man struggled to his feet, the cheeks on his crimson face shaking. "You've never had a problem with me before, Alastair," Amos cried.

"That's not true, you dirty bounder. I've told you to keep your hands to yourself while you're in my tavern. This was your last chance." Alastair crossed his thick arms over his broad chest. To Anne, he looked like an older version of Coyle, with the same smattering of dark freckles across the bridge of his nose and cheeks. The wood creaked beneath his feet as he descended the steps.

Glaring at the stern expression on Alastair's face, Amos must have thought better of arguing with him. He shot one last surly look at Cara, and headed to the door, his friend following on his heels.

Anne exhaled in relief as Alastair wrapped Cara and Coyle in his arms.

Cara's face relaxed somewhat and Anne could not help a twinge of envy. She longed for a connection with another family member; unsure if any still lived, Anne worried such a relationship was impossible. Feeling out of place, Anne clasped and unclasped her hands nervously.

"You're grown into a beauty, Cara Flynn. Perhaps it wasn't such a good idea to have you and your brother come stay with me," Alastair said.

"After what we just saw, I'm not sure I would have made this trip," Cara muttered.

"What happened?"

Cara shuddered. "There was a fight near the docks. Someone pulled a knife and . . ." Her voice trailed off.

"Unless you have an escort, stay away from the docks," Alastair said, his expression fierce.

"It's rather hard to avoid the docks when you arrive on a ship," Cara pointed out.

"And here I'd hoped the years had softened the sharp side of your tongue. No matter. You'll be safe as long as you're with me." Alastair turned to give Coyle an appraising look. "Have you looked after your sister?"

"As much as anyone can look after Cara," Coyle said. "She doesn't listen to a thing I say. Maybe you can do a better job keeping her in line."

Cara shrugged. "I didn't get into any trouble on the ship. After all, I had Anne to keep me company."

Alastair glanced at Anne standing back from the group. Despite his intimidating appearance, kindness flashed in his eyes.

Cara linked her arm with Anne's and pulled her forward. "Uncle, this is Anne Barrett. Anne, this is our uncle, Alastair Flynn."

"Pleased to meet you, Anne. What brings you to Nassau?"

"She needs a place to stay," Cara said, before Anne could respond. "And a place to work. I told her you wouldn't mind employing her."

Anne flushed, wondering how Alastair would react to *Cara's* generosity. It was one thing for Cara to make the offer. It was quite another for Alastair to follow through with it. His smile, however, put her at ease.

"Anyone who can manage to keep Cara out of trouble for an extended period of time has my respect and approval," Alastair said.

Anne answered with a slight smile of her own. "On the contrary. It was Cara and Coyle who came to *my* aid. If it hadn't been for them, I'm afraid my passage from England would have been much different." Her smile faded and she shivered at the thought of the *Providence*.

Cara gave Anne a comforting squeeze, while Coyle took a deep breath. "Uncle, I hate to cut our reunion short, but we're in need of some help. We believe a merchantman was attacked not far from shore."

Alastair's jaw tightened and his eyes narrowed. "When did this happen."

"Two days ago," Anne said. "The ship was the *Deliverance*, the largest of its kind ever built."

"You were supposed to travel on the *Deliverance*. What happened to the money I sent you?" Alastair asked.

Cara blushed and Coyle shot her a dark look. "Cara took a liking to someone on the way from Donegal to Bristol."

"I didn't know he would rob us," Cara cried, looking like a guilty child caught in an act of mischief.

"You should know better than to trust a pretty face."

"He wasn't all that pretty once you were finished with him, now was he, brother dear?"

Rolling his eyes, Coyle took a deep breath. "I recovered what I could from the money, but I wasn't able to get all of it. Once we reached Bristol, we discovered the only ship we could afford passage on was the *Providence*."

Alastair nodded. "I thought you were a mite early. So you think the *Deliverance* was attacked?"

"I do. Two ships approached it as we sailed away," Anne said, as Alastair pursed his lips.

"There was some talk of having an escort sent out to greet it," Alastair said.

Cara looked hopeful. "Perhaps those were the ships we saw."

Both Anne and Coyle shook their heads. "I don't think so," Anne said. "They followed us for several days. If they'd been sent to escort the *Deliverance*, why did they keep their distance from us?"

"Anne's right. They didn't want to show their colors, which is why they didn't approach the *Providence*."

"Why didn't they have an escort when they left England?" Cara asked.

Alastair gave a short laugh. "I heard the owner thought it would be a sign of weakness if he sent it off with an escort. It's a foolish gamble to take with other's lives."

Richard Drummond's reputation has clearly reached the West Indies, thought Anne.

Coyle turned to his uncle. "Is there someone we can notify? Someone who might be able to offer some assistance?"

"Aye. We'll send word to Governor Webb. He'll know best what kind of help, if any, can be provided."

Anne's stomach dropped to her feet. It had been two days since they last saw the *Deliverance*. She hoped it wasn't too late to help the survivors. If there were any.

"Will he listen to you?" Coyle asked.

"Aye, he will. I know Governor Webb personally."

Both Cara's and Coyle's eyes widened in surprise. "You've come a long way from Donegal," Cara said.

"I told your da I'd make something of myself." There was no conceit in Alastair's voice. It was simply a statement of fact.

"Could we send word to the governor now?" Anne asked, desperate to act. Although she didn't know for sure if Teach was on the *Deliverance* or not, there was a part of her that seemed to sense his presence. Or perhaps it was only her wishful thinking.

"I'll go myself. Coyle, you come with me. Cara, Anne, you stay here with Beth and let her show you to your rooms."

"Beth?" Cara asked.

The barkeep had mentioned Beth when they first entered.

A tender smile crossed Alastair's face. "Aye. Beth. She'll be pleased you're finally here." Striding to the swinging door, Alastair motioned with his hand for the others to follow him.

The big and well-equipped kitchen held a fireplace, and shelves filled with brass pots and pans. Garlic, drying peppers, as well as herbs and spices hung from the ceiling over wooden cupboards. A petite woman with mahogany skin stood beside a narrow table, instructing two girls as they chopped carrots and onions.

"Beth, let me introduce my niece and nephew, Cara and Coyle Flynn. And this is their friend, Anne Barrett. Coyle, Cara, Anne, this is Beth Morris."

Beth smiled, her face lighting up as she greeted them. Alastair placed a kiss on Beth's cheek. "I'm off to visit Webb on some business. Will you show the girls where they'll be staying?"

"Of course. Is anything wrong?" Beth's soft and melodic accent drifted into Anne's ears. It reminded Anne of her mother's, the way Beth ran her words together, and her use of soft vowels.

Cara and Coyle watched their uncle with interest. Anne, too, noticed the affection between Alastair and Beth. Although Anne's parents had not been as demonstrative, she could not help thinking of them. Anne warmed to the pair immediately.

"A merchant ship might have been attacked. We're going to see if anything can be done to help. Is Benjamin outside?"

"I believe so," Beth replied.

Alastair led them to a crescent-shaped courtyard between the tavern and a single-storied house. A vegetable garden lined one side of a large wooden barn on the other side of the enclosure. Shutters and flower boxes decorated the structures. "Benjamin, come meet our guests," Alastair called.

A tall, broad-shouldered young man came out of the barn, his brown eyes steady as he shook Alastair's hand. Benjamin's skin was a shade darker than Beth's, and Alastair greeted him in a foreign tongue Anne didn't recognize. Benjamin wore breeches and a brown shirt, the sleeves pushed up to his elbows. Thick, raised scars covered his hands and arms, evidence of a whipping. Anne's breath hitched in her throat, and she felt an intense flash of fury at the unknown person who had performed such a barbarous act.

Alastair nodded to Benjamin after making the introductions. "I'm taking my nephew to meet with the governor. Please keep an eye on things for me."

"Yes, sir," Benjamin said, his English heavily accented.

The three men turned toward the tavern, but Anne couldn't stop staring at Benjamin's scars. "Who did that?" she breathed, unaware she'd spoken the words aloud.

Beth gave Anne an understanding nod. "His former master. Benjamin works for Alastair now. He's free to come and go as he chooses, just like anyone else in Alastair's employ."

Anne bit her lip, grateful Benjamin hadn't heard her. It was one thing to hear about the horrors of slavery, but quite another to actually witness the effects of the barbaric institution.

"You must be very tired after your trip," Beth said, breaking the stilted silence. She led the girls through the front door of the house and down a short hallway. "I'll bring you a tray of food."

"Thank you, but I'm not very hungry," Anne said. Between the scene at the docks and the unknown fate of the *Deliverance*, she doubted she'd be able to rest. Or eat.

"Have you known my uncle long?" Cara asked as Beth guided the girls into a room with a large bed and dresser. Thin lines of light trickled through the shuttered window.

"For nine years."

Curiosity rang in Cara's voice. "Are you in charge of the kitchen?"

Beth gave Cara a knowing smile. "I help your uncle with The Laughing Fox" was all she said.

Before Cara could pose another question, Anne spoke up. "How long will it take to deliver a message to the governor?"

"Not long. If Governor Webb is at home, Alastair will be allowed to see him immediately." Pride filled Beth's words and light shone in her eyes.

Cara let out a low whistle. "I wish my da were here to see this. When Uncle Alastair left Donegal, everyone in the family believed he'd be back within five years."

"Your uncle is one of the most respected men on the island," Beth said. "Governor Webb stops by the Fox at least once a week." The warmth faded from Beth's face and her voice turned hard. She walked to the door. "Stay here and rest. Alastair should be back before long."

"Thank you," Anne said, following her. "For letting me stay here."

Beth paused and gave her a slight smile. She tucked one of Anne's wayward tendrils behind her ear. "I'll send for a bath. And we'll do something about this hair. You'll find the weather here a little more agreeable for your curls."

Anne's chest warmed at the motherly gesture. Beth had a calming presence about her that Anne hadn't felt in quite a while.

The older woman left, leaving Anne and Cara to scrub their hands and faces of the dirt and grime from the *Providence* and Nassau's docks.

"I hope the governor will truly send help," Anne said, getting the feeling that Beth did not care much for the governor.

"Why wouldn't he? It's an English ship and Nassau is an English settlement." Cara struggled out of her dress. "Although I don't know how people can live here in this heat," she muttered. "I wish my da would have accepted the money Uncle Alastair offered him. But he was too proud to take it. Men and their silly pride."

Anne walked to the window. She knew how much Cara

missed her mother. They were the unfortunate victims of a rift between Alastair and Cara's father. Family was important to Cara, and she hoped to earn enough money to send back to her parents. If her father wouldn't accept assistance from Alastair, Cara hoped he'd accept it from his own daughter. Cara's greatest wish was to be reunited with her family. Anne wanted to help, which was why she needed to send word to her father's solicitor immediately to get him to send the other half of her inheritance—if Richard Drummond would still honor his word and send her the rest.

Cara lay down on the bed, dressed only in her shift. "We'll do what we can to help you, Anne. We're your family now. Try to get some rest. When we both wake up, maybe we'll feel better."

Sitting down on the edge of the bed, Anne tried to relax. Cara was right. They were her family now. Although they weren't blood-related, they'd treated her better than most people she'd ever known. She and Cara had slept side by side for weeks, sharing secrets and wishes in the dark, falling asleep exhausted, knowing that Coyle guarded their door. Anne knew about Cara's desire to get married and settle down and Coyle's hopes to follow in his uncle's footsteps and own a tavern of his own one day. And both of the Flynns knew about Teach. Anne wished for the millionth time that Teach could meet them. He'd warm to their kindness, humor, and humility.

Anne leaned forward, resting her elbows on her knees to

ease the tension settling between her shoulder blades. The exhaustion weighed on her, tightening muscles, making her fingers tremble, and drying her eyes. She could not free herself from the tumultuous thoughts haunting her mind. Every time she pictured Teach, pain unfolded in her chest, squeezing the breath from her lungs. She'd give anything to see those green eyes once more.

Cara's soft snores lingered in the room. She had an enviable knack for falling asleep easily, even during squalls aboard the *Providence*.

But Anne always struggled.

Determined to rest, she lay down on her side. She squeezed her eyes shut, her stomach gripped in a vice of fear. Her mother had often told her if one lost courage and hope, one lost everything. The desperate strength of her hope was her one link with Teach. As long as she clung to her courage, all was not lost.

Anne stared at the wall in front of her, until her lids slowly lowered. In the distance a dog barked. Someone shouted. A shot rang out.

Anne's eyes flew open. Nassau wasn't safe.

But please, she prayed. *Let Teach be.*

CHAPTER 6

Teach

"We lost young Daniel during the night," John said, approaching Teach at the helm. Gray clouds hung heavy in the sky as the *Deliverance* limped toward the Bahamas.

John and Teach took turns guiding the ship and did their best to ensure the injured men were as comfortable as possible despite their circumstances. They'd lost the ship's surgeon during the battle, as well as their medicine chest.

The weary and sweat-soaked crew was somber, though the mood aboard had more to do with the heavy burden of lost comrades than it did the weather. Those injured during the battle littered the weather deck. Every once in a while, a painful groan rose up to the heavens. Bloodied bandages covered opened wounds, and the air was hot and smelled of death and rotting flesh.

Teach frowned as he altered their course a point and a half to the south. Daniel had been one of the livelier crew members and had had a penchant for jokes. "If we don't make port soon, I fear we won't have anyone left." The supplies on the *Deliverance* were alarmingly low. One of the cannonballs had pierced the side of the ship, destroying valuable barrels of water for cooking and brandy for drinking, as well as their supply of salted beef.

John's eyes searched the horizon. "We can't be that far off. It shouldn't take us more than a few days to get there."

Drawing a deep breath, Teach nodded. It had already been three days since the attack, but to him it felt like twice that amount. "So long as we don't encounter any storms . . ." His voice trailed off. They both knew the unpredictability of the seas.

"We could always stop at one of the first islands we see. There are enough trees to repair the damage, an' fresh water shouldn't be too difficult to find."

"We can't do that with the injured," Teach said. "They need more help than any of us can provide and that help can only be found in Nassau. Any delay could cost more men their lives." Teach had given their options serious thought. If there weren't any wounded, he would be tempted to repair the ship and try to sell off what cargo they still had to the highest bidder. He could buy a smaller vessel to continue his search for Anne. But that was too risky and too many things could go wrong. The *Providence* was bound for Nassau, and Teach needed to get there as quickly as possible.

"You should get some rest. I can take over for now," John offered.

"I think I'll have another go at the chest," Teach said. He still hadn't found Anne's chest of coins and wondered where Captain Murrell could have hidden it.

"Have you asked Peter? I reckon he'd have an idea of where it is."

"Peter hasn't spoken since the attack."

"Should we beat a call to quarters? That would draw him out an' the coward couldn't hide."

Teach shook his head, reaching automatically for the leather cords around his neck. Captain Murrell had been fond of the practice of beating the drums and causing the men to scurry and gather on deck. He'd said it was to practice in the event of an attack, but a lot of good that had done him. The minute those ships had appeared, Murrell had practically wet himself. "No, there's no need. Let the men rest. I'll find Peter and ask him myself."

"Do you think he'll cause trouble for us when we get to Nassau?"

Teach had wondered the same thing. "It will be his word against ours. If he does charge me with mutiny, it will be on him to provide enough evidence to support his claim."

John scoffed. "He'll get no support from me or the crew. Don't you worry none, Teach. We'll get through this. And we'll find Anne as well. Things will work out. Mark my words."

Grateful for his friend's optimistic presence, Teach remembered another talk he'd had with John in the captain's cabin of the *Deliverance* back in Bristol. Someone had accused Teach of piracy, and John had vowed then he would do everything in his power to make sure nothing happened to Teach.

"You're a good friend, John. I'm lucky to know you."

"Me and the crew feel the same about you. Now go find that chest."

Teach made his way down the stairs to the weather deck, where the wounded were spread out, reminding Teach of pieces of leather drying under the sun. One of the men called to Teach as he passed and Teach knelt beside him. "Are you thirsty?" Teach asked, grabbing a nearby jug filled with brandy. The water had turned brackish in the heat, and they had been forced to dilute the brandy with it, to extend their supply.

The man clutched Teach's wrist and sipped greedily from the mug. "The pain. I need something for the pain," the man choked out, once he'd swallowed.

"As soon as we get to port, I'll make sure you get something for the pain."

With a solemn nod, the man closed his eyes, his chest expanding with each labored breath. Wishing there was something more he could do, but knowing he couldn't do a thing until they reached land, Teach stood with a muttered oath. The men had fought valiantly. They didn't deserve to suffer like this.

Heading in the direction of the captain's cabin, he threw open the door, only to stop short when he saw Peter already there, taking some papers from the desk and stuffing them in the pocket of his waistcoat. In Peter's left hand was Teach's copy of Dampier's book. Peter looked up, startled, and his face turned a furious shade of red.

"What are you doing here?" Teach demanded, his temper already frayed.

"Nothing."

Teach's eyes narrowed at the sullen expression on Peter's face. "Then why are you taking those papers? They don't belong to you."

"They don't belong to you, either. The only reason you're captain is because you disobeyed Murrell's orders."

It was just as Teach had feared. *If* they managed to reach port, Peter would be trouble. Teach would have to tread carefully, so as not to anger him further. Teach spoke calmly, even though his every muscle clenched in anticipation of giving Peter a thorough thrashing.

"Despite what you think, I didn't want Murrell to die like that."

"But you did want him to die," Peter sneered.

True. Grinding his teeth, Teach barely managed to stay in one spot. The desire to drive his fist into Peter's smug countenance was overwhelming. "Get out."

For a moment, Peter didn't move.

"Leave the book," Teach said.

Flushing angrily, Peter threw the book on the floor before stalking toward the door.

"The papers as well."

"I think I'll keep—" Peter cried out as his back hit the wall, Teach's arm pressing against his windpipe.

Teach ripped the papers out of Peter's pocket. The cargo list of the *Deliverance*. "Why were you taking these?"

Peter didn't answer and Teach increased the pressure on his throat.

"I asked what you what you were doing with these?"

"I'll see you hang before I answer to you," Peter choked out, his eyes bulging from lack of air. "Once we get to port, you'll be charged with mutiny."

Teach brought his face close, his jaw clenched. "A dead man tells no tales."

"Is everything all right?" John asked from the door.

"Fine," Teach ground out. Although Peter hadn't answered his question, Teach knew what Peter had planned, and it made Teach sick to realize he'd had the same thought. He tried to tell himself that his desire to sell the cargo was different from Peter's. Peter simply wanted to sell it for his own personal gain, whereas Teach hoped to pay his men and continue his search for Anne.

Slowly, Teach loosened his hold. Peter gasped and jerked out of reach. Backing out of the room, Peter stumbled down the hallway before the sound of his footsteps disappeared.

John gave a low whistle. "What was that all about?"

Teach held up the cargo list. "This."

"What did he want with that? Did you ask him to check what was lost during the fight?"

"No. I think he was hoping to sell some of it when we reach port."

"How? Merchants are expecting their goods. They paid for their transport."

Teach didn't want to tell John that he'd contemplated doing exactly what Peter had considered. Yes, the *Deliverance* was well-known and recognizable, but there were always people willing to bend the rules or break the law in order to make a profit. It was only a question of finding them. And Teach figured breaking the rules was worth it in order to pay his crew and find Anne.

"Keep an eye on Peter," Teach said, sitting in the chair behind the desk.

"Aye, Captain." John turned to leave, but hesitated. "Before I forget, I wanted to tell you that we lost another water barrel. The cooper discovered too late that there was a hole in it."

With a sigh of resignation, Teach shook his head. "Cut the water rations in half."

John nodded and closed the door quietly behind him.

CHAPTER 7

Anne

A sheen of sweat coated Anne's skin, and for a half moment she wondered if her sore muscles and tight skin were the result of some illness she'd caught. Surely if she closed her eyes again, she'd awaken to find herself still in Bristol in Drummond's house. Her dream had been so vivid, so real.

Teach, with his dark hair and vibrant green eyes, was a figment of a fevered imagination. But as Anne rested her wrist across her eyes, blocking out the sun, she realized that Margery would never have allowed her to sleep till the sky was full bright.

Anne sat up, the heat oppressive in the strange room. She was alone. Everything came rushing back. Leaving England and sailing on the nightmare that was the *Providence*. Arriving in Nassau, the loud and crowded streets. The man falling with a knife embedded in his chest. Her surroundings were surreal, and she felt completely out of her element. But this was no dream.

Swinging her legs over the side of the bed, she spied a small tub filled with water. A clean chemise, blouse, and skirt had all been laid out for her.

With a grimace, Anne shed every last stitch of clothing, tempted to set a flame to the salt-encrusted material. As she bathed, she marveled that she hadn't heard anyone enter or leave the room. *Where was Cara?*

After weeks on board the ship, Anne had finally slept deeply. She shuddered as she scrubbed the grime from her skin, grateful for the cool, fresh water and floral-scented soap. She washed her hair with the pitcher of water from the nightstand. Using a blackwood brush to comb through her thick waves, she quickly braided her hair and left it hanging down her back. She looked at her tattered and rotting shoes and decided to leave them behind. Padding barefoot across the courtyard, the packed dirt beneath her feet was warm from the heat of the afternoon sun.

In the kitchen, Anne discovered Alastair and Beth sitting together at the worn wooden table. Once when Anne was little and couldn't sleep, she'd crept down to the kitchen and discovered her parents in a similar scenario. The rest of the household had slept, but Anne would never forget that image of her parents, one of the rare occasions she'd seen them together. At the time, she hadn't understood their whispered discussions or shared smiles. It wasn't until she'd shared similar moments with Teach that she fully grasped their meaning.

"I'm sorry. I didn't mean to interrupt," Anne said, hesitating in the doorway.

Alastair stood, but still held on to Beth's hand. "You're not interrupting. Did you rest well?"

Beth got to her feet and moved toward the fire. She dished something out of the pot that hung there and motioned for Anne to sit down. "Come have some conch stew."

Anne's mother had told her about the large shellfish that lived in the shallow waters surrounding the islands. Anne's stomach reacted to the scent of the rich broth and her mouth watered. "Thank you," she said, sliding gratefully onto the stool Alastair provided for her. She'd been so exhausted, she hadn't given much thought to food, but now that she'd rested, she realized just how hungry she was. She took a tentative bite of the sweet white meat and spicy broth. It was delicious.

"Where's Cara?" Anne asked.

"She's working in the tavern," Alastair said, leaning against the table beside Beth.

Anne flushed guiltily and began to rise, but Alastair stopped her. "There's no need for you to rush out there. It's early yet and doesn't get busy until the evening. Take your time and eat."

"But I don't want to be a burd—"

"You're not a burden. And you'll be pleased to know that Governor Webb said he'd send out two ships for the *Deliverance*."

Relieved at his words, Anne wondered how long would it take for the ships to be ready. She sincerely hoped it wasn't too late. "The captain was a coward not to stay to help."

Alastair nodded thoughtfully. "Perhaps. But he did what he thought was best at the time."

Anne said nothing as she ate. She'd never forget the feeling of desperation and helplessness as the *Providence* had sailed away, leaving the *Deliverance* on its own. If Teach had figured out her note and sailed on his father's ship like he'd planned, that meant the fate of the *Deliverance* was Teach's fate as well.

A loud laugh sounded from the tavern, accompanied by the call for another round of drinks. Anne wondered how Cara was faring. She herself didn't relish the thought of working amongst the rowdy patrons.

Beth placed a tankard in front of her. "This is the juice from a pineapple. Have you ever tried it?"

"No, never." Anne took a sip, surprised by the vibrant flavor. It had a sweet taste with a hint of tartness. "Thank you," Anne said, feeling refreshed after she swallowed the last drop.

Beth smiled and refilled the tankard. "We can't have you collapsing on your first day here, now can we?"

"Is it always like this?" Anne asked, wiping her brow with the back of her hand. Her blouse already stuck to her skin, and beads of perspiration rolled down her face.

Alastair nodded. "Mostly. When the winds come, it will cool off a bit. If you aren't used to the warmth, it can be overwhelming."

"How can anyone possibly cook in this heat?"

"We all have to eat. But people mostly come to The Laughing Fox to drink. Only a few ever require any meals," Beth said.

Alastair and Beth watched Anne take another spoonful of the stew.

"Coyle told me what you've been through. So you know this merchant, Richard Drummond, do you?" Alastair asked.

"Yes," Anne said.

"And he's the one who sent you away?"

Anne's throat closed around her response, remembering the scene at the Drummond household when Drummond had told her to leave. She swallowed, her eyes meeting Alastair's. "Yes."

"The devil hang him. I don't know the man, but he had no right sending a girl off on a ship by herself. What kind of irresponsible—"

"Al, let the poor girl eat. Can't you see how thin she is? We can discuss this later," Beth murmured.

Anne laid her spoon down. "No, it's fine. I appreciate your kindness." Glancing between Beth and Alastair, Anne drew a deep breath. Unsure exactly how much Coyle had said, Anne decided it would be best to be forthright from the start. "My father's name was Andrew Barrett. He was an English merchant. My mother worked for him in his household, but she came from the island of Curaçao."

Beth and Alastair remained silent.

"If it isn't too much to ask, I'd like to send word to my father's solicitor in Bristol. I left before I was able to tell him of my whereabouts. Once I hear back from him, I'll be able to move on."

"Aye, Coyle told me you hoped to find some of your mother's family. Do you know where they might be?"

Anne mentioned the name of the village on the island of Curaçao.

"I'll send someone to inquire after them for you." Alastair exchanged a glance with Beth. "Although if we're being honest, I should warn you not to hold out much hope."

"I'm aware it might be difficult—"

Beth interrupted Anne, her expression kind. "It's not just about finding them, Anne. I don't mean to be cruel, but . . . how long had it been since your mother had any contact with them?"

Anne's chest tightened. She couldn't quite remember the last time her mother had told her about any of her relatives. Anne had an uncle somewhere as well as her mother's cousins, but when was the last time either of her parents had mentioned them? Had it been four years? Or five? What had become of them?

Andrew Barrett had always promised to take Anne to her mother's island, but he'd been a wealthy white merchant. His life was privileged and he knew no restrictions. The reality for Anne and her mother was quite different.

After Anne's mother had died and Anne had arrived in the Drummond household, she'd never felt so alone and out of place. She'd clung to the stories of her mother's people like a lifeline, feeling a tie to her roots. Now, in the harsh reality of day, Anne had to face facts. It was quite possible none of her family members were alive.

Beth cleared her throat. "I don't know what life was like for you in England, but you should know that here in the islands, it's hard and often brutal. Most people don't hold respect for a person of color, whether bond or free. They believe we have no rights. Or opinions. To them, we're expendable, something to be bartered or bought. I'm sure you noticed Benjamin's scars."

Anne nodded dully.

"He's one of the lucky ones. He escaped from a plantation in Jamaica where he attended the stables."

"How did he get here?" Anne asked.

"He hid on a ship. Alastair found him one morning at the docks and offered him a job."

Alastair drew in a deep breath. "He was stolen from his home by the foulest and cruelest of men. Brought to a strange land where he was beaten and starved and held in the same rank as horses and cattle." Alastair shook his head. "It's barbaric. Nobody deserves to be treated like that."

Anne couldn't begin to imagine the terror Benjamin must have felt. Forced to withstand torture that she wouldn't wish on her worst enemy. The fact that he'd actually survived and escaped such circumstances spoke about his strength and spirit. It made her view her own situation in a much different light.

Back in England, she'd been scorned and reviled, but not to the extent that Alastair was describing. She'd heard stories about slavery, but had found it difficult to conceive that anyone would ever feel a sense of ownership over another human being. "My father made a trip to the islands sound wonderful. Adventurous. I always thought I could find my family members." But wouldn't her mother have had the same hopes and dreams? To return to them? To share her culture and history with others?

Beth covered Anne's hand with her own. "I'm sorry. But you should prepare yourself for the worst."

"That's not to say that you have no future here," Alastair said quickly.

At the moment, Anne's future was bleak. Until she heard from her solicitor, she had no money. She hadn't been sure what kind of situation her relatives might be in, which was why she'd planned to steal so much from Drummond. She'd taken a goblet and cutlery, and any of the coins she'd had left over from the market. The most valuable piece she'd taken had been the spyglass belonging to Drummond. But it had all been for naught. Margery had caught her and sent her off on the *Providence* penniless, unable to help herself, let alone her relatives.

If any of them were alive, she would help them in whatever way she could, including purchasing their freedom. She never imagined finding her family might mean rescuing them from the hands of slavers. But she'd do it, even if it meant using the rest of her inheritance. She hadn't allowed herself to think that she was the only one left of her entire family, but it was a definite possibility.

Anxiety crept in once more and Anne pushed the bowl away. "Thank you."

"You're free to stay for as long as you like."

That, at least, was something. Sitting up straight, she met Alastair's eyes. "I can help in the tavern. Or back here in the kitchen with Beth. My mother taught me how to cook."

"Beth has all the help she needs in the kitchen. But I could definitely use your help out in the tavern." He paused, once again exchanging a knowing glance with Beth. It almost seemed as if the two of them could communicate without the use of speech. "They're a rowdy lot, but I'll pay you well, and I'll do all I can to keep you safe."

Working in a tavern wasn't Anne's first choice for employment, but at the moment, it was her only one. At least it provided her with a place to stay until she knew where Teach was. "All right. When shall I start?"

"Tonight will be soon enough. You can keep me company in the kitchen until then," Beth said. "Or you can still rest if you need."

As much as Anne wanted to crawl back into bed, she knew it wouldn't do her any good. For someone who always liked to plan ahead, she'd felt adrift since setting foot on shore in Nassau, not unlike when she first arrived in the Drummond household. Then, the loneliness and sadness had nearly overwhelmed her.

Everything had been so similar and yet so very different from her earlier life growing up in her father's household. After a few weeks, she'd managed to overcome the loneliness and fight back.

Here in Nassau she could do the same thing. Although her surroundings were unlike anything she'd ever experienced before, she wasn't alone, and that gave her courage to fight and move on. Despite the rough introduction to the island, perhaps the Bahamas wouldn't be as bad as Anne had first feared.

CHAPTER 8

Anne

The patrons of The Laughing Fox enjoyed their ale. Anne's arms ached from carrying heavy trays laden with foaming tankards. As soon as one group left, another noisy crowd swarmed in, demanding drinks.

Coyle and Benjamin stood at different ends of the room, keeping an eye out in case anyone became too unruly. Cara wove through the tables with amazing ease, laughing and flirting with the men where they sat speaking loudly and singing off-key.

Anne tried to tell herself that her present situation wasn't much different from working in Drummond's household. Instead of food, she simply served drinks. Alastair had confirmed that many of the patrons were indeed pirates, although Anne had a hard time differentiating between normal sailors and the more outrageous seamen. None of them looked as hardened and cynical as the group of men she'd seen in the streets of Bristol. They'd been taken to London and died on the noose. None of the clientele in the Fox appeared concerned about capture.

Rolling her head from side to side to loosen the tension in her neck, Anne stopped next to the bar and called out to the barkeep to give her three more tankards. Coyle caught her attention and winked at her. Anne rolled her eyes. Coyle might find their present situation entertaining, but Anne did not. Unless anyone caused a problem, *he* didn't have to contend with the thirsty mariners and dockworkers. Anne and Cara did, and it was obvious who did a better job of it. Cara's pockets jingled with coins. Anne's were decidedly bare.

Gritting her teeth, Anne returned with another round of drinks. She longed for her bed, but the tavern would be open for another three hours. Rest would have to wait.

The door to the Fox opened, allowing a fresh ocean breeze to blow through the smell of unwashed bodies and tallow. Four men walked in, dressed in simple breeches, their shirts and waistcoats were more ostentatious and colorful than any of the present occupants. Two of them wore wigs, but the headpieces didn't fit properly. Their appearance caused a stir. The din in the room lessened and the occupants of the nearest table stood up and vacated their chairs. The men took the empty seats without question. Several people eyed the newcomers, their voices lowered.

Anne looked to Benjamin to see his reaction to the strangers. He'd worked for Alastair for some time and knew many of the regular patrons. At the moment, his face was inscrutable, but he no longer lounged against the wall. Instead, he stood straight, his arms folded across his chest as he inspected the table.

Cara was on the far side near the kitchen door, smiling and chatting with a young sailor, who had his hands at Cara's waist. Coyle watched his sister with a frown on his face and took a few steps in her direction, oblivious to the tension in the room.

Knowing it was up to her to approach the table, Anne hoped the four men didn't cause her any problems. There was something different about them, an air of confidence that many others in the room didn't possess. Here, at last, were pirates. "What'll it be?" Anne asked.

"Four ales," a feminine voice replied.

Anne's mouth fell open, shocked to discover that one of the four was actually a young woman. She had tanned skin and deep brown eyes, and she wore her dark hair in multiple braids, pulled back with a thin strip of leather. Her waistcoat and shirt revealed curves that were not immediately noticeable.

Anne had focused on the two men with wigs, and she hadn't paid much attention to the shortest figure in the group. Recovering from her surprise, Anne nodded, flushing as the four of them laughed at her expression.

"She thought you was a lad, Reva," one of the wigged men said.

Instead of being insulted, Reva's smile grew. "I'm a far prettier lad than any of you would ever make." She had a slight Spanish accent.

Anne had never seen a woman wear breeches, not even in the slums of Bristol. She left them to go and place their order.

"Get into the kitchen," Benjamin said, appearing at Anne's elbow beside the bar. His face was hard. Anne followed his gaze, only to discover that he watched the door, not Reva and her trio of friends. "And take Cara with you. There's going to be—" The door to the Fox opened and several men rushed in, their pistols drawn.

Anne finished Benjamin's sentence in her head. *Trouble.*

Benjamin drew his own weapon and Anne rushed behind the bar while the first shot rang out. Crouching low, she searched for Cara and Coyle as chaos erupted around her. People scrambled and overturned tables while the men in the doorway shoved their way inside the crowded tavern.

Coyle dragged Cara toward the kitchen, his eyes frantically searching the room. Clutching the tray in her hands, Anne ducked as a tankard smashed into the wall above her head. Beside her, the barkeep pulled out two pistols of his own. Anne had only a second to drop the tray and cover her ears as he shot into the air. If he'd hoped to gain some kind of control over the fray, he was sorely mistaken. He vaulted over the bar and narrowly missed kicking Anne in the face.

Peering up from her hiding spot, Anne saw Alastair thundering down the stairs, shouting above the commotion, but the breaking of glass and the frenzied cries of the throng drowned out his words.

Coyle dropped unexpectedly to Anne's side and she stifled a

scream. His shirt was ripped and blood dripped down the side of his face from a gash in his forehead. Heedless of his appearance, he caught her to his chest as glass rained down around them.

"I'm all right," she said, her voice muffled. He didn't release his hold. Pushing against his muscled torso, Anne pulled back. "I'm all right. Go help Alastair," she yelled.

Coyle's brown eyes were conflicted. It was clear he wanted to make sure she was safe, but he also needed to help restore some semblance of peace. With a quick nod, he vaulted back over the top of the bar.

Anne crouched low, prepared to race to the safety of the kitchen, but her way was blocked. The sounds of fists striking flesh reverberated in the room, with Benjamin and Coyle in the thick of it. Anne couldn't see Alastair amongst the twisting figures.

Reva was on the ground, struggling against a man kneeling on her chest, his hands around her throat. A wicked-looking knife lay beside them. Wide eyed, Anne watched as Reva's face turned red. Anne's own breath came in short, fast breaths, like she was trying to compensate for the other girl's lack of air. Intent glistened in the man's grim expression as he clenched harder around Reva's throat. He was trying to kill her.

Unable to sit by and watch the girl die, Anne snatched up the nearest bottle and rushed at the pair. She stumbled over her own skirts, barely managing to stay upright before smashing the bottle over the back of the man's head. The glass shattered and the amber liquid rained down on Reva.

The man froze for a moment, before toppling to the ground like a felled tree.

Reva gave Anne a grateful smile as she scrambled to her feet and disappeared through the door to the kitchen, with Anne close on her heels. Cara shrieked as Reva dashed past her and headed out into the moonlit night. Anne braced her hands on her knees, her breathing harsh.

"Was that a girl?" Cara asked.

"It was."

Cara shook her head. "This place is madness."

Anne was glad the pirate had escaped. Living in Bristol, Anne had once accused all pirates of being scoundrels and crooks, but after seeing Reva, Anne had felt a tinge of grudging respect. Something had obviously happened in Reva's life to cause her to wear breeches and carry two pistols. It didn't necessarily mean she was a thief. It meant she was desperate. Perhaps that's why men turned to piracy. They did what was necessary in order to survive. Anne could certainly relate to the feeling.

The girls listened as the commotion in the next room slowly died down. It seemed as if Alastair, Benjamin, and Coyle finally had things under control. The majority of law-abiding citizens had long fled the island, leaving behind only a small number of plantation owners determined to make their sugar crops succeed. The rest of Nassau's inhabitants were a collection of brigands and bandits who were quick to anger and use violence. Anne had heard from sailors on the *Providence* that there were nightly brawls and fights in the streets or taverns. It appeared those reports were right.

"I think I might like to have a pair of breeches, especially if we're to stay here for very long," Cara whispered, a mischievous smile on her face. "Can you imagine what my brother would say?"

Anne laughed, having thought the same thing. "Perhaps you should sew some so we can find out."

A trickle of sweat ran down Anne's back as she pulled out the sliver of glass piercing her palm. The crimson shard caught the morning sunlight streaming in through the windows of the Fox.

Cara sat beside Anne on the floor as they sorted through the unbroken bottles of alcohol. Cara glanced over her shoulder and frowned. "Is that another one?" Cara asked. "I'm sorry, Anne. I thought I swept them all last night."

More than half of Alastair's supply of alcohol was gone, but he expected a new shipment in a few days. They'd cleaned up the majority of the glass and splintered wood the previous night, but Alastair had insisted they get some rest. "This mess will be here for us in the morning," he had said.

And what a mess it was.

Benjamin repaired one of the few chairs that could be salvaged. Most of the tables were still intact, but Alastair would have to purchase new benches and stools, as well as replace the railing leading upstairs.

It was a miracle no one had been killed. Remembering the look on that man's face as he'd knelt over Reva, Anne knew it wasn't for lack of trying.

Coyle strode into the room, interrupting Anne's thoughts. He and Alastair had gone to the docks to commission a carpenter to help with repairs. "Alastair wants you to start carrying these," he said to Anne and Cara as he placed two pistols on the bar.

Wiping her palm on her skirts, Anne eyed the weapons, a cold fist clenching her heart. She'd never held a weapon before, let alone fired one. Once, when she'd accompanied her father to the docks, someone had fired a pistol. To her young mind, it had resembled the roar of a cannon. People had scattered, and although Anne had never seen exactly what happened, she still remembered the fear on people's faces.

Cara laughed outright. "You're daft if you think I'm going to carry one of those."

Her brother scowled. "If you plan on staying here, you're going to do just that, Cara. And so will you, Anne."

An image of Reva flashed in Anne's head. The girl had worn two pistols, although neither of them had helped her in the end. Curious, Anne picked up the weapon. It was surprisingly compact and almost fit in the palm of her hand. It seemed strange that something so small could wield such power.

Seeing her interest, Coyle moved forward. "Don't worry. It's not loaded. These are flintlock coat pistols. You can carry them with your pistolman's pouch, which will hold your ammunition." Coyle took the weapon from her and attached it to the leather pouch hanging across his chest. Lifting it over his head, he draped it across Anne's shoulder, where it fit snugly, resting on her hip.

It felt foreign and heavy. "I can't wear this," she protested.

"It's better for people to see you're armed, so no one will bother you. Besides, that's a dainty pistol."

It might have been smaller than the two Coyle carried with him, but it was still quite solid. "I wouldn't know how to use it," Anne said.

"I'll teach you," Coyle said without hesitation.

Seeing Anne's deliberation, Cara swept by her and stalked toward the kitchen. "I'm going to speak with Uncle Alastair. You can't make us do this if we don't want to."

With a muttered curse, Coyle turned on his heel and followed his sister. "It's for your own good, Cara." His voice faded as they went to find Alastair.

Anne removed the pouch and pistol and placed them on the bar. Looking at Benjamin, she saw him studying her. He could not have been more than three years her senior, but his quiet dignity made him seem older.

He seemed to sense her indecision. "Beth carries one with her whenever she leaves the Fox."

Biting her lip, Anne reached for the watch in her pocket, her gaze returning to the two pistols. They seemed so benign, yet she knew they could inflict considerable damage, even death. "I'd be more afraid of injuring myself than I would of protecting myself."

"You might be surprised what you can do in the face of fear."

Before Anne had a chance to respond, the front door of the tavern opened unexpectedly and in walked two men. She recognized the shortest one. It took her a moment to place him because he wore a powdered wig and a brocaded long coat, but he was the same one who'd tried to kill Reva the night before. He was clearly a man of importance, at least in his own eyes, for he gave Anne and Benjamin a disparaging look when he saw them.

So surprised by their appearance, Anne was unprepared when the taller man kicked over the chair Benjamin had just repaired. She curled her hands into fists as it skidded across the room. Benjamin stayed where he was, his expression cold and unflinching.

"Get back to the kitchen where you belong," the small man sneered at her before turning to Benjamin. "And you, get back to your chores, boy. Don't you have some manure to shovel somewhere? What's Alastair thinking—?"

"I'm thinking you have no business coming into my establishment and telling me or my friends what we can and cannot do," Alastair said, standing in the doorway to the kitchen. "Especially after what happened last night. Did you come to admire your handiwork, Pelham?"

"Someone's got to try to keep the peace."

"Things were plenty peaceful around here until you showed up."

"What would you say if I told you the governor sent me?" Pelham asked.

"I'd say you're lying. Webb's thugs only come in and wreck the place. You tried to kill one of my patrons last night."

Pelham looked unrepentant. "I heard there were pirates in the vicinity and wanted to make sure you and your customers were safe. After all, that's why I was sent here. Webb's not doing a good enough job."

"There are always pirates in the vicinity, Pelham. Save your stories for someone who'll believe them. I know you're after one particular pirate. She's leading you on quite a merry chase."

Anne was even more pleased that she'd helped Reva escape, as color rose in the smaller man's face and fury gleamed in his eyes. "It would be wise to remember who you're dealing with, Alastair. I'm a peer of the realm."

"You might have a title, but titles mean significantly less here in the islands. Your backers are far, far away, so don't you dare come here and threaten me, *Lord* Pelham."

Pelham practically shook, his expression threatening retribution for Alastair's insolence. "It wouldn't be wise to underestimate me or the power of my title. Webb's told us some of the things you've done and we aren't pleased with your decisions."

"Some of the things *I've* done? What about some of the things *Webb* has done?" Alastair demanded.

"Your refusal to join us is unacceptable. We need your ships if we want to compete against other merchants. They're willing to do whatever it takes."

"I'm not. I told Webb the same thing I told Trott. I will not engage in the bartering of human lives. My ships will transport any number of raw materials. Sugar, coffee, tobacco. I will gladly fuel Britain's addictions, but I will *never* transport slaves."

This was news to Anne. She'd believed Alastair was a simple tavern owner, but it appeared he was a merchant as well, and a successful one at that.

"It's only a matter of time before the Royal African Company loses its control on the slave trade. We need to be prepared to act when that happens. The rest of our shareholders will meet in Jamaica within eight weeks. Before then, I suggest you change your position." The cold detachment in Pelham's voice caused a shiver to run down Anne's spine.

"It's a wasted trip, for I have no intention of changing my mind," Alastair snapped.

"We'll see. I believe some of them might be quite convincing in their arguments."

There was no denying the implicit threat in his statement. Without another word, the two men left the tavern. Alastair muttered an oath and stalked from the room toward the kitchen, leaving Anne and Benjamin standing there. Anne couldn't help wondering about the meeting in Jamaica and whether or not she and Benjamin were safe.

CHAPTER 9

Teach

The water was so clear beneath the hull of the *Deliverance* as it limped into the port of Nassau, Teach could see the ripples in the sand twenty feet below. Occasionally a large ray glided under the bow, a fleeting shadow in the shallows of the bay. Anxious to be on land, Teach could not help wondering how he would continue his search for Anne.

The Bahamas was a major shipping thoroughfare that had recently become popular, attracting pirates and buccaneers. The draw of the turquoise waters and long sandbars were an ideal setting to attack unwary ships. Or even wary ones, as Teach had discovered the hard way. Hundreds of secluded cays and islets allowed marauding ships to lie in wait to pounce on unwilling prey sailing by.

It had been seven days since they'd encountered and fought with those ships, but their ordeal wasn't over just yet.

As soon as they dropped anchor, Teach and the rest of the crew began the arduous task of getting the injured to shore first. The *Deliverance* was too large and there were too many ships already dotting the busy water for it to get any closer to the docks themselves.

The city's new fort, in the shape of a four-pointed star, stood sentinel on a hill, with two of its walls projecting northward over the seafront. Figures hurried along the wharves to load and unload the myriad of anchored merchant ships. Was one of the vessels the *Providence*?

With his mind racing, Teach nodded at John. "I'm going to search for Peter myself. If you see him, make sure he doesn't leave the ship."

"Aye, Captain."

Teach swept the quarterdeck as the anchor dropped, looking for any sign of the familiar blond head, but to no avail. Teach pictured Peter hiding in the bowels of the ship like the rat he was. Deciding to head down to check the cargo hold, Teach descended the last flight of stairs when he heard shouting and the distinct sound of a splash. Someone had released one of the rafts and jumped in after it.

Peter.

Rushing back to the top deck, Teach drew his pistol as he spied two figures clambering over the side of the small boat. The bounder had somehow managed to get someone to help him, which meant that not all of the crew was loyal.

Teach tensed against the shaking of his muscles, his finger squeezing the trigger of his revolver as he took aim between Peter's shoulder blades.

It would be so easy to stop the coward from leaving. Peter had carried out every whipping Murrell had ordered on board the Deliverance, and he'd enjoyed it.

This was Teach's chance to carry out his own punishment. He would be Peter's executioner. . . .

"He's not worth it," John said quietly at his side.

With a humorless laugh, Teach kept the weapon trained on Peter's back. Peter shouted at the other man to gain control of the oars. "At the moment, I would have to disagree."

Teach should have gone down to the gun deck. If he'd fired from one of the cannon ports, nobody would have been able to tell where the shot came from.

At John's prolonged silence, Teach glanced over at his friend, noting the disapproval in his eyes. "Don't look at me like that," Teach muttered.

"Like what?"

"Like my father."

With a heavy sigh, Teach slowly lowered the weapon. John reached forward and dragged the pistol out of Teach's grasp. "You're better than this, Teach. You can't shoot a man from behind."

"Then bring him here and I'll shoot him in the face," Teach said, his voice iced with quiet menace.

The two men now had control of the raft and rowed away from the *Deliverance*. Peter glanced over his shoulder, a triumphant smile on his lips. Teach jerked his thumb in Peter's direction. "After everything he's done, he doesn't deserve to get away like this. He might not be shooting us from behind, but we'll all surely hang if he gets away."

"They're only two men. The rest of us are loyal to you, Teach."

Teach gave him a stony stare. "I wonder if you'll feel the same when the noose is around your throat."

"You didn't do anything wrong. Murrell wasn't right in the head. All of us could see that."

"I hope the courts will agree with you." Not waiting for John to respond, Teach gave a short shout, instructing his men to lower a boat over the side. It was time to get the wounded on shore. Lashing several planks of wood together, Teach and his men began the laborious task of lowering the injured men to the small vessels below. John stood on the Jacob's ladder swung over the side to help with their descent.

Since Peter had taken one of the rafts, the rest of the men had only two to transport the entire crew and passengers to shore. Teach's back was covered in sweat, and his face and head burned as he worked for the next hour under the scorching sun.

The last injured sailor only had a broken arm. He climbed onto the Jacob's ladder, gritting his teeth and descending slowly. Halfway down, the sailor lost his footing on the spreaders and fell into the clear water below. Teach dove in, his eyes stinging from the saltwater. He located the boy and pulled him to the surface, where John hoisted him into the skiff. Teach clung to the side of the boat, grateful to be in the cooling sea, if only for a short while.

A large crowd gathered and watched as more weary crew members reached the docks.

"There are soldiers," John muttered beneath his breath, staying the oars. "Want me to talk to them while you go and get the rest off the ship?"

"No. I'll deal with them." Drawing a deep breath, Teach climbed the wooden ladder that led out from the choppy waves, only to stop when a hand reached out to assist him near the top. One of the soldiers, presumably their leader, gave Teach an assessing look.

"Are you the captain of that ship?"

"Aye," Teach said, standing to his full height, and running a hand through his hair. Droplets rained down around him and his clothes dripped onto the bleached boards beneath his feet.

"You've been charged with mutiny. You and your men will come with me."

CHAPTER 10

Anne

Anne took aim, squinting against the brightness of the sun. The roof of the abandoned warehouse they were in was missing parts, but the wooden slats in the walls were surprisingly intact. The noise from the busy waterfront in the distance camouflaged the report of the pistol. Coyle had chosen this spot because they could practice here without fear of interference or detection.

For the past couple of days, while Alastair and Benjamin oversaw repairs to the Fox, Coyle had been showing Anne how to fire a pistol.

Fifteen coconuts lined one wall of the warehouse. Anne squeezed the trigger and the pistol jumped in her hand. One of the coconuts exploded, its shredded husk flying into the sky. Coyle hollered, a proud smile on his face.

Sweat dripped down Anne's brow. With shaking fingers, she poured a small amount of powder into the breech before placing a ball on top of the opening and screwing the barrel of the pistol firmly back into place.

Within seconds, she fired off another shot and another coconut exploded.

"Anne, you've got it!" Coyle cried. She laughed at his exuberance. No matter what she did, he always encouraged her.

"Only if I'm on firm ground and nobody is shooting at me," she said, holstering her weapon behind the pistolman's pouch. She didn't tell Coyle she'd been aiming for an entirely different coconut.

"It's your turn, Cara," Coyle called out.

Cara shook her head. "You can't make me."

"You haven't shot once this week, Cara. As much as you enjoy sewing, you can't protect yourself with a needle and thread."

"Just because Uncle Alastair is forcing me to come with you, doesn't mean I have to do as he says."

"If you don't shoot today, I'll tell him that you refuse to take him seriously," Coyle said. "He might think twice about giving you any money."

Scowling at her brother, Cara marched over to him, and he handed her his pistol. With lightning speed, Cara loaded the weapon and fired off a shot. Another coconut exploded and Anne had a feeling that it was precisely the one Cara had aimed at.

Anne stared at her friend with newfound wonder. Looking at Cara, in her simple dress and with her blond hair hanging in a braid down her back, no one would ever guess she could handle a gun like that. Anne certainly hadn't.

"Just because I don't want to carry it doesn't mean I don't know how to use it," Cara said as she handed the pistol back to Coyle. "Don't you dare say another word about firing that thing, or I swear I'll use it on you."

Coyle holstered the pistol with a satisfied look, clearly unaffected by his sister's threat.

"No you won't. Because you love me. And you know I'm only doing this because I love you as well. I want you to be safe."

Cara rolled her eyes at her brother but didn't argue further.

After their shooting practices, the trio visited the waterfront each day to see if there was any sign of the *Deliverance*. Anne feared that the more time passed, the less likely it was that the great ship had survived the attack.

Anne had become more comfortable with the pistol, something she never thought would happen. She hated to admit it, but Alastair had been right. It was strange to feel both at home and on edge at the same time. Here, she didn't stand out like she had in England. In fact, nobody gave her a second glance. It was Cara and Coyle who attracted more attention with their blond hair and blue eyes.

However, Anne never left the safety of The Laughing Fox unattended. Cara still refused to carry anything, but Coyle always carried two pistols and a dagger. Cara and Coyle were always by her side. The most loyal of friends, they accompanied Anne when they could have remained at the Fox and stayed out of the heat. None of them ventured out past dark.

The weight of the pistol and leather pouch at Anne's waist was a constant reminder of the hazards of the island, but it also served to comfort her. If she needed it, it was there for protection and would hopefully act as a deterrent.

"Where did you learn to shoot like that?" Anne asked as they left the warehouse.

"From our da. He hates the English," Coyle said matter-of-factly.

Cara scoffed at her brother. "So do you."

"I'm English," Anne said.

"Trust me. Coyle doesn't hate you."

Coyle blushed underneath his tan as he shot his sister a quelling glance. "You're only part English, Anne. And you're not like the English soldiers swarming the Irish countryside, taking our farms from us. Da didn't want Cara ending up in one of their beds."

Cara stopped and Coyle ran into her. "I almost want to bring one home, just to see both of your reactions. They're not all bad, you know."

"I won't *let* you bring one home," Coyle said, his voice hard.

Cara turned to Anne with an annoyed look. "That's why our father refused Uncle Alastair's money. He says Alastair's in league with the English and doesn't want anything to do with his filthy coins. Da almost stopped *us* from taking the money, but Coyle here had a bit of a scuffle with one of the soldiers back home. It was better for him to leave. And so I came too."

Despite Alastair's refusal to help Lord Pelham, it was clear the Irishman had *some* kind of business dealings with the English.

It was hard for Anne to erase the threat of Pelham's words. The African Trading Company held the monopoly on slavery in England. Several merchants fought to ban the control and open the practice up for everyone. Anne couldn't imagine what that would look like. She didn't want to.

Although Lord Pelham hadn't visited The Laughing Fox again, Alastair had warned her to stay out of his way if she ever ran into him. Not that she planned to.

By now they'd reached the busy marketplace. Anne still marveled at all the sights and sounds. What William Dampier had described with such vivid detail in his book, Anne now saw with her own eyes. Sweet plantains with yellow peels, raw sugar-cane, plump pineapples, and ripe papayas, Anne had tasted them all. Even the cacao nut, used to make chocolate, was sold amongst the stalls. The flamboyance of the island was in stark contrast to the more somber markets of Bristol.

What she wouldn't give to walk these streets with Teach.

Turning a corner, Anne stopped short when she ran into a stout woman in a blue dress. The woman's hair was a vibrant shade of red, matching the rouge on her cheeks. Anne reached out automatically to steady herself. "Oh, forgive me."

"There's nothing to forgive, dearie. But I'm afraid you're too late."

"Too late for what?"

The woman nodded in the direction of the docks. "If you're wanting a piece of that large ship, you best forget it. Soldiers are swarming the docks. Nobody can get near it."

"Large ship?" Anne leaned forward. "Do you know the name of it?"

"I don't know the name, but it's bloody huge. Looks like it's seen a wee bit of excitement too. I was hoping to provide some excitement myself, but I can't wait around all day, you know. Those sailors will have to come to find me themselves."

Reaching into her pocket, Anne pulled out a few coins Alastair had given her.

"Thank you," Anne said, pressing them into the woman's palm. Coyle and Cara had caught up to Anne and the woman. They gave Anne a curious look, and she returned their looks with a smile.

The woman's eyes widened. "Why're you giving me these?"

"Because your information about the ship has helped me greatly." Before the woman could respond, Anne picked up her skirts and tore off, leaving Cara and Coyle to follow as best they could.

Anne's heart thumped painfully in her chest and sweat covered her back by the time she reached the crowded water-front. It was just as the woman had said. Squinting against the brightness of the sun, Anne could make out a large regiment of men standing on the pier, all of them dressed in red long coats and carrying muskets. The crowd surrounding the soldiers was thick as well. It was hopeless to try to get any closer.

Quickly scouring the area around her, Anne spied three barrels nearby, tethered to a wooden post. She scrambled to the top of one and held on to the rough pole as her eyes darted to the familiar ship in the distance. From this vantage point, she had a clear view of the damaged *Deliverance* and a grateful sob tore from her throat. They'd made it. The *Deliverance* had actually made it. There were fresh patches in the hull, evidence of some recent repairs. The sails, too, looked like they'd been pieced together and hastily sewn.

"What do you see, Anne? Is it the *Deliverance*?"

Looking down, Anne met Cara's hopeful gaze. Anne beamed at her. "It is!"

Coyle helped Cara climb up beside Anne and the two of them clutched each other for support.

"Look at you. You're shaking." Cara gave Anne a squeeze. "Do you see Teach anywhere?"

"Not yet." She looked for the familiar black hair amongst the teeming crowd, but could not see him. Time seemed to stand still for her, now that she was this close. Six weeks of waiting and wondering if she would ever see Teach again. Anne nearly suffocated beneath the weight of her own anticipation. She didn't want to think about the fact that he might not be on board.

One of the soldiers called out an order and the mob parted, quieting down as they made room on the docks. Several men with scruffy beards and unkempt hair formed a line, surrounded by soldiers on each side. They marched single file toward a waiting cart. *There!* Anne's insides tightened and her heart began to drum with furious force when she saw Teach take his position at the back of the line. His broad-shouldered build towered above the rest of the crew, and his clothes were wet and dripping.

"Teach!" Her voice rang out across the horde and his head shot up. "Teach!" Anne yelled once again, not caring about the attention she drew to herself.

His gaze locked on hers across the distance, his features pronounced and striking, even with the growth of facial hair. His skin was bronzed and the sun glanced off his rich black hair. He took a step in her direction. The soldier to his right slammed the butt of his musket into Teach's stomach and Teach doubled over.

"Oi!" Cara cried. "What's that all about?"

Another soldier stepped forward and clasped irons around Teach's wrists and ankles. A pounding sounded in Anne's ears, and her blood pulsated through her body. Desperate to get to his side, she scrambled down from the barrels and attempted to push her way through the crowd, but it was no use. There were too many people blocking their path, and everyone's eyes were riveted on the drama unfolding before them.

Grabbing Anne's hand in his, Coyle managed to shove his way a few feet, but they didn't make much progress.

"Where are they taking them?" Anne asked, trying to peer over the shoulders of other onlookers.

Coyle ran a hand through his hair. "I don't know. Perhaps to the fort."

She could hear the distinct clang of iron and the sound of a struggle, accompanied by the frenzied cheers of the throng. "We must go there."

"They won't let us in, Anne. We'll have to wait to see what's to be done. Uncle Alastair will know what to do."

Wrenching free of Coyle's grip, Anne dove through the mob, ducking between people as they followed the soldiers and the crew of the *Deliverance*. Along the way, several men reached for her, taking the opportunity to grope at her arms and chest, but Anne brought out her pistol. Anger and desperation lent her strength. Using the butt of the handle as a cudgel, she left more than a few of them in her wake, clutching their hands and howling in pain.

But she was too late. By the time she reached the end of the crowded docks, the wagon had disappeared down one of the side streets.

Shaking her head, she tried to breathe, but it felt like iron bands squeezed her chest. The crew of the *Deliverance* weren't the ones who had unlawfully attacked a ship. Somehow, they'd managed to survive the assault, so why were Teach and his men being treated like criminals? What cruel twist of fate would bring Teach to Nassau, only to have him taken from her once more?

The crowds slowly dispersed, going back to their normal routines on the busy waterfront. Anne stood motionless, unsure what to do next. Her mouth was dry and a headache started to coil behind her eyes. She couldn't stop thinking about Teach. He'd looked tired, but his face had lit up at the sight of her. She closed her eyes against the memory of the soldier hitting him in the stomach. She'd never seen Teach brought low by anyone, and the frustration and rage she'd felt was immediate.

"Let's go back to the Fox, Anne," Cara said, putting her arm around Anne's shoulders. Coyle nodded in agreement.

They turned, but movement farther down the docks caught Anne's attention. Glancing up, her pulse thudded darkly at the sight of slaves shuffling forward—men, women, and children— their ankles and wrists in chains as they disembarked from a ship. They were practically naked. Filthy rags hung from their limbs, barely covering them.

Even from a distance, the sores and open wounds covering their skin were visible, with clouds of flies swarming the air around them. Like walking ghosts, they moved forward, their once proud spirits beaten into submission. There were no crowds to gawk at the sight. No gasps of shock or outrage at their treatment.

"We have to do something" Anne said, her voice low and tremulous. Bile rose in her throat.

Coyle hesitated, the color leaving his cheeks. "Let's get back to the Fox, Anne."

One of the older slaves stumbled, his injured leg giving out beneath him. A man stepped forward, his pale skin mottled with pock scars and his clothing stained red. He wielded a braided leather whip and raised his arm to strike. Bright spots danced in front of Anne's eyes and a roar in her ears drowned out the noise of the busy wharf as she squeezed the trigger of the unloaded pistol in her hand. The loud click of the hammer sounded like a clap of thunder. Heads turned in her direction, including the man with the cow skin.

"What are you doing?" Coyle ground out. "Nobody knows that thing isn't loaded. Do you want to get yourself arrested or killed?"

Anne didn't respond. She hadn't realized her hands were on the trigger. Her gaze locked on the slaver. If it had been loaded, that man wouldn't be staring at her with disgust and loathing. Instead, he would be flat on his back, bleeding out.

"We should go," Cara said, her voice subdued.

Anne opened the leather pouch at her side, but Coyle's hand closed over hers. "If you load it and shoot, they will hang you."

"If I don't do something, who will?" Anne asked, gesturing to the people surrounding them.

Coyle shook his head, a pained look in his eyes. "You won't be able to help anyone if you're dead. Especially not Teach."

Anne glared at Coyle, aware her anger wasn't directed at him. He released her hand slowly, as if he still didn't trust her not to act. She wasn't sure herself.

With a shaky breath, Anne turned, noticing for the first time the shiny black carriage stopped nearby, the lacquered sides gleaming in the sunlight. She froze when she saw the familiar face of Lord Pelham watching her with hooded eyes. Anne stared back at him without blinking, without moving, knowing that despite his expensive clothes and carriage, she stood face-to-face with a viper poised to strike.

CHAPTER 11

Teach

Teach paced his cell in circles, like a wild animal in a cage. He rubbed the marks on his wrists where the irons had been, while the hammer of his own pulse caused his veins to hurt. His clothes had dried long ago, but his skin was itchy and tight from the saltwater. With each step, he deepened the path and scattered the straw strewn across the floor. Although the fort was fairly new, the ramparts already reeked of urine and fetid oil. Teach hadn't touched the bread or water the jailer had left for him, completely absorbed in thought.

Anne was alive. She was *alive*.

Teach hadn't even realized he'd taken a step in her direction until he'd felt the punishing blow of the musket. Grimacing, he tested the bruised skin on his stomach.

Footsteps echoed down the stone hallway. Teach stopped his pacing and gripped the bars, rattling them, his knuckles white. Six soldiers appeared, armed with bayonets on the ends of their muskets.

"Governor Webb would like to speak with you."

"I would be happy to speak with your governor, as soon as I know where the rest of my men are." Teach didn't know how he managed to keep his voice level, while his blood teemed with fury.

Upon reaching shore, Peter had slipped away like a serpent in the grass, clearly wasting no time in reporting the mutiny on board the *Deliverance*. Some men had managed to blend into the crowd on the wharf, but once the soldiers had surrounded them, they'd been led to the wagon and taken to the fort. Teach's hands tightened on the bars. He should have killed Peter when he had the chance.

"Your men have been questioned individually. The governor now wishes to hear your report."

"What about the wounded?" Teach had promised they would receive something for the pain, and he didn't want to go back on his word.

"They're receiving medical attention."

Teach didn't believe him. "Where are they?"

"Governor Webb will answer your questions. Now move back."

Slowly, Teach retreated. He watched in grim silence as one of the soldiers struggled with the cell door. When they'd locked him up, Teach had targeted the latch with a powerful blow from the heel of his boot. The soldiers had responded by threatening to shoot him if he didn't behave.

Wary, the lead soldier motioned for Teach to step forward. Once again, the irons closed on Teach's ankles and wrists. He jerked his arms away, but felt the tip of a bayonet in the small of his back. "It makes no difference to me whether you live or die. If you hope to help your men, I suggest you do as the governor says."

Teach followed the soldiers back the way he had come a few hours prior. He wondered where Anne was now and how she fared. If only he could see her, hold her, kiss her. Assure himself that she was indeed real and not a figment of his imagination.

Teach was led down a long, dark corridor and staircase illuminated by torches. They wound their way through the interior of the battlements, stopping in front of a large wooden door. One of the soldiers raised his hand and knocked. Someone called for them to enter.

With irons clanging, Teach shuffled into the office. A large desk anchored the room, with sunlight and heat pouring through a small embrasure on the west wall. There was a map opened on the desk, its edges curling in the miserable humidity and heat. An ornate clock ticked the seconds, keeping time with Teach's heartbeat, but otherwise the room was bare. There wasn't even an extra chair for guests.

No doubt the governor preferred his visitors to stand, while he lounged. Not that Teach minded. He didn't want to spend another minute in this place. He wanted to get to Anne.

Four of the soldiers escorted him in, while the other two

remained outside the door. Teach would have laughed at the situation if he hadn't been so frustrated. He was larger in stature, but they were armed and he was in chains.

"Here he is, Governor Webb."

If it hadn't been for the elaborate white wig perched on the governor's head, Teach would have a hard time believing that the man seated at the desk was the most powerful man on the island. In fact, the governor looked quite ill. His skin had an unhealthy pallor and his shoulders barely seemed capable of holding up the sleeves of his embroidered long coat. The dark circles ringing his brown eyes told of sleepless nights.

"Thank you. You and the others may wait outside."

Without another word, the four soldiers stepped out of the office, closing the door behind them. Teach watched them go, before turning back to the governor, only to find a pistol pointed at his chest.

Teach's stomach tightened and his shoulders stiffened. He'd been threatened before, but never by someone intended to keep the peace. Did the governor intend to dispense with the formality of a trial and simply shoot him outright?

No. I have to get to Anne. Teach's palms grew slick with sweat as he attempted to keep his expression neutral.

"What's your name?"

"Edward Teach."

Tick. Tock. Tick. Tock.

"Tell me about the attack on your ship, Edward." Despite

his haggard appearance, the man still spoke with authority and he gave Teach an appraising look.

Sweat rolled down Teach's face and neck and the clock continued to count the seconds.

Tick.

Tock.

Teach blinked, unable to wipe at his eyes. "As we neared the islands, two ships lay in wait for us. We believed them to be either Spanish or Dutch."

"What led you to such a decision? In my experience, few pirates raise an ensign from where they're berthed."

"They flew no flag. But we thought only the Spaniards or the Dutch would be bold enough to attack an English ship this close to port. In the end, it didn't really matter who the ships belonged to. The attack was thwarted."

The governor lowered the pistol and tapped his fingers on the desktop, a lazy arpeggio. He measured his next words with the trembling rhythm, out of sync with the clock. "Who was captaining your ship at the time?"

"Captain Murrell." Teach answered with no hesitation. It was true, though it hadn't stayed true for long.

"And where is your captain now?"

Where Peter should be. "At the bottom of the sea."

Governor Webb's eyes narrowed at Teach's dispassionate response. "Is it true what this Peter says? Did you lead a mutiny while on board the *Deliverance*?"

"No."

"Another man supported his claim. Are you saying that because you know that mutiny is a capital offense?" Governor Webb's voice was skeptical, his lips pressed into a thin line.

All too aware that lives hung in the balance, Teach met the governor's gaze unflinchingly. "No. I'm saying it because I did not lead a mutiny. Captain Murrell was unable to maintain control of the ship. Before the battle commenced, he relinquished his control to me."

"That's not what Peter said transpired."

Tick. Tock.

A vein began to pound at Teach's right temple. *Stay calm. He has no proof.* "Peter wished to be made captain himself. I'm not surprised by his claim."

Governor Webb remained silent for a moment. Taking a white kerchief, he wiped his forehead and upper lip. It was stifling in the office. Teach could not understand why anyone would choose to spend much time in here.

"I've spoken with the passengers," Webb said. "They said Murrell was excessively cruel."

Teach knew firsthand how true that statement was. "Yes, sir."

"They also said you and the captain were constantly at odds."

It was no surprise that the passengers had noticed the tension on board the ship. Teach didn't try to deny it. "His style of leadership did little to instill loyalty amongst the men."

"Your men are very loyal to you, Edward."

The way the governor said his name was patronizing. It reminded Teach of when his father spoke to him, and Teach felt his body temperature rise with each passing minute, his impatience escalating. "And I to them." It was clear the other members of Teach's crew had stuck to their story. Once Peter left the ship and Teach had realized the young man would make trouble, John had gone to each member of the crew to make sure their stories corroborated.

"I sent out two ships of my own to try to intercept, but they must have missed you."

Interesting. Teach had seen no sails.

Tick. Tock.

"Despite the attack, I'm glad to see you arrived unharmed."

Teach made a scornful sound, his eyes narrowing. "I would hardly say we arrived unharmed. Seventeen of my men were injured. Seven died of their injuries before we made port."

Webb's brow knotted. "And what about your cargo? Was it damaged?"

"My cargo will be delivered as planned."

The governor stared at him in silence. Teach waited, the pounding in his temple increasing with each second. The moment lengthened uncomfortably, until Webb finally spoke. "You must be a remarkable captain to maintain command of such an exceptional ship."

Richard Drummond would be pleased by the fact that even here, the *Deliverance* was viewed with respect and admiration.

Teach didn't know how much more he could take. If he didn't see Anne soon, he would go mad.

"What's your history? Have you captained other ships?"

Biting back a curse, Teach barely managed to keep his voice level. "Yes, I have. It was under similar circumstances, when the captain of another merchant ship on which I sailed died from his injuries during an attack off the coast of Jamaica."

"You seem to have a knack for coming out of encounters unscathed."

Teach shrugged, unsure how to respond.

Governor Webb steepled his fingers, clearly enjoying Teach's discomfiture. Webb watched him as though he was an insect under glass. "I would like you to captain a ship for me."

Not sure he heard the governor correctly, Teach cocked his head slightly, a flush of adrenaline coursing through his body. "I'm sorry, you want me to captain a ship?" Under different circumstances, Teach might have leapt at the chance. But not now. Now he simply wanted this interrogation to end.

"Yes."

"Why me?"

"Why not you? Do you have other pressing matters?" Webb's voice was mocking.

Yes. Now his most pressing thoughts were of Anne. But he couldn't tell Webb that. "Perhaps we could discuss this later. I would like to go and see to my men."

"Of course. That's what a good captain should do. By all

means, go and see to your men. But then you will report back here first thing tomorrow morning."

"And the charge of mutiny brought against me?"

"Dismissed."

"Thank you, sir—"

"For now."

Any relief Teach might have felt at the governor's words faded. "What do you mean, for now?"

"It means that unless you do as I ask, you and the rest of your crew will be charged and hanged for mutiny."

CHAPTER 12

Anne

Anne spun the pocket watch that had once belonged to her mother on its gold chain, watching the way it reflected the light from the kitchen window. Beth had gone upstairs to Alastair's office, leaving Anne alone with only heavy thoughts as company.

She couldn't shake the image of seeing Teach led away in irons. Her insides were tied, like the cordage on a sail.

Twisting the chain into a tight ball, she released the tension and watched it spiral to the last link. The action didn't soothe her; it reminded her too much of her own predicament. She was spinning, spinning, but anchored to a fixed point. Nothing she did seemed to break her free of the dizzying loop of her helplessness. She had done nothing to help Teach, and she failed to help the slaves.

But what could she do? She was a young girl with no money

in a strange land. Her mind circled back to that point again and again but couldn't take hold of a single plan of action.

Once she had money, she could stop relying on others for aid. Alastair had gone immediately to seek an audience with the governor to talk about Teach and his arrest. Anne wished she could have accompanied him, but Alastair had insisted he go alone. Cara and Coyle had gone to the market, to see if they could learn any news.

And, unable to sit idle, Anne had cleaned the kitchen for four straight hours. With nothing left to do, she spun her watch and paced across the small space.

The sound of carriage wheels broke into her thoughts. Rushing out to meet it, she stopped, her stomach plummeting at the sight of a stranger. It wasn't Alastair returning with news after all. Nor was it Lord Pelham's.

Anne eyed the driver, his dark skin glistening, his shirt plastered to his back with sweat. He immediately removed his hat and used it to fan his face.

Curious who it could be, Anne moved forward until she stood beside the door. The linen partition covering the window lifted.

The woman's face inside was older, and marred with deep wrinkles around the mouth. But it was as pale as the underbelly of a fish, as was her hand where it held the curtain aside. Her modest blue satin dress had puffed sleeves that reached to her elbows.

"You're not Beth," she snapped, her green eyes narrowing.

Anne stood up straight, unprepared for the venom in the woman's voice. "No, ma'am. I'm not."

"Where is she?"

"Inside, ma'am. Shall I get her for you?"

"Of course, you fool. I'm not here to bandy words with some ill-begotten monster."

Anne felt the blood rush her cheeks in anger. Still, she held her tongue. "And whom may I tell her is calling?"

The woman's mouth dropped open and she stared at Anne with unconcealed hostility. "Your job isn't to ask me who I am. Your job is to go and get Beth immediately."

Fisting her hands in her skirt, Anne narrowed her eyes. "I meant no disre—"

"I could have you whipped for your insolence."

Anne's mouth snapped shut and her fury flared like the sails on a ship. An image of Benjamin's scars flashed in her mind, as well as the unfortunate souls on the docks. "You could certainly try."

With a curse, the woman reached down beside her and lifted what appeared to be a walking stick. Anne took a step back, wishing for a moment that she had her pistol at her side. She'd taken it off while she was cleaning, and she missed the familiar weight against her hip. How was it possible that in just a few short days, she would come to appreciate the security it afforded her?

"You have the devil in you, girl, and are sorely in need of reverence! Come here!" The woman hit the walking stick on the side of the window and the driver jumped, his eyes widening. It was clear he recognized the sound.

A firm hand on Anne's shoulder prevented her from retorting. Beth looked at the carriage, her lips thinned. "Go inside and wait for me. Alastair should be back soon with some news."

Grinding her teeth, Anne turned and marched toward the kitchen, her back ramrod straight. Never before had she experienced so much animosity for people in such a short amount of time. First Lord Pelham and the slavers at the wharf, and now this woman. Patience, Teach's former betrothed, had been ignorant and cruel, yes. It didn't excuse her prejudice, but she'd grown up sheltered and spoiled. Here in the islands, people of color were everywhere. This woman's contempt was palpable, rolling off her in waves. She made Drummond look almost tolerant.

Drawing deep breaths, Anne stepped inside the door and leaned against the wall, a swift, painful throbbing in her chest. She reached automatically for her pocket watch. Closing her eyes, she tried to listen as Beth spoke with the woman, but she could only make out a word or two of their conversation.

Beth's voice was calm and even, the other was sharp and piercing. Even from a distance, Anne could feel the woman's hatred. Treated poorly as a free person of color, Anne could only imagine what actual slaves had to endure.

A few minutes later, Beth returned to the kitchen, the sound of the carriage fading in the distance. Anne watched Beth closely, waiting, but the older woman said nothing as she moved toward the pantry and withdrew a burlap bag.

"Who was that woman?" Anne asked, anger making her voice sharp.

"That was Governor Webb's wife."

Anne's stomach dropped. "Did she have any news of the *Deliverance* and her crew?"

Beth picked up a small spoon, measuring some of the green leaves from the bag. "No, that's not why she came."

Frustrated, Anne clenched her hands, the pocket watch cool against her hot palms. "What did she want?"

"Would you mind getting the mortar and pestle for me, please?"

Anne hesitated, but only briefly. Slipping her mother's watch into her pocket, she marveled that Beth could remain so calm. Anne's entire body was tense, the blood still pounding in her ears. On the way to the pantry, Anne passed the shelf where she'd placed her pistol while she cleaned the kitchen. Once she had done as Beth had asked, Anne retrieved it and slung the pouch over her shoulder, grateful for its familiar weight. She slipped the pistol free and unscrewed the barrel as Coyle had shown her. Perhaps it was time she kept it loaded.

Beth raised an eyebrow, but said nothing. Anne bit her lip, aware that beneath her anger, there was a layer of fear.

Growing up in Bristol, her half brother Henry had often bullied her, but she had learned how to fight back. She'd endured snide remarks and disgusted looks. This was the first time a complete stranger had ever physically threatened her, and Anne hated to admit that she was frightened. Not only for herself, but for others as well.

"That woman," Anne said, unable to remain silent. "She's evil."

"There are many more like her."

"It's not right."

"No, it's not."

Tears prickled the back of Anne's eyes, and she blinked rapidly, refusing to let Webb's wife have that much power over her. The prejudice Anne had endured in England had not prepared her for this level of hate.

"Come here," Beth said.

Anne shook her head and looked away, toying with the weapon in her hands.

Beth's fingers closed over Anne's, and she removed the pistol. "Come here, child." Before Anne could protest, Beth wrapped her in her arms.

The embrace reminded Anne of her mother, Jaqueline. Aside from Teach, Anne's mother had been the only one to ever hold her. Anne had felt alone for so long. Unable to stop the flood of emotions, Anne leaned into Beth's shoulder and sobbed.

Beth said nothing, she simply held Anne while weeks of frustration, fear, and uncertainty poured out of her. Eventually, Anne drew back and Beth handed her a kerchief to blow her nose.

"I'm sorry," Anne whispered.

Beth smiled, her expression sad. "For what? For being human? There's no need to apologize. You're in a strange place and you've just seen your friend arrested. You've been through a lot. And are sure to endure much more before your journey's through."

Anne sniffed. "I saw a ship this morning. They were unloading slaves."

Beth's expression hardened. "There will always be people getting rich off the misery of others."

"I want to do something, but I don't know what," Anne said, her stomach churning at the thought of the wealth at Drummond's disposal. There was so much injustice in the world, and it seemed as if the wrong people were in possession of the power.

"We each do what we can with what we have. Alastair has helped escaped slaves move on. That's why he keeps the tavern open. He doesn't need the revenue from the Fox, but it's someplace for people to come if they need help."

"Can anything be done to help the slaves who are brought here? To get them away from people like the governor's wife and Lord Pelham?"

Beth's hands stilled. "There was a boy named David, who

wasn't much older than you. He tried once. He was one of the governor's field hands who met Benjamin in the streets of Nassau. Benjamin told David about Alastair. David tried to escape, but Webb caught him before he could get to us. The governor gave him three chances to give himself up. But David refused. By the fourth time, Webb simply raised a musket and took aim. David didn't survive the night."

Anne swallowed, her throat tight.

Drawing a deep breath, Beth looked down at the table briefly before meeting Anne's eyes. "A slave's job is to stand, listen, and tremble. The minute we stop trembling, we become unmanageable."

Anne found that her own hands were trembling. Reaching for the pistol, she caught herself and clenched her palms together. "Can nothing be done?"

"Alastair has tried, but the killing of a slave, or any colored person, is not treated as a crime, either by the courts or the community. Charges were never brought against Webb."

"I hate how that woman made me feel."

"You'll always find people like her. People who must make you feel small in order to feel big. They'll do everything in their power to keep you in the place they've assigned you, but remember, you always have a choice. You can choose to hate them back. Or you can choose to be better than they are," Beth said, picking up the spoon once more to measure out some leaves.

"How you must hate working for her."

"Mrs. Webb has enough hate in her for the rest of us. She makes no secret of the fact that she wishes to return to England. I pray every day that her wish will be granted. It would save me the trouble of making this poultice."

"What's it for?"

"It's a helpful remedy for boils." The hint of a smile appeared on Beth's lips. "Mrs. Webb doesn't like people to know she visits me, which is why she comes in an unmarked carriage and only approaches from the back."

"Surely the governor knows."

"Most likely. But he never speaks of it with Alastair. I suppose she doesn't want anyone to know. I only do it to try to keep the peace between Alastair and the governor. I'm not doing it to help her."

Leaning over the table, Anne bent toward the bag, studying its contents. Reaching forward, she prepared to take a pinch, but Beth raised a hand in warning.

"Be careful. It's black nightshade."

Anne's mother had often spoken of plants and vegetation from the islands. "I've heard nightshade is poisonous."

"It can be if it's swallowed."

"Can you . . . see the boils?" Anne asked. Although she'd only had a brief glimpse of the woman, there hadn't been any evidence of any unsightly sores. Anne couldn't help her smile at the thought of Mrs. Webb covered in oozing cysts and ulcers.

"I wouldn't know. When she comes, she waits in her carriage.

I'm to be ready, hand the poultice through the window, and take the coins for payment. She surprised me today. I hadn't expected her so soon after the last batch I made. But she's the governor's wife, and answers to no one. When she comes again, I don't want you speaking with her."

"Trust me, I have no desire to ever set eyes on that woman again." Alastair had already warned Anne about Lord Pelham. And now she had to worry about Mrs. Webb. There seemed to be quite a few people on the island who posed a serious threat.

"It's a wise person who knows when to stay silent, Anne. She has slaves at home who have no shield against her anger."

Anne hadn't thought of that. She'd wracked her brain to think of some sharp retort to put the woman in her place. She was indeed grateful Beth had come before she had fanned the flames of Mrs. Webb's anger any further. Anne shuddered, hoping that the woman would not cause anyone harm because of Anne's careless words.

Looking out the window, Anne wished Alastair would return with some news.

"Try not to worry about your friend. Alastair knows what he's doing."

"Does Alastair trust the governor?"

Beth gave a short laugh. "Trust is not quite the word I would use. Theirs is a unique relationship. Webb's only been governor for a few months and I've met him only once. There's some concern for his welfare. In the past few weeks, his health has declined."

That wasn't a sound endorsement. Especially not with Teach still in custody. "Will Webb allow Alastair to speak with Teach? To find out what happened?"

"I'm afraid I don't know. It's difficult to tell how the governor will respond. It depends entirely on his mood and on his health. Some days he isn't fit for visitors."

Anne hoped fervently that the governor was in a good humor that day. His wife certainly hadn't been. If only Anne had the money from her inheritance. Not only did she wish to find her family members, if any still lived, but she also wondered what it would take to free the slaves working for the Webbs.

The uncertainty of everything and her inability to act were driving her mad. Normally she had a plan for everything. All she knew now was that she had to find a way to get to Teach. He was so close. . . .

Anne glanced at the door leading to the tavern. It would open later that night. Perhaps that was what she needed. A mindless job that could provide her an escape from her thoughts.

Unexpectedly the door swung open, and Alastair filled the entryway. He was alone, looking drained. "I'm sorry, but I wasn't able to see the governor. He didn't feel well enough to have any visitors."

His voice crackled with frustration, but it was nothing compared to how Anne felt. "Were you able to find out what happened?"

"No, lass. Not yet. By the time I arrived, the crew was already locked up. Nobody was allowed to see them. Not even me."

Anne didn't miss the worried look Beth shot Alastair.

"I'll go first thing in the morning. Perhaps a good night's rest will clear the governor's head. Make him more cooperative."

"Is that man even fit to lead?" Anne cried, throwing her hands in the air. "What could that crew have possibly done to warrant their arrest? They were the ones who were attacked. I saw those ships close in with my own eyes."

Beth placed her arm around Anne's shoulders and gave her a squeeze. "I know this must be difficult for you, seeing your friend like that. But you have to realize that it's easier to get into a prison than to get out."

That was precisely what Anne was afraid of. "There must be something *I* can do," Anne said.

"Unfortunately not. I'm going to do my best to get your friend out of there. But it will take time."

"Time?" Anne mumbled to herself. She had waited weeks aboard the horrendous *Providence* to be with Teach. See him again. Hold him again. Make sure he was okay. And now that he was so close, it seemed he was farther away than ever. "How much time?" she dared ask.

Alastair stayed silent, and Anne knew she got her answer.

CHAPTER 13

Teach

"Move over," John muttered, his words unnaturally loud in the small, dark cell. The rats scurrying along the corridor stopped at the sound of his voice. Most of the crew was asleep, their deep snores reverberating off the walls.

"There's no place for me to go," Jack Thurston grumbled. "Cozy up to the captain if you need more space."

"I'd rather he didn't." Drenched in sweat, Teach felt as if he'd entered the bowels of hell. No light penetrated the gloom and Teach couldn't see the hand he held in front of his face.

Unaware of how many hours had passed since his conversation with the governor, it already felt like an eternity. Pushed tight against the cell bars, with John pressed to his side, Teach attempted to sit up, knowing sleep would be impossible. The stuffy air combined with the stench of unwashed bodies made the space unbearable. He should have simply agreed to captain

Webb's ship, but the request had caught him off guard. Nassau was full of sailors and sea captains. Why would the governor insist on Teach's help? It didn't make sense.

Shifting, Teach leaned against the bars, trying to give John more room. "I'm sorry about this," Teach said.

"Don't blame yourself, Captain. I've been in places much worse than this," Jack said.

John gave a disbelieving snort. "When and where?"

"I was locked up in Madeira once. The place was crawling with all kinds of vermin. Maggots ate the flesh right off the soles of one man's feet, clear down to the bone."

"What a load of poppycock. When were you in Madeira?"

"It weren't more than three summers ago, when you were still plucking up the courage to talk to the lasses. But no jail can hold me."

"This one seems to be doing a fairly good job of it." John's smug words dissolved into a pained grunt. "You throw another elbow in my back and there won't be enough of you for the maggots to feed on."

"Is that a challenge?"

"Enough. Both of you," Teach said, running a weary hand over his face. His eyes were scratchy and dry and he was sorely in need of a drink, but as long as his two friends argued, rest eluded him. Jack was only five years older than John, but he often acted like it was ten.

For a moment, the three of them sat silently in the dark,

listening to the deep breathing of their fellow sailors. Rats scurried in the darkness, and Teach closed his eyes as something brushed by his boot. He kicked out and was rewarded by the sound of an angry squeak as the rat scurried away.

John jumped. "If I ever see Peter again . . ."

"You'll have to wait your turn," Jack muttered. "As soon as I get out of here, I'm going to hunt him down."

"And just how do you intend to get out? Last time I looked, there were at least ten guards between us and freedom."

Teach interrupted them before they could quarrel further. "Webb's coming for me in the morning. I'll get you out."

"We shouldn't even be here. Webb needs to go after the ships that attacked us," John said, his voice rising. "Find those bastards and you'll find the real criminals."

"Right," Jack chimed in. "If Webb was really doing his job, these cells would be filled with pirates, not us. We all know the islands are full of 'em."

"I said I'll get you out of here," Teach said, wishing he could go back in time. Would he have stood up to Murrell? Yes. He would never regret that decision. But it still didn't erase the guilt he felt at their current dilemma. "Now try to sleep. I don't want you to wake the others. Let them have their peace."

Neither John nor Jack responded. Teach closed his eyes, grateful that the majority of the crew already slept. Every one of them had remained loyal to Teach and refused to corroborate Peter's story of mutiny, and for that Teach would always be grateful.

The men ranged in age from twelve to forty, and most of them came from coastal towns in England. Young Matthew had narrowly escaped the press-gang on a naval ship. He'd met twenty-two-year-old Lawrence outside a tavern in Whitby and together they'd made their way to Bristol, one of the busiest ports in England, searching for work. Thirty-year-old Hugh had promised to send everything he earned home to his wife and their three children. Walter was the oldest of the group and didn't have anyone left in the world, and so he'd given some of his pay to Hugh.

Each seaman on board the *Deliverance* had a history of hardship and suffering. On long voyages, the comfort and safety of everyone depended entirely on the character of the crew, and although Richard Drummond had made a colossal mistake by choosing Murrell as captain, Teach had nothing but praise for the other seamen his father had hired.

John's loud snore cut into Teach's thoughts and Teach smiled, grateful to have his friend by his side.

"Jack?" Teach whispered.

"Yes?"

"How did you get out of Madeira?"

Jack cleared his throat. "If I tell you, you have to swear not to tell a single soul. I've never told anyone, for fear of it getting back to my ma. I promised her I'd make something of myself. I don't want to be just a sailor like my pa and my older brother. I promised her I'd make captain one day."

"I swear I won't tell a soul," Teach said, his curiosity piqued by the earnestness in Jack's voice.

"Before I joined the *Deliverance*, I crewed on a pirate ship. I was only with them for a few months when the Spanish navy caught us off the coast of Madeira. Our captain managed to escape and left us to die. Have you ever been in a Spanish prison, Captain?"

"No."

"You never want to be, trust me. They did things to us there . . ." Jack's voice was hard. "Sometimes I can still hear the other men screaming."

Teach didn't know how to respond. At that moment, Jack sounded far older than his twenty-three years. Teach doubted he could say anything that would erase Jack's memories, and so he kept silent.

"I finally told them where they could find the pirate. He'd been stealing from them for years, and I took them right to him and all of the gold he'd hidden. His life for mine. I think that was a fair trade, don't you?"

"Aye, I do."

"I would never do that to you. I would never betray you. You're a good leader and the men trust you."

The crew had proven that by supporting Teach. "And as your leader, I would never abandon you."

"We know. Things have a way of working themselves out, Captain Blackbeard. Just you wait and see. Some opportunity will present itself, just like it did for me in Madeira."

Teach smiled at the nickname Jack had given him, wishing he shared the man's confidence, but he didn't trust Webb at all. "It might not be easy."

"I have no intention of dying here, Captain."

"Neither do I, Jack," Teach whispered. "Neither do I."

CHAPTER 14

Anne

"Are you sure you don't want to come with us, Anne? It might do you good to get out." Cara stood in the doorway to the kitchen of the Fox, her eyes concerned.

Anne had somehow managed to sleep the night before, but only because she suspected Beth had added something to her tea.

"I want to be here in case Alastair sends word." Alastair had already left early that morning to go to the fort.

"All right. We won't be long. Coyle thinks I'm buying material to make breeches for him, which I am. But I also plan to make each of us a pair as well." Cara's smile was mischievous. Ever since she'd seen Reva dressed in men's attire, she hadn't stopped talking or thinking about it.

"Be careful," Anne said, cutting up some of the fruit on the table.

Cara blew her a kiss before leaving.

Using a knife, Anne speared a piece of pineapple. She'd grown quite fond of the fruit in the time that she'd been in Nassau. But she wasn't very hungry at the moment, and after just one bite, she pushed the food aside. Standing, she paced around the table, the pistolman's pouch hanging low on her hip. Ever since she'd met Webb's wife, Anne made sure to keep the pistol with her at all times.

"You're going to wear a hole in my floor if you keep that up," Beth said.

Anne looked up, startled. "Morning."

Beth held a basket overflowing with long stems of grass. "Good morning. How did you sleep last night?"

"Surprisingly well. The tea definitely helped."

"I thought you could use the rest. I only added a bit of chamomile."

"My mother used to do that when I was younger."

"So did mine," Beth said, her voice warm.

A part of Anne was grateful to Beth. She had indeed slept soundly. But Anne also felt guilty. Teach had spent the entire night locked up at the fort, and she'd done nothing to help him. "Can I help you with anything?"

"I just need to dry this fever grass. Alastair woke up with a bit of a headache and I used the last of my supply for him this morning. You can help me tie it up if you like."

The two women worked in silence. Anne kept glancing at

the doorway leading out to the courtyard, but there was no sign of Alastair.

"I understand what you're going through, Anne. There was a time when Alastair was locked up and I didn't know if I would ever see him again."

"What happened?"

Beth took the bunches of fever grass they had tied and hung them in the pantry. Returning to the table, she picked up several more strands and began to tie them as well. "Alastair overheard someone speaking poorly about me. He nearly beat the man to death. Unfortunately, the other man happened to be a member of the aristocracy."

Anne gaped at Beth. "They could have hanged Alastair for that."

The older woman nodded. She stopped working and folded her arms across her chest. "They nearly did. Luckily for Alastair, another aristocrat took a liking to him. He helped Alastair escape, but Alastair's never been back to Jamaica. And neither have I."

"Is that where the two of you first met?"

"Yes. My mother and I sold herbs in the Spanish Town market. I'll never forget the first time I saw him. His clothes were old and worn and his skin was blistered red from the sun, but he was proud and stubborn. He strode right up to the stall and bought our entire stock of aloe. The next day he came and bought all our figs. That continued for an entire week. My mother welcomed the coins he brought, but by the seventh day, she grew suspicious.

"When he came the next morning, she asked him what he wanted from us. He looked her straight in the eye and told her he wanted to court her daughter." Beth laughed, clearly remembering the encounter. "My mother looked him up and down and told him he would have to prove himself to be worthy of me. He spent the next two months trying to do just that. It was only when she heard how he'd nearly killed the man in my defense that she decided he'd done enough."

Anne could easily picture Alastair wielding his meaty fists and pounding someone into the ground. The love between Beth and Alastair was obvious. "And so you left Jamaica?"

"Yes. Alastair paid for our passage. My mother came with us." Tears shimmered in Beth's eyes. "But she wasn't long for this world. We landed in Nassau and she passed away shortly after. Alastair decided we should remain here, where I could be close to her. He named the tavern The Laughing Fox, because that's what she reminded him of. She was always laughing at him and his blustery ways."

Anne hesitated only a moment before she placed her hand on Beth's arm.

"Don't give up hope, Anne," Beth said softly. "Even a faint light will shine far in the dark."

The door leading into the tavern swung open. Alastair filled the entryway, his gaze immediately finding Beth. But over his shoulder, Anne caught a glimpse of a familiar face, with green eyes and hair as black as thatch. For a moment, she couldn't react. Rooted to the spot, the blood coursed through her veins in a dizzying rush.

"You found me," she whispered.

"Always."

CHAPTER 15

Teach

Teach's heart clenched and he was certain it would stay that way until he had Anne in his arms. He was riveted by her. Dressed in a simple blouse and skirt and with her hair hanging in a long braid over her shoulder, she'd never looked more beautiful.

Alastair stepped to the side and Teach reached for her, and only once his face was in her hair, her body pressed tight to his, did the pain in his chest begin to subside, the string of tight knots begin to loosen. He was at peace again, the only peace he had ever known.

"I'm sorry. I'm so sorry, Anne," he murmured against her temple, his voice low and shaken. "I never should have left you. I'm so sorry."

She shook her head, her voice muffled against his shirt. "It's not your fault. I don't blame you. I should never have stolen those things. And I shouldn't have lied to you."

"I understand why you did it. I'm just sorry I couldn't protect you from my father. Or those men." He drew back, his fingers sliding along her arms and wrists as he tried to determine for himself that she was unharmed. Her clear blue eyes glistened with tears, yet the corners of her lips turned up in a tremulous smile. Her velvety skin glowed. There were no discernable marks on her arms or face, but he feared what might lie beneath the surface. He brought her hand to his mouth and kissed it. "Are you well?"

"I am now that I know you're safe." A tear trickled down her cheek. He brushed it away with his thumb, and then kissed the spot, high on her cheekbone where it had crested.

She gave a small sigh of contentment, of relief, and his lips met hers. She tilted up her chin, and her hands reached around his neck, holding him close as if to assure her that their trials were behind them. He melted into that assurance, holding her tight, breathing her in. Nothing save hell's gaping gates would keep him from his Queen Anne again. His fury and grief at their separation melted, and it was difficult to believe that he could need another human being as much as he needed Anne.

When at last he pulled away, he didn't fully relinquish his hold. Now that she was here, it seemed impossible to keep from touching her. Anne's face flushed crimson and she glanced over his shoulder. Teach had completely forgotten about an audience. Looking around the kitchen, he wondered when Alastair and Beth had left them alone.

"How did you get away?" Anne asked.

"It was Alastair. He spoke with the governor. I would have been here sooner, but Alastair insisted we stop. He said I couldn't see you smelling and looking like I did."

Anne wrinkled her nose. "If I'd known it would take this long, I'd have advised him to forget it. But now that you're here, I'm grateful to him." Grasping his freshly clean-shaven jaw in her hands, Anne stood on her toes and brought her mouth to his once more. "I still can't believe you're here. When I saw them taking you away yesterday morning . . . what happened?"

Her words dispelled the magic of their reunion. Preoccupied with her warm body and lips pressed against his, it took a significant effort on his part to focus. He had a thousand questions to ask her about her own trip. Alastair had done his best to tell him about the arrival of the *Providence*, but Teach wanted to hear the story from Anne herself. However, that would have to wait. With John and the rest of his men still locked away in the fort, guilt ate away at him. "There was a mutiny on board the *Deliverance*."

Anne sucked in a deep breath, her eyes wide. "And?"

"I took charge. If it had been up to the captain, we would all be dead and the cargo from the *Deliverance* would be lost."

"Was the cargo so important that you would risk your *life* for it?" Anne demanded.

"No, but my men's lives were."

Anne shook her head, raising her eyes to the sky. "You take far too many chances."

"No longer. I'm not going to risk losing you again. I plan on marrying you at the first available opportunity."

Her face lit up at his words. "Is that a proposal?"

"Patience, my love," Teach whispered, his forehead touching hers.

Anne tensed in his arms. Leaning back she raised an eyebrow at him. *"Patience?"*

"What?"

"You called me Patience."

Teach looked at her blankly. "I did not."

"You did. Just now."

He blinked, trying to concentrate. It was hard with Anne so near. Realization dawned on Teach and he cringed at his word choice. "No. *No!* I didn't mean . . . what I meant was to *wait*, to give me time to . . ." *Damnation!* Marriage was important to Anne, and with one careless word, he'd ruined the proposal. Her father had never married her mother, nor had he ever openly claimed Anne as his daughter. Teach didn't want there to be any doubt in anyone's mind that they belonged together.

Anne simply looked at Teach. One corner of her mouth twitched, as if she was trying to hold back a smile.

"The devil take you," he muttered, reaching for her once more. He kissed her, his lips moving over hers, determined to remove any doubt of his affection. He lost awareness of time, of where they were, as Anne responded in kind.

Eventually he lifted his head, giving a soft, shaky laugh.

He couldn't think clearly. From around his neck, he withdrew the leather pouch he'd carried with him since leaving Bristol. It seemed like an eternity had passed since the day he'd purchased the braided gold ring.

Anne sucked in a quick breath.

Just as he'd hoped, the band fit her perfectly. "Marry me."

Her eyes sparkled. "When?"

"Now."

Before Anne could respond, the back door opened and two people entered. Teach recognized the girl. She'd stood with Anne on the barrels at the dock. The boy stopped short when he saw Anne in Teach's arms, a frown on his face, but the girl rushed forward, a welcoming smile on hers. Despite their differing expressions, there was an unmistakable family resemblance.

"We forgot to take money with us to the market. You must be Teach," the girl said, her blue eyes sparkling. Winking at Anne, she nodded in Teach's direction. "I told you everything would be all right. If something needs fixing, Uncle Alastair can fix it."

Anne introduced the pair. Cara planted an impetuous kiss on Teach's cheek. Coyle sized him up from across the room, his arms folded across his chest, and Teach wondered at Coyle's relationship with Anne. Alastair had spoken briefly about his niece and nephew and how they'd befriended Anne on the long journey. Teach was grateful that Anne hadn't traveled alone and that she was safe. Judging by the expression on Coyle's face, he clearly didn't share his sister's enthusiasm for Teach's arrival.

Beth entered the kitchen from the door behind Teach. He was beginning to find The Laughing Fox far too crowded for his taste.

"Now that you've had some time, Alastair would like to speak with you, Teach. He's waiting for you upstairs."

Teach wanted to tell Alastair to go to the devil, but he needed Alastair's help to free his crew. The Irishman clearly had some sway with the governor, for he'd been able to secure Teach's release.

"Come with me," Teach said, tugging at Anne's hand, her skin warm beneath his touch. Now that he'd found her, he didn't want to let her out of his sight.

"I should help Beth in the kitchen."

"Nonsense. I can handle it. You go ahead," Cara said, waving an impatient hand.

Teach wasn't aware Coyle had followed them through the tavern and up the stairs until he heard Coyle's heavy tread from behind. Glancing over his shoulder, Teach raised an eyebrow at him. "I'm quite sure we don't need an escort."

Anne placed a hand on Teach's arm. "Don't," she said.

Coyle shrugged, unperturbed. "I've made sure nothing's happened to Anne since she left England. I'm not going to stop just because you showed up. I'll leave you alone once you're in the office."

Anne smiled. Rolling his eyes, Teach continued up the

stairs, wondering *again* exactly what Coyle was to Anne. It was obvious they cared about each other, but to what extent?

Once inside Alastair's office, Coyle closed the door behind them. It was a moderate room, with few furnishings, but they were well-made and well-appointed. Teach was surprised at the bookshelves lining one wall. This didn't resemble an office one typically encountered in a tavern.

"Don't look so surprised, boy. I may not look like much, but I know the importance of an education. I might have come to it a bit late in life, but it's never too late. Didn't your father ever teach you that?"

Teach stiffened at the reminder of Richard Drummond. Did Alastair know who his father was? "Actually, sir, education was very important to my father." Anne squeezed his hand.

Alastair snorted, seeing the small gesture. His features softened when he looked at Anne. "So this is the scoundrel you were waiting for, was it?"

Anne's cheeks flushed, but she nodded. "Yes, sir."

"Hmm. He's made quite a mess of things. Did he tell you about the charges?"

"He did."

"And did he tell you that he could hang for mutiny, unless he accepts a job from the governor?"

Anne raised a brow at Teach. "No, he didn't."

Now it was Teach's turn to flush. Hang it all, he'd meant to tell Anne everything, but they hadn't had much time alone.

He'd wanted to have this conversation in private, but Alastair now forced his hand.

"What kind of job?" Anne asked.

"I don't know, exactly. He wants me to captain a ship for him."

Anne frowned. "But how can you accept a job if you don't know what it entails?"

Alastair's face hardened. "That's how Webb operates."

"And yet you have a working relationship with him," Anne pointed out.

"I work with him, yes. But I wouldn't exactly call it a relationship."

"But you managed to secure my release. Surely that means you have some influence over him," Teach said.

Leaning back in his chair, Alastair toyed with an ornate brass letter opener. "Webb allowed your release because it benefited him somehow. That's why you're standing here and not still locked in your cell. He didn't do it out of the kindness of his heart."

A vein pulsed in Teach's neck. "So you had nothing to do with it?"

"I would never presume to be that influential. From time to time the governor listens to me, and I to him. But we go about achieving our goals very differently. The man looks for weaknesses and won't hesitate to exploit them."

Teach wondered what Alastair's weakness was. It certainly sounded as if he spoke from experience.

"Beth," Anne said, stepping forward and clasping the

pouch at her hip. Her fingers traced the wooden handle of the small pistol. Teach wasn't surprised she carried a weapon. He'd spent enough time on other islands like Jamaica and Bermuda to know it was necessary in port towns. But it made him angry that she needed it to feel safe.

Alastair nodded. "Aye, Beth is my weakness."

Teach understood that weakness only too well.

"I'll butcher the man who ever harms a hair on her head. Webb knows the tavern is important to Beth, although she'll tell you it's mine. My name is on the papers, but all the money we earn is set aside to help escaped slaves move on. Every once in a while, Webb will send some men to come in and wreck the place. Just to prove they're in charge."

"But you don't believe Webb sent those men the other night," Anne said.

"No, I don't. Pelham's official business here is to help put a stop to pirating. He's particularly keen on catching a female pirate named Reva. Word is she stole something valuable from him a few years ago. Benjamin said she was at the Fox when Pelham attacked."

"I saw her."

"You were attacked?" Teach asked, his insides turning to ice. He didn't like not knowing what was going on.

Anne glanced at Teach's face and quickly shook her head. "It was a small scuffle. Nothing happened."

Teach didn't believe Anne for a minute, and he felt powerless to protect her. That frustration coupled with the fact that he wanted to be alone with her did not improve his foul temper. This was not how he had envisioned his reunion with the woman he loved.

"Pelham mentioned something about the Royal African Company," Anne said, clearly trying to change the subject.

"He says it's only a matter of time before the slave trade is open to all merchants." Alastair exhaled, running a hand over his jaw.

Teach looked between Anne and Alastair. "What does that have to do with you?"

"Pelham wants to have a large group ready to act if the monopoly breaks. Of course, he wants to be in charge. He thinks he can persuade me, but I have no intention of joining them. Thankfully, neither Webb nor Pelham know about *all* my business dealings. The minute they become more of a threat, and as much as I'd hate to do it, I'll take my leave of the island, assets and all, including my merchant ships."

"But you've lived here for so long," Anne said.

"True, and I had a better relationship with the previous governor, Trott, but he left. He came from a prosperous family and didn't need the hassle of dealing with the riffraff of Nassau."

"Webb said he sent out ships to search for the *Deliverance*. Surely that shows he's fair," Anne said.

Teach's eyebrows drew together. "He told me the same thing, but I saw no sails."

The three of them were silent for a moment. Teach didn't like the picture Alastair painted of the governor. It merely confirmed what he'd first suspected. And he didn't know who this Lord Pelham was, but Teach was certain that anyone working with the governor would be rather shady. "My crew is still locked up."

"John?" Anne's voice was fearful.

"Aye, including John. Those are good men, and they fought bravely." Teach stared down at the floor, his mind racing, but he could not come up with any alternatives. "I've been in the fort. It would be impossible to plan an escape."

"For that many men, yes," Alastair agreed, his eyes glinting. "Now, if you only had to break out one person . . ."

Teach frowned. "And how am I to choose which one survives? No, I'm not leaving any of my men behind. I'll take the job with Webb before I sentence them to death."

"You might be doing just that by taking the job," Alastair said quietly.

"Surely there's some other way," Anne asked, looking between the two of them.

"I'm afraid not. Even if we could, by some miracle, free all his men from the fort, it would be impossible to hide them on some ship sailing out of port. Webb has eyes everywhere, including this tavern. It would only be a matter of time before he rounded the lot of them up."

Pain unfolded in Teach's chest at the thought of leaving

Anne again so soon. Nor did he like being backed into a corner.

"So what are our options?" Teach asked.

"You take the job with Webb. And we go from there."

"I'd hoped to marry Anne. Today if possible."

Alastair shook his head. "That wouldn't be wise. The last thing you want is for Webb to know your weakness. And judging by the way you look at her, Anne is very much your weakness."

The governor's mansion was a large structure, two stories high, made from local quarried coral stone. Wooden louvered verandas stretched around the exterior, to provide privacy, ventilation, and protection from the sun. Its many windows were shuttered, the roof covered in cedar shingles.

At the front door, Teach gave his name. His footsteps echoed off the marble floor as he followed the footman through the halls of the large house. This time there were no shackles around his wrists and ankles. There could be no doubt in the governor's mind that Teach would take the job.

The smell of roasted meat wafted through the air from the direction of the kitchen house. With its hot fireplace, the structure stood back from the main building amidst the densely landscaped property. Farther back, barely visible amongst the thick vegetation, was the low roof of the slaves' quarters.

Frowning, Teach followed the footman into a large office. A mahogany desk dominated the space with potted palms dotting the corners of the room. The books lining the wall mirrored his father's study back in Bristol. Teach shook off the unwanted memory and glanced out the open windows, grateful for the light breeze that blew through the room.

"The governor will be with you shortly." With a slight bow, the man left.

Moments later, the door opened and Webb entered the room, followed by another man wearing a powdered wig and ornate long coat. *This must be Lord Pelham.*

Webb moved to the large leather chair situated beside one of the floor-to-ceiling windows, and sat down, his steps stiff, and halting, as if he was in pain. Once off his feet, his features seemed to relax somewhat. Waving toward Teach, he motioned for him to do the same.

Teach remained standing, as did Lord Pelham.

"Have you thought about my offer?"

"Yes."

"Excellent. I suppose you're curious as to what it entails."

Aside from the clenching of his jaw, Teach gave no response.

"I want you to search for someone."

"Who?"

Pelham laughed lightly, the sound grating on Teach's already raw nerves. "Aren't you going to ask him about the pay? Good Lord, Webb, where did you find this one? He's willing to do it for free."

Truthfully, Teach had not considered that fact. He thought his freedom was his payment. "How much?"

"Five hundred pounds. I will pay you five hundred pounds to search for George Easton."

"Who's George Easton?"

Webb's lips thinned. "A pirate. And he's been plaguing these shores for far too long. I will give you a ship and provisions. All I ask is that you bring the scoundrel Easton to me. Preferably alive."

"Why me?"

With a quick glance in Pelham's direction, Webb scowled. "Sir."

Teach shook his head slightly, not understanding why the governor had addressed him as such. Webb sat up straight in his chair. "You will address me as 'sir.' Is that understood?"

"Yes. Sir."

If Webb noticed the slight hesitation, he chose to ignore it. "As governor of this island, I deserve at least that much from you. Now, you want to know why I chose you. It's because you're a fighter. And you've proven yourself capable of getting out of a tight scrape."

"Has anyone else gone after Easton?"

"Yes, but none of them have returned."

"Is he so dangerous?"

Pelham spoke up again. "The last man Webb sent after Easton came home in parts. The governor received his head on a spit. Is that dangerous enough for you?"

Despite himself, Teach winced at the image. "I wish to use my own crew."

"Fine. But they will stay locked up until the *Triumph* is ready to depart," Webb said.

"That's unacceptable. The more time they spend in those cells, the weaker they'll become. If you truly want me to catch Easton, my men need to be ready."

"I'm sorry, but those are my conditions. I can't have you getting any ideas in your head about quitting the island before you perform your duties. The ship will leave within the week."

It seemed to Teach that the governor was posturing in front of Pelham, trying to make himself appear more threatening. "The ship will leave within three days. And you will make sure my men are given adequate food and water until that time. I also want their quarters changed."

"That's impossible. That's a fort, not an inn."

"Then I want them to be allowed up in the courtyard during the day."

"You remind me of someone," Pelham said, his gaze narrowed. "Have we met before?"

Teach shook his head, an alarm sounding in his head. Was it possible Pelham had met Richard Drummond before? It would be disastrous if that were the case. Pelham would most likely contact Teach's father about his whereabouts, and Teach could find himself on a ship back to England. Without Anne and without his crew. "No."

Crossing his arms over his chest, Webb pursed his lips.

"What makes you think I can have everything ready in that time?"

"You're the *governor*."

Tilting his head to one side, Webb's expression darkened. "I may have underestimated you, Teach."

"I'm sure you won't make that mistake again."

CHAPTER 16

Anne

Standing in the shade of a warehouse lining the docks, Anne eyed the *Triumph*, a painful knot gathering in her throat. It was clearly a warship, small and maneuverable, with several cannons, built with one purpose in mind. And in less than forty-eight hours, Teach would set sail on it and leave Anne behind. Anne still didn't know exactly what job Teach was to perform for the governor. She had considered going with him, but it would be impossible to stow away on the *Triumph*. And if she was honest, she had no desire to return to sea so soon. The crossing on the *Providence* was still too fresh in her mind.

As much as she disliked Nassau, at least she was not alone.

Toying with the pistol at her side, Anne waited for Alastair to finish his conversation with some merchant as the late afternoon sun continued to sink toward the horizon. Alastair had asked Anne if she wished to accompany him. They had not seen

Teach since he left the previous day to go and speak with the governor. He had sent word that the ship would leave within three days and that the governor had kindly made sleeping arrangements for him.

"The governor wrote that," Anne had said. The wording had been too stiff and formal. Teach would never had written a missive like that.

Alastair had agreed with her assessment. "Webb's not letting him out of his sight."

In the hope of catching a glimpse of Teach at the docks, Anne had agreed to go with Alastair, but Teach was noticeably absent. There were other figures striding about the deck, checking the rigging and adjusting the sails, as supplies were loaded on board the *Triumph*. Anne could only imagine how much preparation needed to be done, especially in such a short amount of time. But where was Teach?

"All right, let's go," Alastair said, returning to her side. Giving her his arm, he led the way back along the wharf. Several people nodded at him as they passed. It was clear everyone knew him on the island. And the only weapon Alastair carried was a large dagger hanging from his waist.

Anne felt Alastair's eyes on her. "I'm sorry you weren't able to see him, Anne. Don't worry. I'm sure he's fine."

Despite the heat of the day, a shiver ran down Anne's spine. She did not know what was worse. Sailing on the *Providence* and not knowing Teach's whereabouts the entire time. Or being within reach of him, but not knowing if he was all right. She hated this feeling of vulnerability.

"I want to make the governor feel this powerless," Anne muttered. How she hated the man for putting them in this position.

"There's a way for you to still see Teach. I have a small sloop. If we have to, we can set sail on it. I could try to get word to Teach and we could meet somewhere, once his crew is secure and they've left port."

"You truly wouldn't mind leaving all this behind?" Anne asked, touched by Alastair's offer.

Alastair glanced around, his gaze thoughtful. The docks weren't nearly as crowded as they were first thing in the morning, when people rushed to and from the busy markets. Many people were indoors, resting during the heat of the day, before the evening started and patrons flocked to the many taverns and brothels. "I started the Fox with nothing. I can do it again somewhere else. I'll be damned if Pelham makes me join his group. I'm willing to go anywhere, as long as those I love are with me. Sometimes you have to lose everything you have to get everything you want."

"What about Beth? Her mother is buried here."

"Beth always says wherever we go, we all live under the same sky. She's already told me she's willing to move on."

"Could we do it? Could we really be prepared to leave so soon?" The only way Anne would consider boarding another ship this soon was if Teach was at her side. Surely Alastair's ship would not be as bad as the *Providence* had been. And she'd have her friends with her, as well as Teach.

"It wouldn't be easy. Like I've said, the governor has eyes and ears everywhere. We would have to be quick. We could take the supplies we needed from the Fox. I have a skeleton crew who could help us sail my sloop out of the harbor."

"Where would we go?"

"There are a number of islands nearby, many of them uninhabited. If we wanted to, we could stay on one of them for several months. We'd lie low until Webb stopped looking for us."

"For how long?" Anne asked, warming to the thought.

"It depends how angry the governor is. Until we find out what Webb wants with your friend Teach, I'm afraid I don't have any specifics. But that's not to say it couldn't be done."

Anne remained silent, as Alastair continued to think out loud, her own mind racing with possibilities. She had just sent word to her solicitor in Bristol, but she hoped she could send another missive, notifying him to hold on to her inheritance until further notice.

It took her a minute to realize that Alastair had stopped speaking. Glancing at his face, she noticed the set of his lips and the hardness in his eyes.

Anne followed his gaze, momentarily puzzled. Two dirty, coarse-looking men stood beside a wooden post just off to the side of the docks. Their faces were red from either the sun or exertion. One held a whip in his hand, laughing at something his companion had said. The other man held the remains of a rope, the edges frayed. He was the same slaver she had seen the day before at the wharf.

Anne's blood turned cold when she noticed the dirt at their feet. Painted crimson, two furrows ran from the post, as if someone had recently been dragged away. She looked around, but everyone appeared to be moving of their own accord.

"Ah, Alastair," one of the men called out as Anne and Alastair strode by. "I'm sorry you missed the show. A few minutes earlier and you could have helped us."

Alastair stiffened at his words, but he stared straight ahead. Anne did the same, knowing that the two swine hoped to get a rise out of them.

"We just taught a lesson to one of the governor's slaves."

Anne clenched the pistol at her side. Just a few more feet and she and Alastair would turn the corner and be out of sight.

"What about her, Alastair? Did you bring her for us? She'd fetch a handsome price."

The blood drained from Anne's face and she could scarcely breathe around her rage.

"Pay them no mind," Alastair ground out as they rounded the corner, only to stop. Another man blocked his path. He was smaller than Alastair, but he carried a large knife.

Anne cast a quick glance over her shoulder and noted with

dread that the two men from the whipping post were right behind them. "Alastair," she whispered.

The Irishman stepped in front of Anne, trying to shield her as they faced the three attackers. Anne pulled out her pistol at the same time Alastair whipped out his dagger.

"Oi, lookie here, boys. The lass thinks she's gonna teach us a lesson. Ye tried that yesterday, love. It didn't work. Remember? It's not even loaded."

"We'll have to see what the governor says about that, now won't we?" his companion said.

Clutching the weapon with two hands, Anne glared at the trio. The three of them took turns lunging at them, reminding Anne of cats playing with mice.

Except she wasn't in the mood to play.

The largest one of the group danced forward, his knife narrowly missing Alastair's face. All the helplessness and rage that Anne had felt in the past few weeks rushed to the surface. These men were slavers. They lived to hurt and destroy other people.

Anne was tired of living in fear, tired of seeing people hurt. This was her chance to strike back, to make them fear *her*.

Anne's vision clouded and her arms trembled as she pointed the pistol, squeezing the trigger. *Boom!* Unprepared for the kickback, Anne slammed into the brick wall behind her, her ears ringing, while the acrid smell of gunpowder filled the air.

"She shot me! She shot me!" the man yelled out, writhing

on the ground and clutching his foot with both hands while blood spurted out between his fingers.

Alastair appeared just as surprised as their assailants, his mouth hanging open, but he had no time to respond. After a moment of shocked silence, the two remaining men attacked. With a swift punch to the gut, Alastair managed to knock one of them down.

The other man grabbed Anne's wrist in a bruising grip. She kicked out, connecting with his knee. He fell to the ground, raining foul curses down on her head.

"The governor will hear about his," he cried.

"If he's going to tell the governor, he might as well have something of interest to report." Alastair hit the man square in the jaw. Anne stepped back as he fell at her feet. Two of them were now out cold, the other one still writhing in pain on the ground.

Taking Anne's hand in his, Alastair turned the corner, the man's cries gradually fading in the distance. Anne knew she should feel *some* kind of remorse for shooting him, but all she could see was the blood in the sand and the tracks in the dirt, evidence of someone else's pain and suffering.

"Coyle said you didn't want to carry a loaded weapon," Alastair said. She could detect no censure in his voice.

"That was before I met the governor's wife."

Alastair shot Anne a surprised look. Noting the set of her jaw, he chuckled softly. "Did you mean to wound him? Or did you just want to scare them?"

"I wanted to stop them from hurting anyone else." If only she'd had better aim and more weapons, she would have gladly shot all three men. Could she ever bring herself to kill someone? A week ago, she would have said no. But now . . . Anne would never forget the scene at the docks with the slaves being led away.

"You're learning quickly. There are times it's better to strike the first blow. It took me years to realize that showing mercy to your enemy would only get you wounded."

As sad as it was for Anne to admit, that is precisely what Mrs. Webb was. What slavers were. Her adversaries. Anne could not help feeling as if she was beginning to shed her civility. Despite the fact that Bristol was also a port town, Nassau seemed so much more raw and unruly.

Alastair's smile slowly faded at Anne's prolonged silence. "As much as I hate to say it, I'm afraid you might not be able to see Teach before he leaves."

"He'll come to see me." Of that she had no doubt.

"I wish I had your confidence, but it's most likely for the best if he doesn't come. You don't want Webb to find out about the two of you."

"You don't know Teach like I do. He will find a way to say good-bye."

"I might not know Teach, but I do know the governor. This is all new to you, but I've lived here too long to be shocked by much."

Anne met his eyes, her gaze steady. "If you don't see the bad in some, you can't recognize the good in others."

Patting her hand, Alastair nodded as The Laughing Fox came into view. "For your sake, I hope you've seen enough of the bad."

So did Anne. But until she knew for sure what the governor wanted from Teach, she was afraid of how much worse things could become.

CHAPTER 17

Teach

The alleys of Nassau weren't as crowded late at night. Most of the inhabitants were filling one of the busy inns or taverns lining the wharf. The air was warm and inviting, the black sky overhead littered with sparkling stars.

Teach headed to the Fox. He couldn't wait to see Anne again, but first, he'd had to ditch the two men Webb had sent after him. Teach knew he'd been followed. The governor hadn't come right out and said he couldn't leave the *Triumph* at night, but he certainly hadn't made it easy for him. Teach had been tempted to turn to confront the men, but had decided to have some fun with them instead. After all, it wasn't their fault the governor had appointed them as nursemaids.

It hadn't been easy to lose them. Teach had stopped in at a tavern, knowing Anne was practically within reach, but he'd had to wait until the two sailors were good and drunk. Then he'd slipped out through the kitchen and made his way to the back of the Fox. He was in a better mood than he had been the day before. The crew of the *Deliverance* had spent the afternoon in one of the courtyards of the fort. They'd been under heavy surveillance, but at least they'd seen the sun and breathed in clean air. He still felt guilty that he was free to move about and his men were forced to sleep in their hot, dark cells, but soon they would be reunited.

Turning down an alleyway, Teach stopped when he saw two figures pummeling a form on the ground, cringing at the sound of fists meeting flesh. He worried for the man. The devil knew when or even if the duo would stop. As much as Teach wanted to see Anne, he couldn't have someone's death on his conscience.

The pair were too busy to notice Teach as he snuck up on them.

"This hardly seems like a fair fight," Teach said with a voice that undercut the noise of the struggle.

The duo paused, their chests heaving, evidence of the pounding they were giving their victim. They turned on Teach, their fists still clenched.

A female voice behind Teach caught him off guard, as well as the sharp point of a knife pressed into his back. "Not that it's any of your business, but this man is getting exactly what he deserves." She spoke with a Spanish accent.

"Is it worth taking his life?" Teach asked.

"They're not taking his life. They're simply making him

rethink it. Next time, I believe he'll reconsider trying to steal from me. And you'd do well not to interfere in something that doesn't involve you, caballero." She removed the knife from Teach's back.

Curious, Teach turned slowly, his hands still held aloft. The woman was dressed in a white shirt, waistcoat, and breeches. She wore her hair pulled back in multiple braids and secured with a strip of leather. The brim of her hat hid part of her face in the darkness, but her chin was visible in the moonlight and at the moment, it was set.

With a sharp movement, the woman motioned to the men to follow her. They did, without hesitation. "He's all yours," she said over her shoulder. "But if he crosses me again . . ." Her voice trailed off and they turned the corner, disappearing from sight.

Teach had no doubt that was the pirate Pelham was after. How she managed to avoid capture on such a small island was admirable. Perhaps she only ventured out into the streets after dark.

The man on the ground groaned and Teach approached with care, curious to know what he'd tried to steal. His pale hair practically glowed in the dim light of the moon and looked somehow familiar.

Reaching down, Teach rolled the man over, and muttered a curse.

"I should have let them have at you," Teach growled at Peter. "Sod off."

"What did you do? Try to sell some cargo that didn't belong

to you? Is that why you tried to take those papers from the *Deliverance*?"

Peter's only response was to spit in Teach's face, desperate fury gleaming in his pale eyes.

"Wrong answer." Drawing back, Teach drove his fist into Peter's face. Peter's eyes rolled back and he lay there, immobile. Shaking his hand, Teach straightened, wishing *he* had been the one to see Peter before the two men had gotten to him first. There was no sport beating up on a man who was half dead already. Not that Peter didn't deserve it.

If Peter hadn't accused them all of mutiny, none of them would be in this mess. Teach would be reunited with Anne and the two of them could start their new life together.

Staring down at the unconscious figure, Teach debated what he should do with Peter. They weren't very far from the docks. A part of Teach truly wanted to take Peter and drop him into the harbor.

The world would be a better place for it.

As Teach stood there, debating his next move, a stray dog meandered down the alley, stopping and sniffing at different spots along the way. It came up and sniffed Teach's hand. Teach scratched the dog behind its scruffy ear and motioned toward Peter. "Have at him," he said, half in jest.

The dog looked up at Teach with soulful eyes, before turning to Peter. Approaching the lifeless form, the dog sniffed once, before lifting its leg.

Teach's dark mood lifted as he laughed. Aside from having Peter locked up, Teach didn't think he could have planned a more fitting form of revenge for the coward.

Turning, Teach left Peter splayed in the street and continued toward The Laughing Fox. Bypassing the front door, Teach headed toward the back courtyard. Once inside the enclosed area, he stopped beside a flowering frangipani bush, its soft, fruity scent heightened at this time of night. In a few hours, the sun would rise, drawing one day closer to when he would have to leave Anne behind.

Fingering the butter soft petals in his hands, he broke off one of the largest white blooms. Inhaling, he took a step forward only to freeze, unprepared for the pistol pressed against his back.

"You're lucky I didn't shoot first. Where the devil have you been?"

Teach turned, a grin splitting his face. This was the second time a woman had surprised him. "Pining for you. Now put that thing away before you shoot someone."

"I only shoot people who are wicked."

"There have been times," Teach began, placing the flower behind her ear, "when I have been known to be a bit wicked."

Anne gave a short laugh. "After my day, don't tempt me."

"But I enjoy it ever so much." Putting the encounter with Peter firmly behind him, Teach ran his fingers down her arm, capturing the gun in her hand and placing the weapon in the back of his waistband. He stepped closer, close enough that their breath mingled, and slipped his arms around her, the slim space between their bodies as charged as the air on a stormy night. "What's wrong?"

"I was worried about you."

"I'm sorry. I wanted to come sooner, but the governor insists on keeping a tight rein and a tighter schedule." Every inch of his skin tingled with Anne's nearness, and he ached to get closer.

"Alastair said as much. He didn't think you would come." Her full bottom lip grazed his as she said the words. "But I knew you would."

His mouth was on hers then. Her hands were on his chest, tugging at the laces of his shirt, as if she wanted nothing else to stand between them. With his forearm across the small of her back, he anchored their bodies together. One step, two. He guided her backward to the side of the barn. No one had ever made him feel this aware. This alive.

The pressure of Anne's lips increased, and he felt like they were the only two people in the world.

A not so subtle cough reminded Teach that that was not the case. *Damnation.* Teach had hoped to visit with Anne uninterrupted. He seemed to have had an easier time catching Anne alone in the Drummond household.

"What the devil are you doing here?" Alastair demanded, approaching them in the dark. Teach could make out a scowl on his face. "And where have you been?"

"I'm here to see Anne," Teach replied, standing with his arm around her waist. It felt so good to have her at his side. "And I spent last night on the ship. With departure so close, Webb wants to make sure things go according to his plan."

"We went to the docks today," Anne said. "We didn't see you."

Teach's chest tightened at the thought of Anne worrying. "In the afternoon Webb took me to the fort. That must have been when you came to the docks."

"What does he want you to do?" Anne asked.

"I'm to go after someone."

Anne's eyes narrowed. "Who?"

"George Easton."

"The pirate?" Alastair asked.

Teach cringed, feeling Anne stiffen at his side. He truly hadn't intended to tell Anne much about his plans. The less she knew, the better. Webb had been only too happy to recount stories about the pirate. According to Webb, Easton was savage and desperate, a man of grotesque brutality. He enjoyed torturing his victims. One time, he bound a man's hands together and then set fire to the rope, removing the flesh down to the bones.

Easton was also cunning. Three British warships once blockaded Easton where he anchored, making escape nearly impossible. Under the cover of darkness, the pirate and his men sailed slowly out of the bay, with another ship in tow. As they made their way to the entrance of the harbor, Easton set the second ship on fire and sent it toward the warships. The British scrambled to get out of the way, allowing the pirates to slip past them.

"Does Webb know you're here?" Alastair asked.

"No."

"How can you be so sure? That's an awful risk you're taking."

"I *was* followed, but those men are enjoying multiple pints at the moment and won't even notice that I'm gone."

"I think you underestimate Webb."

Teach's cheeks burned. "And I think you don't give me enough credit. For the past twenty-four hours, I've done everything the man has asked me. Now it's my turn to take something back."

"And what, precisely, were you planning to take back? She's not going back with you to the ship."

"Alastair, please," Anne said. "Give us a moment."

The Irishman shook his head. "I'm sorry, Anne, but the boy is putting too much at risk by being here. After what happened today the governor is sure to be displeased."

"Why? What happened?"

Anne and Alastair spoke simultaneously.

"I shot someone."

"She shot someone."

"What?" Teach gazed incredulously at Anne. She stared defiantly back.

"He deserved it. I only wish my aim had been better."

Shocked, Teach turned to Alastair.

"Aye, it's true. She nearly took off his foot." There was a hint of pride in Alastair's words. "Give her a few more weeks of practice and she'll be a fine shot."

"What exactly happened?"

Alastair opened his mouth, but it was Anne who answered, her voice bitter. "We ran into the town whipper."

Teach closed his eyes. He'd seen the whipping post used in several ports. When anyone wanted their slaves "corrected," they'd pay up to eighteen pence to the town whipper to teach them a lesson. Oftentimes a bell-ringer would stand nearby and draw a crowd. No wonder Anne had been so upset when he first arrived.

"They also said they could fetch a handsome price for me."

His eyes snapped open and he clenched his fists. "Who was it?" he demanded.

"It doesn't matter now."

"Of course it matters."

"I'm fine, Teach. But whoever they whipped, that person is suffering somewhere. And we're helpless to do anything about it."

"All the more reason to finish the job you started."

Alastair stepped in between the two of them. "Stop this. You two are worse than Coyle and Cara. Teach, you have to leave. It's too risky for you to be here."

"But I just—"

"Please," Anne said, placing a hand on Alastair's arm. "Can we just have a moment?"

The Irishman shook his head. "I'm sorry. I understand how you both feel. I do, which is precisely why you must leave now. I will keep Anne safe until we meet up with you again."

"What do you mean, meet up with me?"

"I'm not letting him go after Easton. It's too dangerous," Anne said.

Alastair raised his eyes to the sky, as if asking for patience. "Nobody is going after Easton. We're leaving Nassau. I have a small sloop anchored in the harbor. We spent most of today going over our supplies. Tomorrow Cara and Coyle will purchase the last few items we'll need. Anne and Beth will pack up the rest. We have to keep up appearances that everything is normal, but we plan to meet you on one of the surrounding islands, once you have your crew."

As much as Teach wanted to believe that it would be as easy as Alastair said, he didn't want to leave anything to chance. And he didn't want to jeopardize the lives of his men. "How do we agree upon the island?"

Alastair waved his hand at them. "Come with me."

Teach clasped Anne's hand in his as the two of them followed Alastair into the kitchen.

"Stay here while I go fetch a map." The Irishman disappeared through the door to the tavern. The voices were not as boisterous as they had been when Teach had first arrived at the Fox. Well past midnight, most of the patrons were deep in their cups.

Drawing Anne into his arms, Teach held her, content for the moment to feel her heart beat against his chest. "I don't want to leave you," Teach murmured into her hair.

"We have no choice. We have to trust Alastair. He's gotten us this far."

Her words reminded him of when his father had gone to deal with the piracy charges. Anne had been right then. He hoped she was right this time. "Does Alastair have a crew who can sail the sloop?"

"He has a small number of men who are loyal to him. Coyle went to make sure they're ready."

Teach grimaced at the mention of that name.

"What?" Anne asked, her voice bemused.

Hating the part of him that wanted to know, but unable to stop himself from asking, Teach paused. "Do you . . . care for him?"

"For Coyle? Of course."

A needle of jealousy pierced Teach's heart. "I see."

"No," Anne said, shaking her head. "I don't think you do. Coyle is like a brother to me. He and Cara are like family."

Teach didn't know Coyle, but he could see that Coyle did *not* regard Anne as a sister. But if she didn't realize it, Teach wasn't about to clarify. Instead, he reached for the weapon in the back of his waistband. "I want you to keep this loaded. At all times."

Her blue eyes locked on his. "I will."

"Do you know what they call this pistol?" he asked, the corners of his mouth lifting in a smile.

She shook her head.

"It's called a Queen Anne's pistol."

Anne's fingers tightened, and for a second Teach feared it might be loaded.

"I swear to you, I'm not joking," he said, choking on a laugh. Before Anne could respond, Alastair returned to the kitchen.

The Irishman lit a small candle and set it down on the table before spreading out the map he held in his hands. "Now come here so we can choose where to meet. I'm tired and need to get some sleep."

It didn't take them long to decide where they would meet up with the *Triumph*. It was a small island southeast of the port of Nassau. It would take them two to three days to sail there, weather permitting. They would hide in one of the small cays, out of sight from the shipping lane.

"What does Webb have planned for you tomorrow?" Alastair asked.

"I'm to spend the day at the fort again, visiting with my men and going over maps. Webb thinks he knows where Easton is hiding."

"I've heard stories about Easton. About as ruthless a pirate as they come. Webb's wanted to go after him for several months, but he couldn't find a crew willing to risk their lives for it."

Teach stood up straight. "Webb told me several men have gone after him."

Alastair shook his head. "None that I know of. Webb didn't offer anyone any wages, just a share of the future profits when they captured Easton. There was no guarantee they'd ever capture the man, so you can imagine why nobody jumped at the chance."

"No prey, no pay," Teach muttered.

"Aye. They could callus their hands reefing sails for years before they saw a pound for their efforts."

"Webb's offered me five hundred pounds to capture him."

Alastair let out a low whistle. "That doesn't sound right, especially coming from Webb. The man's a cheap bastard. It's a good thing you're not going after Easton. Even if you did survive the encounter, you wouldn't see a single coin for your troubles."

Rubbing the back of his neck, Teach sighed. He hadn't truly believed the governor when he'd mentioned that amount. "What do you think will happen when I don't bring Easton back?"

"Webb might send someone after *you*. He won't appreciate the fact that you took him for a fool."

Anne frowned. "But we'll be long gone before that happens, won't we?"

"Of course. He won't know where to find us."

"You're awfully confident in your abilities. I like that. It doesn't make sense to go into something already expecting defeat," Alastair said.

"I have to believe in something. I'm the one who got myself into this mess."

"Aye. And I hope you're capable of getting out of it. Now say your good-byes, you two. It's time for you to leave." Blowing out the candle, Alastair stepped outside the kitchen door.

Teach waited for him to walk away, but the stubborn old man wouldn't. He truly intended for Teach to leave.

"I'll see you in a few days. Come and find me," Anne whispered, intertwining their fingers, their palms pressed together.

"Always." Teach stole a quick kiss, then stepped outside and turned to Alastair.

"She can't keep that ring on her finger. They'll find out you gave it to her," Alastair said. "You have to do what I say in this, or else you'll put her life in danger. I know that's not what you want to do."

Teach pulled at the leather cords around his neck, withdrawing the little leather pouch from the inside of his shirt. He'd grown accustomed to it and hadn't taken it off after he gave the ring to Anne. Anne removed the ring from her finger, and Teach put it away once more for safekeeping.

"Promise me you'll keep her safe," he said to Alastair.

"I will, lad. Like she was my own daughter."

"You swear it?"

"I swear. And if I'm unable to keep my promise, may the good Lord strike me down."

CHAPTER 18

Anne

"Will you miss being here?" Anne asked Beth the next morning. The two of them had spent the past hour packing the pantry into crates. They had salted fish and pork, as well as pineapples, limes, and other fruits and vegetables. Cara and Coyle had gone to the market to purchase more chickens. Once they returned, they would take the supplies to Alastair's sloop. By sunrise the next day, they would all be on their way.

"I'll miss what Alastair and I had here," Beth said, wiping her hands on her apron. Looking at the worn table and large fireplace, there was sadness in her eyes. "It wasn't always this bad, but Webb has changed things. He claims he's working for the Crown, but every decision he makes only seems to benefit himself."

Fear gnawed at Anne, but she pushed it aside. She knew she

wouldn't be able to completely relax until she saw for herself that Teach was free of Webb's control. "Will the governor come after us once he discovers we're gone?"

"It won't be us he's after. It will be Teach. But don't worry," Beth said quickly, once she saw Anne's face. "Alastair knows these islands. With a ship at our disposal, we can disappear before the governor has time to send someone after us."

Another thought occurred to Anne and she smiled. "I wonder what will happen to Mrs. Webb's boils."

Beth laughed. "She'll have to find someone else to make the poultice. Someone who will mix it properly for it to actually work."

"You mean you—"

"I did," Beth said nodding. "I purposefully left out the nightshade a few times and substituted something else in its place."

Now it was Anne's turn to laugh. "I'd be afraid to see what she would do if she ever found out. These islands might not be far enough. Perhaps we should return to England."

"Alastair has talked about heading up to Charles Town or perhaps even New York one day. We've always wanted to own some land somewhere and settle down. Perhaps you would consider joining us."

Anne smiled, touched by Beth's words. "That sounds lovely."

Knowing Teach's love of the sea, Anne wasn't sure what

their future held. All she knew was that until she received the rest of her inheritance, her options were limited.

"I have something for you, child," Beth said, taking a beautiful tortoiseshell comb out of her pocket.

Anne regarded the gift with blank surprise. "It's lovely, but you've done enough for me already. I couldn't possibly accept it."

"Nonsense. I want you to have it." Stepping behind Anne, Beth untied Anne's thick tresses from their heavy braid. Anne's scalp prickled, and she enjoyed the feel of Beth running her fingers through her hair. It reminded Anne of when her mother had painstakingly brushed Anne's hair. Jacqueline had often despaired of ever taming Anne's locks.

Stepping in front of Anne once more, Beth smoothed back the tight curls on one side of Anne's face, securing them in place with the comb. She guided Anne to the looking glass near the back door. "I told you the island would be good for your hair."

The image staring back at Anne didn't seem to belong to her. Beth was right. The humidity created long coils that cascaded over Anne's shoulders, nearly reaching down to her waist. Anne fingered a tendril, happy with the effect. In Bristol, Drummond had insisted the household help keep their hair confined under a cap. Anne had been forced to conform to Drummond's supposed high standards.

But here, her dark curls didn't stand out anymore. She'd finally found a place where she belonged.

Smiling, Anne embraced the older woman. "I'm glad I came

to Nassau. If I hadn't, I would never have met you."

"You're a beautiful girl, Anne. Good things are going to happen for you. You'll see."

Anne flushed. She certainly hoped so. "Alastair said I should go through the books in his office and bring some of them with us."

Beth waved at Anne. "Go. I'll finish what's left in here. By the time Alastair returns, we should have everything ready."

The tavern was silent, and dust motes caught the sunlight streaming in through the windows. In a few hours, thirsty sailors would fill the tables, demanding drinks, but for now, the front door remained locked. Anne was grateful for the peace and quiet.

On her way up the stairs, she heard the jangle of a harness and horses from out in the courtyard. Cara and Coyle must have returned. Opening the door to Alastair's office, Anne walked to the bookshelves lining the wall and began to withdraw several volumes, noting Alastair's eclectic taste. He had a worn copy of Nicholas Barbon's *A Discourse of Trade*, surrounded by several editions of Shakespeare's works, as well as John Milton's *Paradise Lost*. Anne wished she had asked Alastair which volumes were his favorites. Guessing by the wear and shape they were in, she left the newer books on the shelves and packed what appeared to be his favorites into the crate, knowing that space on the sloop was limited.

When she ran across a copy of Dampier's *A New Voyage Round the World*, she could not help wondering what had happened to

Teach's. She remembered the first time she'd read to Teach, when he'd been so ill. He'd lost his lunch on his betrothed and Anne had nursed him back to health. In the beginning she'd regarded it as a chore, but by the end of that week, she'd started to care for him. That had been the beginning of their friendship.

Anne slid the book into the pocket of her apron. She would ask Alastair if she could keep it.

When at last she was done, Anne headed down the stairs and returned to the kitchen, surprised to see it empty. The coals in the fireplace glowed, warming the small pot of stew they'd left cooking. The back door stood open, a breeze blowing through the warm space. "Beth?" Anne called out.

Something scraped the kitchen floor, ever so slightly. Following the sound, Anne walked around the table toward the pantry. A red line trickled underfoot. Rounding the corner, Anne cried out at the sight before her, her hand flying to her mouth. Beth lay on the ground, clutching her stomach, while a pool of blood slowly spread beneath her.

No! No! No!

Dropping to her knees, Anne used Beth's apron to try to stanch the crimson flow, her hands shaking as a wave of nausea threatened to overwhelm her. She remembered another time, when her mother had come home, broken and bleeding at the hands of an earl's son. "Who did this?" Anne asked, her voice trembling. She swayed slightly, unused to the sight of so much blood. "Who did this to you?"

Beth's skin was dull. "The governor's wife."

A white-hot rage filled Anne and she bit her lip to keep from shouting. "I have to get help."

Beth clutched Anne's arm, her fingers smearing blood on the yellow sleeves. She gasped for breath, her words choked. "Don't go. Stay. Stay with me."

Anne was unable to prevent the flow of tears down her cheeks, knowing that Beth's wound was grave. A part of Anne wanted to run out of the kitchen as fast as she could. She needed to find Alastair, but if she left now, she might be leaving Beth to die alone. "I'm here, Beth. I'm right here."

"Tell Alastair . . . I thought I could stop her. I should have told him." Beth's face twisted into a mask of pain. Anne wasn't sure what to do, where to touch, what she could do to help her friend.

"Told him what? What did you want to say to Alastair?" Anne shot a frantic look toward the courtyard, but there was no sign of anyone.

"Don't cry. Please don't cry, Anne." Beth seemed stronger for a second. "You need to tell my Alastair that I love him. Tell him he never had to prove himself to me."

"You tell him, Beth. You can tell him. Alastair will be here soon."

Beth winced. "The governor. You must warn the governor. She's using nightshade to poison him. Warn him."

Shaking, Anne slid her arm under Beth's head as the woman

struggled for breath. "Don't go, Beth. Please. Alastair will be here soon."

"You can't let them win, Anne. Don't let them win. Make your place in this world. Claim it."

"I will," Anne whispered.

"Promise me—" Beth's body seized up before lying perfectly still. Anne stared down at her, willing her to finish her sentence, but Beth's eyes stared sightlessly up at the ceiling. The red coals in the fireplace popped and a bee buzzed outside the kitchen door, hovering, as if waiting for permission to come inside. A breeze lifted the hair on Anne's nape. Stunned, she waited stubbornly, but Beth remained motionless.

Fury against the governor's wife threatened to choke Anne, and she took a steadying breath. *Don't let them win. Don't let them win.* Anne had no intention of letting the governor's wife win. Beth's death would not go unavenged.

Hearing a wagon enter the courtyard, Anne slowly lay Beth's head back down on the ground, hating to leave her like that, but knowing she had to tell Alastair. They had to warn the governor.

Anne rushed out, stumbling over her skirts in her haste, her loose hair tumbling over her shoulders. But it wasn't Alastair in the courtyard. It was Coyle, Cara, and Benjamin returning from the market.

"Anne!" Cara cried, seeing Anne's bloodied clothes.

Coyle jumped down before the wagon had come to a complete stop, catching Anne in his arms while Benjamin brought the horses to a halt. "What happened? Are you all right?" Coyle asked.

Breathless, Anne shook her head, swiping at the tears on her cheeks. "It's Beth. She's dead."

Coyle blanched. "What? How?"

"The governor's wife. Beth found out she's been using nightshade to poison her husband. So she killed Beth and left her there to die." Anne choked on the last word.

"Benjamin, you stay here and wait for Alastair with Cara. Let him know where we are," Coyle said, reaching into the back of the wagon to remove the crate full of chickens before handing Anne up to the seat.

"She can't get away with it," Anne said, her voice urgent.

"She won't. We'll warn Webb."

Clutching the rough wood, Anne tried to brace herself as Coyle turned the wagon and left the courtyard at a breakneck speed. She was grateful for Coyle's presence. She didn't have to face the governor alone. When her mother had died, Anne hadn't been able to do anything. She hadn't had the money to even pay for a proper funeral for her mother. Jacqueline was buried in a pauper's grave.

Not this time. This time, Anne was determined to make someone pay for the crime.

Anne paced the room, her skirts stiff with dried blood.

Beth's blood.

With a cry of frustration, Anne pushed the solitary chair out of the way, sending it skittering across the floor. Pushing her hair out her face, she realized the comb from Beth was missing. Her heart ached at the loss.

It had been three hours since she and Coyle had rushed through the streets of Nassau, her promise to the dying woman driving her to the fort. She shut her eyes to try to keep the nausea at bay. Some of the shock had subsided, replaced by anger.

Until today, Anne had only seen the fort from afar. From the outside, it had appeared staunch and stalwart. But from the inside, it was dark and sinister. The governor's wife was much like the fort.

The men at the gates had brought them inside immediately. Coyle had insisted on seeing the governor, warning them that the governor's life was in danger. They'd separated Anne and Coyle shortly thereafter. At the time, Anne had thought they'd believed them, but the more she waited in this room, the more she feared she'd been mistaken. She should have waited for Alastair to return.

Tears sprang to Anne's eyes as she pictured Beth where she had left her. Alone, on the kitchen floor.

Where was Mrs. Webb at the moment? Was she sipping tea in her parlor?

Anne's pulse spiked at the injustice of it all and she strode to the door, wrenching it open. The soldier stationed outside the room jumped to his feet, his chair toppling to the ground.

"Where is the governor?" Anne demanded.

"He's been detained."

"By what?"

"That's none of your business."

Anne gave a short laugh. "This is a matter of importance, but if he doesn't care . . ." She shrugged and moved to exit the room, intent on finding Coyle. Alastair would make sure the governor's wife paid. He would make sure justice was served.

The soldier stepped in front of her, bringing her up short.

"Step aside."

The soldier stared back at her, his expression blank. "I've been instructed to keep you here."

"By whom?"

When he didn't respond, Anne tried to brush past him, but he grabbed her arm. Anne yanked out of his grasp, only to find two more soldiers had joined the first.

"What's going on? Where's Coyle Flynn?"

"He's being questioned."

"For three hours? I want to see him."

"We can't allow that."

Anne frowned. "Why not?"

"Not until his questioning is complete."

"Why hasn't anyone come to question me? We came here together. I want to see him."

The soldier shook his head. "We can't allow that."

"Why not? I've done nothing wrong." Even as Anne said

the words, she realized how ridiculous she sounded. Covered in blood, she'd ranted about the governor's life being in danger. "I wish to return to The Laughing Fox."

Their only response was to shove her back into the room, closing the door soundly behind them.

CHAPTER 19

Teach

Teach strode through the streets of Nassau, enjoying his momentary liberation. The governor's soldiers hadn't come to the *Triumph* like they had the previous day. If Webb hadn't gone on and on about the importance of a schedule and punctuality, Teach wouldn't have been so surprised that the soldiers were late. But he had waited for thirty minutes before he finally realized that for whatever reason, the soldiers wouldn't be accompanying him to the fort.

Since he planned to go and visit his men once more, Teach had decided to call on Anne first at The Laughing Fox. His heart was light at the prospect of seeing her again. If everything went according to plan, they would set sail in the morning and meet up with Alastair within three days.

Teach pulled at the door of the tavern, but it didn't budge. Strange. It was late afternoon. A crowd should have already gathered within the popular pub, especially since they'd repaired the damage from the recent fight. Teach knocked and waited, but there was no response.

The hair on the back of his neck prickled. Alastair wouldn't have left already, would he? Teach quickly shook off the thought. Although he didn't truly know the man, Anne apparently trusted him, and Anne didn't trust easily.

With a growing sense of unease, Teach went around to the back. The courtyard was empty, the barn doors closed. The single-story house also looked deserted. Entering the back of the tavern through the kitchen, Teach was momentarily relieved to see Cara seated at the table, until he saw her tear-streaked face.

"What happened?"

Cara sniffed, the look in her eyes haunted. "Beth's dead."

"What?"

"She was stabbed. Anne found her." Cara pointed to a spot beside the table. Although it was apparent someone had tried to clean the area, Teach knew from experience that the dark stain would remain for some time.

"Where's Anne now?" he asked, a buzzing in his ears growing sharper, more piercing.

"She went to the fort with Coyle. The governor's wife has been poisoning the governor. They went to warn him and to tell him about the murder."

"How long ago was that?"

Cara stared at him blankly. "I don't know. Four hours, perhaps."

What could possibly take that long? "Where's Alastair?"

Cara wiped her face with the back of her hands. "Upstairs. He waited for them to come to take the body and then he said he wanted to be alone. I've . . . I've never seen him like that."

Teach could only imagine the shock the Irishman must be feeling. "I'm going to speak with Alastair. Will you be all right?" he asked Cara.

She nodded.

Running a hand through his hair, Teach strode through the empty tavern and up the stairs to Alastair's office. He tried the handle, but the door didn't move. Teach knocked briefly. "Alastair? Alastair, please let me in. We have to talk."

An interminable silence followed. Teach leaned in, straining to hear any sound from within the room.

"Alastair, please. I'm sorry, but we have to talk. Neither Anne nor Coyle has returned from the fort."

Nothing.

Teach considered breaking down the door when the key turned in the lock and Alastair opened it. The older man's face was drawn and anguished. In his left hand he held a tortoiseshell comb. He looked, quite literally, as if a part of him had died.

Teach didn't know what to do. He didn't know what to say. When he'd climbed the stairs, he'd had a vague idea to speak with Alastair about their next course of action. But looking into Alastair's tormented eyes, Teach hesitated. Alastair had done enough. He'd sacrificed enough.

For a minute, there was no sound or movement.

Alastair was the first to speak. "I told them I'd never join them. And I told them I'd butcher any man who ever harmed her," he said, looking down at the comb in his hand, his voice hoarse. "Never thought they'd send a woman to do the job."

In that moment Teach believed one could die of a broken heart as he looked at Alastair's sloped shoulders. When Anne had left on the *Providence*, Teach had been overcome with grief. For weeks he'd wondered if he'd ever see her again. He couldn't imagine the pain of Alastair's loss, and the corners of Teach's eyes burned as he watched the older man.

Alastair finally met Teach's gaze. "They took her from me. They took the one person who mattered the most to me in this world."

"I'm so sorry," Teach breathed, although the words didn't adequately express how he felt.

Turning the tortoiseshell comb over, Alastair held it tenderly in his palm. "This belonged to our daughter. She died when she was six."

How much heartache could one person bear? Nodding, Alastair took a shuddering breath. "Beth told me she planned to give this to Anne this morning. I found it in the courtyard. Anne must have had it with her when she left."

"That's what I wanted to talk to you about."

Alastair closed his fingers over the comb, a deadly glint entering his eyes. "They'll pay for what they've done. I swear, I'll make them pay."

Loud footsteps sounded on the stairs and Coyle appeared in the doorway, panic gleaming in his eyes.

"Where's Anne?" Teach asked.

Coyle's lips tightened. "They have her locked up."

"Who has her locked up?" Alastair demanded.

"The governor. We went to warn him about his wife and tell him about the murder, but he didn't believe me. Webb says Beth and Anne had some kind of a fight over Alastair and now Anne is trying to cover up her crime."

Teach's blood teemed with fury. "I'll kill him. I'll kill him myself if anything happens to her." If anyone harmed Anne because of that man's assumptions, Teach would rip him apart. They should have let his wife finish the job of poisoning him. Teach turned to the door, but Alastair caught his hand in a viselike grip.

"I'll go," Alastair said, but Teach pulled away.

"No, you've done enough."

Moving with surprising speed, Alastair stepped in front of Teach. When just a few minutes before he'd seemed defeated, Alastair now shook with purpose. "You're in no position to go."

"And you are?" Teach asked, his gaze locked with Alastair's.

Alastair blanched beneath Teach's cold words. "Don't you

understand, boy? You cannot let them see how much she means to you. I'll go and speak with the governor."

"Then I'm coming with you," Teach insisted.

"No you're not. This isn't about you right now and your need to do something. I know you feel helpless, but we have to make sure Anne comes out of this alive. You stay here and wait for me."

"But what will you say? I've already tried to talk to the governor. The man's a fool," Coyle said, his face taut.

"Pelham is behind the poisoning. I'm convinced of it," Alastair said.

"And if the governor doesn't believe you?" Teach asked as Alastair headed to the top of the stairs. "What will you do then?"

Pausing, Alastair turned to look at them, his expression grim. "I don't know. But don't worry," he said as Teach raised his hand to protest. "I'll think of something. After all, I have nothing left to lose."

CHAPTER 20

Anne

Taking a corner of her apron, Anne dipped it in the stagnant cup of water the jailer had left her. She was the only one occupying a cell in this wing of the fort, a dark and humid place with a single torch illuminating the dank, sweating stone of the bulwarks.

Anne sat on the floor, cleaning around each fingernail with nerveless fingers. She had been locked up for the better part of the day. At one point, she'd tried to read Dampier's book, but it brought her no comfort. The last time she had looked, her mother's pocket watch had read half past four in the afternoon.

Through the cell bars, a faint glow appeared down the corridor, accompanied by the clang of irons and swishing skirts. As the light grew, Anne also recognized the sound of heavy breathing. Stealing a glance through her lashes, she saw it was the governor's wife, accompanied by three men. Two of the men were the slavers Anne had seen at the whipping post. The third one she didn't recognize. Although he couldn't have been that old, he was hunched over, and his shoulders appeared frail beneath his long coat.

Bracing herself against the upcoming confrontation, Anne kept her eyes on her task. The footsteps stopped in front of her cell.

"Is this her?" the stranger asked. His breath came in short pants, as if each step was a struggle.

"Aye, it is, Governor."

Anne dipped her apron once more, her fingers starting to shake, trying to suppress the fear welling up inside her. She had held Beth with her right hand, so of course there was more blood there.

"Not much to look at, is she?" He clicked his tongue in disgust. "Nothing more than a common criminal spitting such vile accusations against *my* wife."

So much blood.

"Look at me when I talk to you."

Anne turned her back to them slightly, continuing the study of her nails.

The bars clanged as if they had been struck by something. Anne jumped but did not look up.

"I said look at me when I'm talking to you. Do you know who I am?"

Anne paused and finally met Governor Webb's gaze. "I

know exactly who you are. You're the man being poisoned by your wife."

Mrs. Webb gasped, raising a gloved hand to her mouth. Only Anne saw the act for what it was. The governor put his arm around his wife's shoulders. Perhaps he was afraid she might swoon. In truth, he could have used his wife's support, for his eyes were sunken, deep shadows beneath them.

"Please," Mrs. Webb said, moving her hand on her husband's chest. "Make her stop! I can't bear such lies."

The governor's face contorted with rage as he leaned closer to the bars, his face demonically lit by the torch. "My wife hasn't left my side since I took ill. She's the one who's been nursing me back to health."

Anne gave a short laugh. "If you wish to live, I suggest you have someone else drink the tea she brings you."

For just a fraction of a second, Anne saw doubt in Webb's expression.

Mrs. Webb stepped forward, no longer cowering at her husband's side. "Don't you dare threaten us. *You're* the one who's committed a crime and now you've come here, hoping to cast a shadow on my good name. You're the one covered in blood. Not me."

Anne couldn't believe the woman's audacity. "I saw you. You claimed you needed a poultice for boils. That's why you asked Beth for the nightshade. And then you killed her when she was no longer useful to you." Anne's voice caught.

"Boils?" Governor Webb frowned, glancing down at his wife.

She clutched his arm, shaking her head. "Lies! She continues to tell lies! I've never met that woman in my life." Mrs. Webb rounded on Anne, her limbs shaking. Anne could see the fear in her eyes. "You probably had some petty argument with her and then you stabbed her. Perhaps you want that awful tavern keeper for yourself. He has such a taste for colored girls."

Anne was on her feet, unwilling to sit still any longer. If she'd had her pistol on her, Mrs. Webb would be on the ground right now, bleeding out. "Her blood is on your hands. Has anyone bothered to check the back of your wardrobe? Or perhaps you've already stashed the dress in a fireplace somewhere."

The color drained from Mrs. Webb's face. She shook her head, pointing at Anne. "You have the devil in you."

Governor Webb was silent as he looked between Anne and his wife, his brows drawn together.

"Are you going to let her speak to me like this?" Mrs. Webb demanded. "I told you it was useless coming to see her. Anyone associated with Alastair Flynn is trouble. That man is too powerful by far and needs to be taught a lesson. Who's in charge of this island? A tavern keeper? Or you?"

Her words had their desired effect. The governor shook himself and snapped his fingers. The two men stepped forward, treacherous smiles curving their cruel faces.

"Bring her," Governor Webb said, his voice impassive.

"You'll fetch a good price for her, Governor. We'll see to that."

No! Ice-cold sweat dripped down Anne's spine as she backed away, dread settling like fog around her. The taller slaver inserted the key in the lock and opened her cell. She eyed the irons they picked up, the hairs pricking on the backs of her arms. They reached for her, but Anne jumped to the side, trying to race past them, but a fist to her cheek stopped her short flight. Dazed, she fell back, landing on the floor in a painful heap, the metallic taste of blood filling her mouth.

The governor's wife laughed, a sinister sound that raised gooseflesh on Anne's skin. Turning over, Anne spat a stream of blood on Mrs. Webb's light blue dress. With a shriek of rage, the woman ripped the whip out of the slaver's hand.

Anne shielded her face with her arm. The pain was blinding and instantaneous. Even as Anne cried out, a rag was stuffed in her mouth and her wrists were caught in a painful grip behind her back as she was hauled to her feet. A triumphant look shined in Mrs. Webb's eyes as the governor declared, "We don't need to go to the whipping post for this one."

Fighting in earnest against her captors, Anne kicked out repeatedly. After several seconds of near misses, one of the slavers gave a disgruntled shout. He slammed his fist into Anne's stomach. Doubling over in pain, she gagged around the rag stuck in her mouth. Cold metal clasped around one of her wrists as the men dragged her unceremoniously across the cell. The heavy chain was laced through several bars before another cuff was attached to her other wrist, effectively securing her in place.

Anne didn't have time to brace herself before the first lash sliced through the thin material of her shirt, the searing pain bringing tears to her eyes and she cried out. Time and again, it was brought down across her back in a relentless assault. With each stroke, Anne's skin softened and tore open until she felt the trickle of blood between her shoulder blades. Her back burned where the leather strips cut into her flesh.

After seven lashes, there was a pause. Anne briefly registered the woman's panting over the pounding of her own heart.

"It's my turn," the slaver said.

With a muted cry, Anne fought against her bonds as the slaver took up where the governor's wife had stopped, but there was no escape. Anne had no idea where the whip landed, for every blow was pure agony. Her legs gave out beneath her, and she hung limply by her wrists, her head hanging forward between her arms against the bars. The rag in her mouth muffled her sobs.

Eventually the flogging stopped. The shackles were removed and Anne collapsed to the floor. With shaking fingers, she took the rag from her mouth, watching dully as Mrs. Webb and the governor stopped beside her.

"You'll be put on a ship tomorrow," Governor Webb said.

"If she survives the journey." This from one of the slavers.

Mrs. Webb sniffed, her dainty shoes peeking out from the bottom of her blood-spattered skirts. "Either way, it doesn't matter. The devil will welcome you to hell."

"I'm already there," Anne whispered, her voice hoarse. She didn't flinch when the whip came down on her one last time.

The cell door shut with a clang and they left Anne lying there on the grimy floor. Clenching her jaw, Anne closed her eyes against the searing pain as the footsteps of her tormentors receded down the dark hallway.

CHAPTER 21

Teach

Thunder rumbled in the distance as heavy pewter clouds rolled across the evening sky. Although they weren't unfurled, the sails of the *Triumph* shuddered in the wind. Teach secured the knot of the mainmast, blinking against the raindrops beginning to fall from the sky.

He'd already secured the lines once, but his muscles and fingers twitched, determined to find some task, some kind of release for his frustration. A handful of men clambered over the ship behind him, part of a skeleton crew the governor had allowed Teach to assemble until they were ready to depart. Then he and his men were free to go.

Teach glared at the fort on the other side of the harbor. He shouldn't have listened to Alastair.

"It's not in Anne's best interest to have you go storming in and causing an uproar," Alastair had said. "Wait and see what I can do first. Wait for me at the *Triumph*." He'd instructed Teach to prepare the ship and act as if everything was normal, but nothing about Teach's stay in Nassau had been normal.

"Teach!"

Exhaling loudly, Teach turned. Coyle stood behind him on the deck, his eyes weary, his mouth turned down at the corners. Teach's chest turned hot with fear.

"Where is she? What's happened?" Teach demanded.

"She's still at the fort."

"Where's Alastair?"

"He's at the tavern."

Teach strode across the deck, but Coyle grabbed Teach's arm, halting him. "Let him rest. He's done all he can for now."

Jerking out of Coyle's grasp, Teach rounded on him. "While he's *resting*, Anne is still locked up in that bloody place. And so are my men."

Coyle's eyes flashed with their own fury. "You'll see your men shortly. And at least they're still alive. In case you've forgotten, Beth is dead. Let the man have a moment to mourn."

Teach felt a sharp stab of guilt and tried to draw a steadying breath. Dragging a hand across his face, he gave Coyle an apologetic grimace. "I'm sorry. I truly am, but unless we do something now, I'm afraid I'll experience firsthand what he's going through. I can't allow that to happen. I *won't* allow that to happen. With or without your help, I plan on getting Anne out of the fort tonight. I take it the governor didn't believe Alastair?"

"He didn't get a chance to speak with him."

"Then I'll go and speak with him," Teach growled, but Coyle stopped him once again.

"Would you listen to me? I know you're upset, but rushing off without a plan won't save Anne." Coyle ran his hand through his hair. "Alastair was with the governor when he collapsed. He didn't collapse from hunger or fatigue. The man was spitting blood when they dragged him away. Alastair saw it with his own eyes."

"Then that should prove that what Beth told Anne was true."

Coyle shook his head. "Nobody believes the story. They say Webb's in ill health because he's obsessed with finding Easton. The governor's wife claims ignorance of the entire thing. Says she never set eyes on Beth."

"But her driver—"

"Nobody can find him."

A ripple of dread ran down Teach's spine. How many people would the Webbs kill before they were stopped?

"The most important thing now is to get Anne out of that fort tonight. We'll take her to Alastair's sloop and set sail with the tide. That's why Alastair needs to rest. He said he saw her, but it was only for a moment. She's—" Coyle swallowed, and Teach noticed the hesitation.

"She's what?"

"We're getting her out of there, Teach. I'm just worried about the storm," Coyle said, eyeing the flash of lightning in the distance.

"We sail with the tide. If Alastair's men are as good as he claims they are, you shouldn't have any problem." Teach hoped the squall would blow right past them. Once Teach knew that Anne and the rest of his crew were safe, he wouldn't look back.

"All right. I'm to wait with Cara at the sloop. Benjamin will go with you and Alastair to get Anne out. With the governor sick, things might work to our advantage."

His gaze firmly fixed on the fort, Teach didn't say anything.

"I love her too, you know," Coyle said quietly.

Teach turned to stare at him. He would have preferred to dislike Coyle, but there was something agreeable about the Irishman. He was like a younger version of Alastair, with a healthy dose of arrogance. "I know. And I'm grateful for everything that you did for her when I wasn't there." *But I'm here now.*

Coyle nodded. The two of them regarded each other in total silence, neither one willing to back down.

"Excellent." Coyle rubbed the back of his neck, looking at the surrounding ships. "As much as I hate the thought of setting sail again, it will be nice to leave this place behind. We've had nothing but trouble since we arrived."

If anything happened to Anne, all that trouble would pale in comparison to what Teach would unleash on the governor.

Four hours later, a lieutenant led the way down the now familiar corridor of the fort, the torch in his hand flickering as he moved, causing their shadows to dance along the smooth stone walls. After the fresh night air from outside, the stench of human waste and sweat was enough to bring tears to Teach's eyes. He'd only spent one day in this place and it made him sick to think of Anne and his men within these walls.

Four more soldiers accompanied Alastair, who walked behind the lieutenant. Teach and Benjamin brought up the rear, carrying a rough wooden crate between the two of them. The only sound from the crew of the *Deliverance* was the deep resonance of their snores.

Alastair hadn't said much since listening to Teach's plan to get Anne out of the fort. He was quiet, tormented, no doubt, by his grief. It would be a long time before he came to terms with it. Teach wished he could help Alastair in some way, but Teach was dealing with his own heartache as well.

The first cell housed five men deep in their slumbers, but they jerked awake when the lieutenant banged on the bars. "All right, now. Look lively."

Blinking against the light, the rest of the crew slowly sat up, rubbing their eyes and muttering amongst themselves. Jack Thurston was the first one to set eyes on Teach.

"Oi, if it isn't Blackbeard hisself, come down off his throne to visit us."

Teach knew Jack meant him no ill will, for Teach had spent quite a bit of time with his men when the governor had allowed him to bring food the last two days.

"I've brought you something," Teach said. Placing the crate on the floor, he and Benjamin pried the lid back, revealing some clean shirts and breeches. "There's a storm brewing. If we want to leave before it hits, you've got to be ready within the hour." The fact that the governor wasn't at the fort definitely worked in their favor. Teach hoped to be aboard the *Triumph* and gone before Webb discovered that they'd left twelve hours earlier than planned.

The rest of the men voiced their approval as Alastair and Benjamin began handing out the garments.

"It's good to see you," John said, approaching the bars nearest Teach.

Teach glanced over his shoulder at the soldiers, but the five men stood several feet away and helped with the distribution of clothing. "I need you to start a fight, John," he muttered beneath his breath. "I need you to cause a distraction."

John raised an eyebrow. "How big a distraction?"

"Port Royal." Teach and John had been part of a crew on a merchant ship the year before. After being attacked by Spaniards, they'd barely made it to Port Royal alive. While Teach and John had gone to secure another ship, most of the crew had visited the nearest tavern, intent on draining their pockets on wine and women. Teach later found many of the men deep in their cups and unable to pay the debt they'd accrued. He and John had had no other choice than to start a fight. It had quickly escalated into an all-out brawl, but they'd managed to get their men out of there. The ends had certainly justified the means.

John winked at Teach. "The boys and I have been feeling a bit restless. It might do us some good."

With a nod and a slight smile, Teach stood back. John looked over his fellow crewmen, a calculating look in his eye, until his gaze came to rest on Jack Thurston. Jack was in the cell next to his and was presently taking off his shirt to change into the new one that had been provided. John called Jack over to the bars. Jack strolled over and leaned forward. John whispered something in his ear. Jack jerked away, his face red.

"Take it back!" Jack yelled.

John grinned. "I will not. Any more time in here and you'd find your manhood shriveling. It's a good thing we're heading out to sea. It will save the fair maidens of Nassau from your wastin' disease."

With a roar, Jack reached through the bars and grabbed John by the collar with one hand while raising his other, but John blocked Jack's fist with his arm. Several of the men hollered at the two, calling out names and bets on who would win. Teach was surprised at the speed with which the quarrel spread, like a match to a powder keg. It was a good thing his men were all sober at the moment. Even young Matthew joined the fray with zeal.

The soldiers raced to the bars, yelling at the crew to stop yelling at each other. Alastair motioned for Teach and Benjamin to follow him with the crate. "Bring them to the ship as soon as you can," Teach cried.

The harried lieutenant nodded before placing his fingers in his mouth and giving a shrill whistle.

More soldiers ran down the corridor to their aid, passing Teach and the others. Teach's heart pounded a deafening rhythm in his ears. Alastair took one of the torches hanging on the wall and strode through the darkened hallways, keeping a fast pace. Teach and Benjamin did their best to keep up with him, despite the unwieldy crate. The sounds of the fight lessened as they turned down a different passageway.

"What are you doing here?" A solitary soldier approached them, his weapon drawn.

Alastair slowed only slightly. "Delivering clothing to the prisoners, as ordered. But a fight broke out. You better join your fellow soldiers before it gets out of hand."

Teach held his breath. The soldier stood, uncertain, until a loud shout echoed down the corridor. Slipping his musket over his shoulder, he bolted toward the commotion.

Alastair quickened his pace. "Quickly now. We don't have much time."

"Won't they be punished?" Benjamin asked.

"I think the guards will be pleased to see their backs," Alastair said, and Teach had to agree with him, even though both men knew why Benjamin was concerned. If any slaves had acted out like the crew of the *Deliverance*, they would have been whipped. Or worse.

At the end of the corridor, Alastair stopped while Teach and Benjamin placed the crate on the ground. The air here smelled musty, even more so than the rest of the fort. It clearly hadn't seen as much use as other parts.

Teach's pulse raced and he glanced over his shoulder, but there was no sign of any pursuit. Benjamin took the torch while Alastair fiddled with the lock. After only a moment, Alastair pulled the door open and Teach rushed into the cell toward a figure huddled in the corner. His chest turned painfully hollow and he was filled with a dull ache of horror when he saw Anne's bloody and lacerated back through her shredded blouse. In one hand she clutched her gold pocket watch and in the other was a copy of a book.

Dropping to his knees, Teach hesitated, helpless to know where to touch her. "Anne," he whispered hoarsely.

She moaned, but didn't open her eyes.

"Why didn't you tell me?" Teach ground out, giving Alastair a cold glare.

"What would you have done? When they brought me to her, this had already happened. They wanted to teach me a lesson."

"Who?"

"Webb and his wife. If I'd told you Anne had been whipped, you would have charged in here and put all our lives at risk. I couldn't let you do that. I know you're upset, but as I've said, this affects more than the two of you."

Fighting to remain calm, Teach closed his eyes and drew in a shuddering breath. Alastair was right. Even now, Teach wanted to find the governor and tear him limb from limb.

"We have to go," Benjamin said.

Alastair nodded. "Aye. We have to put her in the crate like we planned."

"Not like this," Teach said, scowling.

"Aye, exactly like this. And we have to do it now. If you want to get her out of here alive, we can't waste more time."

Benjamin and Alastair moved to help Anne, but Teach pushed them aside. He pocketed the watch and the book before turning her gently. He laid her neck on one arm, scooping up her legs with his other.

Alastair arranged the canvas they'd brought in the bottom of the crate and Teach lowered her carefully on her side, praying fervently that she wouldn't wake up. Placing the lid back on top, Teach caught Alastair's wrist as he lifted the small mallet to nail it back into place.

"If we drop it, we can't risk her falling out," Alastair said.

"Then we won't drop it. I won't have her waking up and thinking she's in a coffin."

Alastair winced, but it was too late for Teach to take it back. Muttering beneath his breath, Alastair heaved one side of the crate in his hands, while Teach took the other side. Benjamin led the way with the torch, and together they walked toward the exit.

CHAPTER 22

Teach

Riding in the back of the wagon, Teach pulled the canvas taut over the crate, trying to protect Anne from the onslaught of rain pouring down from the black sky. A stray drop rolled down her arm and Teach gently brushed it away. He'd removed the lid as soon as they were clear of the fort, its thick walls growing smaller in the distance. Anne still hadn't wakened.

Alastair flicked the reins, trying to get the horses to move faster, but the streets of Nassau were slick with mud, and the horses struggled to maintain their footing. Benjamin sat beside him, his shoulders hunched. He looked back every once in a while to make sure they weren't being followed.

Anne groaned, and Teach's soul staggered beneath the blow of seeing her this way. He'd felt helpless before, but never like this. The governor would pay. If his wife didn't finish him off, Teach vowed he would do the job.

Alastair let loose a foul curse and Teach sat up, drawing his pistol. In the distance, an orange glow peeked through the night with several soldiers patrolling the docks.

"That's my ship," Alastair growled.

"Alastair! Alastair!"

Swinging around, Teach pointed the pistol, only to drop it when he saw Cara rushing out of the shadows to meet the wagon. She was soaked to the skin, and her blond hair hung limply to her shoulders. "Turn around. Now!" Teach helped her scramble into the back of the wagon. She gasped for breath.

"What happened? Where's Coyle?" Alastair asked, turning the horses down a side alley. The wagon bumped along the rutted lane, and Teach gripped the sides of the crate, hating the fact that the quick movements jostled Anne.

"The soldiers took him. Somehow Webb knew we were leaving. Coyle fought with them so I could slip away. They burned the ship."

"Blast!" Alastair turned down another road, bringing them parallel with the docks, but going in the opposite direction. "Pelham had a hand in this, but I don't know how they found out."

"Where are we going?" Teach asked.

"I'm taking you to the *Triumph*. Then I'll go back for Coyle. We'll have to find some other way off the island."

"Do you think he knows I'm not going after Easton?"

"I don't know."

Teach's hands tightened on the crate. "Anne comes with me."

"No!" Cara said at the same time as Alastair spoke: "It's too dangerous."

"It's even more dangerous if she stays here with you. You'll have enough trouble going after Coyle. The more time that passes, the more likely they are to discover that Anne's gone."

Cara gazed down at her friend. Frowning, she leaned closer, sucking in a deep breath when she saw Anne's back. "What happened? Who did this to her?" she asked, her expression horrified.

"Webb."

"She can't stay in those clothes. They're filthy. Look how they're sticking to her back."

Teach didn't have to look to know that the dried blood acted like a glue, adhering Anne's shredded blouse to her skin. Although there were extra garments in the crate, he hadn't wanted to remove Anne's, for fear of hurting her even more.

Before Teach could stop her, Cara tipped one corner of the canvas inward, allowing the rain water to wash over Anne's back. Anne winced, but did not wake.

Cara's fingers shook as she gently pried the material away from the raw wounds. Teach took one of Anne's fevered hands in his, watching as Cara continued to work. She gripped Anne's sleeve and tried to rip it, but the material was wet and Cara was shivering. Teach slid a knife from his left boot and sliced through the fabric before handing it to Cara.

"How *are* we going to get Coyle back?" Cara asked her uncle as she exposed Anne's injuries.

Teach looked away, his muscles tensed. The desire to find Webb pumped through his veins with a violent force.

Alastair stayed silent, his jaw clenched. Teach knew he was going over their options, but Teach also knew they were extremely limited.

"I wish I could help you somehow," Teach offered, but Alastair was already shaking his head.

"No. You're right. You need to get Anne and your men away from here. It won't do us any good to be stuck here. I'm the one Pelham and Webb want."

"I can take Cara with me if you like," Teach said. "It won't be easy for her, but it will get her away from Nassau."

Cara jerked her head up, her hands stilled over Anne's skin. "No! I'm not going anywhere without Coyle."

Alastair sighed. "Cara, you have to be reasonable—"

"Uncle, I am not leaving you behind. Together we'll think of some way to free Coyle." Cara wiped at her eyes, her expression determined.

"I can't run the risk of you getting caught as well," Alastair said.

"You can't do everything alone. I can help. *Please*. He's my brother."

Running his hand over his face, Alastair sighed in resignation. "All right. Anne will go with Teach. Cara and I will get Coyle. If the governor knew about us trying to leave on my sloop, I dare say he'll have other ships watched. I might have to call in a few favors with some people to get us out of this blasted place."

Cara bit her lip, the tears on her cheeks mixing with the rain. She gave Teach a solemn look. "You'll take care of Anne for us, won't you?"

"With my life."

Smiling slightly at Teach's response, Cara took a portion of her own sodden skirts and gently wiped at Anne's back. But a wheel hit another hole in the road, and Cara cried out in frustration.

Teach placed a comforting hand on Cara's shoulder. "We'll take her to the captain's cabin. You can finish once we're on board."

They pulled up beside the bobbing *Triumph*, ocean water splashing up between the ship and the wharf.

"I'll go speak with the port officials," Alastair said. "I'll arrange for a pilot cutter to take you out of the shallows. The last thing we need is for you to ground the *Triumph* as you leave."

Grateful for the older man's assistance, Teach replaced the lid on the crate and slid it toward the back of the wagon before he jumped down and took one side in his hands. Benjamin grabbed the other side and the two of them hefted it in their arms. Teach backed slowly over the slick plank leading from the dock to the deck as the rain continued to fall. Once they were safely on board, they moved to the stairs leading down to the belly of the ship, but Teach stopped when he saw torches in the distance.

Cara reached for the crate where Teach held it. "They're bringing your crew already. We'll take Anne down. You stay here to meet them."

"It's too heavy for you," Teach said.

"I grew up carrying newborn calves on a farm. I'm quite sure Benjamin and I can handle a crate," Cara said, shouldering Teach aside. "Besides, I wish to tell her good-bye." Her voice was unsteady, her eyes glittering.

Teach nodded in understanding. He didn't see anything wrong with allowing Cara these last few minutes with Anne. "At the bottom of the stairs, turn left. The captain's cabin is at the end of the hallway."

The two of them disappeared, and Teach moved to meet the oncoming party. The soldiers outnumbered the men of his crew.

Striding to the plank, Teach stopped the lead sergeant from boarding the *Triumph*. "Where are the rest of my men?" He saw John, but Jack Thurston and several others were noticeably absent.

The man held his torch aloft and Teach noted the triumphant gleam in his eyes. "The rest of your crew will wait here for you until you return with George Easton."

"That wasn't my agreement with the governor," Teach said, his voice sharp.

"The governor has had a change of heart. Don't worry, you won't be left short-handed. My men and I will be accompanying you. I'm your new first mate."

"I'm not leaving my crew behind." The thought of Jack, Matthew, and the others spending any more time in those dark cells make Teach sick. And he wouldn't be there to ensure their well-being.

"You're free to speak with the governor tomorrow."

They had to leave now or risk being discovered. "Do you even know anything about sailing?" The first mate was second in command to the captain, and like the captain, he never pulled, hauled, or did work with his hands.

"Of course," the man said, clearly affronted.

"I already have a first mate," Teach said, pointing to John. "And I wasn't aware the governor was in a position to make such changes. Last I heard, he'd taken ill."

The sergeant's face showed surprise. "Where did you hear that?"

"From me," Alastair said, coming up from behind. The soldiers parted, allowing Alastair to approach the plank. It was clear they respected the tavern keeper. "I was with the governor when he took ill. What are you doing here, Kitts?"

"That's Sergeant Kitts to you. The governor wishes to have a word with you, Alastair."

Teach shot a glance at Alastair, but the Irishman appeared unruffled.

"As I said, I just spoke with him. I can't imagine what else he would like to discuss with me again so soon."

Kitts smiled, but it didn't reach his eyes. "Nevertheless, you're to be escorted to his house."

Alastair motioned to the men on the docks. "I'm sure I won't need that much of an escort."

"As I was just telling your friend here, part of my men will sail with him. The rest of his crew will remain here. For their well-being, of course."

Teach shifted, torn between wanting to set sail as quickly as possible and making sure Alastair and the rest of his crew were all right. "It could take weeks to find Easton."

The sergeant stepped forward on the ramp, coming nose-to-nose with Teach, a clear threat in his posture, his wide-set eyes intense as they locked on Teach's. "In that case, your men will be well-rested when you return."

Sucking in a deep breath, Teach drew up to his full height, but Alastair gave a slight shake of his head. "I'll make sure they're taken care of, Teach. I'll speak with the governor myself."

It was too risky for Alastair to stay, made clear by the burning of Alastair's ship. Alastair staying in Nassau was precisely what the governor wanted. And Lord Pelham too.

Cara and Benjamin joined them. The sergeant's eyes raked Cara from head to toe, and Teach's hands curled into fists.

"Were you planning on one last visit before you set sail?"

Kitts asked Teach. "That might be allowed elsewhere, but there's no room for whores on this trip."

Alastair moved quickly, grabbing the sergeant by his collar and planting a fist in his stomach. Kitts toppled into the choppy waters below. Two other soldiers scrambled to pull their comrade up to safety. Teach's crew laughed, joined by some of the men in uniforms. Apparently Kitts didn't have the respect of all his men. Teach motioned for the men to come on board.

"I wish you hadn't done that," Teach muttered beneath his breath.

"Why?" Alastair asked, coming to stand by his side on deck.

"I should have been the one to hit him," Cara said.

"You're my niece. I won't allow anyone to call you that."

"He deserved much worse," Teach said.

Cara nodded. "True. Plus he'll be in a devil of a mood when they fish him out."

"Which is why I should have done it. He's sailing with me, remember? The last thing you need is more trouble with the governor."

"I'll handle the governor. And Pelham. You just make sure you find Easton and bring him back as quickly as possible." Taking Cara's hand in his, Alastair helped her onto the plank. "This is your last chance. Are you sure we can't take Anne with us?"

Looking at the sputtering sergeant coming out of the water, Teach wasn't exactly sure he'd made the right decision. There was no question their mission to go after Easton was dangerous. And with the soldiers on board, Anne would be forced to stay in the captain's cabin. She was essentially a prisoner.

But it was also clear the governor no longer trusted Alastair, and the minute they discovered Anne was missing, they would search for her. The island wasn't large enough to hide anyone in Anne's condition for an extended period of time. "I'm sure."

"Some of her cuts are deep. She'll need to be sewn up," Cara said, her voice apologetic as tears filled her eyes once more. "There was no time."

"I'll see to it," Teach said.

"What about you, Benjamin? What do you wish to do?" Alastair asked.

Benjamin looked between Alastair and Teach, before taking another look at the port of Nassau. At night it looked practically harmless, with lights flickering in the windows of the taverns and houses, giving it an almost cozy atmosphere, as if the rain washed it clean. But Teach knew the hazards and perils lurking in the shadows, and the man entrusted with keeping peace on the island was the greatest threat of all.

"I wish to leave this place," Benjamin said. "I wish to start new."

Nodding, Alastair clasped Benjamin's hand in his. "I was hoping you'd say that. There's no future for any of us here. But this isn't good-bye."

Benjamin smiled. "No, it's not."

"I'll see you again soon, my friend," Alastair said. Reaching into his pocket, Alastair pulled out a familiar tortoiseshell comb. He handed it to Teach. "Give this to Anne."

"I will. Make sure the crew of the *Deliverance* are cared for."

"Aye, I will." The rain subsided as Alastair joined Cara on the dock. A handful of soldiers quickly surrounded them.

Teach hated to leave them behind, their safety uncertain. But he wasn't in a much better position. And neither was Anne.

The sergeant stood dripping on the wharf, shouting in Alastair's face and calling for one of the soldiers to place him in irons.

"Kitts!" Teach called out.

The sergeant whipped his head around, scowling.

"If you don't wish to be left behind, I suggest you come on board. I'm still captain of this ship, and unless you want to explain to the governor the reason for our delay, we need to sail now."

With a jerk of his head, Kitts instructed the soldiers to lead Alastair and Cara away. John gave a low whistle, coming to stand at Teach's side. "This should make for an interesting journey."

Teach pictured Anne below in his cabin. His friend had no idea. "I'm sorry we couldn't bring the rest of the crew with us. I should have known better than to trust Webb."

"It's not your fault, Teach."

"But it is my fault that you started that fight. I wouldn't

have asked you to do it, but I needed your help."

"None of us blame you. From the sound of it, Webb had this planned all along. He just didn't tell you about it. Let's just hope there aren't any more surprises."

What would John say when he found out Anne was on board? Teach would have to tell him sometime. "As soon as we hit the open sea, I wish to speak with you in private. But for now, we must profit by the wind, John. It's time to make sail and put as much distance between us and Nassau as possible."

John grinned. "I thought Kitts was your new first mate."

"I saw no papers. The governor said I could choose my crew. Sound the call."

Turning, John reared back and shouted, "All hands, prepare to make sail!"

The men scrambled to prepare the *Triumph* as the moon came out from behind the clouds. Steam rose from the deck as the crew rushed about, climbing to the yards, canvas in hand.

Kitts stalked up to Teach, reminding Teach of a drowned rat. His once impeccable uniform now hung limply from his thickset frame. "The governor said *I* was to be first mate," he snapped.

"Then you can take it up with the governor when we return."

The pilot took the helm, prepared to guide the *Triumph* away from the full quay. On John's orders, the men let some of the sails fall, the sheets unfurling in the wind. A gentle tug brought the *Triumph* away from the dock, followed by another. Once they were clear of the other ships, the pilot quickly handed over control of the *Triumph*, climbed down the Jacob's ladder, and untied the small skiff being pulled alongside. Once he was aboard his own cutter, he waved a lantern in his hand, signaling the go ahead.

Another shout from John and more sails opened up. The *Triumph* made her way, eventually picking up speed, and cutting through the waves leading out of the harbor.

As the lights of Nassau grew smaller in the distance, Teach should have felt relief. Instead, it was as if a yoke had descended on his shoulders, with a heavy load harnessed to it. He was finally captain of his own ship, but the price he'd paid had been a steep one. And unless he succeeded in bringing Easton back to Nassau, the weight of innocent lives would be added to that burden.

CHAPTER 23

Anne

Pried from the numbing cocoon of sleep, Anne slowly opened her eyes. She lay flat on her stomach on a table or desk of some sort. Two of the table legs were attached to the cabin wall. A large piece of canvas stretched out on the other side, ready to catch her if she fell.

The strange room swayed. She could hear low voices, but she didn't have the strength to turn to see who spoke. Her limbs were heavy, and she was dressed in a large tunic at least two sizes too big. The skin on her back burned as if on fire.

Her throat was dry and scratchy, and she closed her eyes against a wave of dizziness.

I've died and gone to hell.

Except she'd expected hell to be louder, with heat and smoke and the moans of the damned rising up. In the background, all she heard was the rhythmic splash of water, accompanied by the familiar scent of the ocean.

She was on a ship. A trickle of fear ran down her spine. *"You'll fetch a good price for her, Governor."*

Anne's fear spiraled into panic as she remembered the scene at the fort. The last thing she recalled was watching the governor and his wife walk away. After the whipping. Squeezing her eyes shut, she tried to picture what had happened next, but she couldn't. Her mind was a fog, her memory blank.

The door opened. Anne's muscles clenched. She wanted to move, to turn to look, but she was too tired. Too exhausted. Her spine blistered with bruises and her back was scorched.

Footsteps approached the table where she braced herself. A hand moved gently over her head, massaging her scalp, and she opened her eyes. "Teach?" The word came out as a mere whisper as Anne leaned into his comforting touch with a soft sigh.

Teach knelt beside her, his green eyes locked on hers. His face was pale beneath its tan. "I'm here," he said, his voice low and shaken. He leaned forward and pressed a kiss to her forehead. "I'm so sorry I couldn't stop this. I'm so sorry I wasn't there to protect you."

Anne swallowed, rolling her tongue over her cracked lips. She tried to rise, but the tight skin on her back protested against the smallest movement.

"No, don't move. You'll open the wounds again." Teach leaned a flask against her lips, and she lifted her head a fraction so she could drink. Brandy trickled into her mouth and down her cheek. Teach paused and put the flask down, and Anne held still as a damp cloth moved over her skin, erasing the liquid trail.

Still thirsty, her gaze found the flask where it lay near her head. "More."

After he placed a rag under her cheek, Teach complied. It seemed as if most of the brandy stained the fabric rather than find its way into her mouth, but what did manage to go in helped to mute the pain in her limbs. When she was finished, Teach removed the rag, and Anne laid her head down once more. She touched his face, wondering at the feel of him under her fingertips.

Teach watched her for a moment, the strain around his eyes noticeable. He took her hand in his and brought it to his lips. "I'll see that they pay. I swear to you they'll pay for this," he murmured, almost to himself. Desperate fury gleamed in his eyes.

Cara. Coyle. Alastair. Benjamin. Were they aboard Alastair's ship? Had they already met up with Teach's crew? Anne's lids were heavy and she found herself giving in to the weariness that once more overwhelmed her. It simply hurt too much to stay awake. Closing her eyes, Anne gave herself up to the dark.

She slept fitfully. When next she stirred, shadows filled the room. Teach stood at the windows lining the back of the wall, looking out at the darkening sky. The gentle rise and fall of the ship lulled her back to sleep before he turned around.

Unaware of the passage of time, she dozed and woke again, searching the cabin, and only going back to sleep once she knew he was there.

Fingers of light crept into the room when at last she roused, her head resting on her arms. It must have been early morning. A pink tint of sunlight streamed through the windows.

Teach sat by her side, reading Alastair's copy of Dampier's book. His hair was mussed, and his shirt was rumpled, as if he'd been there for quite some time. A brown leather baldric hung from one shoulder across his chest, holding three pistols. One of them was hers. In his left hand he toyed with her pocket watch.

Someone shouted overhead and Teach glared up at the ceiling.

"Alastair?" she asked.

Teach glanced at her, and closed the book. "No." He held a skin of water to her lips and Anne welcomed the cool rivulets that escaped and ran down her neck.

Something heavy dropped on deck, causing the windows to shudder.

Closing her eyes briefly, Anne tried to take a deep breath, but a hollow pain unfolded inside her chest. Beth. Beth was gone. Although she hadn't said the words aloud, somehow Teach had heard them.

"I'm sorry about Beth," Teach murmured. "If I could go

back and do things differently . . ." His voice trailed off.

Anne lowered her head and pressed her cheek to the back of Teach's hand. None of this was his fault. The blame lay solely with the Webbs. "Where's Cara?" she asked at length, still finding it difficult to speak.

Leaning forward, Teach stroked her hair back from her face. His eyes were grave as they met hers. "We're not on Alastair's sloop, Anne. We're on the *Triumph*."

Anne puzzled over his words. Something must have happened to Alastair's sloop. "Where are they?"

"You should rest—"

"Tell me," she croaked, wishing she sounded more firm.

"They're still in Nassau. The governor destroyed Alastair's ship, and they were forced to stay behind. We had to get you out of there."

Shaking, Anne attempted to sit up, but her back screamed in protest.

"Don't move. You'll rip the stitches. Alastair knows what he's doing. They'll try to find passage on another ship," Teach said, but she noticed the hint of uncertainty in his voice.

"I dreamed Alastair came to me. He promised me he'd get me out of there."

"That was no dream. Alastair did visit you. Together we planned your escape."

Anne pictured the governor and his wife as they'd stood over her, remembering Mrs. Webb's words. *That man is too powerful by far and needs to be taught a lesson.* Alastair and the others were in danger. Anne's hand shook as she reached out. Teach looked down, placing the gold pocket watch in her palm.

"No," she said, shaking her head. As much as she cherished the watch, it no longer brought her the comfort she sought.

Next he handed her Dampier's book, but she rejected that as well. "The pistol." She pointed at his chest.

With obvious reluctance, Teach handed her the Queen Anne's pistol.

"You won't need it aboard this ship," he said. Anne wanted to believe him, but there was an unfamiliar tension in the lines of his mouth, as if he was trying to convince himself.

"I'm growing to like it," she whispered, fingering the smooth handle where it lay wedged between the hammock and the desk.

"Well, perhaps you'll like this one more." Teach withdrew another Queen Anne's pistol from the baldric across his chest. It was the same shape and size as the one Alastair had given her, but it was not as ornate. The brown wood grain of the handle was polished to a sheen. "I thought to give it to you for your birthday, but it never hurts to be prepared."

Anne smiled slightly, her cheek tugging at the hammock beneath her. He was learning, and really beginning to understand her. Knowing that he had promised to protect her was a lovely sentiment—and she knew without question that he'd give his life to save hers— but with this simple gift, he'd finally recognized her desire to protect herself. "It's beautiful. Thank you." Anne closed her eyes briefly, her limbs still weak. "How long have I slept?"

"Two days."

Anne nodded, not surprised by his answer. She felt as if she could sleep for another two. "Isn't it too early for my birthday?"

"It's never too early to celebrate." And with those words, he removed the gold ring from the small leather pouch that hung around his neck and placed the gold band on her finger.

CHAPTER 24

Teach

"Aren't you going to eat with the men?" Kitts asked, blocking the way as Teach attempted to leave the galley. The ceiling in the hallway was low and cramped and Teach had to hunch his shoulders so as not to hit his head on the crossbeams. The *Triumph* had been at sea for over twenty-four hours.

Balancing the plate of bacon and biscuits in one hand, and the full bucket of water in the other, Teach didn't bother hiding his annoyance. "No. It's not common practice on a ship for the captain to eat with the crew. And I'm fairly certain it's the same on a naval ship."

"But aren't you going to address the men?"

"We all know why we're here." They were essentially privateers, tasked with searching for and apprehending a pirate. Teach couldn't help wondering what his father would say if he could see him now. With a disgruntled shake of his head, he

227

attempted to step past Kitts, but the sergeant remained where he was.

"Your men are insubordinate and don't listen to me."

"That's because when I'm not on deck, John is in charge. Not you."

An angry flush surfaced Kitts's cheeks. "But it's your duty as captain to gather the crew and discuss the nature of the voyage. It's up to you to make the rules of conduct perfectly clear."

"Then let me start with you. I wish to eat my meals in peace. Alone. In my cabin."

"Not four hours ago, you took in an entire pineapple. If you continue to eat like that, our rations won't last long," Kitts said, eyeing Teach's plate.

Teach gritted his teeth. How did the blasted man know that? In order to conceal Anne's presence on board, Teach had decided to stockpile some food to help her regain her strength. That way, he wouldn't have to traipse to and from the galley like he was now. "I've made sure there are enough rations to last us for several weeks. And since we aren't leaving the islands behind, if we need more supplies, we can always stop." He shouldered his way past the sergeant, drawing some satisfaction when Kitts bumped into the wall with a loud grunt, not caring that some of the water spilled down the front of the man's shirt.

Walking up the stairs, Teach was aware of Kitts following him, and Teach stopped mid-stride. "I'm sure you have more pressing duties than to follow me around the ship. I suggest you get to them." Not waiting for a response, Teach turned and continued up the stairs and down the hall before arriving at the captain's cabin, where he set the bucket down at his feet. Reaching for the handle he glanced one last time over his shoulder. Kitts watched him from the top of the stairs.

Teach opened the door and quickly entered, before shutting it behind him. Exhaling, he waited until he heard Kitts's footsteps continue up to the top deck. He wouldn't put it past the man to come barging in. Kitts was proving to be even more of a problem than Teach had first anticipated. But Teach's annoyance with Kitts faded when he was confronted with the sight of Anne's back.

Before she'd left the ship, Cara had dressed Anne in a pair of breeches and one of Teach's large shirts. She'd also cut the material, so that Anne's back was fully exposed. Angry red welts crisscrossed her skin, stretching from her neck down to her waist. Teach had stitched the largest gash shut, while Anne was still unconscious. It had been one of the hardest things he'd ever done. John had held a candle for him, while he'd pinched the skin together, trying to maintain his footing as the *Triumph* had sailed out to sea. As soon as she was well enough to move, he intended to switch out her clothing as well as the hammocks beneath her.

As if sensing his presence, Anne stirred, her crystal blue eyes blinking up at him.

"Hello," he said softly.

"Hello."

"Would you like something to drink?"

She nodded and Teach put the bucket of water down as well as the plate of food. Refilling the skin of water, he held it to her mouth.

"I have some food. Do you think you can eat it?" Teach asked, once she'd satisfied her thirst.

"Please," she said.

Bending forward, Teach picked the plate off the floor. "I was hoping your appetite would return." He lifted a piece of crispy bacon and held it up to her mouth.

"I can feed myself," Anne said, her voice tired.

"If I remember correctly, I was a model patient when you nursed me back to health."

Anne snorted. She opened her mouth to argue, but Teach popped the bacon between her lips, preventing further comment. Scowling, she began to chew.

"And now I'm asking you to do the same." He held her gaze intently. "I need you to do this, Anne. You have to get better, so that when this is over, we can go away somewhere. And start new."

Teach was relieved when the corners of Anne's mouth tilted up into the semblance of a smile. "All right," she said.

Despite the obvious pain in her voice, Teach could see a glimpse of the Anne that he knew. She needed time to work through what she'd endured, and as much as he wanted to help her, he didn't want to force her to talk about it. Anne would dictate the pace of her own healing.

Standing upright, he went and opened the small, circular window on the starboard wall, allowing the sea breeze to blow through the cabin, before returning to her side.

"When will you tell your men?" she asked.

About to hand her another piece of bacon, Teach paused. "About what?"

"That I'm here."

"We can't let the others know that you're here."

Anne's eyes widened. "But I thought you trusted them."

"I do, but Webb didn't trust *me*. He kept part of my crew back in Nassau, and replaced them with his soldiers."

Anne was silent for a moment. "And you're still supposed to go after Easton."

"Yes."

Closing her eyes, she drew in a shallow breath. It was clear when he'd said they were on the *Triumph*, she'd assumed they were escaping. "So I'm to remain in this cabin?"

Teach didn't respond, noting the hint of desperation in her voice. She detested being confined, and he detested telling her that that was exactly what she had to do.

After a moment of silence, Anne opened her eyes once more, pinning him to the spot. "What about Alastair and the others? Will we still be able to meet them as planned?"

"Benjamin is here. Apparently he did some work as a carpenter before, and we're lucky to have him on board. As for the others, Alastair said they'd find passage aboard another ship." Teach seriously hoped they'd been able to do just that.

"Who will go after Webb?"

"Right now, all I care about is that you get better and that we find Easton as quickly as possible. I have no plans beyond that." He didn't tell her that once his men were safe, he intended to have his revenge on the governor and his wife.

A knock at the door prevented further comment. Teach held his finger up to his lips and stood. Anne glared at him, but remained quiet. Opening the door a crack, Teach glanced out to see one of the soldiers standing there, his expression grim. "What is it?"

"Excuse me, captain, but there's a problem on deck."

"Surely John or Kitts can deal with—"

"They're the problem, sir."

With a curse, Teach shook his head. "I'll be right there," he said, shutting the door. He returned to Anne's side. She didn't move, she simply looked at him. "Anne, I'm so sorry . . ."

"Go," she said at last. "You know where I'll be."

With each step his irritation with Kitts rose. By the time he reached the upper deck, he was in a foul mood. There were things Teach wanted to discuss with Anne, especially now that she was regaining her strength. Teach could hear the powerful blows before he saw John and Kitts hammering each other with their fists. The scene tempted Teach to join in the fray to release some of his pent-up frustration.

John was an exceptional fighter and he clearly had the upper hand against Kitts. Teach thought about letting it play out, but he didn't wish to have Kitts's blood on his hands, no matter how much he irritated Teach.

The last time Teach had tried to stop John from fighting had been at his home in Bristol. John had discovered his betrothed, Mary, a maid in the Drummond household, in a compromising circumstance with the horse groom. For his efforts, Teach had received a fist to his stomach. Not wishing to relive that experience, Teach decided to haul Kitts to his feet instead of John. Kitts strained against his grasp like a charging bull, his face red as he kept swinging. Teach had to hand it to him, the man refused to give up.

John wiped a hand across his bloody lip, panting as he glared at Kitts. A mocking smile played at the corners of his mouth. Teach had a sneaking suspicion John had picked the fight with the soldier.

"Unless you wish to spend tomorrow scrubbing decks, I suggest you both stand down."

"He started it," Kitts yelled, jerking out of Teach's grasp.

"I don't care who started it. It ends now. And there will be no more fighting amongst the crew, is that understood?"

Kitts stared at him sullenly. Even John appeared a bit surprised that Teach included him in his reprimand, but Teach didn't care. He had enough concerns without worrying about his crew tearing one another apart one by one.

"We need to save our energy for when we face Easton. And face him we will. Tomorrow we sail for the cove where Webb says he was last seen." Teach eyed his men, striding up and down their ranks. "If he isn't there, we'll move on to the next one, and the next, until we find the bounder and take him back to Webb. Once we're back in Nassau, you can do what you like. But as long as you're on my ship, you'll do as I say. Is that understood?"

A few of the men grumbled their acquiescence. Teach realized that perhaps Kitts had been right. He should have addressed his men earlier, but he'd been so concerned with Anne that he hadn't given his crew much thought. He would never regret the time he'd spent with her, but he recognized it had cost him in regard to his men. If he wanted them to work as one against Easton, he needed to devote some time to them.

"What we've set out to do won't be easy. We've all heard accounts of Easton's cruelty and cunning. He likes to torture his victims. Once we find him, we'll have to strike fast. We can't let him get the upper hand. And when we emerge victorious, there will be a reward."

Teach ignored the twinge of guilt he felt, knowing that the governor had no intention of paying these men. Looking at their dirty and scarred faces, he knew they hadn't come from a privileged background like he had. Many of these men had grown up on the streets of Bristol, fighting for their very survival. Teach knew a portion of them well and trusted them with his life, but it was time to get to know the others.

"Whatever spoils we discover, we will give the governor one half of the net gains. The rest will be split equally. From the bosun to the cooper, all the way up to me. Each man will get his fair share. But we have to work together. And we have to find Easton."

Kitts's outrage was instantaneous. "You can't promise that! Whatever plunder Easton has goes directly to Webb."

"You can give your portion to the governor, then. I plan to pay these men for their time."

"The governor won't allow it!"

"Who's going to tell him?" Teach asked, motioning to the outraged crew surrounding them. "It might be uncomfortable for you in Nassau if these men know you prevented them from collecting their coin."

With a surly look, Kitts's shoulders slumped. "The governor will hear about this."

"If you manage to live that long," Teach said.

CHAPTER 25

Anne

The skin on Anne's back throbbed with every heartbeat, but the pain wasn't as intense as it had been. Teach had broken her out of the fort four days ago, but she was grateful she'd slept for most of that time. He'd checked to make sure her stitches were still intact. Some places on her back were so painful, she'd shuddered where he'd touched her.

She looked out the windows of the *Triumph* as the ship rose and fell in rhythmic motion, glad that her position on the table afforded her a decent view. She lay on her stomach with her chin resting on her hands. If she closed her eyes, she could almost imagine she was flying.

As much as she disliked being on a ship again, she had to admit it was rather beautiful. The sapphire sea was topped with white-tipped waves, colliding and breaking into wisps of spray. The sky was dotted with feathery clouds, the afternoon sun low on the horizon. It was times like these when she could understand why Teach had fallen in love with the sea.

A soft knock at the door interrupted Anne's reverie and she turned to see John poke his head in, a sheepish expression on his face. He sported a black eye and a swollen lip. She motioned for him to enter. Teach had made it very clear that she needed to remain quiet. If any of the crew discovered her presence on the ship, it would prove disastrous.

That was probably why Teach had only come to check on her once during the night, when half of the men were asleep. The other half were on deck, keeping watch for any sign of Easton. They'd anchored in the cay where the pirate was last spotted, but of course there had been no sign of him or his ship.

"It's good to see you awake, Miss Anne," John said as he took a seat on the chair at her side. His movements were guarded, as if he feared making too much noise.

Anne smiled at John, noting how he kept his eyes strictly trained on her face. She knew how unconventional her attire was, but she had to admit, she was grateful she wasn't trapped by layers of petticoats and skirts. Not to mention the comfort the breeches provided. During the day, the cabin was hot and stuffy, despite the open window. Anne pictured Reva racing out the back door of the Fox in her breeches and Cara's reaction. If only Cara could see Anne now. "Did Teach ask you to keep me company?"

John flushed. "Aye."

She waited for him to say something else, but he simply sat

beside her, an awkward silence filling the space between them as he played with a hole in the knee of his breeches. Only the sound of the waves against the hull disturbed the quiet. Anne could imagine how uncomfortable it must be for him to see her like this. The first few times she'd seen the scars on Benjamin's arms, she hadn't known where to look either.

"What happened to you?" she asked at length, motioning to his bruised face. She had enough silence when she was alone, with nothing but her thoughts for company.

John grinned slightly, a glint in his eyes. "I had a bit of sport with Kitts."

"Who's Kitts?" she asked, finding herself returning his smile. He reminded her of an unruly boy, caught doing something wrong, but unrepentant about it.

"An arrogant arse."

Anne couldn't stop her bark of laughter. Both she and John froze, looking over at the door to determine if anyone had heard her. After a moment, their eyes met and the two of them dissolved into muffled laughter, each of them shushing the other one. Anne tried to remain still, aware of the pain her movements caused. Tears rolled down her cheeks, and she wasn't sure if it was because of the soreness of her back or John's expression.

Eventually, they quieted down.

"I'm sorry, Miss Anne. I shouldn't have said that in front of you."

With her chin resting on her hands once again, she shook

her head. "There's no need to apologize. I appreciate your honesty. But now I'm curious to meet this Kitts for myself."

"Oh no. You don't want to do that. He's a pain in the—" John stopped himself just in time. "He's not someone you can be around for long. I think Teach is ready to have him committed to the sea."

"Is he so terrible?"

John nodded. "Aye. Webb sent him to keep an eye on Teach, and the bounder is doing a good job of it. That's why Teach can't spend as much time with you, now that he knows you're on the mend. He can't risk anyone finding out about you."

"Surely Kitts isn't that severe."

"Kitts makes a clergy look like a sinner. I've never seen anyone so intent on following the letter of the law."

"And you say he's giving Teach trouble?"

"Aye. Every time Teach turns around, Kitts is there to remind him of his duty. He's a bit like Richard Drummond in that regard. Just not as old."

"I thought he would be free of that once he left his father's house."

John shook his head. "I'm afraid there will always be a small part of Teach who longs for his father's approval. Kitts is obedient, something Teach will never be."

Anne raised an eyebrow at him. "It sounds like Kitts truly is an arse. If that's the case, perhaps he and Teach have more in common than they realize."

It was John's turn to raise a brow at her. "For shame, Miss Anne. I'll pretend I didn't hear that." She rolled her eyes and he winked at her. "Teach won't let me come back if he knows I've been a bad influence."

"I don't care what Teach says. He might be in charge of this ship, but he's not in charge of me. And I'll be hurt if you don't come back to visit. You're saving me from boredom, a most terrible fate."

John's smile faded. "Actually, it was Teach who did that. He came to us while we were still in the fort. Asked me to cause a distraction. That's when he got you away from Webb. Broke you clean out of jail. So you see, he'll never be submissive like Kitts." He glanced around the cabin. "I know you don't like being shut up in here, but this was Teach's only option."

Anne cleared her throat. "I know. But maybe I don't have to stay here the entire time. Perhaps I could come out at night. Dressed like this, nobody would suspect I'm a girl." Even as she said the words, Anne realized how ridiculous they sounded. By now the entire crew must recognize everyone on board. She would certainly stand out, but she'd never been one to sit idly by and wait for things to happen. And she didn't suppose Teach would agree to leave her on one of the islands either. Too much could go wrong.

"If it was just the men from the *Deliverance*, Teach might agree to it. He blames himself that this whole thing happened. He didn't want to lead the mutiny, but if he hadn't intervened, the lot of us would find ourselves in Davy Jones's Locker."

"I don't blame Teach. He saved my life."

John looked relieved. "It's Kitts's fault you have to stay in here. With Webb's men on board, we don't know exactly who we can trust."

"I'm beginning to dislike Kitts as well," Anne muttered.

"I could deep-six him if you like."

She had no doubt that John would use any opportunity to throw Kitts overboard. "I don't think Teach would allow you to do that."

"He'd probably like to do it himself. He's worried sick that Kitts and the others will find out about you."

Anne couldn't imagine the stress Teach was under. "You're a good friend, John. Teach is lucky to have you."

John grinned again. "He tells me that all the time. But I'm the lucky one. He gave me a chance when nobody else would. It's because of him that I'm able to send money home to my family."

"My mother always said your friend is your mirror."

Red suffused John's cheeks. "That's sounds rather nice. I like it more than what my ma used to say to me."

"What was that?"

"She said there can be no friendship between a wolf and a goat. Back home, I used to run with a rough crowd. That changed when I met Teach."

"Are you saying you've always been the goat?" Anne asked.

John sat up straight. "Of course not. I'm the good-looking one, so naturally, I've always been the wolf."

Anne smiled.

For a while, they sat in companionable silence. How Anne wished things were different. If only they'd been able to carry out their plans and leave on Alastair's ship. They could have rendez-voused by now with Cara and the others. Anne sincerely hoped she could introduce John to Cara in the not so distant future. She could imagine the two of them getting on quite well.

But Cara and Coyle were stuck back in Nassau. With Webb. Beth was dead because of Webb's wife. And because of the gov-ernor, Teach was now in pursuit of a pirate. How Anne hated the governor and his wife. She longed for the day they'd be free of the Webbs' influence.

"What do you think will happen when we catch Easton?" Anne asked.

"I don't know. Take him back to Nassau, I suppose, just like Webb wants us to. The rest of the men from the *Deliverance* are still locked up."

Although he hadn't said much to Anne, she knew it weighed heavily on Teach. "And then?"

John met Anne's eyes, his expression somber. They both knew the *Deliverance* itself wouldn't be a viable escape for them when they returned to Nassau. It required far too many repairs. "Let's worry about catching ourselves a pirate first. The rest will come to us as we go along."

"Webb is a powerful man. Look how many lives he's ruined. And will continue to ruin. Someone has to stop him."

"What are you thinking of doing?" John asked, his voice wary.

"Nothing," Anne said as she picked up the pistol by her side.

"I don't believe you."

"John, would you do me a favor?"

"That depends what it is."

A smile lifted the corner of her mouth. He sounded so suspicious. "Can you please bring some extra powder and balls so I can practice loading my pistols?"

His answer was swift. "Teach wouldn't like it."

"Again, Teach is not in charge of me. I'm asking you as *my* friend."

"Wolf," John muttered under his breath.

"I know you don't want me to refer to you as a goat. I simply wish to be prepared."

John raised an eyebrow at her. "Prepared for what?"

How could Anne make John understand the fear and vulnerability she felt simply because of the color of her skin and because of her gender? "I want to protect myself."

"By learning how to shoot?"

"Not just shoot. I already know how to do that. I want to be able to shoot *first*."

"And you wish to shoot Webb, is that right? You're mad."

Anne's smiled. "To begin something without fear is the same as victory."

"That may be, but my ma always said to retreat before an inevitable defeat is not cowardice."

"I thought you didn't like her advice."

"I didn't always. But I do love her something fierce. I think Marian would like you," John said, his expression softening.

"Is that her name?"

"Aye."

"It's lovely. And I'm sure I'd like her. She raised a fine son. One who doesn't turn from his friends when they're in need."

John whistled under his breath. "You're a cold one, Anne Barrett. I'll have to warn Teach about you."

"So you'll do it? You'll bring me the powder and balls?"

"Wait here." And with that, John stood and exited the room.

CHAPTER 26

Teach

The dappled gray skies signaled an approaching gale. The wind buffeted his hair and shirt, and Teach braced himself, the spray from the ocean dampening his face and cheeks. He had a feel for the sea and its moods and he could tell that the approaching storm was a big one, bigger than some of his men had most likely seen.

"Reef the sails," Teach called out.

Kitts was by Teach's side in an instant. "Sir, isn't it too soon? We need to reach the next cay before the storm hits. Perhaps we should wait."

By now, Teach was used to Kitts questioning his every move, but it still grated on his nerves. "If we don't reef now, it will be too late." A significant gust could easily capsize the ship, especially if it heeled over from the wind.

"But, sir," Kitts continued, walking with Teach as he strode across the slick deck. "The ship will be more protected in the cay—"

Teach rounded on Kitts, his muscles clenched. "A storm is even more dangerous in shallow waters. Waves become steeper and are more likely to break. We have a better chance by riding it out where we are. Now stop questioning me and do as you're told."

Kitts's nostrils flared and his eyes narrowed. "Aye, Captain," he snapped.

"Drop the anchor and heave to!" Teach shouted, continuing across the deck as the crew of the *Triumph* raced to carry out his orders. It was imperative that they turn, with the helm locked into position and the jib backwinded, so the ship could slowly jog along without turning broadside to the waves.

Anne. He needed to warn her. He hadn't spent nearly as much time with her as he'd wanted, and she would provide him with a little peace before the storm.

Bracing himself against the railing, Teach descended the stairs, bumping into the wall as the ship rose on a large swell. Opening the door to the captain's cabin, he stopped, experiencing a sharp pang at the sight before him. John and Anne stood at the window looking out at the rolling waves. John's arm was around Anne's waist, lending her support. She'd changed into another one of Teach's shirts. The collar was large, exposing one of Anne's slender shoulders, but the back hadn't been removed. Neither of them had heard his approach.

Teach shut the door with a little more force than necessary.

Anne jumped. John's head whipped around. "It's getting bad out there," John said. "We're in for a rough night."

"You shouldn't be up. Do you want to rip the stitches?" Teach asked Anne. He ignored John, not liking the poisonous resentment he felt toward his friend at the moment. It wasn't as if John had strong feelings for Anne. Unlike Coyle.

Anne's mouth tightened. "My stitches are fine."

It had been five days since Teach first sewed Anne up. By now her wounds had scabbed over. It was a good sign that she was mobile, but it wouldn't do to rush her healing. It would be at least another week before the stitches could be removed.

He knew she hated being stuck in the cabin, but they had no other choice. Giving the room a quick sweep, he noticed that the hammock had been removed from the table. "That is the only thing that will keep you safe." He grabbed the hammock and proceeded to hang it near the armoire in the room.

"I'm aware of that, but I wanted to take a look before it got too bad out there."

"John's needed on deck. Now."

The hint of a smile touched John's lips. "Aye, Captain." Turning to Anne, he gave her arm a squeeze. "I'll be back later."

"No you won't."

Both Anne and John raised a brow at Teach. Feeling like a fool, he returned their gazes. It had been Teach's idea to have John keep Anne company while Teach was on deck. Technically, Teach didn't have to perform any manual duties, but he'd found it the best way to gain his men's trust. He wouldn't ask them to do anything that he himself wasn't prepared to do.

This was the first time that Teach felt torn between the two things he loved most. If he devoted his time to captaining the ship, he neglected Anne. But if he devoted all his time to Anne, he neglected the ship and her crew. He felt much like the *Triumph* as it prepared to meet the coming storm: unsure of which way to go as the two greatest things in his life warred with each other.

"I'll see you later, John," Anne said pointedly.

John left, slanting a grin at Teach before closing the door.

"What was that about?" Anne asked, gripping the table to keep her balance.

"It's time for him to return to his duties. The entire crew will have to work through the night if we hope to weather this storm."

"Did you have to be so short with him?"

Teach shrugged, reaching up to ease the cramp of tension at the back of his neck. "I wanted to make sure you were all right."

Anne held his gaze as she moved toward him. Placing a hand on his chest, she pulled his head down for a kiss. He dropped his hands to her waist, worried he'd undo the very stitches he'd made a fool of himself to keep intact. He had to remind himself that she was still injured, even though she wasn't making it easy for him.

"There's no reason for you to be jealous," Anne whispered in between kisses.

"I'm not."

He felt Anne smile against his lips. "Good. And there's no reason for you to be worried about my stitches. I'll be careful."

The ship listed beneath their feet, pushing them closer together. This was not being careful. The storm. The crew. It was time for Teach to leave. Drawing back, he motioned to the hammock swinging behind her. With a sigh, Anne let him clasp her beneath the knees. She kept her back straight as he lifted and then lowered her into the hammock. The sides came up and instantly cocooned her within. Leaning over, he gave her another kiss on the lips. Every touch between them was like a stamp on his soul.

"Stay here."

Anne shook her head at him. "I've been on a ship before, remember? And we weathered many a storm."

Teach debated telling her about the extent of the approaching squall. He didn't want to worry her needlessly, but she should be prepared. "Stay here unless I come for you."

Some of his concern must have shown on his face, because her brows furrowed. "It's bad, isn't it?"

"We'll get through it."

"Be careful."

"Always."

By four bells, the men of the *Triumph* were soaking wet and exhausted. All hands were on deck and had been for the past hour. There was no sign of the storm lessening. Rain lashed at them like needles, and the drop in temperature caused their limbs to shake and their teeth to chatter.

The bare poles overhead swayed, their canvas tightly rolled to protect the sails from the wind. The occasional flash of lightning lit up the night sky, and the thunder in the distance bellowed its response.

"Teach!" Bent over at the waist and with his stance wide, John attempted to approach Teach, but the wind and lurching deck beneath his feet made it difficult. "We saw a light in the distance."

Teach wiped the rain from his eyes. "It could have been lightning."

"It was steady."

Before Teach could answer, a wave rolled over the deck, sweeping his feet away. The deck slammed upward, smashing into his back. A pained grunt escaped his lungs, but he couldn't hear it over the roar of the water in his ears.

"John!" he shouted, flailing for something, anything. But the sea was the master, dragging its wayward servant into its eternal prison.

One boot smashed into the railing, sending a bolt of pain clear up to his hip. It hurt like the devil's hottest poker, but he scrabbled for a handhold. Suddenly he found it, a bit of wood. One hand stable, then the other.

"Teach!"

The voice came from Teach's left, and he turned toward it, still blinded by the salty spray.

John gave a watery cough, and shouted for his friend once more.

Releasing his grip on the railing, Teach lunged toward the sound. For a moment, his surroundings receded, his entire attention focused on John. As Teach neared, the whites of John's eyes were all Teach could see as John tried to find some purchase on the deck. The waves bashed relentlessly onto the sides of the *Triumph*. If any other men noticed or attempted to help, Teach couldn't tell. Perhaps they were battling to save their own lives.

Just when it appeared that John would be swept overboard, Teach grabbed his friend by the arm, his fingers digging desperately into John's flesh. Teach was quickly followed by more members of the crew. They heaved and pulled John and Teach to the center of the ship. With a mighty tug, the two collapsed onto the deck, struggling to regain their breath, wet hair hanging in their eyes.

"I guess this means you're no longer mad at me," John yelled at length, his voice carrying over the strength of the wind.

Teach gave a shout of laughter. "No, John. I'm not mad at you."

Drawing a deep breath, John smiled. "Good. Because you're a fool if you think she'd care for anyone the same way she cares for you."

Getting to his knees, Teach grimaced as he held out a hand to John. Teach was a fool. But when it came to Anne, he couldn't seem to control his reactions.

They both struggled to their feet.

"Come. I think you deserve a break."

John shook his head. "No. I saw a light."

If it had been anyone else, Teach would have questioned their eyesight. But John was an experienced sailor and wouldn't make such claims if he wasn't sure. "You think it was Easton," Teach said.

"Aye, I do."

A part of Teach wanted to find Easton immediately. The sooner they found the pirate, the sooner they could return to Nassau and free the others. But another part of him dreaded the upcoming confrontation. If the rumors about the pirate were true, Teach feared that not all of his men would survive the encounter.

CHAPTER 27

Anne

Anne stood at the windows, steadying herself against the pitching of the ship as she watched the endless procession of waves threatening to capsize the *Triumph*. It was just before dawn, and the sky outside was gray. The rain came down in horizontal sheets, and the wind screamed, drowning out any sound of the men's shouts on deck. She was actually grateful to be in the shelter of the cabin, and hoped that the rest of the crew would be protected against the storm. It appeared to be abating. *Somewhat.* Of course, it hadn't completely passed.

The hull creaked ominously and Anne moved once again toward the safety of the hammock. Wondering what time it was, she reached for the watch in her pocket, but a sudden shift in the floor sent her sprawling. Her arms flew out as she tried to catch herself, popping a few of the stitches in her back. The watch sailed across the room, and landed near the armoire in the corner.

Grimacing against the pain, Anne went to retrieve her timepiece. She had just picked it up and was checking the glass when the door to the cabin began to open. Conditioned to duck out of sight, she automatically crouched down, praying it was Teach. But as the door swung shut, any words she might have uttered died on her lips when she saw that it wasn't Teach. Or John or even Benjamin.

The man before her was a stranger. He was sopping wet and had a large dirk slung across his back, sheathed in a baldric. His hair was gathered in a queue at the nape of his neck. It was too dim in the cabin for her to make out the exact color. It could have been dark brown or perhaps even black. She couldn't see his face, but he was broad shouldered and stout, much like John.

Anne's breath caught in her throat and she went still and cold. Her eyes found her revolvers, tucked neatly into the baldric lying beside the solitary chair in the room. *Blast!* There was no way for her to retrieve them without him noticing. She wasn't sure she even wanted to retrieve them.

All she knew was that whoever this person was, he wasn't supposed to be here. Apprehensive, she watched and waited as he looked from side to side before he moved toward the desk, his gait unsteady with the tossing of the ship.

Feeling a trickle down her back, Anne wasn't sure if it was blood or sweat. What would happen if he saw her? Deciding she didn't want to find out, she searched desperately for something to hide behind, but aside from the armoire and the desk, the only other object in the room was a long crate behind the door. Anne crept toward the crate. It slid back and forth, back and forth, as the *Triumph* listed with every wave.

He searched through every drawer, tossing maps and scattering papers across the floor. As far as Anne knew, there was nothing of value on board.

When he was done at the desk, he turned to the armoire, pushing the hammock out of the way before continuing his search.

Anne crouched low behind the crate, grateful for the gloom of the cabin and the howling of the wind. The storm outside cloaked her in darkness. But the storm seemed the exact reason he was here. While the rest of the men were up on deck, trying to prevent the ship from sinking, he was free to search the room. *But for what, exactly?*

Cursing, he spun, taking in the rest of the furniture. His eyes fell on the glint of the pistols. Anne tensed in anticipation. Her small movement must have caught his attention, as ever so slightly, he turned his head and looked directly at her. Their gazes locked and the two froze, glued to each other's stares. She didn't know if he could tell that she was female. Her hair was caught back in a braid and she still wore breeches and Teach's shirt. Nonetheless, the man's jaw dropped and he looked as startled as she felt.

Something in his posture announced his intentions a second

before he moved. Anne lunged for the pistols, the motion of the ship launching her just as he slammed into the wall.

Clutching the weapon with two hands, she pointed it at him. A poisonous alarm crept through her, and her finger touched the trigger. *What would he have done if he'd reached the weapons first?*

She'd never find out. With one last look in her direction and a chilling smile, he rushed toward the door, slamming it shut behind him.

Anne tried to catch her breath. Shaking, she pulled herself up by the desk and made her way to the hammock, clambering into it, and lying with her feet toward the door. She'd forgotten all about her stitches and cringed as her bloody back contacted the canvas.

With her eyes on the door, Anne aimed her pistol at the lock, ready for the next time the stranger burst into the cabin. She wasn't about to be surprised again.

CHAPTER 28

Teach

Weary, sore, and concerned, Teach stood inside the captain's cabin with his back against the door, surveying the chaos before him. The hopeful rays of the early morning sun broke through the last lingering clouds, tinting the windows with bright patches of light. It was a sharp contrast to the storm from the previous night. Maps and papers littered the floor.

In the midst of it all, Anne slept peacefully in the hammock, with her head tilted to the side. Her long lashes created shadows on her cheeks, and her lips were relaxed in sleep. That same mouth could curve up in the most beautiful smile, or a thin scowl when she was upset or angry.

The sight of her was knee-weakening, and sometimes it frightened Teach how much he cared for her.

He approached the hammock, wanting to reassure himself that she was all right. Reaching out to brush a stray hair off her face, he wasn't prepared for the pistol pointed at his head. Startled, his eyes held hers, and she cursed beneath her breath.

"I'm beginning to think you enjoy pointing that thing at me," he muttered, his pulse driving in constant spurts.

After a brief hesitation, Anne lowered the weapon. "I wouldn't point it at you if you didn't keep sneaking up on me."

"I wasn't sneaking up on you."

She raised an eyebrow at him. "Then what, exactly, were you doing?" she whispered, her voice fierce.

"Coming to see if you were all right. What happened here?"

"Someone came looking for something."

Teach scowled. "Who was it?"

"Someone I didn't recognize. He was built like John, but his hair was dark brown or black."

"Most of the men on the ship are built like John. That's why they're sailors." His voice came out sharper than he'd intended. They spoke in hushed voices, not wanting to draw any attention, but Teach couldn't hide his unease. Her description of the man only narrowed his hunt down to half the crew.

Anne grimaced as she shifted slightly in the hammock. "I tried to look for any marks or scars that would help to distinguish him, but it was too dark."

"Did he see you?"

"Of course he saw me."

Damnation! Teach's instantaneous response was to find whoever had entered the cabin and remove his head from his body. "Did he hurt you?" he asked, his eyes running down the length of her. She was still dressed in breeches and one of his shirts, and aside from a thin scar on her shin, she showed no outward signs of abuse.

Except for her back.

"No. I think he was more surprised than anything." Anne's brow furrowed. "I just can't imagine what he was looking for. When he saw the pistols, he almost took them, but I don't believe that's why he came."

Teach could guess why the man had come in here. When Teach had spent the first few days of their voyage locked in the cabin, no doubt his crew had thought he was hiding something valuable. He was, but not quite what the men imagined. He didn't think it had been anyone from the crew of the *Deliverance*. Those men trusted him and he had no reason to suspect any of them would be so bold as to break into the captain's cabin. They'd been through too much together.

It was Kitts and his men Teach didn't trust.

"Do you think he'll tell anyone about me?"

"A lot depends on if he could tell if you were a woman or not. If he didn't see you clearly, he might wonder who you were and what you were doing in here. In which case, he probably will come back, because he'll believe I am indeed hiding something in my cabin."

"Which you are."

"Aye, which I am."

"And if he *did* notice that I'm female?"

"He might tell the others. *And* he might come back." In which case, Teach would most definitely remove the man's head from his body. He hated feeling out of control, especially when it came to Anne's safety. There were too many unknowns in this entire situation. "It could be that Kitts sent one of his men to search my cabin. And if Kitts finds out you're here, when we get back to Nassau, he won't let you leave this ship without an escort."

"Then I'll have to leave the ship before we return to Nassau."

"First let's concentrate on finding Easton. We can worry about the rest later."

"You men are very narrow minded. That's exactly what John said to me when I asked him about Webb."

"What about Webb?"

Anne clenched the pistol from Teach, her knuckles turning white. "He cannot be allowed to continue to destroy people's lives. Someone has to stop him."

"He's the bloody governor of Nassau. How exactly do you expect someone to stop him?"

"I haven't gotten that far."

"All right. Well, while you're planning his downfall, I'll make sure you're not left alone. Between John, Benjamin, and myself, we should be able keep you company." He'd expected

Anne to be pleased, but from the look on her face, it was clear that she wasn't. "What's wrong?"

"Nothing," she said.

Only then did Teach notice that Anne still lay unmoving in the hammock. "Would you like to sit up?"

"No. I'm fine."

She was not fine. She'd barely moved since he'd entered the room. Even before the storm had hit, she'd stood at the window with John. There was no storm now.

"Would you like me to open the window?" Teach asked, watching her closely.

"I can manage. I'm sure you're busy," she said.

"Remember when I asked you to be truthful with me?" he asked. Anne nodded, not quite meeting his eyes. "I'm asking you now to tell me what's wrong."

"It's nothing I can't take care of," she said, glaring at him.

"Is it your stitches? Because if it is—"

"Go away."

"—I need to take a look at them."

She squirmed beneath his gaze, but remained silent. Frustrated, Teach ran a hand over his face. "Do you want them to become infected? If they do, you'll have the devil of a time going after Webb." Teach had cleaned the wounds before he'd sewn her up, but it wouldn't take much for infection to set in.

A knock at the door interrupted them. Teach opened

the door a crack. John looked back at him, his expression earnest.

"May I have a word, captain?"

Teach stood back, shutting the door once John had entered.

"How are ye? Did ye weather the storm?" John asked, glancing at Anne.

She gave him a small smile. "Yes, thank you. Was it terribly difficult on deck?"

"No, nothing that I couldn't han—"

"What do you want?" Teach snapped.

John's eyes widened. "I thought you weren't mad at me?"

"Why would he be mad at you?" Anne asked.

For the love . . . "I'm not mad. I simply want to know what you wish to discuss. It had to be important, otherwise you wouldn't have left your position on deck," Teach said pointedly.

"The men have returned to their watches. First watch is on duty while the rest sleep."

"Good. You should go and rest as well," Teach said dismissively. Since he'd just spent the past five hours on deck, he could bloody well spend the next half hour with Anne, making sure she was all right. "You pulled your stitches." He didn't know for sure, but he had a sneaking suspicion that was precisely what Anne had done. Her next words confirmed it.

"Not on purpose."

"They'll have to be sewn back up."

Anne shook her head, her eyes wide. "No."

"Why not?" Teach demanded. "I did it once before."

"Yes, but I wasn't awake while you did it."

Teach was astounded. She had endured a flogging. How could she be afraid of some stitches? "I'll be careful."

"If you come after me with a needle, I will shoot you. Just so you're aware," Anne said, tightening her grip on the pistol. As much as he liked the fact that she now favored the weapon he'd given her, he should have removed it from her grasp.

"I have a fine hand. I can sew her up," John volunteered.

Teach shot John a dark look. "Then *I'll* shoot *you*."

"This is getting us nowhere. You've been awake for most of the night. You need rest as much as the others," Anne said.

"In case you've forgotten, you're in my hammock."

Anne pursed her lips.

"Let me check your stitches. It's too soon for them to come out, Anne. You have to be reasonable."

The two of them stared at each other, neither one willing to back down. Looking between them, John shifted his weight uncomfortably. "He's right, Anne. He should at least check them."

Anne rolled her eyes. "Fine," she muttered at length.

Clearly pleased that she'd listened to him, John turned to leave.

"Bring me a bottle of brandy before you go up on deck," Teach said.

John nodded and shut the door behind him.

Folding her arms across her chest, Anne speared him with a glare. "If you think I'm going to let you get drunk and then try to stitch me up, you're mad."

"The brandy's not for me, Anne. It's for you."

CHAPTER 29

Anne

The brandy left a trail of warmth in its wake. After two full cups, Anne felt as if she was glowing from the inside out.

"Lie down," Teach said, indicating the desk.

"I'd rather sit."

He muttered something under his breath, but Anne couldn't hear precisely what it was. She sat on the chair while Teach pried the shirt away from her back. The blood had dried, sticking the fabric to her skin.

"How bad is it?" she asked, holding her breath.

"I'm going to have to cut the shirt a bit."

Not quite an answer. Anne laughed nervously. "You're going to run out of them if we continue like this."

"I won't have to cut much. The lower stitches are fine."

"How many will you have to replace?" she asked, her stomach already churning.

There was no response. Perhaps it was better that way. Anne glanced over her shoulder at Teach, noting the tense lines around his eyes and lips. He didn't enjoy doing this any more than she wanted it to be done. But he was right. The last thing she needed was for her back to become infected. This was all the Webbs' fault. How many slaves had they whipped who had later died from their injuries? She could feel her hatred of the governor and his wife increase with every minute.

Anne stiffened when Teach sliced through the material with his knife. This time she didn't bother pouring the brown liquid into the cup, but took a large swig straight from the bottle instead.

"Do you want me to warn you when I—"

"No. Just . . . no." She knew she was being ridiculous, but she couldn't help herself. When she was younger, she'd had stitches twice and it had been a painful experience, leaving her physically ill from anxiety afterward. And, with the recent crossing on the *Providence*, stitches signified death. It was one thing to sew someone else up, but to be on the receiving end of the procedure . . . This was the one fear Anne couldn't seem to conquer.

"I'll need that," Teach said, taking the brandy out of her hands. Before she knew what he was about to do, he poured the alcohol over the wound. Anne shot up out of the chair and rounded on him, her back scorched beneath the fire of the brandy. She felt the watery sting of tears in her eyes. "The devil take you," she hissed, looking around for her new favorite pistol. It was lying on the hammock, but Teach swept it into his hand and tucked it into his waistband before she could take it.

"I'm sorry, but you told me not to warn you."

"Are you daft? I didn't want you to warn me about the *needle*," she said, looking around for her other weapon.

"I'm sorry. I misunderstood." And from the look on his face, she could see he truly was repentant. His hands shook slightly and he took a gulp from the bottle before handing it back to her. Leaning forward, he gave her a swift kiss and she tasted the fruity flavor of the brandy on his lips. "Forgive me."

With a shuddering breath, she nodded and sat down, her back tensed, deciding another swig couldn't hurt. "Do you see this scar?" Anne asked after she swallowed. She lifted her left leg and pointed to the thin white line on her shin.

"Aye."

"I had to have stitches—" She jerked away as the needle punctured her skin.

"Be still. I don't want to hurt you."

"Then don't—"

"Finish your story."

She turned her head slightly, not trusting herself to move for fear of bumping the needle. "Has anyone ever told you, you sound just like your father? So commanding," she muttered, tilting the bottle to her lips. Teach waited until she was still before he moved again.

For a second, Anne's vision clouded as he tugged on the thread. Feeling slightly light-headed, Anne was sure she was going to be sick.

"Would it help to know that I understand what you're going through?" Teach asked.

Once again, the needle pierced her skin. One stitch complete. She was afraid to ask how many more were needed. "You do?" *Focus on his voice. Focus on his voice.*

"Aye, I do. The captain of the *Deliverance* had me flogged when I disobeyed a direct order."

"Why didn't you tell me?"

"It's healed."

"But there are scars," Anne said.

"Wounds always turn into scars, but that means the pain is over."

"No, that just means the wound has closed. Every time you see the scar, you'll be reminded of the pain."

"If you choose to be. But if you're able to move on, you're stronger for it."

Anne bit her lip and Teach worked quietly. His breath, slightly faster than normal, fanned the nape of her neck. Sparks of awareness chased along her nerves as his fingertips brushed lightly against her skin. Anne stared straight ahead, her heart lurching in an unsteady rhythm. She closed her eyes against a wave of dizziness that had nothing to do with her fear of needles. "May I see them?"

His hands stilled. "My scars?"

"Yes."

She could practically hear his indecision. She suspected his injuries had been worse than he let on.

"All right," he said at length. "Once I'm done with you."

By the time Teach finished, Anne was much more relaxed. The alcohol had worked its way into her head like warm clouds, diluting the pain, but also dissolving any self-consciousness.

Anne stood and turned, meeting Teach's eyes. She raised the bottle to take another drink, but Teach quirked a brow at her.

"Don't you think you've had enough?"

Unperturbed, she took a sip. Wiping her mouth with the back of her hand, she motioned for him to turn around. "Show me."

Teach's color heightened as he stared at her, his green eyes darkening. "I should go up on deck."

"You said you'd show me your scars."

Teach was motionless as a flush burned across his cheeks. With unsteady hands, he reached for the bottom of his shirt and pulled it over his head.

His broad bronzed shoulders sloped down, flowing into the powerful lines of his arms, and Anne could feel the heat of his skin. Somehow she managed to drag her mesmerized gaze away from his chest. He didn't turn.

Anne paced around him slowly, her head buzzing with more

than the alcohol. When she saw his back, she realized why he'd been so hesitant to show her.

He claimed he no longer felt the pain, but she certainly did. Tears slipped from beneath her lashes, even as she tried to blink them away. Her fingers traced the thick, uneven scars crisscrossing his back. Teach shivered beneath her touch.

She didn't know what was worse: having suffered under the sting of the whip herself, or knowing that Teach had suffered as well, and she'd been helpless to do anything about it. Whoever had sewn him up had done a terrible job. There were jagged edges of skin that would never lie flat or smooth again. She covered a scar tenderly with her palm. The gold band on her finger winked up at her and she realized that she'd never answered him. "Yes," she whispered.

Teach turned. "Yes, what?" he asked, his voice low.

"Yes, I'll marry you," she murmured, tilting her head back to meet his eyes.

Teach's lips lifted at the corners. His hands skimmed down her sides, careful to avoid the wounds on her back. Taking the bottle from her, he placed it on the chair before returning his palms to her waist. He used his grip to bring her closer until she listed against him, his mouth briefly touching hers. Anne responded to the tender kiss before she turned her head and leaned her cheek against his chest. For several moments they simply held each other, their connection strong and unshakeable.

Someone knocked on the door. Reluctantly, Anne pulled away. She put her hand to her midriff, her nerves trembling.

Teach fell back a step. "What is it?"

"It's important," John said, his voice muffled. "Otherwise I wouldn't bother you."

Teach opened the door and peered out before allowing John to enter.

John quirked a brow at Teach's state of undress. Anne hid a smile at John's expression as Teach hastily donned his shirt.

"What's wrong?" Teach asked, his voice slightly hoarse.

"We spotted a sail. From the same direction I saw the light last night. In the next cay."

"Do you think it's Easton?" Anne asked.

"Can't be sure, since we only saw them through the spyglass. Their sails were torn and it looked as if they might have to repair one of the masts. We lowered our canvas and dropped anchor. I simply came down to see what the captain wanted us to do next."

"Well done," Teach said. "How far away are we?"

"At least a league, if not more."

Teach nodded. "Have the men who are awake prepare their weapons. We'll rouse the second watch as soon as the others are finished."

"You should rest as well," John said. "How much sleep have you had in the last twelve hours?"

"There will be plenty of time for sleep when this is over.

I'll take the second watch ashore. Once we land, we can set out and observe Easton from a distance. You remain with the boat. Before sundown, bring the *Triumph* in closer to the head of the cay. You'll cut off any plans they might have for escape."

John nodded and exited the room.

"And what am I supposed to do?" Anne asked, regretting the brandy. Her speech was slurred and her limbs felt heavy.

"Stay here. I'll send Benjamin to keep you company. Don't open the door for anyone."

Mindful of her back, she caught Teach by the front of his shirt and tugged gently. He went willingly, his gaze locked with hers. Standing on tiptoe, she kissed him. "Be careful," she whispered against his lips.

Brushing his knuckle down her cheek, he nodded. This time he didn't say "always." It was understood.

To pass the time, Benjamin straightened the clothes in the armoire, while Anne organized the papers and maps from the floor. To Anne's surprise, she found extra clothing in the crate. John had told her how Teach and Alastair had helped her escape, and Anne ran the material through her fingers, wondering how her friends were doing. They'd risked a lot to get Anne out of the fort. If Webb had done anything to hurt them . . . Her chest tightened at the thought and she closed her eyes. Webb would pay.

"Are you all right?" Benjamin asked, his kind brown eyes

watchful. In the brief time they'd known each other, he'd become like an older brother to her. He wasn't loud or blustering, and his quiet strength was comforting.

Anne nodded, drawing a deep breath. She attempted a smile, grateful for his company.

"You're tired of being in here." It wasn't a question.

"I am."

Outside the cabin, heavy footsteps traipsed up and down the stairs leading to the deck. The men were preparing to go ashore and they called out to one another.

Benjamin was quiet for a moment. "Would you like me to bring you some water? To bathe?"

"I would like that very much."

With a nod, Benjamin slid out the door. Anne could hear one of the longboats being lowered over the side. She longed to leave the confines of the ship as well, but she was stuck. What a horrid world in which women were born. Subject to the whims and fancies of men, dependent on them for everything.

Benjamin returned, a bucket of fresh water in his hands. "I'll go and get you some food as well."

"Thank you for this."

Smiling, Benjamin left. While he was gone, Anne cleaned herself the best she could. Hoping to protect her wounds, she ripped Teach's shirt into strips and wound them carefully around her chest and back. When she was done, she donned one of the smaller shirts that Cara had made.

All the while, the men of the *Triumph* marched up to the deck and down to the belly of the ship. Another longboat splashed into the water, punctuated by shouts. Once Teach departed with the shore-going party, the men left on board would rest.

A light tap on the door alerted Anne to Benjamin's presence. Assuming his hands were full, she opened the door, only to slam it shut when she saw the leering face on the other side.

"What's the matter, love? Aren't you happy to see me?"

She shivered, the voice giving her chills. She had a clear image of his face now. His bulbous nose looked as if it had been broken numerous times. His neck was thick and his shoulders wide. He pushed against the wood, his hand snaking in, and Anne's feet nearly slid out from under her.

With her heart in her throat, she realized she'd left both pistols in the hammock. Rage at her helplessness leant her strength and she smashed her back into the panel, forgetting about her stitches. The man howled and Anne grinned with grim satisfaction as he withdrew.

"You'll be sorry for that. Once I take care of him, I'm coming back for you!"

The door buckled beneath the weight of his fist before his steps faded down the hall. Not trusting that he truly left, Anne waited, holding her breath. She needed to warn Teach. Now that she'd seen the man's face, she could easily identify him.

Except what would she accuse him of? Searching the captain's cabin? If she came out of hiding, then everyone would know she was on board.

But it was clear from the man's comment that Teach was in danger.

The door behind her opened and Anne practically dragged Benjamin inside, his face startled.

"Teach is in trouble and I'm going to need your help."

CHAPTER 30

Teach

Teach was quiet as the blades of the oars rose and fell in precise sequence, cutting through the water and leaving bright whorls upon the blue-green surface. The water darkened, but only briefly, as they passed over rocks lurking beneath the surface. It wasn't long before the turquoise shallows welcomed them into the shelter of the cay.

Looking ahead, his eyes scoured the lush green tree line of mangroves, bougainvilleas, and coniferous pines. Although it would take them a few hours to hike through the vegetation to get to the neighboring cay, there would be plenty of cover for them to observe Easton and his men.

John had been left in charge of the *Triumph* while Teach had taken Kitts and his men in the two skiffs, armed with guns and swords.

He hated leaving Anne behind, but he'd had little choice. It was safer for her to remain on board with Benjamin and John than to accompany him. Despite what she claimed, Teach knew her wounds were still too fresh. Closing her stitches the second time had been difficult. The sight of those crude gashes marring her beautiful skin had caused him more anguish than his own lashing. The brandy had helped to ease her pain, and for that he was glad, but it hadn't helped him at all. The memory of Anne's hands on his scars went straight to his gut.

Sand grabbed the bow of the longboat and they jarred to a stop. Teach leapt ashore, his boots splashing in the water. After days at sea, the land felt hard beneath his feet as the surf rushed up to greet him. His hands were clammy and he wiped them down the legs of his breeches, aware of the oppressive heat. Shading his eyes, he looked at their surroundings.

Anne would love it here. The sand glowed a bright pink, and the sky overhead matched Anne's blue eyes. The dense tangle of prop roots made some of the trees look as if they stood on stilts. Coconuts littered the ground and there were sufficient fish in the water to provide an endless supply of food. Teach could imagine the two of them living in a place like this, with a small hut and a boat anchored in the sparkling waters.

Truly, this was paradise.

Anne had always wanted to find a place where she could belong. Maybe this was it. With no one around, Teach's greatest wish was to spend time with Anne here. Instead of trying to fit their lives into someone else's mold, they could make their own place in the world.

With that thought in mind, Teach marched across the sand dunes and into the mangrove forest, leaving the ocean and the *Triumph* behind. Kitts kept pace with Teach while the rest of the crew followed in their wake. The soldiers no longer wore their uniforms, and Kitts's men blended in with the others. There were thirty in all.

Teach watched the sergeant out of the corner of his eye, wondering if he was the one who'd searched the captain's cabin and discovered Anne. Teach didn't think so, otherwise Kitts would have confronted him before now.

Then again, Teach didn't know Kitts that well. Perhaps he was adept at playacting. Trying to think of some way to trick a confession out of him, Teach was quiet as they entered the foliage.

"Have you always wanted to captain a ship?"

They'd walked for several minutes, and Teach was caught off-guard by the question.

"Aye," Teach answered truthfully. This was a good enough start. Heaven knew they had plenty of time before they reached the cay where Easton was moored. "Have you always wanted to be a soldier?"

"My father and grandfather were soldiers before me."

"But is that what you wanted?"

"I want to make my father proud."

Teach could understand that desire all too well. However, in Teach's case, it had come with too high of a price, one he hadn't been willing to pay. "What would you be if you weren't a soldier?"

Kitts gave him a blank look. "What kind of question is that? I'm a soldier. I've chosen my course."

Teach had to give Kitts credit. He was single-minded and dedicated. From what Teach had seen of the man's actions on the deck of the *Triumph*, and his interactions with the rest of the crew, Teach couldn't imagine Kitts doing anything half-heartedly or against the rules.

They walked in uncomfortable silence for several minutes, broken occasionally by the shrill cry of a tropical bird. As they passed under a tall tree, something dropped from an overhanging branch and Teach pushed Kitts to the side. The thick corded length of a boa constrictor hung suspended between them, its forked tongue snaking out. Kitts eyes were wide and he gave Teach a small nod. "Thank you."

With a slight shrug, Teach moved on. The rest of the men made a wide arc around the snake.

"I suppose if I weren't a soldier, I might be a farmer," Kitts said unexpectedly, sweat beading on his forehead.

Teach gave him a curious look. "Truly?" Kitts's response surprised him. As did the fact that Kitts had given Teach's question more thought.

"Yes. I would have five acres. Nothing large, but enough to support myself. I'd also have cattle, chickens, and an ox."

He'd clearly given it some *serious* thought. "And would

livestock be your sole source of companionship?" Teach couldn't help himself. Kitts was so easily annoyed.

Sure enough, Kitts stiffened, his mouth turned down at the corners. He reminded Teach of a raccoon with his two black eyes. His nose was still swollen after his run-in with John. "It might surprise you to know this, but at one time, I cared deeply for someone."

Teach couldn't imagine the rigid Kitts doing anything as "impractical" as falling in love. "What happened?"

There was a pregnant pause, as if Kitts debated telling Teach the truth. A lizard underfoot skidded away, rustling amongst the fallen leaves of a nearby bougainvillea bush.

"Her father did not support the match."

"Why not?"

"An earl's daughter doesn't marry a soldier."

"Ah," Teach said, feeling contrite. Although Teach's circumstances had been somewhat different, he could understand Kitts's frustration. "Is she already wed?"

"Not to my knowledge, no."

"When you return to England, perhaps you could search her out again. After you've sacrificed your time and freedom for country and Crown, of course," Teach said, ducking beneath an overhanging branch.

"Society would frown upon it."

Teach gave an incredulous laugh. "Hang society. If you truly loved her, you wouldn't let her go so easily."

"There are rules—"

"Bugger the rules! I wouldn't listen to anyone who told me to stay away. Only an act of God would be able to keep me from the woman I loved."

Kitts's lips twisted. "If there weren't rules and administrations, the world would be in absolute chaos."

"But sometimes the rules are made by unjust men."

"If everyone rebelled, the result would be disastrous."

"Do you realize how close you are now to overstepping the boundary between the law and lawlessness?"

"What do you mean?" Kitts snapped, stumbling on a mangrove root.

"For all intents and purposes, you're a privateer. In my opinion, that's only one step away from piracy."

Kitts stopped, drawing himself up to his full height. "I am a soldier following the command of the sovereign governor of Nassau. I am *not* a privateer."

A few of the men stopped behind them, their expressions curious as they watched the exchange.

Teach almost felt sorry for Kitts. He clearly lacked imagination and the ability to think for himself. "We've been sent to capture Easton. A letter of marque is the only thing separating us from them."

"Except that we won't be keeping any of the plunder. Webb is expecting us to return everything, and I am here to ensure that happens."

"Do you honestly believe Webb is going to pay you?"

Kitts shifted from one foot to the other. The sunlight filtered down through the green canopy overhead. "He informed me we would be paid for our time and trouble."

"How much?"

"That's between the governor and my—"

Some of the men came forward. "How much?" one of them asked.

Scowling, Kitts shot Teach a murderous glare. "That information is confidential."

"Tsk, tsk," Teach said, enjoying the look of frustration on the other man's face. "Is that any way to earn your men's trust? Is that any way to lead them?"

"He takes his orders from Webb. He doesn't *lead* anyone," someone called out.

Kitts's head whipped around as he searched for the source of the comment. Nobody moved. Turning back to Teach, he leaned forward and poked Teach's chest. "Since you know so much, *Captain*," Kitts said, his jaw clenched. "Why don't you tell us what Webb said to *you*."

Teach shrugged. "He told me he would pay me five hundred pounds if I bring Easton back alive." A rumble rose through the men as they muttered amongst themselves. "And I pledge to share it with the crew equally. But I don't truly believe Webb will pay us when we return."

"Are you saying the governor is a liar?" Kitts asked.

"I'm saying I don't believe everything that comes out of his mouth." Teach turned to address the crew. "How many of you have ever *seen* Easton's ship? Or how many of you *know* anyone who *claims* they've seen Easton's ship?"

Two hands went up. In a group of thirty. Admittedly, only eighteen of them were Kitts's men, but they'd been stationed in Nassau. Surely more people would have witnessed Easton's ship if the pirate plagued the shores as much as Webb had led Teach to believe.

While Teach had cared for Anne in the captain's cabin, he'd been giving their situation serious thought. Webb had told Teach he'd sent people after Easton before. But Alastair had said that wasn't the case, and that Webb had had a hard time gathering a crew. Teach was more prone to believe Alastair than Webb. Which made Teach wonder who, exactly, George Easton was. And what was he to Webb?

"Our job is not to question the orders we've been given. The letter of marque Webb gave you proves we are innocent of any criminal act. I trust—"

"I have no letter of marque," Teach said.

Kitts's frown deepened as his face reddened. "What do you mean?"

"Webb didn't give me one. I assumed you would have it, since he sent you as well."

"No. He told me he'd given it to you."

The crew grumbled, their voices caught in the sticky air, their frustration palpable.

"Do you still believe you'll be paid for your time and trouble?" Teach asked, leaning in close.

The look of doubt on Kitts's face was answer enough.

Teach turned to the crew, raising his hand to get them to quiet down. "In light of the situation, I propose a small change. We won't be giving Webb one half of the net proceeds. Whatever spoils we find, we keep. All of it. But we will bring Easton back alive. Are we all agreed?"

Not even Kitts voiced his dissent.

"Excellent. And I would like to add something else to that agreement. Consider it our code, if you will. If any person steals or is caught stealing any part of the prize or prizes, or he's found pilfering any money or goods, he shall forfeit his share to the rest of the crew. Is that understood?"

The men nodded in agreement.

Teach drew a deep breath, giving them a hard look. "Furthermore, if any person be found a ringleader of mutiny, or causing a disturbance on board, he shall forfeit his share, to be divided amongst the ship's company. And if any person refuses to obey my command or behaves with cowardice, he shall be punished according to law. Do you have any questions?"

Other than a few headshakes, there was no response.

"Good," Teach said. "Now let's go catch ourselves a pirate."

CHAPTER 31

Anne

"You're not leaving the ship," John said, running his hands through his hair. "Teach would kill me."

"Someone will kill *Teach* if I don't," Anne snapped. Her hands shook as she loaded both pistols. Benjamin had told John that Anne wished to see him. She could not wait to leave the confines of the ship.

"Maybe he's still here. If he is, it's too dangerous for you to leave the cabin."

Anne placed the pistols in the baldric slung across her chest. "I have no intention of staying here and waiting for him to come back. Where is Kitts?" When she'd first described the man to Benjamin, he'd said it fit Kitts's description. Except at the moment, Kitts sported two black eyes. Although she'd only seen the man briefly, Anne couldn't be sure if he'd had two black eyes.

"With Teach," John muttered.

Benjamin entered the cabin, his expression grave. "Most of the men are resting now. I did not see the man she described on board," Benjamin said. "She's right. He went with the others."

"Teach said you should stay here."

Anne threw her hands in the air. "He didn't know someone would try to kill him. If you won't take us, Benjamin and I will take the longboat ourselves."

"You can't. There's only one left," John said. "We'll need it to go after Easton when we reach the cay."

Anne reached for the large dagger at John's waist. Startled, he raised his hands in defense, but she simply took ahold of her hair where it was pulled back in a braid and sliced through the thick strands. The curls bounced up, relaxed and free around her shoulders.

John gasped. "What the devil are you doing?"

Benjamin's jaw dropped, his eyes wide as he looked at the length of hair in her hand.

Dropping the hair into the hammock, she loosened the leather strip that had held it together and retied her shorter hair. "I can't go ashore looking like this."

"You're not going ashore," John insisted.

"We don't have time to waste arguing. Either you take us or we'll go ourselves."

John looked at Benjamin. "What do you think about this?"

"I think a weak man has a long tongue."

Anne laughed out loud as John jerked back. "What does that bloody well mean?" he snarled.

Benjamin shrugged. "It means we are wasting valuable time. Anne is right. We need to go now." Anne handed the dagger back to John, hilt first. "You're both mad," John muttered, looking at the two of them.

Finished arguing, Anne moved toward the door, but John's voice stopped her. "Wait. You can't go like that. I've got something to help you." Walking to the armoire, he pulled out a floppy hat and placed it on Anne's head. It was too large, and came down to her eyebrows, shielding a good portion of her face. "I don't know how your boots will hold up. They're not exactly made for this kind of thing."

Benjamin bent down to tug off his boot, but Anne stopped him. "What will you wear?"

"Where I come from, people do not wear shoes."

She shook her head. "Your boots will be far too large for me. I'll wear mine for as long as they'll last." Holding out her arms, she looked at them. "Well? How do I look?"

"Like a mad woman," John said without hesitation.

"Like a mad *boy*," Benjamin corrected.

John muttered something beneath his breath and handed the dagger in its sheath back to Anne, but she held up her hands. "I prefer pistols," she said.

"You'll need more than a single shot."

"Which is why I have two."

"What happens if you miss?"

Anne raised her chin at him. "I won't miss."

"Have you practiced with those? They're only for close range."

"Then I'll have to get close enough, won't I?" she said, resisting the temptation to practice on *him*.

"For someone so small, you're awfully fierce."

Benjamin took the dagger from John and slung the sheath over one shoulder. "Even a mosquito can cope with a lion at times," Benjamin said with quiet confidence. Anne could have kissed him.

John whirled, pointing a finger in his face. "I've had just about enough of you and your smart comments."

Anne smirked at the innocent look on Benjamin's face. John turned his attention back to her. "Just how do you propose you get back to the ship? If you truly shoot the man, and save Teach, there's no guarantee you'll make it back before everyone discovers you're a girl, including Kitts."

Anne stopped at the door, gripping the handle. "If it is Kitts, then he'll be dead."

John quirked a brow at her. "And if it isn't?"

"I haven't gotten that far." She'd once accused Teach of not seeing the broader picture, but she didn't have time to go over the pros and cons of her decision. She simply needed to get to Teach.

Grabbing the two water skins that Benjamin had filled,

John followed behind, muttering under his breath as they took the stairs. Only a handful of men were on deck. They were clearly still exhausted from battling the storm. Nobody gave Anne a second look, her hat pulled far too low for them to make out her features. John and Benjamin untied the ropes and started to lower the longboat to the crystal clear waters below.

"How will you know which way they've gone?" John asked.

Anne gripped his arm, wishing she could smooth the furrows from between his brows. "There were thirty men who left with Teach. I'm fairly certain they've left a trail even I could track. Now, are we going to continue discussing this or can we get going?"

"I wish I could go with you," he said, his voice strained. Anne knew John was worried. Not only for her safety, but for Teach's as well.

"You're needed with the ship. I'll be careful, John. I promise."

John gave her a long hard look. Finally, he nodded. "All right, then. Let's get to the longboat.

As Benjamin and Anne followed the clear path left by Teach and his men, the sun's rays beat down on them in relentless waves. If not for the breeze, Anne was fairly certain they would have been devoured by mosquitos.

The afternoon dragged on, the only real mark of the passage of time was the moving shadows across the ground. Anne was grateful for the hat John had given her, but she wished she hadn't wrapped her wounds. The extra material caused sweat to run down her back in unending rivulets, and her head started to pound.

Ever attentive, Benjamin was quick to catch her when she stumbled. She hadn't fully recovered from her injuries and marching through the heat was exhausting. By the time they came to a large pool of water, Anne had already finished the skin she'd brought with her. She felt nauseous, her muscles cramping and fatigued.

"You need to rest in the shade," Benjamin said.

Anne eyed the brown surface of the pool, littered with leaves from the surrounding trees, and wondered if it was safe to drink.

Benjamin didn't hesitate. He took the skin from her and filled it before handing it back. Then he filled his own. "It's safe," he said, taking a large drink. "The fresh water is on top. The saltwater is far below. There are no large animals to taint it." It was obvious he'd benefited from pools like this before.

Anne filled her skin three more times and downed it all. "Okay, let's move on," Anne said, eager to keep going.

"You need to rest."

"I can rest later."

"You won't help him if you collapse from the heat. We can't be far behind. Even they must have taken a short break." Benjamin sat and removed his boots.

Torn between wanting to press on and recognizing the need

for a rest, Anne stepped carefully to the limestone edge of the pool and looked into its shadowy depths. "Are you going in there?" she asked.

Benjamin nodded, his forehead gleaming under the sun. "It will help us cool off. But you must be careful of your stitches." He dove in, fully clothed, and surfaced a few feet away with a smile splitting his face. He made it seem so easy.

Unlacing her boots and removing her stockings, Anne placed them at her side. Her back was still tight and bruised. Inching forward, she dipped a toe into the water. It was definitely cooler than the air around them. In England, she'd never learned how to swim, and she envied Benjamin's confidence in the water.

"Where did you learn to swim?' she asked, sticking her legs into the pool. She relished the feel of it gently lapping against her warm skin and wished she could fully submerge in its cool depths. But if she did, her stitches would soften and pull out.

"My father was a fisherman. I had to go and gather the nets for him." He swam to her side, somehow managing to stay afloat by waving his arms and legs back and forth. "When we have time, I can teach you."

His smile and warmth were contagious. Anne didn't think she'd met anyone as caring as Benjamin. "I'd like that." Dipping her hat into the water, she leaned forward and poured it over head, feeling instantly refreshed, her fatigue momentarily forgotten. Drenching her hair again and again, she closed her eyes, grateful for this brief respite from the blazing sun. She hoped it wasn't much farther to the next cay.

Benjamin filled the skins, insisting Anne drink as much as possible. "I've watched people die because of the sun," he said. "Alastair wouldn't forgive me if anything happened to you."

"Nothing's going to happen to me," she assured him, but did as he asked. The small break had certainly helped and the pounding in her head had receded somewhat. It was time to continue their journey.

Using her stockings to dry off her feet, Anne slid them on. As she picked up one of her boots, a tiny head popped out. With a small shriek, Anne dropped it, the hair on her arms standing on end. The lizard disappeared inside the dark cavity of leather.

Benjamin reached over, but Anne grabbed his arm. "Wait! What are you doing?"

"I'm removing it from your shoe."

"But you don't know if it's dangerous."

"It's not. It's seeking shelter." Just as Benjamin said that a large white bird flew overhead, its shadow darkening the ground briefly beside them before disappearing amongst the trees.

Wary, Anne watched as Benjamin calmly removed the lizard, holding it gently in his hand. She couldn't help the shiver that ran down her back as it turned its head, its beady eyes staring at her. "What are you going to do with it?" she asked.

"Set it free." Lowering his hand, he placed the lizard in

some sand. It scurried away, its tiny legs carrying it as fast as it could run.

"But what happens if the bird comes back?" she asked, feeling rather silly. The lizard had startled her. Just to make sure there wasn't another one hiding in her other boot, she picked it up and shook it out before sliding it on.

"Then it will seek shelter elsewhere. If it escaped once, it can do it again."

Something in his voice caused Anne to pause. He wasn't simply talking about the lizard. "How many times did you try?" she asked.

Benjamin drew a deep breath. "Twice." He gave her a wry smile. "The moon can be both a blessing and a curse. It can light a darkened path. But it can also betray you. The second time I learned and left when the moon was small. I hid in bug-filled caves and came to appreciate the lizards. They kept the bugs away."

Anne marveled at Benjamin's ability to overcome any situation. "How terrifying that must have been."

"It was. But these were more terrifying," he said, running his hands over the scars on his arms and motioning to his back. "I couldn't stay and let them do this to me. They'd already killed my family."

Anne felt sick. She didn't press and instead waited for Benjamin to talk. He picked up a stick and turned it in his hands.

"You know, some slavers keep families together. But they

don't do it to be kind. No such thing as a good slaveholder. They do it to make escape more difficult." He looked up at Anne, his eyes sad but hard. "They killed my father when he tried to stop the overseer from—" He broke the stick, his fingers trembling. "Hurting my sister."

Anne stiffened as she shared his hatred and his pain. A tear slid down her cheek, but she couldn't move to wipe it off.

"Marie died that night. She was only ten."

"That's barbaric," she whispered, unable to bring strength to her voice.

"I ran the next night. Didn't know where I was going, but I ran. I ran for my father. For all the ones I left behind . . ." He looked down at his hands and said softly, "I ran because Marie couldn't. And I wouldn't hesitate to do it again. I will never go back to being a slave," he said, meeting her eyes once more.

"I won't let that happen," Anne resolved, thinking back to the fiery rage she'd felt when the hilt of her gun had burned in her hands as she'd pointed it at the slaver. The next time it would be loaded and she wouldn't miss.

Anne and Benjamin shared a look of understanding and determination. The thick scars marking their skin would always remind Anne of the cruelty and depravity of men. And women. But they would also symbolize survival. And strength. "Are you ready to go?" she asked.

He nodded.

"The path leads this way. Let's go."

CHAPTER 32

Teach

The ship anchored in the clear blue waters of the cay was the same one that had attacked the *Deliverance*. Teach was sure of it. His pulse pounded as he thought of all the men who'd lost their lives.

His nails bit into his palms as he glared at the ship. Where the mast had once stood tall and proud on the deck, it was now split in half, with sharp spikes of wood reaching up to the sky.

The rigging was taut, but with no canvas. The *Deliverance* had punched three holes in the side of the ship and they'd been hastily patched. This vessel had been built for speed and maneuverability, but without a working mast, it sat in the shallow waters like a duck bobbing in the waves.

From his vantage point, Teach could see several sailors working on repairs. The rest of the men were scattered across the sandy beach, performing different duties.

A fire burned in their midst, and one or two members of the crew roasted something over the open flames. The men were thin and their clothes hung from them in dirty tatters. It had been more than two weeks since the attack on the *Deliverance*. Shocked at their appearance, Teach wondered how Easton and his crew had deteriorated in such a short amount of time. Or had they already been in this condition and Teach had somehow overlooked it? During the fight, they'd seemed much more robust. Admittedly, Teach had been intent on securing the *Deliverance*'s escape, but could he have overlooked their state? It was obvious to him that Easton's men had needed the cargo of the large merchant ship. And because they hadn't secured it, they'd paid a steep price.

"Which one do you suppose is Easton?" Kitts whispered.

Teach shook his head. "We'll have to watch them for a bit. We don't want to rush into anything."

Kitts nodded. Motioning to the men behind them, Teach gestured for them to spread out. They crept like spiders stealthily through the vegetation, the white sand muffling their footsteps.

For the next several minutes, they watched the pirates, noting their lack of energy. Strips of canvas were spread before them as they attempted to repair some sails. Others dragged buckets of water into their camp. They'd no doubt filled them from one of the freshwater pools that dotted the island. The pirates' movements were slow and labored. It wouldn't take much to overcome the group.

The snap of a twig caught Teach's attention and he and Kitts ducked under the awning of a large cork tree. Teach held his breath as a thin young man attempted to close his breeches as he returned to the camp. Just as he reached Teach's side, Teach jumped out, stifling the young man's shocked cry with the palm of his hand, and dragging him backward. Kitts reached for his feet, but the pirate kicked out, his foot connecting with Kitts's jaw. At the same time, the young man sank his teeth into the soft flesh of Teach's hand. Teach threw him to the ground. Kitts drew his pistol and pointed it at the young man's head. He stilled instantly.

Shouts sounded from the camp and Teach pulled out the pair of revolvers hanging across his chest, ready to fire. But nobody came charging through the brush. The shouts continued, but remained on the beach.

The pirate in front of Kitts opened his mouth to cry out, but Kitts pistol-whipped him, and his eyes rolled back in his head. Ripping strips of material from the bottom of his own shirt, Kitts hastily secured the young man's hands behind his back, and stuffed another tattered cloth into his mouth. "That should keep him quiet," Kitts muttered, rubbing his jaw, which was already beginning to bruise.

Peering through the trees, Teach watched as the men on the beach argued over the smoking skewers, charred pieces stuck to the ends. They were clearly suffering if they were prepared to come to blows over that amount of food.

A tall thin figure with light brown hair limped toward the group, and despite his scruffy appearance, Teach knew they had their captain. It was obvious the pirates respected Easton and his command in the way they parted for him to walk through their midst. They quieted down instantly. Although his words didn't quite carry all the way to where Teach and the others hid, there was no mistaking the confidence in his stance.

"Now?" Kitts asked.

"Now," Teach said. With a loud cry, Teach led the way, storming onto the beach, his pistols drawn as he fired once into the air.

The pirates scattered, a few of them scrambling for their cutlasses. The clang of steel hitting steel rang through the air, but Easton's men were quickly subdued. Teach and his crew clearly had the advantage and surrounded the pirates, their weapons drawn.

Considering how Webb had built up Easton's reputation and ferocity, Teach had expected much more of a fight from a much larger opponent. Easton wasn't as broad as Teach and he stood a few inches shorter. His clothing hung on his thin frame, but he stood straight, with an unmistakable air of authority.

"George Easton, surrender now, and we'll let you live," Teach said, his second pistol pointing straight at Easton's chest.

The pirate smirked, his brown eyes wrinkling at the corners. "I must say, that's very generous of you. But who the devil are you?"

"The name's Teach."

Easton tilted his head to the side, considering Teach. "What kind of a fool name is that?"

"The only one you'll get from me. Now tell your men to lower their weapons."

"And if I don't?" Easton asked casually, glancing around. His nonchalant attitude was deceptive. Easton's men watched him closely, clearly prepared to fight on if he gave the order.

"We'll show no quarter." Although Webb wanted Easton returned alive, Teach would not allow any men on his crew to die at a pirate's hand.

"A man sure in his strength does not threaten." Easton appeared to have a response for everything.

"You and your men will return with us to Nassau. From there you'll be sent to England, where you're to be tried for your crimes," Teach said.

Easton eyed him, a slight smile lifting the corners of his mouth. Teach wondered if he ever took anything seriously. "Well, *Teach*, I'll happily go back to England. I'll even help crew your ship if you have the supplies to take us now. But there's nothing you can say or do to make me return to Nassau. Strand us. Take the ship and go. We have a better chance surviving on this island with nothing but fish and lizards to eat than going anywhere under Webb's control."

"You fear Webb more than the law?" Teach asked.

"Of course I do. The law is hard, but at least it's just on occasion. Webb has never been honorable or just."

Teach tightened his grip. "I'm afraid you have no choice."

"Do you really believe that Webb will send me back to London? If we go with you, we'll die in Nassau."

"The law says you're to be taken and tried in England," Kitts said.

Easton scoffed at him. "Perhaps I didn't make myself clear. The law is a weapon Webb bandies around on the rare occasion it serves him. It's like a dinner knife versus a dagger. Webb will always let you see him politely using his dinner knife, but you'll be surprised every time when he sneaks up on you in an alley and stabs you with the dagger."

Kitts and Teach exchanged a confused look. Clearly this man had spent too much time in the sun.

"In short," Easton continued, "you're a fool to trust Webb."

How often had Teach thought those very words? "Nevertheless, you'll be taken to England and hanged for piracy."

"That's not much of an incentive for me to go with you. You've already determined my guilt."

"Do you deny that you're a pirate?"

"Whether I deny it or not, what evidence do you have?" Easton asked.

"I recognize your ship. You attacked me and my crew aboard the *Deliverance*. I believe that's evidence enough."

Easton narrowed his eyes at Teach, any trace of his earlier nonchalance gone. "So you're the one who nearly committed me and my men to the bottom of the ocean."

"No. You did that when you decided to attack us."

"Would you like to know who gave those orders?"

"Who?" Even as Teach asked the question, he had a feeling he already knew the answer.

"Governor Webb."

"That's a lie," Kitts sputtered, his hand shaking as he pointed his weapon at Easton. "The governor works for the Crown. It's his job to uphold the laws of our country."

The pirate ignored Kitts, continuing to watch Teach as he said, "You forget, there were *two* ships that attacked the *Deliverance* that day. The captain of the second ship was every bit as bloodthirsty and ruthless as Webb. Nelson liked to see people suffer."

"Webb said *you're* the one who likes to torture his victims."

"Of course he did. And do you believe everything that comes out of his mouth?"

Teach hesitated, his confidence in Easton's guilt shifting like the sand underfoot. "Where's the other ship?"

"I'm afraid I don't know the answer to your question. But don't you find it interesting that Webb only sent you after me?"

Kitt cleared his throat. Teach could feel the uncertainty of some of his men, because he felt the same doubt.

Easton continued. "Surely you realize that as soon as we return to Nassau, your worth and usefulness to the governor will conclude. And you and anyone close to you is as good as dead. Webb doesn't leave anything to chance."

"I'm not the one Webb is after. You are."

"True, but by taking me back to Nassau, you've spent time with me. I could tell you things about Webb that he doesn't want you to know. You're now a threat to him. Guilt by association."

Before Teach could respond, a shot rang out, followed closely by another. Several men ducked, desperately looking around to see where the shots had come from. Easton staggered back, clutching his right shoulder. Teach leapt forward to catch him as he collapsed to the ground. Two of Easton's men tackled someone near the tree line.

The fighting resumed, even as Teach yelled for his men to stand down. Turning to Easton, Teach pressed a hand to the wound, trying to stanch the flow of blood. "Stand down!" Teach yelled, but only a few of his men responded. They were too busy defending themselves from the pirates. "Call your crew back before we kill the lot of you!"

After only a slight hesitation, Easton let out a sharp whistle. He had to repeat it several times to be heard over the sound of the fighting, but eventually his men obeyed.

"Hillel, get over here," Easton called out. A pirate approached Easton, the same one Teach and Kitts had encountered in the trees. Somehow he'd freed himself from his bonds. Teach traded places with Hillel, and the young man pressed a rag into Easton's wound.

Teach stood and walked over to the man who'd been tackled

by two pirates. He recognized Nathan from his stocky build and dark brown hair. He was one of the soldiers who'd come with Kitts. A musket lay by Nathan's side and a crimson stream spurted from a gaping wound in his stomach. It took Teach a moment to realize that Nathan had shot Easton, but the acrid smoke of gunpowder lingered in the air. Who had shot Nathan? And who had shot first?

The ball had entered Nathan's back, and judging by the amount of blood spilling onto the white sand at his feet, he wouldn't make it. Teach yelled for Kitts to scour the nearby forest.

A short laugh burst through Easton's lips, only to end in a coughing fit. "Don't quite know who to trust, do you?"

Teach ignored him, unwilling to let the pirate know just how accurate his statement was. He had never had any reason to suspect Nathan would do something like this. The young man always stayed in the background, going about his work quietly.

But he wasn't quiet now. In shock, Nathan's body shook violently from the loss of blood.

"Why did you shoot Easton?" Teach demanded.

Nathan spit a stream of blood at Teach's feet. "Webb's coming for you. All of you." He looked at Teach with cold and flinty eyes, his skin already turning the color of ash.

Teach crouched low, his pistol pointed at the man's face. "What do you mean, he's coming for us? What do you know?"

Nathan cringed and stiffened, before releasing a drawn out breath. "I know you're all dead men."

Teach wondered if the threat was the sailor's pathetic attempt to strike one last hefty blow. Perhaps Webb wasn't coming after them. "I'm afraid you'll be the first to die." Teach stood and turned away.

"I saw—what you're hiding in your cabin."

Teach whirled around, his eyes narrowed.

"Don't worry, Captain. I already took my share."

With a roaring in his ears, Teach's vision clouded. His rage, held so long in check, drove deeper and spread wider than ever before in his life. Nathan's voice erupted in an anguished scream as Teach dug his boot into the man's wound. Ignoring the blood spilling over the worn leather and the agonized cries of the man at his feet, Teach felt more like a raging beast than a civilized man. And to his surprise, he embraced that feeling of power.

Easton laughed as several men pointed off toward the trees. Teach looked, recognizing a familiar figure, wearing a floppy hat, a baldric, and a pistolman's pouch, striding from the brush, escorted at sword point by Kitts and his men.

CHAPTER 33

Anne

Although Anne wasn't close enough to see the fury in Teach's eyes, she could certainly feel it rolling in waves toward her. He marched purposefully across the beach, and she noticed the white sand stuck to his right boot, with the occasional glint of red. *Blood.*

Her gaze darted to the man lying on his back, surrounded by a crimson stain. She'd just shot a man with what appeared to be a deathly blow. Her hands shook. Her ears rang. And only after a few deep breaths did her pulse begin beating at a normal pace.

She should have felt remorse at shooting another human being. After all, this was the second time she'd done it. In England, she would never have considered owning a weapon, let alone actually using it. But when she saw the man who'd threatened her, who'd raised his musket to shoot Teach, Anne could only feel a sense of relief as he bled out. She no longer feared him.

"Lower your weapons," Teach called out.

The man beside Anne stiffened. "But we caught—"

"I said lower your weapons!"

The rage in Teach's voice surprised Anne. He stopped in front of her, the air charged between them. "What the devil are you doing here?" Teach growled, his eyes scanning her from head to toe. "Are you all right?"

"You know her?" The sailor who'd captured Anne snapped, his face twisted in shock.

Anne and Teach both looked at him. Anne recognized him as the same soldier who'd guarded her at the fort. Right after Beth's death. Anne had been as astonished to see him as he was to see her.

Anne let out a swift, shallow breath. "I'm fine."

"Then why did you come?"

"To save your life!" she retorted, glaring at him.

"By risking your own? I told you to stay on board—"

"You *know* her?"

"Yes!" Anne and Teach shouted simultaneously.

"Kitts, go and see if you can get a confession out of Nathan as to why he shot Easton and why he searched my cabin. He didn't respond well to my interrogation. Now!" Teach added when the man continued to stare blankly at the two of them.

Kitts stalked off, as did the men who'd accompanied him. Only Benjamin stayed nearby, his expression watchful and wary.

Anne shook her head at Benjamin, and Teach followed her gaze. Pointing an accusing finger at the young man, Teach's eyes narrowed. "You disobeyed a direct order."

"She was not to be stopped."

"You left John shorthanded."

Anne rolled her eyes and sighed. "Don't be ridiculous, Teach. John has plenty of men." Anne had been so focused on getting to Teach that she hadn't given much thought to what would come after. She hadn't a clue now as to how to proceed.

"When I see him, I'm going to wring his neck. What you did was . . ."

"Brave?" Anne offered.

"Foolish!"

Scowling, she bit her lip. "I saved your life."

Shaking his head, Teach grasped Anne's hand in his and marched her over to the assembled crowd.

"Do you mean to tell us what she's doing here?" Kitts demanded from where he stood.

Teach responded with an immediate, "No."

"She shot and killed a man," Kitts barked.

Anne dared another glance at the man she shot. He stared sightlessly up at the sun, his mouth partly open. The air reeked with the coppery scent of blood. Her stomach churned at the sight of the bullet wound and she turned away.

"In case you've forgotten, that man shot *me*, so I'm obliged to her."

Teach pointed a finger at the pirate. "Nobody asked you, Easton."

So this was Easton. He didn't appear that intimidating. Anne met Easton's eyes and he nodded at her in thanks. He wasn't exactly handsome, with his narrow forehead and strong chin. His eyes were bright with sharp hollows beneath. There was an irreverence about him, with his thin lips tilted up slightly at the corners, as if he was always secretly laughing at someone or something. Still, he wasn't unpleasant to look at. Anne guessed he was in his twenties.

"Where's your medicine chest?"

Easton motioned toward the water. "On the *Kelly Killorn*."

"Then we need to get you to your ship."

"My men will take me. You can stay here."

"And have you fire a cannon at us? I don't believe that's a good idea," Teach said. "Besides, I have more questions for you about Webb."

"There isn't enough room in the skiffs for all of us."

"Then you'll have to trust me. And I'll have to trust you. Truce?"

Anne waited, her pulse pounding as each man sized the other up. Her two pistols were primed and loaded.

"Truce," Easton said. He nodded at his men. "Stand down. The first person to raise their weapon will answer to me. Understood?"

"The same goes for my men. Ten of you will come with me.

The rest of you stay here." Teach turned to Easton. "Can you walk?"

"Of course." Easton stood, only to sway precariously on his feet. It appeared he'd lost more blood than anyone realized.

Teach spread out one of the sails lying on the ground. He and a handful of Easton's men lifted the pirate up and placed him carefully on top. They carried him slowly down to one of the waiting skiffs. Anne and Benjamin followed.

"I demand an explanation," Kitts sputtered, striding down to the edge of the water.

Teach turned, the gentle waves washing his boots clean. "About what?"

"Her!"

Startled, Anne stumbled backward as Kitts pointed a shaking finger in her direction.

"The last time I saw this woman, she was being questioned for the charges she brought against the governor's wife."

"No, she was being held against her will while she was trying to save the governor's life. Not that he deserved it," Teach said.

"What is she doing here?"

"She's coming with me."

Kitts's face flashed a bright red. "This is outrageous. There are laws to be—"

"Look around you, man! This isn't England and it isn't even

Nassau. There are no laws or rules out here." A vein pulsed at Teach's temple. Anne knew the tether on his anger was about to break.

"For your information, I was never *questioned* about my involvement. The governor's wife killed a woman in cold blood. I was found guilty of that murder without the benefit of a trial. Now, if you will excuse us," Anne pointed to Easton, his wound bleeding out, "we have to see to this man's injuries."

"What exactly do you expect me to do?" Kitts demanded.

"Wait here." Anne allowed Teach to assist her into one of the skiffs.

Benjamin placed a hand on Kitts's chest as the outraged soldier stepped forward. A group of men moved to the other skiff, leaving Kitts standing in the sand.

They rowed toward the pirate ship. Anne sat in the longboat facing the beach, with Easton stretched out in front of her. Kitts stared after them, his mouth open. Anne almost felt sorry for him. The day had clearly been full of surprises.

"How did you do it?" Easton asked.

"Do what?" The pungent smell of blood filled the air and Anne tried to hold her breath, but that only increased her light-headedness. The ringing in her ears had finally stopped. *I shot and killed a man.*

"How did you get close enough to shoot the man who shot me?"

Anne forced herself to focus. "You all made it very easy,

actually. With the three of you arguing, nobody paid us any attention. Benjamin and I crept through the trees. As soon as I recognized him, I moved in from behind," she said.

Teach looked over at her sharply. "Did you shoot first?"

"No. I saw him raise the musket. I thought he was aiming for you, but he shot him instead." If she hadn't suspected Teach was in danger, would she have fired the weapon? It was too late to second-guess herself. If faced with the same choice, Anne didn't think she would have done anything differently.

"We were standing side by side. It is possible he meant to shoot *you*," Easton said.

"Why would Webb want *me* killed? He gave me the task of bringing you back to Nassau."

"I told you, you're a threat to him. You recognized one of the ships that attacked the *Deliverance*."

Anne looked up to the sky. "Does it really matter who he meant to kill? He said Webb was coming for us. Do you think there is any truth to his words?"

"Absolutely," Easton said. "If not here, then when you get back to Nassau. The minute you agreed to work for him, you signed your death warrant."

"I had no other choice. Part of my men from the *Deliverance* are still locked up in the fort."

"And so are some of our friends," Anne said.

Easton grimaced. "I hate to be the bearer of bad news, but I wouldn't hold out much hope for your crewmates or your friends.

If you were smart, you'd sail from here and never return."

Refusing to give credence to his words, Anne turned away, trying to breathe around the tightness in her chest. She would not give up on saving any of them, regardless of how difficult it might be. Looking over her shoulder, she watched as they approached the ship. It was a three-masted vessel, and Anne counted twelve guns plus twenty oars to maneuver it in calm winds. The mainmast was in the process of being repaired, and some roughly patched holes in the side were testament to its most recent battle.

"Admiring your handiwork?" Easton asked Teach.

"My first mate told me we'd ruined your looks. It appears he was right."

"Ah, but that's merely on the surface. Her true beauty lies within."

"Why did you name it the *Kelly Killorn*?" Anne asked.

"I was sweet on a girl when I was a lad. But she married another."

The men on board the *Killorn* threw down a Jacob's ladder and Benjamin went up first. Anne and Teach followed behind, while Easton and his men came up last. The pirate captain threw one leg over the railing at a time, but it was clear it took considerable effort on his part to remain upright.

"Welcome aboard," Easton said. "You'll forgive me a proper tour of the ship, but I'm a little under the weather at the moment."

Beneath Easton's bravado, Anne could see he was in considerable pain. His shoulder blades protruded through the back of his shirt and his skin was wan, sweat glistening on his forehead in the late afternoon sun. He was clearly undernourished.

The other skiff with Teach's men arrived and they boarded as well. Anne wasn't sure if Teach had made the right decision to trust the pirate so easily, but she supposed it was better than staying behind and possibly having a cannon fired at them.

"Take him to the captain's cabin," Teach said. Easton's men led their captain down the stairs. Teach took Anne's hand in his and they followed behind, into the belly of the ship.

CHAPTER 34

Teach

Easton was addled. As far as Teach could see, there was nothing special about the *Killorn*. There were no carvings or extra scroll-work in the wooden railings. The lines of the ship were smooth and well made, but the *Triumph* had been just as serviceable. The pirate had an overinflated ego.

In the captain's cabin, there was nothing out of the ordinary in the stark furnishings. A simple desk, chair, and an armoire were the only pieces of furniture inside the stuffy room. A hammock swung gently from side to side, swaying with the ship. The vessel was quite clean and well maintained, even with the repairs that took place.

Easton's shirt had been ripped open, his bloody shoulder exposed to the air. The bullet had missed the bone, burrowing through the flesh like a large earthworm. Somehow he'd survive. Teach wasn't certain whether or not that was a positive.

Easton sat on the desk, a dark brown bottle in his hand.

Easton nodded to the single chair. "Have a seat," he said, speaking to Anne.

"Thank you, but I'll stand."

Grinning, the pirate took a long swig from the bottle. He wiped his mouth. "Would you care for a sip?" he asked, pushing the bottle toward her.

"I'm not thirsty."

"What information do you have about Webb?" The muscles in Teach's hands twitched. He wanted nothing more than to wrap them around Easton's throat. If the man wasn't careful, Teach would finish what Nathan started.

Easton's amused eyes landed on Teach, as if he could read his thoughts. "Lots." The pirate wasn't in a hurry. After another lengthy drink, he took the bottle and upended it over his shoulder, letting loose a string of curses that would make a dock worker blush.

Anne swayed slightly on her feet.

Easton's face twisted somberly. "I apologize. I'm sorry for offending you."

"It's a bit too late for that," Teach snapped. Turning to Anne, he noted the sheen of sweat on her forehead. Knowing how she felt about needles, he didn't think it wise for her to be present for the rest of the ordeal. She'd already been through a lot. "Would you like to go up on deck for some fresh air? Benjamin could stay with you."

She drew in a shaky breath and sat down on the only chair in the room. "No, I'll be fine."

"How about I hold your hand?" Easton offered. "Sometimes it makes it easi—"

Teach clutched Easton by the shirtfront and dragged him to his feet, not caring about the pirate's injury. "If you don't want to lose your other arm, I suggest you keep your hands to yourself."

Toe-to-toe, the two men stared each other down, neither one willing to look away first.

"Teach," Anne said quietly.

Teach looked over his shoulder. Three pistols pointed at him, a reminder that he was still on Easton's ship. Loosening his hold, Teach slowly released the pirate. Easton's eyes gleamed with triumph. Teach made a mental note to visit with Easton later. Alone. "You were talking about the information you have against Webb."

"Ah, yes. It's not here. I mean, it is *here*," Easton amended, pointing to his temple when he saw Teach clench his fists. "But who would believe a pirate? When I began to work with Webb, it became apparent that I'd need to document everything. At the time, Webb was new to this whole pirating thing and so he did as I asked."

"What do you mean, new?"

"Before I came to Nassau, my crew and I had worked in the Indian Ocean."

Teach scoffed at him. "By 'work' you mean 'stole.'"

Easton hissed as the sailor stitching him up inserted the needle. Teach didn't bother to hide his smile.

"We came to the islands with a significant fortune in tow. The former governor of Nassau, Nicholas Trott, offered us refuge in exchange for some of the treasure. When Trott returned to England, Webb seemed eager to take his place. He gave me a list of ships he wanted us to attack. All of them English."

"Let me guess, you had a twinge of conscience."

"Not at all. I don't feel an ounce of guilt taking money from those bloody merchants. And neither did Webb. But it didn't take long for me to realize that I'd agreed to make a deal with the devil. Trott was corrupt, but the only word to describe Webb would be evil."

"What happened?" Anne asked.

"As you've seen, I assembled my crew from all corners of the earth. It doesn't matter to me what a man looks like or where he comes from, as long as he's willing to work, and work hard. I'll take a chance on him. Webb isn't as open."

Teach chanced a glance in Anne's direction. Her mouth was set into thin lines and he could almost see the progression of her thoughts. Anne wanted to make Webb suffer.

"At first, I just wanted to agitate him. You know, make him wriggle a bit. Whenever Webb came to my ship, I made sure he was treated to a meal that would only be served in Sumatra or Java. For someone who strictly enjoyed meat and potatoes, even the smell of the spices set him off. But one day, he'd had enough." Easton's mouth hardened. "It was the same day he came to tell us about the *Deliverance*. When he left, he asked one of my crew members to deliver a message. Fool that I was, I didn't think anything of it."

"And?" Anne asked. Teach wondered if he should insist she go up on deck.

It was clear Easton had the same thought. "The story isn't meant for female ears."

Anne stood. "I've experienced firsthand the cruelty of that man. If you don't believe me, ask Teach. He sewed me up after Webb and his wife were finished with their handiwork."

Easton swallowed. "Seems we all have a reason to make Webb pay. I'm not innocent. I've done my share of killing, but Webb's different. He does it for sport."

"What happened to the messenger?" Anne asked. Teach hated to admit it, but a small part of him was curious as well.

"Webb sent him to me in pieces with a note suggesting I use him in the next meal." Easton didn't even flinch when the needle pierced his skin this time.

Nobody spoke. Webb had accused Easton of doing that very thing, but Teach was more inclined to believe the pirate. For a thief, the man was surprisingly honest. "So all the rumors about you . . . are they all a lie?"

"Most times rumors are more exciting than the truth," was all Easton said. "And if you make the rumors bad enough, people will fear you and the sound of your name."

The only noise in the room was the thin sound of the thread being pulled through Easton's shoulder. In the distance Kitts could be heard yelling at his men.

"You said you have documents," Anne said. "Could they bring Webb to justice?"

Easton nodded. "If it comes to that. Like I said, Webb asked me to steal from several British merchants."

Teach was beginning to understand Webb's desperation to kill Easton. "Would those happen to be the same merchants Pelham has approached to join their venture?"

"So you've heard about their scheme. Yes, those are the same merchants."

"Which is why you let everyone think you're Spaniards," Teach said.

"That was Webb's idea. At the time it was a good one. I'm sure he didn't think that one day he might need to do business with the same men he'd robbed."

"I would have loved to see Webb's face when Pelham first told him the names of their future associates," Anne said. "Can you imagine how shocked he must have been?"

Easton chuckled. "I'd like to think there's a better way of going after Webb and thrashing him at his own game. Besides, I'll be implicated if any of the information I have gets into the hands of a judge. My head is happily attached to my body and I would like to avoid the gallows."

"But it's important for us to know what kind of arsenal we have at our disposal," Anne said.

Teach tried to catch Anne's gaze, but she avoided looking at him. "Anne."

"What?" Her eyes flashed fire.

Teach didn't want to have a discussion in front of Easton. Teach knew Anne was upset, but nobody had said anything about going after Webb. Teach simply wanted to free his men and Anne's friends and leave Nassau as quickly as possible. "We can discuss this later."

"Why not now?" Easton asked.

The man had a death wish.

"I have some papers signed by Webb. Supply lists for the *Killorn*. In the beginning, Webb signed and paid for everything. He left a trail of bread crumbs leading back to him. But it didn't take long for him to catch on. It didn't matter. By then, I'd already managed to mimic his signature."

Teach gave a short laugh. "Which means the only evidence you have against him are forged documents. Nothing that would hold up in court."

"How good are the forgeries?" Anne asked.

Easton winked at her. "I like you. If you were mine, I'd name my ship after you."

"She's not yours," Teach snapped.

"She could be," Easton said.

Teach took a menacing step forward, but Anne placed her

hand on his chest. "Stop. This is ridiculous. Circumstances have made Webb our common enemy. Now we need to work together to fight against him."

"All I have to do is take Easton and his men back to Nassau," Teach said. "That should be enough to grant me clemency."

"You won't take me back alive."

"Judging from the look of you and your crew, you won't last much longer on your own."

For the first time Easton glared at him. "Does the sight of us starving to death amuse you?"

Heat suffused Teach's face. "I was simply pointing out that you're fast running out of supplies."

"And do you know why? Because we didn't deliver the *Deliverance* to Webb. Everyone had heard about Richard Drummond's mighty ship, and Webb wanted to be the one to take it. Ironic, isn't it? Once we captured it, we were supposed to rendezvous with Webb and split the spoils. He usually left supplies for us in the cay. But thanks to you and your men, the *Killorn* was badly damaged. It took us more than a week to get to the rendezvous point. But there was nothing waiting for us. And I knew then that we were all dead men. Webb wants me gone before the documents and papers I have against him can get into the wrong hands."

Teach knew that if any of the merchants found out about Webb's dealings, they wouldn't be so keen to join Pelham and Webb.

"Which is why Webb sent Nathan with specific instructions to kill you," Anne murmured.

"I'm truly grateful you shot the bounder," Easton said.

Teach didn't know what to say. He didn't know what to do. He wasn't convinced he wanted to go after Webb, especially not with so many lives at stake. But something had to be done.

"There's more," Easton said.

What else could there be, Teach wondered.

"Webb's just the beginning. As wicked as he is, he's almost tame compared to his colleagues. They've scheduled a meeting in Jamaica and should arrive within three months."

"Seven weeks, actually," Anne said.

Both Teach and Easton threw Anne a surprised look.

"I was at the tavern with Benjamin when Pelham stopped by one day. Pelham was upset that Alastair refused to join their group. They want to challenge the monopoly the Royal African Company has on slavery. Pelham said others would be arriving soon and Alastair would need to rethink his position."

"I know who those men are. And they all deserve to hang."

"But who would believe a pirate?" Teach asked, giving Easton a skeptical glance.

"I know you don't believe me, but I do have documentation of Webb's crimes. In the beginning, he trusted me. Later, when Pelham arrived and told Webb his plans, Webb asked for the papers back, but I said they'd been destroyed. I don't think he believed me. In fact, he had the *Killorn* searched twice. But I don't keep any of those things on me. I keep 'em somewhere safe. I consider it a form of insurance, if you will."

"That was an awful gamble to take," Anne said. "Especially now that you know how desperate he is."

"I know. But like a cat, I have nine lives."

Teach rolled his eyes at the same time that Benjamin appeared in the door, a relieved look on his face. "Captain?"

"Yes," Teach and Easton replied, simultaneously.

There was a slight pause as Benjamin looked between the two until Teach spoke up. "What is it?"

"It's still my ship," Easton mumbled.

"The *Triumph* just entered the cay and is preparing to drop anchor. Looks like John is here."

"It's about time," Teach muttered. Turning to Anne, he motioned to the doorway. "Let's go and see what John has to say about his tardiness."

"Should I be worried?" Easton asked, as the man at his side wrapped a bandage around his shoulder.

Anne quirked a brow at him. "About what?"

"That more of your friends have shown up."

An image of John fighting Easton flashed in Teach's mind and he smiled. "Perhaps."

Just as Teach had finished speaking, a familiar hum burst through the air. A half second later, the deep boom of cannon fire shook the ship. The *Killorn* rocked, riding the waves caused by the cannonball.

"Did your men just shoot at us?" Easton's voice was incredulous.

Shocked, Teach met Anne's wide eyes. "There must be some mistake," he said. "I never told him to open fire."

"Perhaps he's worried because he hasn't seen you," Anne offered.

"Right. We'll go up on deck and—" A second cannonball striking the hull of the ship cut off Teach's words. *That was no mistake.*

"Blimey! Get up there!" Easton yelled. "Before they tear my bloody ship apart."

"Stay here," Teach said to Anne before turning to the door. "Easton, try to make yourself useful."

"I'll keep her safe," Easton called after him.

Shooting the pirate a murderous glare over his shoulder, Teach raced up to the deck, his heart lurching in painful strikes against his ribs. His crew looked to him, waiting for orders, while Easton's men busily loaded their weapons.

Benjamin handed Teach a spyglass. He quickly scanned the *Triumph.* "I don't recognize any of them," he muttered, giving the deck another once-over. He strode to the railing in an attempt to make himself visible. And he waited. *Where is John?*

Benjamin jerked his head sideways just as the sound of a musket shot exploded from the deck of the *Triumph.* The young man raised his hand to his ear, blood pouring down his arm. Stooping over, Teach hurried to Benjamin's side, snapping the spyglass shut and reaching up to check the wound. "Are you all right?" Teach asked.

Benjamin nodded. "It just grazed me."

Teach breathed a sigh of relief. "Go have Anne take a look at it. And tell her to stay out of sight. John's not in command of that ship."

"What?"

"There's no sign of him or any of our men. I know they saw me and they still opened fire."

"Webb," Benjamin said, his voice grim.

They'd clearly underestimated the governor. Nathan had been right. "He must have had us followed. And now they've overtaken the *Triumph*." Signaling to his crew, he motioned for them to follow him to the stairs leading belowdecks. To Easton's men he called out, "Are your guns trained around?"

"Aye, sir."

"Good. You there, stay here and open fire with your muskets. Shoot for their portals and make them scatter. The rest of you come with me and prepare to cast loose your guns!"

"But John could still be on board," Benjamin said as they rushed down the wooden planks.

Teach had already considered that thought, but he wasn't about to sit around and wait to be blown out of the water. John would never fire on a sitting ship without first knowing where his friends were. It was possible John was already dead. Another cannonball hurled toward them, the echo of the gun sounding across the open cay.

"We don't have another choice."

With a sad nod, Benjamin headed off in the direction of the captain's cabin.

The low ceiling of the gun deck caused Teach to crouch. Normally the crew had plenty of time to prepare a ship for action when the watch in the crow's nest spotted a sail at sea. But they only had a few minutes to prepare for this battle. Teach called for his gun captains to work together and Easton's men to man their own cannons. They were shorthanded, but Teach refused to consider the odds of them not coming out of this encounter alive.

The men were quiet, waiting for their next command. "Level your gun and load with cartridge!" With a burst of frenzied movements, the men did as he ordered. "Out tampions!"

Once they'd removed the muzzles of the cannons, all eyes were once again on him. "Number one and three guns, you fire on my command." Teach paused only a fraction of a second, then, "Fire!"

The world exploded around them as the guns let loose their deadly arsenal. Acrid smoke filled the cramped space, and the fading light of day had difficulty breaking through the wispy mists choking the men. The spongers immediately wiped out the guns, preparing for the next volley.

Too slow. They were too slow. Three cannonballs shot from

the *Triumph*, but only one broke through the hull of the *Killorn*, sending a shower of sharp, splintered wood in the air. "Fire!"

The ringing in Teach's ears intensified. He heard a shout. "Captain!"

Teach turned to see Easton stumbling and carrying one side of a crate with his good arm and Benjamin carrying the other. "What are you doing?" Teach demanded.

Easton dropped the crate and pulled up the lid, revealing short iron bars bundled together with a length of rope. Bundle shot. They were normally used to take down rigging and masts, but because it wasn't very accurate, could only be used at close range. But they were also known to cause devastating damage to flesh and bone.

"Where did those come from?" Teach asked.

"I told you the beauty of this ship came from within. You didn't believe me." Easton's men rushed the crate and removed most of the bundle shot, just as another cannonball struck the *Killorn*.

"Did you have them when you went against the *Deliverance*?"

"Aye."

"But you didn't use them."

"It wasn't our intent to send you to your deaths." He jerked his thumb in the direction of the *Triumph*. "But that's exactly where they're going. Fire when ready!" Easton yelled.

The ship jumped beneath the explosions, and Teach held on to an overhead rafter as more smoke filled the air. Still pale from blood loss, Easton's eyes were focused, his expression unforgiving. Gone was the flippant air of the rogue pirate. He was clearly a man intent on survival.

Teach's men, now prepared to launch their own cannonballs, looked to him for permission. "Show them no quarter, for they'll give you none!" Teach braced himself for the volley sure to come from the *Triumph*. Easton called out more preparations to his gunners.

"Fire!"

With teeth-rattling intensity, the cannons shattered the air once more. As the smoke cleared, Teach realized that there had been no answering strike from the *Triumph*. Easton raised a brow and made a motion with his hand. The men paused. Had the *Killorn* inflicted enough damage that the others had already given up?

One minute passed and then another, but the cannons of the *Triumph* remained silent. Leaning forward, Teach peered through the nearest gun port, careful not to expose himself to the enemy muskets. The *Triumph* had several broad holes in her hull. They'd managed to inflict significant damage.

The hair on the back of Teach's neck stood up as he saw the men of the *Triumph* scrambling on her deck. But they were scrambling to the other side of the ship, out to the open water and away from the *Killorn*.

"Something's not right," Teach said, straightening. He headed for the stairs, but Easton reached out and stopped him.

"It could be a trick on their part."

Teach shook him off. "I don't think so. I'm going up." With Easton following close on his heels, Teach reached the top, careful to keep low. Debris covered the deck, bits of canvas and chunks of wood. Easton growled, but the sound died in his throat when they saw the oncoming sails of an approaching ship.

"That's the *Fortune*," Easton said. "It belongs to Webb."

As more of the sails and rigging came into view, Teach recognized the same simple lines and curves that matched the *Killorn*. The *Fortune* was the sister ship that had taken part in the attack on the *Deliverance*.

The knot in Teach's stomach tightened. The assault on the *Killorn* would now be doubled, unless they sank the *Triumph* where she lay, preventing the *Fortune* from entering the shallow waters of the inlet. But that would leave them trapped as well.

A white cloud of smoke erupted from a gun port of the *Fortune*, sending a cannonball slicing through the air and hitting the *Triumph* with a resounding crack.

Teach and Easton shot each other confused looks.

"Did they just fire on their own ship?" Easton asked. He'd no sooner finished his question when another gun erupted, followed by another, with both balls hitting the *Triumph*.

Raising the spyglass to his eye, Teach scoured the deck of the *Fortune*, and he gave an exultant shout when he saw John's face amongst his familiar crew.

Turning, Teach raced back down the steps to his own gun deck, calling out commands to prepare the cannons.

When the men were ready, Teach raised his arm. "First and third guns, on my command. Fire!" he yelled.

The world exploded at the eruptions.

"Fifth and seventh. Fire!" Teach was astounded at the detonation that rocked the *Killorn* beneath his feet. Even his men froze and paused, until they heard an exuberant shout.

Easton crouched on the stairs between the gun and upper deck, a jubilant smile on his face. "Well done, lads! We live to see another day! The *Triumph* will plague us no more!"

Leaning forward, Teach saw the burning remains of the *Triumph*. Most of the ship had been blown apart, with only the stern remaining. The *Triumph* hadn't stood a chance against two well-armed vessels.

Bounding toward the captain's cabin, Teach found Anne where he'd left her. Benjamin sat on the table, holding a rag up to his ear and Anne stood by his side, a beautiful smile lighting her face. In two steps, he reached her. Mindful of her back, his lips met hers. Her arms went around his neck, her fingers sliding into his hair. His desire to be alone with her overwhelmed him in every way.

But someone gave a low whistle, reminding Teach that they were so very far from being alone.

Easing Anne away with a quiet murmur, Teach saw that Benjamin had turned his head politely. But Easton leaned against the door frame, a smile stretching his thin face.

"If that's the prize *you're* awarded, what will the *real* hero receive? Since it was my ship that saved us—"

Teach stepped forward, prepared to inflict bodily harm, but Anne stopped him, rounding on Easton. "Your reward is your life. If you make one more comment like that, I won't stop him from coming after you. You might be entertained by your own wit, but the rest of us are not."

Easton looked between the two of them. Something in Teach's expression must have convinced him that Anne spoke the truth, for he gave them a brief nod. "All right, then. I'll consider myself thanked. Shall we go up on deck and see where your men are?"

CHAPTER 35

Anne

Teach sent a skiff to shore, bringing Kitts and the rest of his men to the *Killorn*. Some of them were already collecting planks of wood that dotted the water's surface from the destroyed *Triumph*. They could be used to repair Easton's ship.

By the time John pulled up in a longboat, the deck of the pirate ship was teeming with men. Kitts, Easton, and Teach had formed some kind of uneasy truce, at least for the moment.

As John's grinning face appeared over the railing, relief unfolded in Anne's chest and she met his smile with one of her own. John had left the *Fortune* anchored out in the open water.

Striding toward Anne, John took her hands in his. "Happy to see me?"

Teach slapped John on the back, slightly harder than necessary. "Of course we are! But how did you get from the *Triumph* to the other ship?"

Kitts's astonished voice cut through the celebration. "You're a woman!"

Anne turned to see everyone staring at a slight figure wearing a hat pulled low. Reva's dark brown hair was long and pulled back in multiple braids.

"Muy bien." Shaking her head, Reva looked in Easton's direction. "Are they all this intelligente, Easton?"

"Only the ones that survive. What are you doing here?"

"Saving your life, querido."

Anne smiled at the expression on Easton's face as he gaped at Reva. The girl certainly enjoyed surprising people.

"What do you mean?" he asked.

Reva gave Anne an exasperated look. "Los hombres," she said, rolling her eyes.

"She means *she* is the reason we're all still alive. After I took Anne and Benjamin ashore," John said, purposefully avoiding Teach's eyes, "I returned to the ship and saw the *Fortune* from a distance. I'd hoped that they would sail past, or if they did stop to offer help, we could simply tell them to move along. But when they arrived, they didn't offer any warning, opening musket fire on our ship, and taking out two of ours before we knew what they were about. Their captain said that if we came without a fight, they'd let us live."

Teach stiffened at Anne's side, his hand tightening momentarily around hers.

"They took us to the *Fortune* and set off on the *Triumph*

to catch you off guard. I'm sure it's no surprise to anyone that Webb sent them after us," John said.

"How do you know for sure?" Kitts asked.

"They were only too happy to tell us." John gave Kitts a cold stare. "Apparently, Webb never planned for any of us to return to Nassau. Or anywhere else, for that matter. They were told not to leave any survivors."

"I told you," Easton said grimly. "Anyone who comes in contact with me and the information I have is considered a threat."

Anne shook her head, trying to make sense of it all. "But how did you overtake their ship?"

"Reva and her men were already part of their crew. They were the ones left to guard us. They set us free and we sailed here as fast as we could."

"Why were you part of the crew?" Easton demanded.

"And how did you hide the fact that you were a woman?" Anne asked, fascinated.

"Los hombres son estupidos. They only see what they want to see. The captain needed more sailors for the *Fortune* and I needed a way to leave Nassau and come after Easton. I slept during the day and kept to the crow's nest during my watch at night." Reva pointed a finger at the pirate. "You stole my ship."

"No, I borrowed it."

"I want it back."

"I'm afraid that's not possible."

"You sank the *Maldicion*?" Reva's lips twisted into an ugly snarl as she let loose a string of Spanish curses, accompanied by rapid hand gestures.

The rest of the group was silent for a moment, watching her.

Anne chanced a glance at Kitts, trying to determine his thoughts. The governor whose orders he so blindly followed hadn't thought twice about killing him.

Eventually Reva stopped, but she continued to glare in Easton's direction. "I should never have trusted you."

"I'll find you another ship. I promise."

Reva let her hands express what she thought of Easton's pledge.

For the first time since he'd boarded the *Killorn*, John took a hard look at Easton. "Who're you?" John asked.

"George Easton."

"The pirate?"

"One and the same. And you are?"

Anne tried to smother a laugh at the shock on John's face.

Teach grinned. "This is John Collins, my first mate."

Easton gave a slight bow. "Well, John Collins, I'm pleased to make your acquaintance."

John raked his hand through his hair. Anne could practically see the wheels churning in his head. The pirate they'd been sent to capture had just greeted him as if they were at a simple dinner party. And he wasn't in any form of restraints, even with

Kitts standing right beside him. "We'll explain later, John. First we have to decide what to do now."

"We head back to Nassau."

Every head turned in Easton's direction.

"What? It's our only option at the moment." Although Easton's voice was light, the look in his eyes was hard.

"You said you'd never go back to Nassau alive," Teach said.

"That was before I knew Webb would try to have me killed *twice* in one day. We have to go back. Do you think he'll let me live with the information I have?" Easton asked. "He sent *you* to find me, that dirty bounder to *kill* me, and then he sent another ship to make everything and everyone disappear. Once he finds out I'm still alive, I'll be a hunted man for the rest of my life, constantly looking over my shoulder. If the *Fortune* doesn't return, he'll know immediately that something is wrong. I wouldn't be surprised if he hasn't already sent another ship after us."

"But he thinks we're dead. If we go back, he'll know his plans failed," Kitts said. This was the first time the soldier had voiced anything that remotely resembled insubordination. Perhaps he wasn't so loyal to the Crown after all.

"Which is precisely why we need to go back. He'll figure it out eventually, but if we strike now, we can catch him off guard. We have to take the fight to *him*."

"That would be a suicide mission," Kitts said.

Easton gave the soldier a patronizing smile. "If you were in charge, yes. You'd walk through his front door and announce yourself. But that's not the way I fight."

Kitts flushed a dark crimson. "We have to seriously think about this. We can't just attack the governor of Nassau."

"That's exactly what we'll do. And we'll do it now. Remember, he tried to kill each and every one of us today. And he won't lose a single night of sleep over it." Easton stepped up to Reva at the same time that she whipped out a long dagger.

"I'm not going back," she hissed. "I had to sleep in the belly of that ship for six days. Today was the first time I saw the sun since I left Nassau. When I go after Pelham, I plan to do it with a ship of my own."

Wisely, the pirate moved on, motioning to Anne and Teach. "Webb's holding your friends hostage until you take me back. So go back we shall. But we'll make it worth our while. Webb is our true enemy. He can't be allowed to continue destroying lives."

"He's right," Anne said. "Webb has to be stopped." She was grateful to Easton. He'd put into words exactly what she'd been feeling ever since she'd first met the governor and his wife. But she knew that as a woman, no one would have listened to her.

"We can't all return on the *Fortune*," Teach pointed out.

"Of course not. We'll need some men to remain here and continue repairing the *Killorn*."

"What about supplies?" Kitts asked.

John stepped forward. "The *Fortune* is well equipped. They took the supplies we had left on the *Triumph* and transported them before they went searching for you. But even if they hadn't, it's obvious Webb made sure they were well stocked."

"Ah, yes, Webb mustn't let his mercenaries starve, must he?" Easton muttered, his voice bitter.

"You were once one of his mercenaries," Kitts pointed out.

Easton scowled at him as he held his arms wide, showing his emaciated form. "And we've seen how well that went."

"We need to make haste," Teach said. "We'll leave enough supplies here for the men who stay and make sure we take enough with us to make the trip to Nassau and back. We won't have time to resupply while we're there."

Excellent. Anne had been about to say the same thing. "The trip there should only take us five or six days, depending on the—"

"You're not going," Teach and Easton said simultaneously.

Anne scoffed at the two of them. "Why not?"

"Because it's too dangerous." A fierce frown cracked Teach's face.

"You'll be too much of a distraction. And it's too dangerous," Easton added, after catching Teach's eye.

"This isn't your decision to make. I have as much right as any of you to go after that man, especially after what he did to me and what his wife did to Beth. And those are *my* friends he's holding hostage, not just your men."

"I'm sorry, Anne. I understand how you must feel—"

"Don't you dare pretend to know how I feel," she ground

out, her face flushing with heat. "This is as much my fight as it is yours." The governor had threatened to sell her. Teach would never understand how that felt.

Teach's mouth thinned, his expression thunderous, but surprisingly it was Kitts who spoke up next.

"He's right. It's too dangerous. You escaped Webb once, but if you go back, and he catches you, you *will* hang. Webb can't be trusted."

"If *any* of you go back and are caught, you'll all hang," Anne pointed out.

Easton shook his head. "We won't get caught."

"How can you be so sure?"

"Because we know how to fight," Easton said, his voice unapologetic. "I meant what I said. You'll be a distraction. A lovely one, but a distraction nonetheless. If you get caught, Teach wouldn't hesitate to go after you, which could compromise all our lives. It's too great a risk."

"So you expect me to stay here with a bunch of strangers while you all sail off?"

"Reva has already said she's staying," Easton said. Reva looked as if she wanted to hurl her dagger in his direction. "And I'm sure the two of you will get along."

"John and Benjamin will stay behind," Teach said. "And some of the men from my crew. They're fit and will be able to repair Easton's ship faster. If I didn't trust them, I wouldn't leave you here."

Frustrated, Anne looked to John for help. Surely he would

make them see reason. But her friend only gave her a sympathetic smile, his mouth firmly shut.

Without another word she stalked off toward the captain's cabin.

Three separate campfires lit up the night sky. The musky scent of smoke rose in lazy spirals toward the stars. From the windows in the captain's cabin, Anne watched the men on the shore laughing together. Correction, the men and one woman. Reva sat comfortably on a log, her legs crossed in front of her. Since her men were excellent fighters and in good shape, several of them would sail back to Nassau as well.

In an effort to help some of Easton's men gain strength, they'd slaughtered two of the pigs from the *Fortune*, and Anne's stomach rumbled, the smell of roasted pork reaching her across the cay.

An overwhelming feeling of loneliness washed over her. Would she ever find a world in which she belonged?

"We're ready to leave," Teach said.

Anne maintained a stony silence. She hadn't heard the cabin door open, but she didn't turn around.

"Please don't be like this."

The scent of food had intensified. Teach had brought her something to eat, and Anne's mouth began to water. His footsteps sounded on the wooden planks behind her, and the plate clanked on the desk as he set it down.

"I'm not sorry for leaving you behind. I would never forgive myself if anything happened to you."

"That's unfortunate, because I won't forgive you if you leave me behind."

"Anne."

"What?" she snapped, whirling on him, the firelight in the distance flickering across his face. "What do you want me to say? I'm not going to make this easy on you."

"None of this is easy on me. But I stand by my decision." He reached for her, but she raised her hands to ward off any contact. He ran a frustrated hand over his jaw. "Do you have any idea of the danger we face in returning to Nassau?"

"Of course I do."

"Then you should know that I would never want you anywhere near there again. When I saw what they did to you." Teach's voice cracked. "Losing you is the one thing I could never recover from, Anne."

She stared back at him defiantly. "And you think I'll be able to go on if something were to happen to you? The danger exists for you, just as it does for me."

"But Easton was right. You would be a distraction. I couldn't focus, worrying about you. It's bad enough that I have to leave you here, but at least Webb won't be able to get to you. You'll be safe. The men I'm leaving behind are good men, Anne. And so are the ones I'm going back for."

The two of them stared at each other, neither one willing

to look away first. Teach was still. Anne understood what lurked beneath his stillness, because she felt the same flow of yearning, but she was too angry right now to give in.

John appeared in the doorway, but he hesitated, as if sensing the tension in the air. "Easton is waiting for you."

Teach nodded. "Tell him I'll be there."

Ducking out of the room, John retreated.

"I suppose I'll see you in a fortnight," Teach said.

Anne's throat was tight and she simply nodded.

"Look for Easton's colors when we return. We're taking his Jolly Roger with us. If all is well, we'll fly his flag." Leaning forward, Teach pressed a swift kiss on her forehead before pulling away. "We'll celebrate your birthday when I get back. I love you," he murmured, and strode from the room, closing the door soundly behind him.

Anne turned, staring sightlessly out the windows at the group on the beach, resentful of their freedom, and wishing she'd told Teach she loved him in return. Unaware of the passage of time, she jumped when she felt a hand on her shoulder. It was John.

"So you're my appointed nursemaid, are you?" Anne asked.

John shook his head. "I'm your friend. And I'd rather spend time with you than the likes of them."

Sighing, she attempted a smile.

"It wasn't an easy decision for him to make," John said.

"I know."

He motioned to the plate of cold food on the table. "You haven't eaten anything. I'm supposed to make sure Teach finds you in the same condition that he left you in."

"I'm not hungry."

"Could you pretend to be? I take my job seriously and would prefer Teach not come back and beat me to a pulp."

Anne laughed outright. "I've heard of your fighting skills. I doubt even Teach could best you." She didn't imagine the straightening of John's shoulders or the proud tilt of his chin. If there was one thing John was good at, it was a physical fight. A sudden thought occurred to Anne. "If I eat, will you promise me something?"

"Anything," John said, completely unsuspecting.

"I want you to teach me how to fight."

CHAPTER 36

Teach

"Looks like Webb decided to practice in my absence," Easton muttered. A single figure swung suspended in a metal cage over the low-water mark of the bay.

Teach shivered at the sight. It was too dark to see him clearly, but from the way the body slumped, Teach guessed the man had been alive when he'd been gibbeted. It was common practice to punish the condemned by leaving them to die of thirst.

The flickering lights of Nassau glittered like stars in the dark as Teach and the others rowed through the shallow waters of the port toward the dock. They'd agreed it would be best to arrive at night, when no one would be able to recognize the *Fortune* and alert Webb. Although it was dangerous, Easton had managed to convince them to leave the ship anchored farther out than Teach would have liked. But because of it, they'd managed to slip undetected into the harbor.

There were fifteen men in all in the skiff. Four from Easton's crew, four of Kitts's soldiers, and four of Reva's men. The rest they'd left on the *Fortune*. Six days prior, they'd left John, Anne, and Benjamin behind with Reva and the others to repair the *Killorn*.

The thought of Anne made Teach's insides contract painfully. He could still picture her face, the sting of his betrayal in her eyes. He vowed to make it up to her somehow.

But first, they had to get to Webb.

Navigating through the water to a dark inlet of the port, they secured the longboat before climbing up the wooden stairs to the wharf. It seemed as if a lifetime had passed since they'd last been there, but it had been just more than three weeks. Teach remembered the first time he'd arrived in Nassau, with the threat of mutiny hanging over his head. The threat was still there, and Teach wondered if he'd ever come to view this city with anything but dread.

Easton pointed in the direction of the fort and moved off with ten of the men in tow, including Hillel, his first mate.

Teach and Kitts headed toward the governor's mansion with two of Kitts's men accompanying them. Nobody spoke, fearful of bringing attention to themselves. The four of them walked with purpose, even though the outcome of their mission was unclear. So many things could go wrong, but Teach had come too far to turn coward now.

There were two guards at the gate to the governor's mansion, with more stationed inside the courtyard. They held up their lanterns and muskets as Teach and his companions approached, but relaxed visibly when they saw and recognized Kitts and his men.

"It's good to see you're back, Kitts," one of the guards said, eyeing Teach. "What brings you at this hour?"

"Webb gave me specific instructions to come to see him when I returned, regardless of the time. I'm simply following orders."

Even Teach was convinced of Kitts's sincerity. Teach shot him a guarded glance, but Kitts didn't return his gaze.

They were waved through, their footsteps echoing in the courtyard. Teach looked at the mansion, noting that only one window was illuminated from within. The butler opened the front door, seemingly unfazed by their appearance, although it was past nine. Since they'd made it past the guards outside, the older man clearly wasn't concerned.

"I'll let the governor know you're here."

Instead of waiting in the foyer, Teach and Kitts followed the butler. The older man looked at them over his shoulder. Teach smiled. "We don't want you to have to walk all the way back to let us know he'll see us."

The butler's gray eyebrows drew together. "That's not necessary. I'm not sure if he will want to see you. Perhaps it would be best if you waited—"

Both Kitts and Teach pounced on the man, smothering his cries with a rag and a hastily tied kerchief around his mouth.

Teach attempted to secure the butler's hands behind his back, while Kitts's soldiers picked up his legs. The muffled sound of their struggle echoed down the hallway as they dragged the butler into one of the spare, dark rooms. Panting, they waited for footsteps, but heard nothing. In the dim moonlight shining through the shuttered windows, the whites of the butler's eyes showed as he looked frantically between them.

"You two stay here and make sure he doesn't get loose," Kitts instructed his men.

"Give us ten minutes to return. If we aren't back by then, get out," Teach said. He opened the door cautiously, peering down the hallway. Somewhere in the distance, a door opened and closed. Other than that, there was no sound. "Better yet, give us fifteen minutes. We don't know who we'll encounter."

Teach headed toward the one lighted room, with Kitts on his heels, only to duck into a nearby alcove when they heard voices coming from the back of the mansion. With a house this size, the governor would need a large staff. Teach simply wished they would all retire so that he and Kitts could get this over with.

Once the voices had faded, Teach and Kitts crept forward, glancing over their shoulders to see if they were being followed. A thin strip of light spilled out beneath the door on their right, but there was no detectable movement from within. Teach bent in front of the keyhole, spying a familiar head leaning over the desk.

Teach took the handle and pressed down, his palms sweaty

and his breathing fractured as he tried to control it. The door opened noiselessly, and the two of them slid inside.

Webb glanced up, a pistol in his hand and a smirk on his face.

Teach's stomach dropped.

"You're back," Webb said.

"No thanks to you and your efforts," Teach said. "You're looking surprisingly well, Governor. Have you started drinking a different brand of tea? Where's your wife?"

The smile on Webb's face vanished. "That's no concern of yours. I sent you out on a fine ship, with plenty of supplies, and how do you repay me? By sneaking into my house like two thieves in the night?"

"We did come through the front door," Teach reminded him, sparing a glance at Kitts. The man's face was devoid of emotion. It was impossible to know what he was thinking.

"And? What news do you have for me?" Webb demanded, waving the pistol.

"Easton's dea—"

"Alive," Kitts said.

The sound of Teach's indrawn breath cut through the air like an axe. "Curse your eyes, Kitts," Teach muttered. The man was incapable of telling a lie.

Webb looked between the two of them, his expression triumphant. "I knew I could count on you, Kitts, which is why I sent you in the first place."

Kitts stood up straight, his chin jutting forward. Even now, the slightest bit of praise from the governor could affect him. It was enough to make Teach sick.

"If you knew you could count on him, then why did you try to have him killed?" Teach ground out.

"My men are willing to die for me. Just as yours were willing to die for you." Webb studied Teach as he allowed the information to sink in. "They faced the gallows without flinching, by the way. As I said before, your leadership is to be commended."

Scorching fury throbbed through Teach's veins as he pictured the faces of young Matthew and Jack Thurston and the others who'd stayed behind, locked in the fort. All because Teach had been arrogant enough to believe he could handle the governor alone. He'd told Jack he wouldn't abandon them, yet that's just what he'd done. "You're a dead man," Teach whispered, his voice hoarse.

Webb stood up from his desk and leaned against the corner, the pistol still in his hand. "Idle threats. I've half a mind to shoot you here. Did you speak with Easton?"

"Aye," Teach said. "And he told us how you stole from English ships. That's piracy and it's a hanging offense."

"And you believed him?"

"Why wouldn't we?"

"Because Easton's a liar and a —" There was a flash of movement behind Webb and the governor stiffened, his eyes growing wide. His mouth opened and closed, but no sound escaped.

Easton stood up from behind the desk, his expression grim. In his hand was a crimson-stained knife that glittered in the candlelight. "I told you he wasn't to be trusted."

Kitts shook his head, glaring at Easton. "It took you long enough."

"It wasn't as easy slipping past the guards as I thought. I'm out of practice," Easton muttered, opening the drawers of the desk. "And someone planted rose bushes outside the bloody windows. I'm surprised you didn't hear me when I crept in."

"I was too busy listening to Webb tell me how invaluable I am," Kitts said.

With shaking hands, Teach grabbed the governor by his shirtfront, bringing him close. "Where's Alastair?" he asked, barely managing to keep a tight rein on his anger. He was tempted to take the knife from Easton and carve Webb up in pieces. Easton had warned him not to expect his men to live, but to hear that Webb had actually gone through with it . . .

Dazed, Webb glanced down. The governor was clearly having trouble grasping that he was bleeding out and would die within minutes. Determined to get an answer, Teach gave the governor a swift shake that rocked the man's head back and forth on his shoulders. "I'll ask one last time, where's Alastair?"

A choked noise gurgled out of the governor's throat and Teach threw him back into his chair. Easton rifled through the governor's pockets, withdrawing a small key that the pirate used to open a drawer on the bottom right of the desk. In it was a stack of papers that Easton tucked into the back of his waist-band.

"What're those?" Teach asked.

"I don't know, but I'm fairly certain they're valuable. Otherwise he wouldn't have them locked up. I'm taking them to add to my growing collection."

Teach was amazed at Easton's cunning. He seemed to have a sixth sense when it came to second-guessing Webb. It had been Easton's idea to trick the governor into believing that Kitts was still on his side, and the governor had played right into their hands. Some of Teach's amazement must have shown on his face, because Easton paused. "When you've known men like this for as long as I have, you learn to fight like they do. You can't expect justice or fairness from them, because they won't give it to you."

"We need to leave," Kitts said.

Teach still hadn't found out where Alastair was being kept.

Easton strode to the window, but ducked back inside when a shot was fired and the ball narrowly missed his head. Splinters of wood flew where the shot embedded itself in the paneling. "We're going to have some difficulty."

Just then, a voice trickled in from the hallway outside the door. "Governor Webb, is all well?"

The governor's eyes were still opened, but his chest was still. He wouldn't be answering in this lifetime. Kitts waved furiously at Easton to be quiet, but Easton shrugged his shoulders and called out, "Aye. Leave us!" His voice was a rough imitation of Webb's.

Teach was both fearful and furious. He'd clearly underestimated the governor and so much of the situation. Picking up the pistol the governor had held, Teach discovered it wasn't even loaded.

More footsteps shuffled in the hallway. "Governor Webb, are you quite sure you're all right?"

Before anyone could respond, the door flew open. Six soldiers burst in and quickly surrounded Kitts, Teach, and Easton, stripping Easton of his knife. They led the three men from the room, down the hall, and into the courtyard, where even more soldiers waited. Some soldiers held torches, while the rest were armed with muskets and cutlasses. Pelham stood before them, robed in a dressing gown, his powdered wig slightly askew.

"Governor Webb is dead, Lord Pelham," one of the soldiers said. "They used this." Easton's knife glinted in the torchlight, still stained with Webb's blood.

"The three of you are charged with the murder of Nicholas Webb, the proprietary governor of Nassau," Pelham said.

"Technically, *I* killed Webb. These two men were innocent bystanders," Easton said.

Pelham snorted. "I would hardly call them innocent."

"And I would hardly say you know the true meaning of the word. How I wish I could say it was a pleasure to see you again,

Lord Pelham. Gentlemen, may I introduce you to a man whose hands are even dirtier than mine."

"Easton," Teach muttered under his breath. The pirate was not exactly helping the situation.

"Webb doesn't deserve your loyalty," Kitts said, addressing the soldiers surrounding them. "And neither does this man. Don't be fooled by anything he says."

"Like you were fooled by Easton?" Pelham sneered. "My men tell me you were a soldier under Webb. And now you're a pirate. How does it feel to be a traitor to the Crown?"

Kitts tried to school his normally expressive face into an impassive mask, but not before Teach saw a flash of emotion, something between shame and resentment. "I have no trouble sleeping at night," Kitts said.

Pelham ignored the comment, his eyes turning to Teach. "What about you, Drummond?"

The world tilted on its axis. Teach had not expected to hear that name again so soon. Pelham licked his lips, obviously enjoying Teach's shock. "Ah, you're surprised I know your real name. You shouldn't be. I told you when I first saw you that you looked familiar. It took me a while to figure it out, but I've dealt with Richard Drummond in the past. In fact, I supported him when he wanted to build the *Deliverance*. Does your father know the path you've chosen?"

Teach went cold, then hot. "I suppose you'll be only too happy to tell him."

"On the contrary. I think it would be best if *you* told him. Take him," Pelham said, motioning to the nearest soldiers. "Line the others up against the wall. If anyone asks, they were covered in Webb's blood and caught escaping."

"What? No trial?" Easton asked as they pushed him to the side.

Pelham smiled, but it didn't reach his eyes. "These islands are lawless. A firm hand is required to rid it of pirates."

"The men of the *Deliverance* were not pirates," Teach said.

"No. According to Webb, they were mutineers. You no doubt saw one of them as you came in. What was the name of the little one?" Pelham asked, looking around at his men, but no one responded. "Was it Matthew? He's the one we placed in the cage. I haven't been out to the docks lately. Is there anything left of him? Or have the birds done their job?"

No! Teach's pulse skipped a beat, and he clenched his hands into fists, the nails digging into his palms as he pictured Matthew's body slumped against the side of the cage.

"The big one, Jack, put up quite a fight as we took the little one away. Because of that we simply decided to hang the others. They deserved to die. And so did your other friend Alastair Flynn. Webb told me all about how you and Alastair helped a murderer escape from the fort. Troubling news, to be sure." Pelham's shrewd eyes watched Teach's every move. "But I need Alastair. More importantly, I need his ships."

"There are other merchants," Teach ground out, wondering at the man's obsession with Alastair.

"True. But they don't have Alastair's extensive knowledge of these islands. It took some convincing on my part, but he's come around. I simply found a price Alastair was willing to pay. Family can be such a motivating factor in one's decisions."

Teach shut his eyes, picturing his hands closing on Pelham's throat and choking the life out of him.

"Steady," Easton whispered.

Pelham made a tsk-ing noise. "You need to choose your friends more wisely, Edward. A father is cursed because of a bad son."

Teach blinked against the black dots swimming in his vision. Those black dots coalesced into figures scurrying into the courtyard. "If anyone's cursed tonight, I dare say it would be you," Teach said, grateful for the steadiness of his voice.

For the first time since he'd confronted them, Pelham frowned. "Why?"

"Because you're surrounded."

Pelham and his men turned, just as Teach's and Easton's men opened fire. Several of the soldiers fell to the ground, their own muskets going off haphazardly.

Teach grabbed the cutlass of a downed soldier nearest him, as Kitts and Easton did the same. The soldiers who hadn't been hit started toward them. Kitts hesitated, and Teach lunged, barely managing to block the sword thrust at Kitts's side.

Kitts gave him a grateful nod, before raising his own cutlass and fighting off the oncoming rush of soldiers. The clash of steel on steel rang throughout the courtyard. Teach and Easton fought back to back, lunging and parrying with their swords.

"We have to go," Easton said, his breathing labored. "Before more soldiers arrive from the fort."

Not until I finish Pelham. Using his size to his advantage, Teach took the legs out from under his opponent with a vicious swipe of his cutlass. The man fell on his back, hitting his head and stirring no more. Teach attacked the next soldier, and the next, cutting through them like a knife through butter. His rage gave him added strength as he stalked his target.

"Teach!" Easton called.

Jerking around, Teach saw Easton motion to the docks, but Teach wasn't ready to leave just yet.

Charging yet another opponent, Teach slammed through two additional soldiers, but Pelham rushed through the throng and into the house, slamming the door shut behind him. Teach started toward the house, but Easton grabbed his arm. "If you want to get out of here alive, then we need to leave now."

With a muttered curse, Teach rushed after Easton, the rest of their men falling in behind. They raced toward the gate and the darkened streets of Nassau. Shouts burst from the courtyard as Pelham's soldiers attempted to rally and give chase.

Teach followed the men darting down side alleyways and passages, breathing through the stitch in his side. As much as Teach wanted to see Pelham suffer and save Alastair, his biggest concern now was to get back to Anne. It was too dangerous to stay in Nassau.

Easton held up a fist and the group slowed to a stop, hiding in the shadows of a warehouse along the docks. Hillel stood beside Easton. Teach glanced at Kitts, and noticed that he was bleeding, his left arm hanging limply down his side.

"Kitts is hurt," Teach said.

"It's not bad," Kitts insisted.

Easton peered through the darkness. "Did you find a ship, Hillel?"

"Aye. It's right there."

The ship in question was a long, slender craft, renowned for its speed. Teach had only seen one once before. It was armed with big guns at the bow and several swivel guns mounted along the side rails. The figure of a woman rested under the bowsprit.

The pirate grinned. "Reva will love it." He led the way, and several of the men followed, crouched low. Hearty laughter drifting from the waterfront tavern nearby drowned out their footsteps. Once they were safely on board, they provided cover for the next group.

Teach and Kitts were some of the last men to leave the shelter of the warehouse. They'd only taken a few steps when several shots rang out as soldiers barreled toward them, their footsteps echoing along the wharf.

"Move!" Easton yelled as the soldiers reloaded their muskets. The ship was already pushing off from the dock, under the control of oars.

Teach and Kitts both ran headlong toward the escaping vessel. Taking a flying leap, Teach soared over the clear water below, hoping he hadn't misjudged the distance due to the gloomy night. Landing on the deck with a grunt, he rolled and came to his feet. He grabbed the weapon Easton shoved at him and took aim, holding the wooden stock flush with his shoulder. The rifle cracked and a soldier on the wharf dropped where he stood.

Kitts wasn't so lucky. With his injured arm held against his chest, he barely cleared the water. His chest slammed into the railing and as he started to fall backward, Easton grabbed hold of his shirt. Several of his men rushed forward and pulled him on board.

The distance between the dock and the ship grew as they continued toward the entrance of the harbor. Soon they were out of gunshot range of the wharf. A cannon fired from the fort but the ball fell short, the command given much too late. The stolen ship drew alongside the *Fortune*, but they didn't stop. Easton shouted at his men on the *Fortune* to ready for sail. It didn't take long before both vessels were streaming toward the open water of the sea, and Easton yelled for more canvas to be raised.

Panting, Teach leaned against the railing, the rifle still in his hands. The weapon was smooth and well made, much more

accurate than the muskets the soldiers had used. The owner of
the ship they'd just stolen was obviously wealthy.

Easton crouched low and patted a hand on Kitts's back, the
moonlight illuminating his features. "I'm sorry you got hurt,
lad. But better you than me."

"Sod off," Kitts choked out.

For all the things Kitts wasn't, he *was* a man of honor and
good intentions, and Teach was glad he'd survived. If only
they'd been able to rescue Alastair and the rest of his crew. Just
thinking about them caused Teach's fury to rise. "That's not
very sporting of you, now is it? Go and have one of my men
take a look at that," Easton said.

"It's nothing," Kitts insisted, blood pouring down his shoulder.

"Excellent. So you won't mind if you lose the use of that
arm. Then, by all means, stay here and enjoy the view. Did you
enjoy your time in Nassau?"

Kitts muttered something beneath his breath, but Easton
simply waited, a serene look on his face. Rolling to his feet,
Kitts headed off in the direction of the stairs leading belowdecks.

Once Kitts was gone, Easton looked back at the lights of Nassau. "As soon as they get a ship ready, they'll be coming for us."

With his breath at last under control, Teach stood. "I know."

"We'll be ready for them."

Teach said nothing as he stared down at the deck, clenching
the rifle in his hands, his knuckles white. He felt guilty at the

number of lives lost. He wracked his brain, thinking of things he could have done differently, but there was no guarantee any of them would have worked. And now Teach had to return to Anne and tell her he'd failed.

"I'm sorry you lost your friends back there. I know what that's like."

"You know nothing," Teach growled, his head snapping up as he rounded on Easton. "My men were innocent! They died because they placed their trust in me and I let them down. I told them I wouldn't abandon them, and that's just what I did! You and your crew chose this life. The life of a pirate."

"And yet here we are, sailing on the same ship, having just worked together to bring a corrupt man to justice."

"There's a big difference between us. I came back to Nassau to try to save lives. You merely came back for revenge."

"Don't you dare judge me," Easton said, his voice low. "You have no idea what I've been through or why I've made the choices I have. You asked once if the rumors about me were true. Like I said, I'm not innocent. When Webb agreed to work with us, he wanted Nelson to take the lead because Nelson had the same merciless streak as the governor. But most of the men followed me. Nelson was bitter and angry and often took it out on the victims of the ships we attacked."

"Why didn't you stop him?"

"I tried. When you figure out a way to be on two ships at the same time, then please let me know the secret to your success."

Loosening his hold on the rifle, Teach averted his gaze.

"Listen, I understand your guilt. And your anger. But just because we got rid of Webb doesn't mean this fight is over."

"It is for me," Teach said. "At least until I can speak with Anne. Together we'll figure out what to do. We're through taking orders from others." First Teach's father, then Captain Murrell, and finally Governor Webb. Teach was ready to take matters into his own hands. He wanted to go after Pelham and save Alastair, but it would be dangerous to get involved, and Teach wouldn't make any decisions until he'd spoken with Anne.

Easton nodded, giving Teach's words some thought. "Now that Pelham knows who you are, he won't rest until he sees you dead."

"If he can find me."

"I'm afraid that won't be a problem for Pelham," Easton said. "You might be able to disappear for a while, but you won't be able to escape forever. Believe me, Reva tried once."

"What's the story between Reva and Pelham?"

"They have a long and ugly history together, which is precisely why she's going to help us stop Pelham and his associates. He killed her father, and she's made it her life's mission to make him pay."

Teach guessed Reva couldn't have been much older than twenty. Pelham was responsible for a lot of suffering in the world.

"You didn't tell us *your* papa was rich," Easton said.

"Does it matter?"

The pirate's eyes widened. "Apparently not to you."

"If you're thinking of using me for ransom, you'd be wasting your time."

"Ah. Let me guess. You and your father had a disagreement."

"Do you *ever* stop talking?" Teach looked around, wondering where he could go to get away from Easton's endless chatter. Jumping into the sea was one of his options.

"Was it because of *her*?" Easton asked, clearly unperturbed.

Teach fingered the rifle in his hands and Easton took a step back.

"All right. Don't tell me. But your silence says more than you know." Easton took a few steps before turning back to Teach. "Oh, and you needn't worry. Your money is safe from me. Reva is typically flush with coin if I need anything."

"Does that mean she's a better pirate than you?"

Easton smirked. "Don't be ridiculous. Nobody's better than me. Reva came from a wealthy family. Spanish aristocracy."

Teach was astonished at the man's ego. "One day you're going to overestimate your abilities, Easton. I almost wish I could be around to see it."

"Yes, well, don't hold your breath," Easton said. "Tomorrow we can plan our revenge. Right now, I have something to show you."

What Teach wanted most was to be alone with his anger and his grief.

Easton must have sensed Teach's hesitation, because he

motioned for Teach to follow him. "We have a guest on board."

"Who is it?" Teach asked.

"A friend of yours."

With heavy steps Teach followed Easton across the moonlit deck, but he stopped when he saw the familiar blond hair. It was Cara.

CHAPTER 37

Anne

Strong fingers circled Anne's throat, threatening to choke the life out of her prone figure. Sweat dripped down her face and neck as she glared up at her opponent where he straddled her. Her fingers curled in the warm sand beneath her as she scooped a handful.

John caught the movement and he released his hold immediately, sitting back on his haunches. "That's not playing fair, Anne."

"I didn't throw it," she said, a guilty flush spreading across her cheeks.

"All you had to do was roll your hips like I taught you and bring your hand like this." John thrust his hand, palm up.

"I thought it was a brilliant move," Reva said. She lay in a hammock, a few feet from where Anne and John sparred, using her hat to fan her face. "I would have done the same thing."

"Besides, I didn't think you wanted me to break your nose again." John had shown Anne a few sparring moves, ones that would work in her favor, especially for her size, but she'd broken his nose the third day. Apparently her elbow was an effective weapon.

John scowled. "I *do* want you to take our sparring seriously." He rolled to the side and helped Anne up. "It's a good idea with the sand, but you need to learn to fight without any added props. You won't always be on a beach."

"I know. I'm sorry," Anne said, looking automatically in the direction of the bay, where the gentle waves kissed the sandy shore. The evening sun sank low, giving everything it touched an amber glow and leaving the horizon dipped in a thin line of silver.

John sighed, following her gaze. "Don't worry, Anne. They'll be back soon."

It had been twelve days since Teach and Easton had left and Anne was restless. And irritated. And worried. She shook the sand from her hair with several sharp flicks, unwilling to give in to her melancholy. "I think it's time for you to teach me how to load a cannon."

She'd lost track of the number of times she'd asked John to show her how to fire a cannon. Each time his answer was the same.

"Teach wouldn't want me to."

"Do you think Teach wants me to cower and hide in the captain's cabin every time we're fired at?"

John laughed. "Maybe not cower, but he wants you safe, and standing on the deck in a fire fight is certainly not in your best interest."

"The cannons aren't on the top deck. And he left me here, which proves my point that he won't always be around. It's better that I can take care of myself," she said, her voice bitter.

"I'm not going to show you how to fire a bloody cannon, Anne. I value my life more than I fear your ire."

"Let me show her again," Reva said, a sly grin on her face. The pirate had been more than willing to show Anne how to load and fire a cannon, and the two girls had snuck aboard the *Killorn* one afternoon while the men were resting.

"You two aren't allowed on that ship until the others get back."

Anne shook her head at John. "You're being ridiculous. We didn't hurt anyone."

"No, but most of us had to search for a clean pair of drawers after your stunt. Nearly scared us to death. And we can't have you wasting our ammunition."

"You let me practice shooting. Is that wasting ammunition?"

"Bullets are easier to come by than cannonballs."

While her Queen Anne's pistol from Teach was still her weapon of choice, thanks to John and Reva, Anne could load and fire a musket as well as a blunderbuss. And in a one-on-one altercation, she could manage to get away. What mattered most was that she'd mastered the loading of the weapons and could be useful in a fight without getting caught.

Reva strolled up to Anne, her hat in her hands. "They're overprotective of their balas. Don't worry, Anne. Once I get a ship, we'll shoot cannons as much as we like. And we won't have to ask for anyone's permission."

While Anne appreciated Reva's offer, she wondered how long they'd have to wait. Frustrated, Anne walked away, her eyes scanning the horizon as she'd done so often since the *Fortune* had left. Reva returned to the hammock, swaying back and forth beneath the trees. Benjamin was out in the cay with a spear in hand, the crystal clear water reaching up to his chest. His fishing skills had helped feed them. Just the other day, he'd managed to catch a turtle that Anne had cooked.

She'd used the time during Teach's absence to her advantage, and the days had passed quickly, including her birthday. She'd been in no mood to celebrate. Her back was healing and Reva had removed her stitches. With Benjamin's help, Anne had learned how to swim somewhat. She preferred the mobility and freedom she had wearing trousers to the constraint she felt in skirts.

They'd repaired the *Killorn* and it stood ready for action, its smooth lines bobbing gently in the water. Two storms had hit and they'd been forced to take shelter in the vessel. Anne had almost come to think of it as home, but she knew how ridiculous that sounded. The only people who spent the majority of their time at sea were either pirates or sailors, and Anne was neither.

She stood on shore as the waves lapped gently around her ankles, the sand sifting away beneath her feet as she watched Benjamin track a dark object beneath the surface. He'd explained to her that fishermen needed to change fishing spots to avoid sharks. Once the *Fortune* returned, they too would need to move on.

The only question was where would they go? So much depended on what happened with Webb. Had they managed to bring the governor to justice and free their friends? Were they now on their way to England, to testify in a trial against him? Would anyone believe them? After all, Easton was a pirate, and the soldiers were more likely to fire first, ask questions later. What they'd done was dangerous, and she couldn't bring herself to even address the issue of whether or not Teach was alive.

The constant barrage of questions and uncertainty kept Anne awake at night. Physically, she was exhausted, but different scenarios of what might be happening in Nassau plagued her until she reached for her pistols and practiced loading them by the light of the moon, determined to never be left behind again.

An excited shout broke into her reverie, and Anne looked up. The topsails of a ship floated into view and soon the smooth lines of the *Fortune* entered the cay. Easton's Jolly Roger, with its white skull and crossed swords, was visible for everyone to see. Anne scoured the line of men striding across the deck, preparing to drop anchor, but she didn't see the tall figure or broad shoulders of the man she loved.

A second vessel came into view, this one smaller and sleeker than the *Killorn* or the *Fortune*. Beneath the bowsprit at the prow of the ship was a glossy carving of a woman, with long dark hair and a bright red dress.

"Who do you suppose that is?" John asked, walking up to her side.

Anne felt her chest tighten. "I have no idea."

Wary and tense, the group on the beach watched the second ship drop anchor. Was this some sort of a trick?

Then Easton was there, giving a shout and raising a hand in greeting.

And beside him was Teach.

The sight of Teach sucked the air out of her lungs and she fell back a step, scarcely able to breathe. Spanning the distance, her eyes met his. As the men on both ships lowered longboats over the side, she held still, sorting through a mixture of emotions. Relief that he was back safely. Joy that they appeared none the worse for wear. Worry when she didn't see Cara, Alastair, or Coyle amongst the group. And finally, anger that Teach had left her there in the first place. She wasn't sure how she would greet him.

By the time he waded through the shallows toward her,

a pulse drummed in the backs of her knees and in the pit of her belly. He was disheveled and looked as exhausted as she felt. His hair was longer and hung loose, and the scruff on his face was several days beyond a shave. Yet the sight of him was captivating. He was so striking, so dear and familiar.

The saltwater sprayed into the air as she launched herself into his arms.

"I'm sorry," he said, burying his face in her hair. "I'm so sorry." His words, spoken softly, melted her anger. His hands roved over her back, his grip strong, as if he feared she might disappear.

"It's all right," she said, reveling in his embrace. She drew back at length, cupping his face in her hands. "I love you. I'm sorry for being so upset—" Anne paused when he shook his head, a swallow rippling down his throat. There was sadness in his eyes, not merely regret at leaving her behind. With a mounting sense of dread, she scanned the two ships over his shoulder once again. Men rowed longboats to shore and unloaded supplies, but there was no sign of any of Anne's friends.

"Where's Jack?" John asked, as he too searched the sailors.

"We were too late," Teach said, his voice low.

The knot in Anne's throat threatened to choke her. "No," she whispered. "What about—"

Then Anne saw a familiar figure. There was a defeated curve to Cara's spine as Kitts helped her into one of the skiffs with the rest of the crew and they began rowing inland.

"Coyle and Alastair?" Anne asked. Teach's hold on Anne tightened, his expression filled with compassion. She fought against the biting pressure of tears welling in her eyes. "Where are they?"

Teach drew in a ragged breath. "Pelham has Alastair. He's taking him to Jamaica. Coyle is dead, and so are the others."

Hardly able to bear the pain, Anne leaned into Teach's chest as tears ran silently down her cheeks.

"What happened?" John asked, his voice low.

"Pelham used Coyle. They tortured him in front of Alastair until Alastair agreed to hand over his ships. Cara almost met the same fate, but one of the soldiers at the fort set her free. She hid in the stables behind the Fox and managed to live off the meager supplies that were in the pantry. Since Pelham had what they wanted from Alastair, they didn't bother searching for her."

"How did you find her?" Anne asked.

"Easton sent his first mate to the Fox, to look for Alastair. He found Cara instead and she told him what happened."

Anne's insides felt hollow, gutted. First Beth, and now this. The knowledge that she wouldn't see Coyle's smiling face again was difficult to absorb. Anne stayed within the protective warmth of Teach's arms, too numb with grief to move until Cara eventually reached shore. Teach loosened his hold and Anne walked toward her friend.

Cara's eyes, usually so warm and friendly, were hard and

bleak, and her dress hung on her frame. Yet, despite Cara's appearance, her arms wrapped around Anne with surprising strength. Anne hugged her back, as sobs wracked Cara's shoulders. Kitts stood nearby, his serious expression even more somber than usual.

"I hate Pelham. I hate him," Cara muttered repeatedly. "I'm going to kill him. He took my brother from me and I'm going to find him and kill him. I want to see the look in his eyes when he breathes his last."

The sound of Cara's weeping and her pledge for revenge caused something inside of Anne to shatter. But instead of feeling defeated and broken, the sharp edges were new and dangerous. Anne met Teach's gaze above Cara's head. He raised a brow at her, as if he could read her thoughts, but Anne turned and led Cara away, those sharp edges taking shape.

Moonlight skimmed the bay and the smell of smoke drifted toward Anne where she stood in the trees. Most of the pirates, former soldiers, and what remained of Teach's men from the *Deliverance* sat around the campfire, their voices low. They were a motley group who didn't seem to have anything in common apart from unknown histories, unclear ethics, and unswerving loyalty. And yet Anne felt no apprehension in their midst.

Teach broke away from the crew and strode toward her. He had a force of character that was hard to overlook and the sight of him eased the tightness in her chest. Anne left Cara where she slept in a hammock between two palms, and walked into Teach's outstretched arms without hesitation, closing her eyes against a rush of raw emotions.

"I missed you."

"I know. Promise you'll never leave me behind again," Anne said.

He brought his lips to hers. "Promise," he whispered against her mouth.

The kiss was fleeting, gentle, yet shockingly intense. Despite the heat of the night air, Anne shivered in his embrace.

"How are you?" Teach asked. He smoothed her hair back from her forehead, frowning as he studied her appearance in the flickering firelight. She couldn't imagine how she must look to him. Her hair was much shorter, and she was dressed in masculine attire, with her pistols at her sides. Benjamin had fashioned holsters for her for when the baldric across her chest became too heavy. She knew she'd lost weight, despite the fish Benjamin had caught for them, but she'd been too worried about Teach and the others to bother with food.

"Tired. Sad. Angry."

Teach nodded. "And how is Cara?"

"Tired. Sad. And angry." Anne had listened to Cara describe in detail what had happened after Teach had left them in Nassau. Locked separately in the fort, Cara hadn't seen Coyle or Alastair. But she'd heard Coyle's screams.

"I should have taken them with us," Teach muttered, his mouth turned down at the corners, his eyes on the ground.

Anne placed a hand on his cheek and forced him to meet her gaze. "It's not your fault. You can't take the blame for this. Cara told me you offered, but Coyle was already locked up. She wouldn't have left without him. I think at the time she hoped Alastair could talk to Webb and they could all leave."

Teach turned and placed a kiss in the palm of her hand, the scruff on his face prickling her skin where it touched. "They might have if Pelham hadn't interfered. I think some part of Webb actually liked Alastair."

"Where is Webb?" Anne asked.

"He's dead."

"Did he suffer?"

"It wasn't an easy death."

Good. At least Webb wouldn't be able to hurt anyone else. "And his wife?"

"She's still in Nassau. Easton told me she and Pelham had a relationship in England. It ended when Webb was assigned governor of Nassau," Teach said.

Anne frowned. "How does Easton know that?"

"You'd be surprised what Easton knows. Pelham came to Nassau to put a stop to piracy. Mrs. Webb wasted no time informing her former lover of her husband's schemes. And starting their relationship all over again."

"So did she poison her husband to stop his involvement

in piracy, or did she poison her husband so she could be with Pelham?" Anne shook her head, shocked by what she was hearing. The twists and turns of life on the island were dizzying.

"Does it matter?"

"Of course not. But she has to pay for what she did."

Before Teach could say anything, Easton marched up to them, a torch in one hand, a small box in the other. "We need to set sail with the tide if we have any hope of escaping. It won't be long before Pelham sends a ship after us. Have you made your decision?"

"I told you I wished to discuss this with Anne in private first," Teach said, his jaw clenched.

"Right. And I believe you've had enough time for that."

Anne narrowed her eyes. "Discuss what?"

"Going to Jamaica with us," Easton said, quirking a brow at Teach's glare.

"Why wouldn't we go with them?" Anne asked Teach.

Teach rubbed the back of his neck. "Because, technically, it's not our fight."

"Of course it's our fight. He has Alastair. He killed Coyle and your men. That makes it our fight."

"We don't know for sure that Pelham has Alastair," Teach said. "Frankly, I don't trust anything that comes out of Pelham's mouth. But even if he does have Alastair, Alastair's not a fool. He knows these islands, and if I know him, he already has a plan to get away from Pelham. This is our chance to flee. To get far, far away. To make a life for ourselves somewhere where Pelham and his ilk will never find us."

"But you'll always be looking over your shoulder," Easton said, shaking his head wearily. "This is not done until we've rid the world of these monsters. And now that Pelham knows who you are, Drummond, you can't run far enough to hide from him."

Anne gasped. It was a shock to hear that name again. "What exactly happened in Nassau?"

Teach sighed. "Everything went according to plan. We killed Webb—"

"Technically, *I* killed Webb," Easton said. "But Pelham didn't seem worried about those minor details. He's charged us all with the murder of Nicholas Webb. And he knows who Teach is."

"How?"

"He recognized me. I thought the name Pelham sounded familiar. Now I know why. He's done business with my father in the past."

Bile rose in Anne's throat, as the worst of two worlds came crashing together. "What does Pelham want?"

"What does any tyrant want? Wealth and power and he'll hurt, maim, or kill anyone who gets in his way. And so will his business partners. Right now, we're in their way," Easton said.

"But we haven't done anything to them," Anne said.

Easton's eyes were cold. "Yet. But they've done plenty to

us. And to others. It's just like I told you. Although the most visible, Webb's hands weren't the dirtiest of the bunch. The souls of those men are as black as the ashes they leave behind," Easton said.

"And that's precisely why our association should end here." Teach drew Anne aside, but Easton stayed where he was, watching them.

"Where will we go if not with them?" Anne asked.

Teach had clearly given it some thought. He didn't hesitate with his answer. "To the colonies. We can go to Charles Town or Boston. We can start new." Although his words were immediate, she sensed the reserve in him. His words spoke of running, yet the Teach she knew would stand and fight.

"And what will we do there? Work in a tavern? Or perhaps settle on a farm, where everyone will regard me as your slave or your whore? I have no desire to do either of those things, and neither do you." She could have the rest of her inheritance sent to one of those cities, but she couldn't imagine Teach being happy doing anything that took him away from the sea. Besides, she already knew she would never be accepted into "polite" society. She'd seen firsthand how *polite* they could be.

"That doesn't mean we have to go with them. We could look for your family."

Anne winced, remembering that Alastair had already sent someone to do just that. No matter what she'd asked of him, he'd always been willing to help her. Anne glanced at where Cara slept. "I won't know for several weeks if any of my family are still alive. And you might be right about Alastair having a plan to escape, but what if he doesn't? Cara and Alastair are my family now. If we don't fight, then Coyle died in vain. And if Easton thinks we have a chance to go after Pelham, then I say we should at least try."

"It's dangerous. There's no guarantee we'll succeed."

"It was dangerous going back to Nassau, but you still did it." Anne was filled with bitterness and fury, as well as fear. "If those men continue to go unchecked, there will be no stopping them. We have the chance now to do something about it. And Easton's willing to help."

"So is Reva," Easton called out.

Teach fixed his deathly stare firmly on Easton.

Easton looked back at him with wide eyes. "What? It's true. I brought her a ship. She's forgiven me."

Reva approached the group. "I still like my old ship more," she said, passing Easton. She stopped beside Anne, her brown eyes narrowed. "He's afraid for you, mi amiga," she said, nodding in Teach's direction.

"He doesn't need to be," Anne replied.

"He's right here," Teach muttered.

Easton motioned for Teach to keep quiet. "Let them talk."

"I know Pelham, and what Easton says is true. Webb took his instructions from Pelham. And there are several more men just like him. If we go after Pelham, we cut off the head of the snake." Reva turned to Teach. "As I see it, you have two options. You can cut and run, but know that those men have resources and power that will shock you. They'll stop at nothing to catch Easton and Teach, now that they're both wanted criminals."

"Is this supposed to convince them, Reva? Because even I'm having second thoughts," Easton muttered.

"You have to ask yourselves how far you're willing to go to get what you want," Reva said, as if the other pirate hadn't spoken. "If you truly wish to stop Pelham and save your friend Alastair, then you'll come with us to Jamaica."

"Why do you want to go after him so badly?"

"He killed mi padre."

Anne gasped, shocked by Reva's revelation. "When did this happen?"

"Five years ago, when I was fifteen. I want to punish him. I want to see him suffer like I suffered. But I can't do it solo. I've tried, but it's impossible. Easton and I both know others who would be willing to join us."

"Other pirates?" Anne asked.

"Not all of them," Reva said.

Easton stepped forward. "*Most* of them. But I also have other connections. And let's not forget the documents I stole."

"I think it's time you showed us what you have in your arsenal, before we commit to anything," Teach said.

"Gladly. But that requires us to leave here as quickly as possible. I didn't want to leave them where Webb could get to them, so I hid them elsewhere."

"Let me guess," Teach said. "You have them in Jamaica."

Easton shrugged his shoulders, as if to say *guilty as charged*.

"It won't be easy. And once you start on this path, there's no going back. I know, because I've tried." For all the girl's bravado, Anne sensed a layer of vulnerability beneath the surface. Reva was scared.

Teach turned to Anne. "It's up to you. I will go wherever you choose."

Anne took a deep breath. She could tell that despite Teach's concern over her welfare and safety, he wanted to bring Pelham to justice. Teach was willing to do whatever that entailed, even if it meant breaking the law. Anne had the feeling that if it wasn't for her, he would have already committed to the fight. "We'll go to Jamaica."

"Excellent," Easton said, clearly pleased. He turned to Reva. "This is who we'll need to contact."

As the two pirates began to make plans, Teach drew Anne into his embrace and she slipped her arms around his waist. "You're sure about this?" he asked quietly.

"Absolutely."

"Do you still want to be my wife?"

Anne smiled. He knew how important marriage was to her. That was one of the reasons she'd refused to run away with him while they were still in Bristol. As much as she'd loved her parents, she didn't want there to be a question in anyone's mind that she belonged with Teach. "Of course I do. I need you to make me an honest woman, before I become a criminal."

Easton made a strangled sound in his throat, overhearing the last part of her sentence. "Not just any criminal. A *pirate*."

"To be proper pirates, they'll need a ship," Reva said.

"You may have the *Fortune*. Although if I were you, I would rename it," Easton said. "Of course, that requires a de-naming ceremony."

"You're making this up," Teach said, with a look of exasperation.

"He's not, actually," Reva said. "It's considered bad luck to change the name of a ship."

"We've already renamed the ship I brought back for Reva. It was a bit maudlin, but she insisted on calling it the *Maldicion*." The expression on Easton's face was smug as he bent and picked up the torch where it burned in the sand. "Now, to do this right, I already wrote down the current name of the ship and placed it in this box. Once the box is burned, we'll take the ashes and throw them into the sea. Only then can you rename the ship."

"I thought you said we were in a hurry," Teach said.

"We are. I doused the box in oil. I won't start this venture off on the wrong foot. We'll rename the ship the proper way."

Teach eyed the box, before leveling a cold stare at Easton.

"You're awfully sure of yourself. What if we hadn't agreed to go to Jamaica?"

Easton grinned and held the flame over the box in the sand. It didn't take long before it caught fire. "Deep down, you always knew you would go after Pelham. You just needed to ask for *her* permission," he said, nodding in Anne's direction.

Anne hid a smile at the look on Teach's face as Easton continued to speak. They'd be lucky if the two men didn't kill each other before they reached Jamaica.

"I think that's why you and Kitts didn't get along at first. You both want to do the right thing, because of some unresolved business with your fathers. But you'll see. You were born for this kind of life. Sometimes doing the right thing means doing the wrong thing."

Teach took a threatening step in Easton's direction, but Anne stopped him with a firm hand on his arm. Easton pressed his lips together and didn't say another word.

The four of them watched the flames as they licked at the wood at an alarming rate.

Reva looked up. "I hope you have a new name in mind. The *Fortune* is no more."

Teach regarded Anne. The gaze in his eyes made her stomach flip. "We'll call it the *Queen Anne*."

Anne tilted her head to the side, regarding Teach, and loving the way the light flickered over his features. He looked fierce, like a pirate, and a small thrill shot through her to know that he was hers. "No," she said, shaking her head.

"Why not?" Reva asked, clearly shocked. "I think it's a lovely name."

Easton was quick to nod his assent. "Aye, I agree."

"It is a lovely name, but I have one that I think would work better."

Teach quirked a brow at her and waited.

"We'll call it *Queen Anne's Revenge*," Anne said, her lips curving up in a smile.

ACKNOWLEDGMENTS

It took a large and competent crew to sail a pirate ship successfully. Captains had to be bold and fearless, but they couldn't navigate the stormy seas on their own. The same can be said about writing a book. While the author writes the story in solitude, without the help of a talented and dedicated crew the book would not find its way onto bookshelves.

If I'm the captain of this ship, then my editor, Nicole Ellul, is definitely the quartermaster, nearly equal in power. Without her valuable insight and asking me to take the story further, this book wouldn't be what it is today. We even had a hurricane named after us, but thankfully, our ship wasn't lost. To the rest of the publishing team at Simon Pulse: Mara Anastas, the admiral, who keeps many ships afloat; Mary Marotta and Liesa Abrams, both captains in their own right; Chelsea Morgan, Carolyn Swerdloff, and Audrey Gibbons, some of the most capable seawomen around. Thank you so much for all your tweets and support! It's a pleasure to be part of the Simon & Schuster crew. Lauren Forte, you're the best copy editor and gunner around for making sure all the words were kept in good repair. Karina Granda, you're a pirate queen, and I absolutely love the cover for *Blacksouls*. You came up with the perfect Jolly Roger for this book and I don't know how to adequately show my gratitude.

Tracey Adams, über agent and sailing master, in charge of navigation and making sure I stayed on course, not an easy job, considering the shifting tides of the market and unforeseen storms that come up in any book's path. Thank you for being such a fierce advocate and all-around great person, and thanks as well to all of Adams Lit. It's such an honor to be a part of the family.

When I finished *Blackhearts*, I knew exactly where I wanted the story to go, and like any historical novel, it required research. The most crucial titles to creating an accurate portrayal were *Daily Life in the Age of Sail* by Dorothy Denneen Volo and James M. Volo and *Narrative of the Life of Frederick Douglass* by Frederick Douglass. Both books were vital to giving the story authenticity, although I admit to taking some artistic license with facts. If there are any glaring mistakes or inaccuracies, I take full responsibility.

Becky Wallace, from now on I will refer to you as Becky Boatswain. You took your duty of inspecting the ship (my manuscript) and the rigging (my characters) very seriously. You're an amazing critique partner, a gifted author, and a wonderful friend, and I consider myself lucky to know you.

Angie Thomas, Nic Stone, and Robyn Lucas were invaluable as I drafted this novel. They were the carpenters, responsible for repairing any damage to the hull by making sure Anne's story was watertight and accurate. In many instances, carpenters also acted as ship surgeons, using the same tools to perform operations and amputations with no anesthetic. Angie, Nic, and Robyn were no different, suggesting I cut anything that wasn't true to Anne's narrative. Ladies, y'all are insanely talented and immensely fierce and I am truly grateful for your insight.

Kelly Elliot, Molly McAdams, Stefani Sloma, Jessica Cluess, and Kerri Maniscalco, your enthusiasm for this story was the backbone of my crew; as my beta readers, you knew how to read the skies, the weather, and the mood of the captain. I am forever grateful to you for taking the time to read this when it was in its less-than-polished form.

There have been so many readers and book bloggers who've been influential in promoting and marketing my books and I am forever in your debt: Sarah K (@thebooktraveler) and Sarah (@whatsarahread), Kristen (@myfriendsarefiction), Brittany (@bbookrambles), Nicole (@blackbeakbooks), Bridget (@darkfaerietales), Rachel (@yaperfectionist), Karina (@MermaidsReadToo), Rachel (@BeautyandtheBookshelf), Fallon (@bookinneverland), Nicola (*Queen of the Bookshelves Blog*), Jaime Arnold of Rockstar Book Tours, Ben Alderson (@BenjaminofTomes), Stephanie (@Chasm_of_Books), and many, many more. I've met some of you already and hope to meet more of you in the very near future. *Mundie Moms* and Vilma Gonzalez, THANK YOU for the amazing cover reveals for both *Blackhearts* and *Blacksouls*. Prepare yourselves for when

I finally get to meet you ladies in person. And, of course, I'm incredibly grateful to the librarians and booksellers who have put my books into the hands of people who needed them.

I also have some good friends in my corner who've continued to show me love and support. Janine Simpson, Holly Loveland, Amie Fagg, and Julie Nelson. Our road trips and lunches have helped me more than you could ever know. I think we need to go on another cruise for more research. Also a special shout-out to Connie Baxter, Christa Tady, Melissa Newman, and Demi Bush. You know what you did in your own special way.

To my parents, James and Doris Platt, I can't remember a time when the two of you weren't reading. Your love of books was definitely passed on. To my siblings, Andrea, Cameron, Kirsten, and your families, thank you so much for helping to spread the word. Love you all! And many thanks to Heidy, Romina, Carlos, and Ida as well.

I don't know what I would do without my own crew at home who always encouraged me to follow my dream. Sophia and Anthony, I LOVE YOU and I love being your mom. "You make me cry." And to my Miguelo, you are my anchor and my best mate. Te amo mucho. Families are forever.

AUTHOR'S NOTE

When I set out to write the story of Blackbeard, I wanted to add flesh and bones to a legend—to create a backstory for a man who chose the life of a pirate and who historians claim was cruel and unruly. But recent studies have people questioning those reports. Some say Blackbeard wasn't as evil as formerly believed, and that he was a type of Robin Hood of the seas. The Edward Teach of *Blackhearts* and *Blacksouls* is a work of fiction based on a few details in various historical accounts. The world he lived in, however, was very real.

I fiercely love my characters and wanted to be true to their narratives. I knew from the beginning I needed a strong female who could go toe-to-toe with the young man who would go on to become the most infamous pirate to sail the seas. An image of Anne came to mind immediately, a beautiful biracial girl with a fierce spirit and a longing for freedom. *Blackhearts* ended with both Anne and Teach on separate ships heading for the West Indies. The more I researched, the more I discovered that the story would be much broader in scope than I first anticipated.

In writing *Blacksouls*, it would have been impossible to ignore the subject of slavery, nor did I want to. I believe it's important to confront the past, to learn and grow from our predecessors' failings. I can only hope *Blacksouls* opens the door for deeper conversations on this topic in the future.

If you're interested in more information about the actual history of slavery, I suggest reading the works of Frederick Douglass himself, including *Narrative of the Life of Frederick Douglass, an American Slave*.

Another book I would recommend is by Andrea Stuart, entitled *Sugar in the Blood: A Family's Story of Slavery and Empire*. One of Ms. Stuart's ancestors fell into the life of a sugar plantation owner, quite by chance. Incredibly well researched, this book details the horrors of the transatlantic slave trade and how absolute power corrupts.

Of course I also needed help with the nautical aspects of my book. I turned to *Daily Life in the Age of Sail* by Dorothy Denneen Volo and James M. Volo. It provided a wealth of information that I hope added to the authenticity of the readers' experience.

These works combined to help me craft *Blacksouls*. At its heart, my story is about a young man's descent into the world of piracy. But it's also about the young woman he loves and their journey together to find their place in a sometimes cruel and unfair world.